FOUNDERS

Also by James Wesley, Rawles

Patriots: A Novel of Survival in the Coming Collapse
How to Survive the End of the World as We Know It
Survivors: A Novel of the Coming Collapse

FOUNDERS

A NOVEL OF THE COMING COLLAPSE

JAMES WESLEY, RAWLES

EMILY BESTLER BOOKS

—

ATRIA

New York   London   Toronto   Sydney   New Delhi

ATRIA BOOKS

A Division of Simon & Schuster, Inc.
1230 Avenue of the Americas
New York, NY 10020

First Emily Bestler Books/Atria Books hardcover edition September 2012

EMILY BESTLER BOOKS / ATRIA BOOKS and colophon are trademarks of Simon & Schuster, Inc.

For information about special discounts for bulk purchases, please contact Simon & Schuster Special Sales at 1-866-506-1949 or business@simonandschuster.com.

The Simon & Schuster Speakers Bureau can bring authors to your live event. For more information or to book an event, contact the Simon & Schuster Speakers Bureau at 1-866-248-3049 or visit our website at www.simonspeakers.com.

Designed by Rhea Braunstein

Manufactured in the United States of America

10 9 8 7 6 5 4 3 2 1

Library of Congress Cataloging-in-Publication Data

Rawles, James Wesley.
Founders : a novel of the coming collapse / by James Wesley Rawles.—1st Emily Bestler Books/Atria Books hardcover ed.
    p.   cm.
1. Financial crises—Fiction.   2. Survival—Fiction.   3. Political fiction.   1. Title.
  PS3568.A8437F68 2012
  813'.54—dc23

                                                    2012013276

ISBN 978-1-4391-7282-7
ISBN 978-1-4391-7285-8 (ebook)

Disclaimers

Dramatis Personae

James Alstoba—Baptist minister and part-time metal detectorist, near Williams, Arizona

Dale Bennet—grasslands biologist and rabbit breeder, Scottsbluff, Nebraska

Peter Blanchard—first lieutenant, USAF, missileer at Malmstrom AFB, Montana

Chambers Clarke—fertilizer and pesticide salesman, Radcliff, Kentucky

Hollan Combs—retired property manager and soils analyst, Bradfordsville, Kentucky

Brent Danley—trauma nurse from Waterville, Vermont

Jennifer Danley—wife of Brent Danley

Ron Emerson—father of Rebecca (Emerson) Fielding

Adrian Evans—a Nashville attorney and friend of Ben Fielding

Ben Fielding—attorney in Muddy Pond, Tennessee

Joseph Fielding—son of Ben and Rebecca Fielding; thirteen years old at the onset of the Crunch

Rebecca (Emerson) Fielding—wife of Ben Fielding

Dan Fong—industrial engineer from Chicago; member of Todd Gray's Idaho survivalist retreat group

Ignacio García—leader of the criminal gang La Fuerza

Todd Gray—leader of a group retreat near Bovill, Idaho

Chet Hailey—owner of Chet's Crawlers and Haulers, a four-wheel drive vehicle repair and modification specialist garage in Chicago, Illinois

Dustin Hodges—deputy sheriff in Marion County, Kentucky

Maynard Hutchings—member of the Hardin, Kentucky, board of supervisors

Tom "T.K." Kennedy—Todd Gray's dormitory roommate and cofounder of The Group

Captain Andrew "Andy" Laine—Army Ordnance Corps officer

Lisbeth "Beth" Laine—wife of Lars Laine

Grace Laine—daughter of Lars and Lisbeth; six years old at the onset of the Crunch; nicknamed "Anelli"

Kaylee (Schmidt) Laine—wife of Andy Laine

Major Lars Laine—disabled U.S. Army veteran

Cliff Larson—HVAC technician from Scottsbluff, Nebraska

Ken Layton—off-road vehicle mechanic, Chicago, Illinois; member of Todd Gray's Idaho survivalist retreat group

Terry Layton—wife of Ken Layton; member of Todd Gray's Idaho survivalist retreat group

Kevin Lendel—computer programmer living near Bovill, Idaho; member of Todd Gray's Idaho survivalist retreat group

L. Roy Martin—owner of the Bloomfield Refinery; nicknamed "El Rey" by his Spanish-speaking employees

Curt Mehgai—oilfield worker and U.S. Army veteran

Jim Monroe—rancher near Raynesford, Montana; father of Kelly (Monroe) Watanabe

Rhonda Monroe—wife of Jim Monroe; mother of Kelly (Monroe) Watanabe

Carl Norwood—rancher in Butte County, South Dakota

Cordelia Norwood—wife of Carl Norwood

Graham Norwood—son of Carl and Cordelia Norwood; sixteen years old at the onset of the Crunch

the Old Man—nickname of the anonymous leader of a Kentucky-based resistance reconnaissance unit

Brigadier General Edward Olds—Mechanized Infantry brigade commander, Fort Knox, Kentucky

Francisco Ortega—ranch hand, Raynesford, Montana; sixteen years old at the onset of the Crunch

Jedediah Peoples—resistance infantryman from Westmoreland, Tennessee

Durward Perkins—farmer in West Branch, Iowa

Karen Perkins—wife of Durward Perkins

Larry Prine—farmer near Morgan City, Utah

Lynda Prine—wife of Larry Prine

Sheila Randall—general store owner and widow of Jerome Randall

Tyree Randall—son of Sheila Randall; ten years old at the onset of the Crunch

Major General Clayton Uhlich—post commander at Fort Knox, Kentucky

Lily Voisin—grandmother ("Grandmère") of Sheila Randall and great-grandmother of Tyree Randall; eighty-five years old at the onset of the Crunch

Joshua Watanabe—senior airman (E-4), Missile Maintenance NCO, Malmstrom AFB, Montana

Kelly (Monroe) Watanabe—wife of Joshua Watanabe

Brigadier General Anthony Woolson—base commander, Malmstrom Air Force Base, Montana

Author's introductory note: Unlike most novel sequels, the story line of *Founders* is contemporaneous with the events described in my previously published novels, *Patriots* and *Survivors*. Thus, you need not read them first (or subsequently), but you'll likely find them entertaining. They will also fill in the backstories for several characters.

FOUNDERS

1

Hammer Time

"Liberty must at all hazards be supported. We have a right to it, derived from our Maker. But if we had not, our fathers have earned and bought it for us, at the expense of their ease, their estates, their pleasure, and their blood."

—John Adams, *A Dissertation on the Canon and Feudal Law*, 1765

Nashville, Tennessee
Eight Years Before the Crunch

Adrian Evans had asked Ben to meet him at the bar after work. This was a meeting that wasn't in Ben's comfort zone. Ben Fielding only rarely set foot in a bar, and the only drinking that he did was tiny little communion cups of wine. But since he was about to move his family and he probably wouldn't see Adrian again for many months, he reluctantly agreed.

Ben had just seen Adrian three days before, at a Sunday afternoon farewell barbeque. Nearly everyone from the law firm, and a couple of Ben and Rebecca's neighbors, came over for the party. Because Ben was moving his family to the country, the get-together had been organized by Ben's secretary as a theme party. Many of the guests wore colorful cowboy shirts or coveralls and straw hats. Most of the gifts were back-to-the-land tools. These included a push cultivator, various hand tools, a scythe, several shovels, and a hay fork. The latter, as everyone insisted, became a prop for Ben to hold for clichéd portraits of Ben and Rebecca standing together, looking like the stern-faced couple in the Grant Wood painting *American Gothic*.

When Ben Fielding arrived at the Full Moon Saloon, he found that Adrian was already there, nursing a gin and tonic. They sat briefly at the bar while Ben ordered a glass of Sprite. Then they moved to a booth to talk. Adrian carried over a paper bag that was gathered at the top. It looked like it held a bottle of liquor for a goodbye gift. Ben was hoping that he wouldn't have to come up with a "Thanks but no thanks" speech, to explain again that he was a nondrinker.

Their conversation started out essentially as a repeat of what they'd talked about at the farewell barbeque. Adrian wished Ben the best for his move to the largely Mennonite community of Muddy Pond. "I'm really jealous of you, Ben," he said. "I'd love to move out to the country, and have a place to shoot my guns without having to pay to go to a range."

Then their conversation moved on to expectations of what things would be like at the law firm after Ben left, and a bit about Adrian's failed marriage.

Adrian noticed Ben glancing at the paper bag on the table and said, "After the party last weekend, I found a couple of more tools that I'd like to give you. Sorry that I didn't wrap them or anything."

He slid the bag over to Ben. Opening it, Ben found that it held a hammer and screwdriver.

Adrian explained, "I hope you like these. The screwdriver is pretty cool. It's an original Winchester brand, from back when they had a chain of hardware stores, in the 1920s and 1930s. The Winchester-marked tools and signage are quite collectible, especially with gun enthusiasts looking to branch out. I already put together a full set of their screwdrivers for my collection, but this one was a duplicate, so it's yours."

"Thanks, so much. This is great."

Adrian pointed to the well-worn hammer and said, "Now, that belonged to my grandfather. It was supposedly handmade by a blacksmith that he knew in Hartsville. The handle is hickory, and is just as stout today as the day it was made back in the 1930s."

Ben hefted the short-handled hammer, which had a head that must have weighed a pound and a half. He said again, "Thanks, Adrian. You've been very generous. I appreciate the socket set and the gardening tools that you gave us at the party, too. They'll all come in handy."

Their conversation wandered into politics, then sports, and finally back to Adrian's marriage. At just after 10 p.m., the bar's cocktail waitress walked by and asked, "Would y'all like another?"

Ben waved her off and said, "No, thanks." He turned to Adrian and said, "I've got to get home to Rebecca and the kids."

Adrian nodded. "I understand."

They both stood up, and Ben picked up the bag. The tip of the screwdriver was poking through the paper bag, so Ben shifted it to his coat pocket.

They went out the bar's front door and shook hands. Adrian gave Ben a wink, and said, "You take good care of yourself, Ben. Where you parked?"

"Around back."

Adrian pointed to his BMW across the street and said, "I'm right here." He waved and dashed across to the car, taking advantage of a gap in the traffic.

As Ben walked to the back parking lot, he was thinking about some of the things that Adrian had said about his ex-wife. He wondered if there was anything that he would have done differently, under the circumstances.

Two tall figures loomed up in the alley in front of him. One of them said, "Give me your wallet, 'tard." The man raised his hand, and in the glow of the vapor light Ben could see the bare edge of a knife.

Instinctively, Ben swung with the hammer, still in the paper bag. The hammer connected with the man's forearm in a half-glancing blow, and he dropped the knife. The other man moved in. Ben assumed that he also had a knife, so he swung with all the strength he could muster, and planted the hammer's head in the side of the man's neck. The attacker went down in a heap.

The first man shouted at Ben, "You're dead, 'tard!" He reached behind the small of his back, as if pulling a gun. Ben stepped in and swung, again aiming for the neck. But the robber ducked. This time the hammer hit the man in the side of the head, making a strange slapping noise. The man fell to the ground next to the other robber.

Ben didn't wait to see if they'd get up to charge at him again. He ran for his car, hopped in, and zoomed out the back of the parking lot.

His mind was racing. "What on earth just happened?" he asked himself aloud. He quickly got on I-65 and set his Ford's cruise control at sixty. He was afraid that he might speed if he didn't. He started praying. Ten minutes later, he was safely parked in his driveway. When he turned off the ignition, his hands were shaking. Growing up, Ben had never so much as been in an elementary school hallway fistfight. He felt overwhelmed by the enormity of what he'd just gone through. He fought to keep control of himself.

Ben picked up the hammer—still in the paper bag—and examined it under the car's map light. There was no blood on the bag, but he decided to burn it regardless. He turned off the map light, and tried to get his breathing under control. He decided that it was best that he didn't tell his wife what had happened. "I can't burden her with this," he said resignedly.

It took him a long time to get to sleep that night.

It wasn't until two days later that Ben read in the online edition of the *Tennessean* that both of the robbers had died. One was dead at the scene, and the other died in the hospital emergency room of internal bleeding. The paper reported that both of them had long criminal records. Two knives and a .380 pistol were found on the pavement. Ben was amazed that just one hammer blow to the head or neck could kill a man. But obviously it could.

After much prayer, Ben decided not to talk about the events with the police. He burned the bag and ran the hammer through an ultrasonic cleaner just in case. Then it went into his tool chest. He didn't use it again, until after the Crunch. Whenever he saw the Winchester screwdriver or the hammer, they reminded him of that night.

Malmstrom Air Force Base, Montana
September, the First Year

Joshua Watanabe was bored. As he told his squadron mates, "There's bored, and then there's world-class bored."

Alerts were always interesting for the first couple of hours, but once the two duty officers were sealed in behind a blast door down in the launch control center (LCC) capsules, seventy-five feet underground, and after all the systems checks were complete, the boredom set in. Joshua had watched all his DVDs several times each. He disliked playing cards. Instead, he often read his Bible and by-subscription Bible study and devotional magazines.

Joshua was a senior airman missile maintenance NCO stationed at Malmstrom AFB, Montana. Malmstrom had the largest ballistic missile field in the United States. The array of silos was spread out over 23,000 square miles. The LGM-30 Minuteman missile launch facilities and LCCs were each separated by several miles, and connected electronically. This distancing ensured that a "full exchange" attack by incoming nuclear missiles or bombs would disable only a few of the ICBMs. This would leave the rest capable of being launched in retaliation. The downside of this wide separation was that huge distances had to be driven by alert

crews, security response teams (SRTs), and maintenance personnel. Montana was a huge state, and at times it seemed as if the
missile fields occupied half of it.

Each squadron at Malmstrom was a grouping of fifty Minuteman silos, controlled by five missile alert facilities (MAFs).
The MAFs housed the on-duty "60 Teams" and the off-duty
"70 Teams." Three squadrons constituted a "Wing." Each MAF
"Flight" controlled ten missile silos. The silos were also known as
"launch facilities" (LFs). The MAFs each had several buildings,
including a main office building, a garage building with roll-up
doors, and two outlying radar buildings, each equipped with small
white radomes. The taller of the two radomes was an EHF antenna
shelter, designed to send and receive traffic using secure satellites
via EHF radio. The short cone-shaped dome was a hardened UHF
antenna, used for the line-of-sight UHF radio located in the MAF.
The MAF crews used this radio to communicate with aircraft that
were within line of sight.

Each MAF had a small sewage lagoon aeration pond, often positioned right in front. To a casual observer, these looked a lot like
the livestock watering ponds that dotted the cattle ranches in the
region, but they were constructed differently, with a rubber pond
liner. At a staff briefing a few years before the Crunch, a major
who had recently transferred into his first missile unit assignment
from the Strategic Air Command (SAC) was watching an overview
PowerPoint presentation about the LGM-30 system. Seeing a picture
that included a sewage lagoon in front of an MAF, the major naively
asked, "Do you ever swim in those ponds in the summer?" His question was answered by howls of laughter. Ever since then, the sewage
lagoons were referred to as "SAC Officer Swimming Pools."

Before the Crunch, there was almost always one or more
camouflage-painted up-armored Humvees or ubiquitous Air
Force Blue commercial pickup trucks parked out front of every
MAF. During alerts, there would often be more vehicles.

The 341st Strategic Missile Wing was part of the Air Force Global Strike Command. There were three missile squadrons at Malmstrom. Joshua was assigned to the 10th Missile Squadron, nicknamed "the First Ace in the Hole." They often jokingly called their headquarters "Burpelson" in honor of the fictional Air Force base in the movie *Dr. Strangelove*.

Joshua's biggest frustration with the Air Force was the countless number of mandatory-attendance training sessions, refamiliarization classes, qualifications ("quals"), and briefings that he had to attend. Not only were these sessions often lengthy, but the requisite driving time was also onerous. Frequently, he would have maintenance tasks scheduled at a remote MAF or silo in the morning, but then he would have to drive more than two hours to attend a one-hour briefing in the early afternoon at the main Malmstrom complex. This would usually burn up the otherwise productive hours of the rest of the day. Most of the briefings were incredibly boring, with half-hour PowerPoint presentations on details of the latest Timepiece software, or documentation changes, or changes in regulations, or infinitesimally small changes to maintenance and repair procedures.

The Minuteman system hardware and software was relatively stable throughout Watanabe's PCS tour at Malmstrom. The flurry of activity that had followed the 9/11 attacks was just a memory, and there were no major hardware or software changes during Joshua's time.

Most Minuteman missiles carried a single warhead, although some were equipped with up to three Multiple Independently targetable Reentry Vehicles (MIRVs). Many of these MIRVs were only "penetration aids"—including radar-reflecting chaff, designed to confuse enemy missile defense radars. The missile warheads and penetration aids were a top item of interest for the logistics and maintenance staffs, and of course under extreme scrutiny and security procedures.

Most of the conversations that followed the logistics and maintenance briefings were more about the idiosyncrasies of the briefers, rather than the content of the briefings themselves. One of Joshua's standard comments was "Gee, they crammed a twenty-minute briefing into two hours." His NCOIC referred to such briefings as "Death by PowerPoint." Whenever he heard this, it became a standing joke for Joshua to always correct him with "More accurately, that's *slow* death by PowerPoint." The same NCOIC's favorite saying was "I seem to be rapidly approaching the apex of my mediocre career."

As an "E-4 Over Four" Joshua's base pay was only $2,266 per month. But he received $705 per month basic allowance for housing (BAH) and $348 per month for basic allowance for subsistence (BAS). He was able to rent a two-bedroom house on five acres for $950 per month. His rental house was on Red Coulee Road, two miles east of the hamlet of Fife. Though it was a named town, it was little more than a road junction. The Fife junction was six miles east of Malmstrom AFB, so his driving time to the main gate was about fifteen minutes in good weather.

The house had been built in the late 1980s, so it had double-pane windows and was well insulated. The woodstove in the house was rusty, but it still sealed tight and put out plenty of heat. The biggest attractions of the rental house were a small shop building, a combination horse and hay barn with two stalls, and good smooth wire horse fencing with a smaller-gauge top wire that was energized by an electric fence charger. Like his father, Joshua avoided pasturing horses inside barbed wire fences. He had seen too many horses injured by barbed wire.

Joshua's specialty code was 2M0X2: Missile and Space Systems Maintenance. Most of his duties were preventive maintenance inspections, diagnostics, and LRU replacements at the MAFs. He also spent many hours assisting contractors as they swapped out the "limited life" components in each missile and its associated systems. This included their peripheral part of the $2.5 billion program to replace Minutemen rocket engines.

Less than 20 percent of Joshua's hands-on time was at the individual missile silos. And of that, it was nearly all just visual inspection, lubrication, and spot painting at exterior doors and in access stairways and tunnels. Very little of his time was spent around the missiles themselves. His standing joke was "Inspection complete: The bird is still present or accounted for."

Joshua commuted to work in a re-engined four-wheel drive 1980 Dodge Power Wagon pickup. His squadron mates all jokingly called it the "Rust Bucket." Joshua had bought the truck because he wanted a vehicle with four-wheel drive to negotiate icy roads, and one that could tow a horse trailer. His squadron's NCOIC had encouraged Joshua to buy a late-model Toyota Tundra pickup like his own. But again following in his father's footsteps, Joshua insisted on buying only American vehicles, and avoiding debt. Part of this stance, although he wouldn't admit it, was that he didn't want to be seen as a Japanese American who drove a Japanese-made vehicle.

The Rust Bucket had peeling paint on its hood and rusted-through spots at the top of both of the rear wheel wells. Despite umpteen wire brushings and spot paintings with brown Rustoleum, the pickup's rust patches continued to grow. Mechanically, he kept the pickup in the best condition possible, given its age. From the exterior, the Rust Bucket looked like it was ready to expire, but under the hood it was in excellent condition. As the Crunch set in, there were only 22,000 miles clocked on the new engine.

Watanabe dreaded getting promoted to E-5. He knew that a promotion would mean that he'd probably have a headquarters desk job at Malmstrom, rather than his usual Maintenance Team member job out at the squadrons. Most likely he'd have several boring years as an NCO at the Base Trainer, an aboveground simulator of an LCC capsule. Or he might get assigned as a liaison or "shepherd" for contractors, as MAFs were sequentially "dealtered" for equipment modifications or upgrades. That job would mean countless hours on the road, but without the fun of actually handling the equipment. With those prospects in mind, he applied for a slot at Officer Training School at the Air University, located at Maxwell Air Force Base, Alabama. But his application was still pending when the Crunch came.

Joshua had proposed marriage twice to Kelly Monroe before the Crunch. But each time she had put him off, saying that she wanted to finish her degree before committing to marriage. When the Crunch came, Kelly was just starting her second year in business administration at Montana State University, Great Falls. She was hoping to get a job in Great Falls after she graduated so that she could live near her family.

Living in Montana, the Crunch seemed less traumatic than it was being described on television. There were no big riots in Montana. Society remained more or less intact and functional. There were 2.5 million cattle in Montana, but only 990,000 people, so Joshua didn't expect that he would experience starvation. But the big cities on the east and west coasts had him worried. Those folks could indeed begin to starve.

The scarcity of gasoline, the hyperinflation, and the collapse of the electric power grid were the biggest effects felt in Montana. Everyone seemed intent on the huge scramble to stock up while their dollars could still buy something. The gas stations sold out of regular unleaded gas first, then premium, and finally diesel. It became impossible to find propane cylinders or ammunition. Soon after, the grocery store shelves were stripped clean.

As the news of the inflation and the rioting in the big cities reached a crescendo, Joshua drove out to the Monroe ranch and ran to the front porch. He knocked forcefully on the door. His knock was answered by Kelly's father, Jim Monroe. Joshua said agitatedly, "I'm here to propose to her again, and this time I won't take 'maybe later' for an answer!"

Jim grinned and said, "Good for you, Josh. That's the right attitude. I'll let her know that you're here."

Chicago, Illinois
October, the First Year

It was a moment that Terry Layton would never forget: Her favorite morning talk radio host on WLS-AM was reading newspaper and Internet headlines. The host paused, audibly took a deep breath, and said, "This is it, folks. Inflation has gone triple digit and there's no end in sight. This is the final destruction of the United States dollar. We can kiss it goodbye."

They called it the Crunch. It was a credit collapse and economic depression that made the Great Depression of the 1930s seem small by comparison. The global credit market had come unglued. All around the world, markets were in free fall. Credit had dried up. Cities, counties, states, and even national governments were in default. Consumer prices soared. Interest rates skyrocketed. The price of precious metals soared. Bonds collapsed. Derivatives contracts cratered, leaving counterparties for trillions of dollars in contracts twisting in the wind. Television news commentators droned on and on about "hopes for a recovery." Corporations of all sizes announced huge layoffs.

Terry's husband, Ken, was worried. All the things that his friends Tom Kennedy and Todd Gray had been warning them about for so many years were coming true. When Ken walked through the waiting room at the shop, all the customers were transfixed, staring at the big HD television. CNN was reporting that the economy was crumbling, inflation was out of control, and now there were riots in cities all over the country. Ken got a cup of water at the water cooler. He lingered by the television for a minute. He caught one of the news analysts saying, ". . . so this is where all that monetizing of the debt—the Quantitative Easing—has brought us, to the point of irreversible hyperinflation. Ron Paul was right after all. This is like some enormous boulder rolling downhill, picking up speed, and nothing can stop it now." Ken shook his head in disgust, and headed back out to the bay in the shop to continue installing an RCD heavy-duty suspension kit on a 2012 Jeep Wrangler Unlimited Rubicon.

Ken was the assistant manager at Chet's Crawlers and Haulers, which specialized in four-wheel drive vehicle modifications and repairs. It was one of the largest such specialty shops in the Midwest. Ironically, many of the shop's customers were yuppies who rarely, if ever, drove off-road. They just wanted to make their trucks *look* tough.

Three years earlier, Ken had been invited to join a fledgling group of Chicago "preppers" who were planning to buy a survival retreat property in Idaho. Ken was recruited by Tom "T.K." Kennedy, a bachelor in Ken and Terry's Young Adults group at church. Ken had been of interest to T.K. because he was an automobile mechanic. Since they both liked to shoot and were interested in outdoor activities, both Ken and Terry were enthusiastic about joining the unnamed group. It was dubbed simply "The Group." Ken of course became the group's vehicle and generator mechanic, while Terry served as a logistician, coordinating group buys— mostly of long-term storage foods. The Laytons' home garage was often heaped with boxes before each group buy was broken up and taken home by the members. After Todd and his wife, Mary, bought their ranch near Bovill, Idaho, more than half of the group's supplies were tucked away in the Grays' basement, carefully labeled with the members' names and purchase dates.

Although he had the requisite academic prowess, Ken had shown no interest in pursuing college when he graduated from high school. Instead, he started working full-time as an automobile mechanic. Ken enjoyed the satisfaction of turning wrenches. By the time he'd joined the group, Ken had changed jobs twice. He had also earned several ASE certifications and was about to become the assistant manager at Chet's shop.

Ken enjoyed the pace of working at the shop, which was more relaxed than at the general auto repair shops where he had worked before. He also liked having a short commute from home—just nine minutes on average, all on surface streets. It was close enough that he even went home to be with his wife for one or two lunch hours each week, or on special occasions she would join him for lunch at a nearby restaurant.

The Laytons' small two-story house was on South Campbell Avenue in Chicago, northeast of Douglas Park. It was an older neighborhood where houses were affordable, but the crime rate was high. Their house had been built in the 1930s and remodeled in the 1970s. They bought it in 2008, just before the peak of the housing market. When the Crunch came, Ken joked that with the rapid inflation they'd soon be able to pay off the $157,000 balance remaining on their mortgage. But this didn't happen because his income didn't increase rapidly enough to match the inflation. Inevitably, the hyperinflation was short-lived.

Since they owed more on the house than what they had paid on the principal, there was no way that they could sell it and move to Idaho, as they had hoped to do. Their only viable solution was "jingle mail"—abandoning their house to the bank, by mailing the bank the house keys with an explanatory note. Feeling overwhelmed by the prospect of moving out west without a job waiting for him, Ken stayed, and prayed.

The Laytons attended St. John Cantius Parish church in Chicago, three miles from their home. The trip to church was a straight shot up West Ogden Boulevard that took less than ten minutes. They had chosen to worship there because they celebrated Mass in

Latin. The church's brochure and website read: "St. John Cantius Parish is also privileged to offer daily the Holy Sacrifice of the Mass in the Extraordinary Form of the Roman Rite, commonly referred to as the Tridentine Latin Mass."

The Latin Mass meant a lot to Ken because that was his parents' preference, and he had grown up hearing it. His parents were part of what was then a "renegade" church—back when the Latin Mass was banned. Terry was also raised Catholic, but had never attended a Latin Mass until just before she married Ken. She grew to love it. They decided that when they had children, they would give them a classical homeschooling, and include Latin in their curriculum.

Unlike most young Catholic couples, the Laytons consciously delayed having children, using the church-approved rhythm and symptothermal method. They wanted to be more financially secure and have a good supply of storage food before starting a family. They followed the lead of Todd and Mary Gray, their survivalist group's leaders, who had declared that they wouldn't have kids until after they had their "beans, bullets, and Band-Aids together."

For their own vehicles, Ken painstakingly restored a 1968 Ford Bronco and a 1967 Ford Mustang. Both vehicles had 302-cubic-inch engines—both rebuilt with .030 oversize pistons, hard piston seats, oversize Clevite bearings, advanced cam shafts, synthetic suspension parts, new radiators, and new exhaust systems from the manifolds back. Since these restorations replaced all of the major engine and driveline components, they were nearly "Zero Time" rebuilds—creating the equivalent of new vehicles with "zero time on the meter." Ken also replaced the Bronco's original steering-column-mounted gear shifter with a Hurst brand floor shifter—which he preferred.

The goal in restoring a late 1960s vehicle was to end up with an extremely reliable vehicle that was easy to work on. Unlike the modern monstrosities that had been coming out of Detroit since the 1980s—with umpteen electronic components and a huge array of sensors, emission control tubes, and mostly plastic parts—the old Fords were old-school designs with plenty of sturdy steel, and a minimum of frippery. Opening the hood, the owner could immediately recognize the alternator, master cylinder, water pump, and power steering pump. Getting access to them for replacement was a breeze.

Another advantage of starting with the older vehicles was that they had traditional "distributor, points, and plugs" ignition systems. This made them virtually invulnerable to the effect of nuclear electromagnetic pulse (EMP), or its natural equivalent, caused by solar flares. Todd Gray's philosophy was that the members of his group should make themselves ready for any and *all* eventualities.

One advantage of having Ken as a member of the group was that he had access to the garage at Chet's after normal working hours. Although he volunteered to do most of the restoration work himself, at cost, he insisted that each group member be there and assist him during the most important phases of the work. This way, Ken reasoned, every group member would know how their vehicles were put together, how they worked, and, hopefully, how to handle most minor repairs.

The vehicle restoration process that Ken insisted on turned out to be relatively expensive and time-consuming. He started by pulling the engine and transmission from each vehicle and farming them out to other shops to be completely rebuilt. Next he would make minor body repairs, sand out the bodies, and put on a flat paint finish, usually in an earth tone. They used standard glossy car paint with a special flattener added. This gave much better rust protection than regular flat paint. At roughly the same time, he would either rebuild or replace the carburetor. Next, when the engine and transmission came back, he would reinstall them, replacing all of their auxiliary equipment, aside from carburetors, with brand-new components. This included radiators, starters, alternators, fuel pumps, water pumps, batteries, voltage regulators, starter solenoids, hoses, and belts.

Next, Ken would rework the vehicle's suspension, usually modifying it for tougher off-road use, and do an alignment and brake job, sometimes involving replacing the master cylinder. In most cases, the vehicle's existing wiring harnesses did not need to be replaced. By the time he was done, Ken had in effect built a whole new vehicle that would be good for at least ten years of strenuous use.

2

Getting Out of Dodge

"These derivatives are the root of the credit crunch. Why? Unlike all other property paper, derivatives are not required by law to be recorded, continually tracked and tied to the assets they represent. Nobody knows precisely how many there are, where they are, and who is finally accountable for them. Thus, there is widespread fear that potential borrowers and recipients of capital with too many nonperforming derivatives will be unable to repay their loans. As trust in property paper breaks down it sets off a chain reaction, paralyzing credit and investment, which shrinks transactions and leads to a catastrophic drop in employment and in the value of everyone's property."
— **Peruvian economist Hernando de Soto Polar**

Chicago, Illinois
October, the First Year

Packing up was a nightmare. Even though Ken and Terry had prepositioned the majority of their storage food and field gear in Idaho, fitting everything that they wanted to bring in their Bronco and the Mustang was impossible. This cost them valuable time in prioritizing and repacking.

Their goal was to get to Todd and Mary Gray's ranch in Idaho as soon as possible. But Ken and Terry still spent too much time in front of the television, transfixed by the news updates on the unfolding economic collapse.

Terry shook her head and said, "I sure hope the government will take some steps—some measures that'll work. They've got to be able to put things back in order."

Ken shook his head. "I really doubt that. The inflation is totally out of control, and the economy is cratering. It's like what happened in Zimbabwe, only worse. The only way out of this is to hit the reset button and start from scratch, with a new currency. It's game over."

Terry frowned, and then Ken continued: "Look, we did our best to warn our families. We promised all the members of the group that we'd get out there to Todd's ranch in a disaster. And they were nice enough to let us store our extra food and gear there. We're committed. If we stick around here our life expectancy is going to drop to nil. So let's *go*, without any regrets."

Terry blinked twice, and then nodded in assent.

After the power went out, they spent the rest of the day packing up their Bronco and Mustang. But after they'd loaded the heaviest items, Ken noticed that the rear end of the Bronco was sagging. With no grid power, he couldn't even use his air compressor to raise the adjustable gas shocks. He had to use a hand pump instead. This turned a two-minute job into a forty-minute one.

By 10 p.m. they had the two vehicles loaded. They changed their clothes, donning British army surplus camouflage fatigues. These disruptive pattern material (DPM) clothes were sturdy and blended in a wide variety of foliage. They were the standard uniform for their Idaho retreat group. Much of their storage food and extra equipment was already in Idaho, at Todd and Mary's retreat. But even the small amount that they had at the house was a challenge to shoehorn into the two vehicles.

While they were packing, they heard gunshots in the distance. Each time that she heard shots, Terry gave Ken a nervous look. After the third time, Ken muttered, "Don't worry, that's just some lowlifes taking advantage of the blackout to settle old scores."

After some discussion, they decided to have Terry lead off in the Mustang. Terry summed up what they had both been contemplating. "Of our two vehicles, we've got to consider the Mustang semi-expendable, and the Bronco irreplaceable, since that's our four-wheel drive. So if we run low of fuel, we ditch the 'Stang. And if the Mustang gets blocked, or pinned, I'll bail out and run back to the Bronc. Hopefully that will distract any looters and give us time to get away."

Ken sighed, and said, "That's hardly like sacrificing a pawn. But under the circumstances, I guess that's the best we can hope for, if we get into a jam."

Ken and Terry worked by the light of flashlights while they packed. As they did so, they listened to the car radio in the Mustang, tuned to the WGN news broadcasts. The reporters mentioned that the station was operating on backup power. The litany of rioting, looting, and arson reports was nearly continuous. At 10:30 p.m., the traffic reports were still bad. There were traffic jams caused by collisions, car fires, stalled cars, and "police activity." That was the euphemism used by the local traffic reporters for gunfights in progress. There were dozens of these incidents throughout the metropolitan region.

Ken intentionally left their rifles and ALICE backpacks as the last items that they would pack on the passenger seats of both vehicles. These packs had been the standard U.S. military issue for many years. With an aluminum frame, olive drab nylon bag, and comfortable hip pad and shoulder straps, the ALICE was the pack carried by two generations of American soldiers. If they had to abandon their vehicles they might have to do so very quickly, and Ken insisted that the most important items be kept close at hand. Their backpacks and their weapons were by far their top priority.

Terry felt that it was best to get on the road as soon as possible. They hoped that leaving at night would minimize the traffic. But the news broadcasts spoke of traffic snarls at all hours. At 10:43, they started the engines of both the Bronco and the Mustang. Ken reached over the hood of the Mustang and pulled down the emergency release for the electric garage door opener. He yanked it backward, rolling the garage door up. In the Bronco, Ken followed Terry's Mustang slowly out the driveway into the street, which was lit only by their headlights.

3

True Believer

"Great works are performed, not by strength, but by perseverance. Yonder palace was raised by single stones, yet you see its height and spaciousness. He that shall walk with vigor three hours a day will pass in seven years a space equal to the circumference of the globe."
—Samuel Johnson (1709–1784)

Richmond, Virginia
Seventeen Years Before the Crunch

Being born and raised in the upscale Carytown district of Richmond, Virginia, Ben Fielding was not very well prepared for the Crunch. His education as a lawyer didn't help him much, either. If it weren't for the fact that he had moved to a rural area a few years before the Crunch, he probably wouldn't have survived it.

Ben's parents were Reformed Jews. His father was a farm credit union loan officer and his mother was a "professional volunteer" who had spent all of her married life donating her time to the PTA, the Red Cross, Women of Hadassah, Habitat for Humanity, and the Democratic Party at the precinct level.

Ben attended the prestigious Yeshiva of Virginia for high school and then pre-law and law school at Virginia Commonwealth University. As he grew up, even though he attended Yeshiva, Ben felt that he was more Jewish by birth than he was by faith. After graduating from high school, he only rarely attended temple services.

Ironically, it was one of his Gentile classmates from his law study circle who invited Ben to attend a Saturday Shabbat service at Tikvat Israel ("Hope of Israel"), a Messianic Jewish congregation on Grove Street in Richmond. The congregation was a mixture of "Jewish Believers"—Jews who had come to faith in Yeshua Messiah (Jesus Christ) and Gentile followers of the Messiah who enjoyed delving into the more Hebraic roots of their faith, including celebrating the Feasts of the Lord, accompanied by some Shabbat service liturgy. About 10 percent of the congregation was black.

The Tikvat congregation met in an old synagogue building that had been the meeting place for Beth Israel from the late 1940s to the early 1970s. The building had sat vacant for fifteen years before the Tikvat congregation noticed it in 1990 and found that it was available to rent. One of the Elders had a vision which indicated that this old building was to be their new congregational home. The Tikvat group held their first service there during Chanukah in December 1990.

Occasionally at Tikvat there would be "black hat" visitors to the Shabbat service—Orthodox Jews. Many of them were just curious about the Messianic Jewish movement, but a few were business travelers who were "walk-ins," assuming that it was a typical Saturday Jewish temple meeting. Very few of them visited more than once. They seemed offended, either by the modern worship service and the band's electric instruments being played on the Sabbath, or by the references to the Messiah, Yeshua. Other Jewish visitors, like Ben, who were Reformed seemed more receptive to the Good News of Messiah, and less offended by the contemporary aspects of the service.

Ben was intrigued by the services and what he heard. He wanted to know more about Yeshua. Shortly after beginning to attend, Ben decided to take the Messianic rabbi's new member class. He heard provoking and expositional teaching of the scriptures.

These proved to him without a shadow of a doubt that Yeshua was indeed the long-awaited Jewish Messiah. Ben spent a lot of time studying the scriptures on his own, praying, and fasting. One day he got on his knees and cried out to Jesus to forgive him for his rebellion against God and for sins he had committed in his life. Ben recognized that he could never keep the Law perfectly, and that all men are sinners. He asked Jesus to come into his life and to save him. Jesus sent the Holy Spirit at that moment and Ben felt a glorious in-filling and cleansing. Immediately, Ben knew that he had become born-again, a "completed Jew." Full of that indescribable joy, he jumped up from his bedside and began praising God and worshipping him with all his heart, mind, and soul. At the next Shabbat service, Ben confessed to the congregation that he had repented and that Yeshua had come into his life and that he knew that he was saved from his sins. Four months later Ben took part in a Mikvah service, being immersed for baptism in the York River, along with some other new believers from Tikvat.

Ben tried to explain to his parents and show them how Jesus fulfilled many of the scriptures prophesying the future Messiah: Jesus as the Suffering Servant of Isaiah 53, Daniel's prophecies of the coming Messiah, and how the Seven Feasts of Israel pointed to his birth, life, death, resurrection, and ascension. He did his best to articulate why he believed that Yeshua was the Messiah. He often invited them to come to the congregation but they politely declined. They felt that Ben was simply infatuated by this new congregation, and being "a nice Jewish boy" would eventually, as his mother put it, "give up this meshuga nonsense." He and his father often had antagonistic conversations about whether Jesus was the Messiah, and sometimes his father became angry and sarcastic and referred to Jesus as "your heretical rabbi."

Ben loved Jesus' Hebrew name and often said "Yeshua" to his father, but his father would refer to Jesus as YESHU: using the Hebrew acronym, which means, "May his name and memory be

blotted out forever," a term coined in extra-biblical rabbinic litera-
ture and used by many Jews who are opposed to Yeshua being the
Messiah. It is traditionally forbidden by many Jews to even mention His name. The irony in all of this was that Yeshua in Hebrew
means "salvation." Ben was sad that his father had so hardened
his heart against Yeshua that he couldn't listen.

After seven months of attending Tikvat, as a third-year law
student (a "3L") Ben met his future wife, Rebecca.

Rebecca Emerson was a Gentile. She played the guitar in the
Tikvat band, danced with the Tikvat Israel Dancers, and was con-
versant in Hebrew. She even taught Hebrew in Tikvat's Hebrew
school. She was studying to become a midwife. She had long light
brown curly hair, hazel eyes, and a lovely smile. She had been
homeschooled and was just nineteen years old when she and Ben
met. She had grown up attending Tikvat.

When Ben first started to attend Tikvat, Rebecca was away,
traveling on an eleven-month Christian medical mission trip to
Ethiopia to witness to and physically help the Falasha Jews who
were preparing to make aliyah—immigration to Israel. Rebecca
took this trip along with her parents and her younger siblings.
When they returned to the United States they resumed attending
Tikvat.

Ben was captivated the first time that he saw Rebecca. Who
was this young woman who sang and played the guitar so well?
Both Ben and Rebecca soon joined the staff of the Youth Group.
They became fast friends and spent a lot of time together during
Youth Group meetings and activities. Ben found Rebecca to be
grounded in her faith, confident, intelligent, and well educated.
She could speak knowledgeably on nearly any topic, especially
apologetics, history, politics, economics, biblical prophecy, natural science, creationism, and biblical law. She was much more con-
versant in Hebrew than Ben.

Along with Ben, Rebecca had taken the Messianic rabbi's biblical law class, in which they had studied all of the ancient biblical laws in the book of Leviticus and also Talmudic law studies. So she had learned to discern circular logic and fallacies, and to recognize the original intent of the law and its later overamplification in modern Jewish life.

Ben found Rebecca to be vivacious and funny. He soon began to learn about her dreams and aspirations for the future. She wanted to be a midwife, a wife, mother, and a homeschooling mom, raising a family out in a rural area, living a homesteading life. Even though much of that was foreign to Ben, he was beginning to think she was a wonderful young woman.

Rebecca's father, Ron Emerson, was a dentist and had led a medical mission team into Gondar, Ethiopia. Because he was a dentist going into villages free of charge, the Ethiopian government allowed him and his team in. Her father said that his family was "part of the team," so they were also able to get visas and accompany him for the year they were there. Rebecca and her siblings quickly learned the Amharic language once they were in Ethiopia. They helped both her father and the doctors on the team with language translation and doctoring. She even witnessed and assisted with some childbirths. Even though her skills as a dental assistant and her knowledge of midwifery were rudimentary, she was considered an expert by the Ethiopian people. They assumed that anyone with white skin was a trained expert.

When Rebecca's family returned to the United States and Tikvat, Rebecca's family was asked to lead a Chavurah. These groups—based on the Hebrew word root *chaver*, which means "friend"—are study cell groups. Their Chavurah met on Thursday nights. Every year the groups switched around their congregants so everyone could eventually meet the other folks in the congregation. Propitiously, Ben was assigned to Ron's Chavurah. A typical Chavurah meeting began at 6:30 and went until 9:30. They usually consisted of potluck dinner, dessert social time, and a Bible study on various topics such as health, hermeneutics, creationism, eschatology, and prayer—followed by more general talk.

During the Chavurah study on biblical health Ben noticed that Ron began questioning the group members about their personal health issues. Ron seemed to be subtly sizing up Ben's health history. It was not until then that Ben realized how obvious Ben's and Rebecca's interest in each other had become.

One time while visiting the Emersons' home, Ben was walking in their backyard and noticed an old well. At first he thought it was merely a decorative wishing well. But then Ron mentioned that it was a hand-dug well from the 1800s that had never been filled in, even after city water had been provided to the neighborhood. The well shaft was more than forty feet deep and three feet wide. Ben pointed out that in the eyes of the law the well was considered an "attractive nuisance." He advised Emerson to put a locking cover over the well's mouth, to prevent any neighborhood children from falling in. Ron thanked him. The following weekend, Ben helped him construct the hinged cover and install a lock hasp. It was through this experience that Emerson's opinion of Ben moved up a notch and they began to think of each other more as equals.

As the months passed, Ben's parents realized Ben was not just infatuated with *"this Jesus"* and with Messianic Judaism, but was completely embracing Yeshua and the Messianic lifestyle. This new faith of their son's began to alarm them and was unacceptable in their eyes. They were beginning to feel like Ben had been brainwashed and drawn into a cult. They tried to talk him out of being a Believer. They asked him to renounce "Yeshu" from being his Savior. They consulted their rabbi on what they should do. He said to send Ben to him for a meeting. Ben refused to go. Next, their rabbi suggested a clandestine gathering at their home to which they would invite a group of rabbis from the New York branch of an Israeli organization that specialized in "deprogramming" Jewish people who have come under the sway of missionar-

ies. They invited Ben home for dinner and "to meet some friends and have a discussion."

Ben didn't stay even long enough for his mother to serve dinner. The agenda of the four strangers became immediately apparent. Ben tried reasoning with them. They refused to listen to him, even when he quoted biblical prophetic passages from Isaiah that clearly foreshadowed Christ's First Coming. After answering several of their questions, and after it became apparent that they had no intention of rationally debating him—only browbeating him—Ben said, "Well, it was nice meeting you all. I have to go now. You will be in my prayers." He bolted out the door.

His parents never spoke to him again.

As two of the oldest members of the Youth Group and designated "staff," Ben and Rebecca joined Tikvat's group trip to Israel for a combined one-month missionary trip and celebration of the Feast of Tabernacles in Jerusalem with the International Christian Embassy. After the feast, the Youth Group traveled to Tel Aviv and assisted a couple of the Messianic Jewish congregations in a joint broadsiding campaign on the Tayelet—a boardwalk along the shore of the Mediterranean that continues for about five miles from the north of Tel Aviv south to Jaffa. There are many restaurants and hotels along this stretch of sandy beaches and rocky outcroppings.

Four large Messianic Jewish congregations and outreach organizations of Tel Aviv and Jaffa (Adonai Roi, Trumpet of Salvation, Beit Immanuel, and Tiferet Yeshua) would, on a regular basis, go out together on the Tayelet to witness and to hand out tracts and Bibles in many languages—not just Hebrew. They also put on street dramas which included worship and dance that depicted the life, death, and resurrection of Jesus. Afterward they would sing praise and modern Christian worship songs in Hebrew, hand out tracts, and talk to and pray with individuals who had questions about Yeshua Messiah.

One morning later in the Israel trip, Ben had woken up early and, as was his practice while in Israel, he went out for a brisk walk on the beach for his prayer time. Some of his prayers had been asking God for a godly wife. Ever since meeting Rebecca, he had been asking in his prayers if she was the one for him and when it would be appropriate to ask for her hand in marriage. He greatly enjoyed her friendship. He felt incredibly alive in her presence. She had become precious to him, but he had been biding his time, patiently waiting for the Lord to confirm if she was to be his bride.

This particular morning, Ben felt a special need to fervently pray about and for Rebecca, asking that God give him a sign that she was the wife that He had chosen for him. As he walked and prayed he looked down at the sand. Suddenly, he saw a small pearly white donut-shaped seashell fragment that had been worn smooth by the tides. He picked up the ring-shaped shell and slipped it onto his pinky finger. It fit perfectly, stopping at just above the knuckle. Just then he heard God's quiet voice in his heart say that this shell was for Rebecca's engagement ring and that he was to ask Rebecca to marry him that night.

That afternoon, the tour group leader unexpectedly told the Youth Group that their evening plans had been canceled and that this would be a free night for everyone. Ben realized this was the open door to ask Rebecca to go for a walk with him. As the group broke up, Ben approached Rebecca. Looking at her clear face, bright hazel eyes, and slim form, his heart swelled with a very protective love. When he stepped into her space, she looked up at him with a warm smile. Ben smiled in return, leaned over slightly, and whispered, "I'd like to talk with you this evening. Could you meet me down in the lobby at seven o'clock?"

Rebecca looked up at him with a twinkle in her eye and answered him, "Okay, I'll come down." Immediately after this, Ben walked down to the lobby and nervously called Rebecca's father, back in Virginia, using his international calling card. Ron an-

swered the phone. When he heard that it was Ben calling from Israel, Ron was alarmed that something had happened to Rebecca. Ben reassured him that she and everybody with their group was fine and spoke briefly about all that the Youth Group had been doing.

Then Ben took a deep audible breath and told Ron how much he had come to love Rebecca over the past months and that he had been praying, asking God if she was to be his wife. He told him about that morning's prayer time and the donut-shaped shell he had found and the small still voice of the Lord saying that the shell was for Rebecca. Ben then asked Ron if he could have permission to ask for Rebecca's hand in marriage and, if so, he felt that he would ask her that very night.

When Ben finished, Ron was quiet on the other end. Ben began to get nervous, wondering if the phone connection had been interrupted. Suddenly, Ron began to speak in his familiar clipped style. Sounding a bit choked up, Ron shared with Ben stories about Rebecca's life: her birth, toddlerhood, elementary years, and of the most funny and touching things she said and did. He described the uncanny wisdom and knowledge she possessed as a young girl. He told Ben about what he knew of her dreams and aspirations for life. He told of her personality and idiosyncrasies, her weaknesses, their challenges and joys in training and raising her, and how proud they were of her. He told him how often his wife and he had prayed for a godly, righteous young man to marry their daughter.

Then Ron said that he had been observing Ben and asking people about his character, kindness, generosity, honesty, work ethic, self-control and self-governance, health, love for the Lord, and dedication to the Word. He had been watching Rebecca interacting with him and listening to her praise him to her family. Ron told Ben that he was very impressed with his character and attitudes. He said that their family had come to love and respect Ben and that they could see that God had made him and Rebecca a match and that the Emersons would love to have him as a member of their family. Ron finished by saying, "You have my blessing." He then prayed for them.

When Ben got off the phone he felt relieved and exhilarated. The phone call had lasted for more than an hour, burning up more than half the minutes on the calling card.

Ben raced up the stairs to his hotel room. After pacing for a minute, he lay down on his bed to praise and thank the Lord. He spent some time praying and reading the Word before a late afternoon meal. After dinner he showered, shaved, and dressed in a white linen short-sleeved shirt and light khaki pants and went down to the lobby to await Rebecca. He prayed and nervously rolled the ring-shaped shell in the palm of his hand.

A few minutes later she appeared on the stairs. Ben's heart flip-flopped for a moment at the sight of her. Quickly, he pocketed the ring, while he observed Rebecca's jaunty descent of the last few steps. She was wearing a green light cotton dress and Teva sandals. Her curly hair looked darker than usual, because she had just taken a shower.

Ben smiled and greeted Rebecca, and her eyes sparkled back as she asked where they were going. Ben whispered mysteriously, "We are going for a walk, because I wish to talk to you and show you something." Ben had said this twice before to Rebecca, so she happily thought it would be another interesting sightseeing adventure. He had seen a lot of the city during his early morning walks and would tell Rebecca of them. She hadn't yet seen as much of Jaffa as Ben had.

Ben lightly guided Rebecca with his fingers barely touching her elbow, out of the main door of the lobby of the hotel, into the parking lot, around the corner, and down the alleyway to Auerbach Street. From there, they turned left onto the dirty, dingy, "concrete jungle" of Eilat Street. Rebecca disliked this street that often

smelled like urine. She preferred grass and yards to only buildings and concrete and always walked quickly, looking forward to
reaching the sea. Along Eilat Street there were large Mylar-backed
glass storefront windows that reflected like mirrors. As Rebecca
and Ben would pass them she would surreptitiously look at herself
and Ben and size up whether they looked like a matching couple,
and she liked what she saw. Later, she learned that Ben was also
sizing them up in those same windows.

They reached the point where Eilat Street Ts off with Professor
Yehezkel Kaufman Street. There, they turned right and walked
west to the grassy parks of the Tayelet along the Mediterranean.
Here the street opened up, with buildings on one side and open
lawns on the other, the Tayelet, the beach, and sea. Rebecca loved
this part of Tel Aviv–Jaffa. Looking north one could sea the beach
curving around the edge of the city of Tel Aviv and its skyline.
Looking south one could see the little hill on which Old Jaffa sits
and its fishing port. She had read that this was the town where
Peter the Apostle visited Cornelius, the God-fearing Gentile who
wanted to learn of the way of Salvation after his vision of the sheet
and a command allowing the eating of unclean beasts.

The sun was near setting when they reached the sea. The sky
was a golden hazy blue, the wind had just reversed its normal flow
and was now coming in off of the mainland. It had a lovely warm
caress and wonderfully fresh salty smell.

Ben turned Rebecca to the south and they walked the Tayelet
toward Old Jaffa. They walked to Retsif HaAliyah HaShniya
Street, where they cut back inland until they reached the Clock
Tower on Nahum Goldman Street. Walking around the *kikar* (a
traffic circle), they continued walking south until they reached Mi-
fratz Shlomo Promenade. A bit up the promenade, Ben veered off
onto the grass and took Rebecca up to the top of the hill to show
her the Statue of Faith, a square arch. He pointed out to her how
the left side shows Jacob's Dream; the right, the Sacrifice of Isaac;

and the top, the fall of Jericho. Rebecca was fascinated. They walked around some of the ruins on top of the hill of Old Jaffa, then walked down to the Church of Saint Peter. Next, Ben took Rebecca to the restaurant behind the minaret. (Jaffa is mainly an Arab Israeli–Muslim town.)

At Ben's request, they were given a table out on the balcony overlooking the sea. It was now twilight. They could see the lights of Tel Aviv. They ordered hummus, pita, and mixed salads for their appetizers. Ben and Rebecca loved the many vegetables in the mixed salads: tomato, cucumber, peppers, radishes, lettuce, eggplant, olives, cabbage, and onions. Ben loved to sprinkle zatar on his hummus. For their main course they ordered lamb kabobs on the stick with *"cheeptz"*—the local name for French fries.

Over dinner, Ben and Rebecca talked of all they had seen and what they had been doing with the Youth Group, their successes in witnessing, how the trip was turning out, and about the things they wanted to do with the Youth Group when they returned home. Ben also talked about what he was planning for his future with his law career, and missionary work, later in life.

After dinner, Ben took Rebecca back out onto the promenade and they walked back up the hill toward the Statue of Faith where it overlooked the sea. He found a private bench, away from the streetlights, where they could have a good view without distracting lights. He invited Rebecca to sit down. They sat quietly together for a few minutes enjoying the view of the city lights, the Mediterranean, and the light breeze. As they looked out to sea, they could also see the navigational lights of airliners stacked up for their approach to Ben Gurion Airport, not far to the south.

As they looked out at the lights, Ben said, "I called your dad this afternoon, and we had a long talk before he went to work. It was nine in the morning his time."

"A long talk?" asked Rebecca quizzically.

"Yes."

"And so?"

"So, I asked him for his blessing, and he said yes."

"That's kind of a roundabout way of asking me . . ."

"Yes, but I was getting to that. I mean, I *am* asking you, I mean . . ."

Rebecca gave a nod and gently urged, "So what exactly are you asking?"

"You are a gift from the Lord, Rebecca. You've become my best friend. I find myself constantly thinking about you. I have thoroughly enjoyed working beside you with the Youth Group and the service projects that we've done. I love the way you think! I love communicating with you and can't wait to ask you questions, getting your opinion and hearing your insights. I have come to love you with all my heart and soul. I would be incredibly blessed if you would become my wife. I believe that the two of us together will be a strong team for furthering Adonai's Kingdom."

Ben then reached into his pocket and pulled out the ring, saying deliberately, "I want to give you something that I found on the beach this morning during my quiet time. I have been praying for you and about you for more than a year now. I've been asking Adonai for the timing and the confirmation. And seeing how much you love God's creation and enjoy finding perfectly created natural objects, I believe this find is a gift to us, a gift to you from the Lord. It is His confirmation for us to marry."

He held out the seashell, clutched between his thumb and forefinger.

Unexpectedly, Rebecca extended her ring finger, and Ben slid it on. She gave a gentle laugh, as she carefully turned the ring around on her finger and murmured, "It's beautiful, Ben! So perfectly shaped and such a pure unblemished white! You really just found this on the beach this morning? It's a miracle. I believe it *is* confirmation and I say 'Yes.' Yes, Benjamin, I will be your wife! I love you and I've been praying and hoping, too, that you were the one and that you would choose me!" She smiled and laughed out loud, shouting "Hallelujah," and began dancing around. Ben stood up and Rebecca ran into his arms and gave him a warm hug and a kiss on the cheek. Ben lifted Rebecca and swung her around, laughing, praising Adonai and telling of his love for her.

They stopped dancing and Ben took both of Rebecca's hands in his and facing her he said, "I will always protect you."

Rebecca replied: "Ben, I will respect you, and I will honor you. I will listen to you. I will pray for you."

Then and there he prayed that God would orchestrate the timing of the wedding and that he would give them much self-control and that he would train them and use them for His kingdom.

They slowly retraced their steps back to Beit Immanuel, talking the whole way about their dreams for their future. They married eighteen months after their first meeting, just shortly after Ben took the Tennessee State Bar exam. The wedding band that he then slipped on her finger was a platinum casting of the seashell that he had found on the beach in Israel. Rebecca often wore the fragile original seashell as a necklace, on a light gold chain.

Following law school, Ben's first job was with a firm in Nashville. In Nashville, Ben and Rebecca found Beth Israel, a small Messianic Jewish congregation. A few of the members of the congregation were standoffish and associated only with other Jewish Believers. They thought of Ben and Rebecca as a "mixed" couple. But most of the congregation was friendly.

Discouraged to find that a small, vocal minority of members of Beth Israel were over-legalistic and some too rabbinical, Ben and Rebecca were happy to find a new congregation when they eventually moved to rural Muddy Pond, Tennessee.

Rebecca had grown up in Richmond, but many of her childhood friends in her homeschooling co-op group had lived in the country outside town. This made Rebecca long for a home in the country, a large garden, and livestock. It was not until the Fieldings moved to Muddy Pond that her dream came true. Drawing on the wisdom and experience of Dorris, a widowed "ex-hippie" grandmother who lived just a quarter mile away, Rebecca gradually accumulated a useful assortment of livestock. She had a Guernsey cow named Matilda, dozens of chickens, a few ducks, some sheep, and a few barn cats. When Rebecca would go out to milk Matilda she would dance out the kitchen door with her milking bucket singing "Milking Matilda" to the tune of the Australian folk song "Waltzing Matilda." Rebecca loved drinking their own fresh raw milk, making their own butter, yogurt, cheese, and ice cream; and growing, canning, freezing, and drying her own homegrown fruits, vegetables, and herbs.

Although he was a city boy, Ben learned to love their place in the boonies. The wild game was abundant, and the fishing was good, both in ponds and in the local streams and rivers. Under the tutelage of a retired neighbor, Ben learned how to shoot, and he in turn started teaching his son to shoot when he was just six years old.

Later, after the Crunch, when Ben and Rebecca's oldest son, Joseph, had turned thirteen, he was trusted to hunt on his own. He hunted on the Fieldings' own property and the 320 acres of adjoining timber company land. Joseph dearly loved fishing and hunting. After his homeschooling was completed each day, if the weather was passable, the thirteen-year-old would go out with either his fishing pole or his Mossberg single-shot .22 rimfire rifle. He was proud that he could help feed the family in a substantial way, and his parents were appreciative of his efforts. Joseph was a patient, self-taught hunter, and was famous for rarely missing a shot. (His .22 rimfire cartridges were strictly rationed, and the use of every one had to be accounted for.) He often brought home bullfrogs, grouse, opossums, quail, rabbits, raccoons, and even armadillos. (The latter they called "possum on the half shell.") Less frequently, he would bag wild turkeys and deer with head shots.

In all, Joseph made a substantial contribution to the family's food needs.

Ben preferred trapping and snaring to hunting. As he explained it, "A trap is hunting twenty-four hours a day." He used wire snares in various sizes ranging from squirrel size to deer size. Most of his success around the house was with rabbits. He also used Conibear #110 traps for squirrels. Between Joseph's hunting, Ben's trapping, milk from Matilda, and Rebecca's big vegetable garden, the Fielding family ate much better than most other families in Tennessee in the aftermath of the Crunch.

4

Rushes

"A nuclear-missile silo is one of the quintessential Great Plains objects: to the eye, it is almost nothing, just one or two acres of ground with a concrete slab in the middle and some posts and poles sticking up behind an eight-foot-high Cyclone fence; but to the imagination, it is the end of the world."

—Ian Frazier, *Great Plains*, 1989

The Monroe Ranch, Raynesford, Montana
October, the First Year

Joshua and Kelly's wedding was at the outset of a socioeconomic collapse that made the Great Depression of the 1930s seem mild by comparison. The Crunch was a devastating global banking and currency collapse without precedent. Seemingly overnight, stock and bond markets fell into turmoil, the U.S. dollar was declared "trash" by foreign investors, and mass inflation ensued. The price of gasoline vaulted to $6 per gallon, then $10, and finally $25 before becoming virtually unobtainable. The price of groceries followed a similar trajectory. Nationwide, there was a mad scramble to convert paper dollars into practical, tangible items. People stocked up on anything and everything they could find. The gas stations, grocery stores, gun shops, and pharmacies were the first stores to have their shelves cleaned out. Toward the end, even sacks of livestock feed, bundles of rags, and thrift store castoffs were eagerly sought. Ultimately, those who foolishly held on to their dollars saw their value melt away in the blast furnace of hyperinflation.

Kelly's diamond wedding ring was a gift from her mother, Rhonda. It had been her grandmother's wedding ring. For many years, Rhonda had hoped that Kelly would someday wear it. The rushed circumstances didn't leave much time for the usual bridal shower. But a visiting neighbor did ask, "What would you like for wedding gifts?"

Kelly answered without hesitation, "We need .30-06, .243 Winchester, and .22 Magnum ammo. We could also use a good pair of binoculars."

They could have been married in Great Falls—which was closer—but Kelly had the idea of getting married at the county courthouse in Stanford. After seeing the store shelves in Great Falls devastated, she was hoping that the hardware stores, sporting goods stores, and ranch supply stores in Stanford would still have some inventory since it was a smaller town. Unfortunately, she was wrong. In visiting seven stores in the towns of Geyser and Stanford the only useful items that they bought were a few pieces of horse tack, two grain buckets, one can of Coleman white gas, and three bottles of Hoppe's #9 rifle bore cleaner. The store shelves looked like those they had seen at grocery stores in news footage from the Gulf Coast just before a hurricane hit.

The county courthouse in Stanford was uncharacteristically crowded. Not only were there several other "hurry up" weddings like Joshua Watanabe's, but there was also a flurry of mortgage settlement filings—as people had just recently taken advantage of the hyperinflation to pay off their home and ranch loans. Simultaneously, there were also a large number of land subdivisions, swaps, and grants that resulted in deeds being filed. Many of these were "In Exchange for $1 . . ."—quit claim deeds, caused by families "doubling up" or otherwise co-locating for mutual security.

Under a quit claim deed, title was conveyed without any significant amount of cash changing hands. The grantee would then assume responsibility for any claims against the property.

The civil ceremony was rushed and informal. Rhonda came with them to sign as a witness. She consoled Kelly, saying, "Don't let it bother you, Kel. You'll have a big church wedding after all this economic mess blows over."

Another exigency of the Crunch was that it went without saying that Joshua would move into the Monroes' ranch house, rather than Kelly moving into Joshua's rental. In the new paradigm, safety in numbers trumped all. Moving to the Monroe ranch took only a few hours, accomplished the same day and evening as the wedding. Like many young men in the Air Force, Joshua didn't have many possessions. His pickup and horse trailer made the move easy. By 11 p.m. he had his horse and tack in the barn and his uniforms, civilian clothes, and camping gear piled in Kelly's room.

Kelly said, "We'll go back and get the straw and hay bales tomorrow. And speaking of hay, how about our consummating roll in the hay?" She locked the door.

Chicago, Illinois
October, the First Year

Ken and Terry Layton were nervous and they chattered anxiously on their two-way radios as they drove through the blacked-out streets. "I can't believe we just walked away from our house."

"You gotta do what you gotta do," Ken radioed back.

Over the sound of their engines, they could hear the low staccato of numerous gunfights. One of them was close enough that they saw muzzle flashes. There were no streetlights, no traffic lights, and no house lights. Just a bit of candlelight visible in a few windows.

Ken was disappointed when they had to diverge from their

planned route. Terry touched her microphone button. "We can't take the Eisenhower Expressway. Just look at it: It's jammed up, bumper-to-bumper. Let's head west on the surface streets."

"Okay, how about we head out West Fillmore?"

"Roger that."

Shortly after they got on West Fillmore Street the cars ahead came to a stop. Apparently there was a stalled vehicle ahead. They backed up slightly and turned south on Ayers Avenue. Then Terry led them west on West 14th Avenue. Ken didn't like the look of the neighborhood. There were a lot of run-down houses. Ken was also apprehensive that now their car was the only one moving on the street.

They had driven just another five blocks west when suddenly from the right side a trash dumpster was pushed out into the street in front of the Mustang. Immediately after, a seven-foot-tall cable spool—one that had originally held large-diameter telephone wire—was rolled in from the left. Ken and Terry slammed on the brakes.

Just as they came to a full stop, gunfire erupted around them. All of the side and back windows on both the Bronco and Mustang collapsed. Their front windshields each also took several hits, but remained intact. The passenger-side tires on the Bronco burst, and Ken felt the vehicle list to that side. He bruised his ribs on the Hurst floor shifter lever as he rapidly bent down to avoid the gunfire.

Also prone on the front seat of the Mustang, Terry flipped the selector lever of the car's automatic transmission into reverse. She stepped on the gas, trying to back out of the roadblock. The back end of the Mustang collided with the front of the Bronco with a sickening crunch.

Ken shouted over his TRC headset walkie-talkie: "If you can, *bail*!"

The gunfire continued, though less rapidly. Ken and Terry both

grabbed their rifles and backpacks. They then almost simultaneously crawled out of their cars and hastily shouldered their packs.

Without even thinking about it, Terry's field training under
the tutelage of Jeff Trasel from Todd Gray's group kicked in. She
keyed her TRC-500 and said, "By bounds, follow me. I'll fire, *you*
move."

She thumbed her AR's selector switch, and aimed at the muzzle
flashes of their attackers, firing five rounds.

Ken scrambled to the side of the street and squatted down behind a parked car. He radioed: "Okay, Joe, I'll fire, you move." (In
their "bounding by pairs" training, all the participants referred
to each other as "Joe," and that stuck.) Just before Terry started
her bound, Ken started firing. Compared to his wife's AR-15, his
larger-caliber HK clone made a much louder boom, and had a
larger muzzle flash.

She replied in a singsong, again from their training. "Okay,
Joe, I'll fire, you move."

Taking turns, they made five bounding rushes, using parked
cars for cover. After the fourth bound, all return fire had ceased.
At the end of the block, they knelt down behind a raised brick
hedge and checked each other over for wounds. They found only
that Ken had one bullet hole through the armpit of his shirt and
jacket. The bullet hadn't touched his skin. Terry had scratches on
her right hand and right cheek from broken glass, but they weren't
bleeding. They reloaded their rifles with fresh magazines. Altogether, they had fired ninety rounds while executing their with-
drawal.

Terry had accidentally dropped the magazine that she had expended between her bounding rushes, but Ken still had an empty
magazine that he'd tucked into one of the cargo pockets on his
trouser leg.

Ken whispered, "Not bad for 'withdraw by fire.'"

"Yeah, Jeff Trasel would be proud."

A moment later, a road flare was ignited near the Bronco and Mustang. The night was so dark that the flare seemed quite bright. Ken and Terry watched with a mixture of fascination and horror a bonfire of wooden pallets, accelerated by a small bucket of gasoline.

By the light of the bonfire, the dozen gang members who had ambushed the Laytons began pillaging the contents of their car and truck. There were loud exclamations as each item was extracted from the vehicles. There were repeated shouts of "Oh yeah!" and "Check it out!" and "This is sick!" One of them hoisted Ken's Remington riotgun in the air and gave a "Woot-woot" shout.

Seeing and hearing this, Ken and Terry were seething. "Those heathen bastards! They're taking all our stuff," Terry muttered.

Ken suggested, "What do you say we make 'em pay for it?"

"I don't know. Do you think that's right?"

Ken nodded and answered, "It's as right as anything could be. Hey, they just did their best to kill us, and they're taking almost everything in the world we have that's worth anything. I say make 'em pay for it, *with interest*."

Terry reached out to tightly grasp Ken's hand, in affirmation.

They dropped down on the sidewalk to the right of a hedge, and got into good prone shooting positions, side by side.

Terry said, "I've got the guys to the right of the bonfire, you take the ones on the left."

"Give me a sec," Ken answered. He shifted his position slightly, and thumbed the HK's safety to the "E" position.

His first target was the man who held the Remington riotgun. By now, he was shouting, "I got the power! I got the power!" Ken waited until he had several other targets close to the bonfire. Then he whispered: "One, two, *three*!"

They each fired a full magazine. The man with the riotgun went down hard. They killed or wounded at least five others.

After there were no more distinct targets standing, they expended the rest of their magazines shooting at likely places where the looters might have taken cover. They rose to their feet and ran around the corner, reloading their guns as they ran.

Halfway down the block they stopped to check each other for injuries and to talk. They decided that to get around the riffraff that ambushed them, they would walk another two blocks south, and then turn to resume traveling west.

They moved in tactical bounds for seven blocks, constantly watching for threats. The sound of gunfire and sirens was almost continuous in all directions. Some of it sounded as if it was within a couple of blocks, but most of it had to be farther off. With their movement in buddy rushes, they were soon feeling exhausted.

Ken trotted up to Terry and whispered, "There's got to be a better way. We'll never get out of town by dawn doing it this way." They crawled behind the concealment of some large bushes next to a Lutheran church, and draped a poncho over themselves to consult a street map with a subdued flashlight.

Terry pointed out their location on the map. "It's ten-plus miles to even get out of Chicago itself, and then there's suburbs," she whispered.

"So, shall I call for a cab?" Ken joked.

Then, more seriously, he added, "Our chances of walking out of this without getting ventilated are about one percent."

He gazed down at the map again, and prayed silently. The map showed no parks or other breaks in successive city blocks for miles ahead.

Terry said, still in a whisper, "Why not go underground, down in the storm drains, just like we talked about for nuke scenarios?"

Ken beamed. "Oh, I love you! That sure beats staying up here in the free-fire zone."

Terry looked up at Ken and asked, "How are we going to get down there?"

"Remember that illustration in T.K.'s book *Life After Dooms-*

day, where you take two big bolts and join them with a piece of wire? Then you stick one of them down into the pry hole on a manhole cover, and pull up."

Terry nodded.

He opened the top flap of his backpack and started to dig though its contents. He soon found a coil of wire. After some more searching, he pulled out a 1970s-vintage Boy Scout knife-fork-spoon kit that had belonged to his father. He twisted two thicknesses of the wire around the spoon and then the same for the knife, with one foot of wire between them.

The knife ended up working well as a toggle, because it had a bottle-opening notch in the middle. That held the wire in place perfectly.

Ken reassembled the contents of his pack and reshouldered it. He then began searching the block, looking for a manhole cover. It took a few minutes to find one marked "Storm Sewer," visible by the dim light of Terry's tiny single-LED flashlight.

Ken handed his rifle to his wife. After inserting the knife into the manhole cover's one-inch aperture, he pulled up on the spoon connected by the wire. The knife had toggled over and held firm. Ken squatted, beefed the manhole cover up, and slid it aside with a clank that sounded uncomfortably loud. He then retrieved his utensils and wire and stuffed them into one of his pants cargo pockets.

Terry descended first. She said quietly, "Okay, it looks doable. There's just a trickle in the bottom. Hand me my gear."

Ken handed down her carbine, then her pack, then his pack, and then his rifle. He lingered at the uppermost ladder rungs to slide the lid back in place over his head. It closed with a reverberating thud.

5

Trogs

"'It has never happened!' cannot be construed to mean, 'It can never happen!'—might as well say, 'Because I have never broken my leg, my leg is unbreakable,' or 'Because I've never died, I am immortal.' One thinks first of some great plague of insects—locusts or grasshoppers—when the species suddenly increases out of all proportion, and then just as dramatically sinks to a tiny fraction of what it has recently been. The higher animals also fluctuate. During most of the nineteenth century the African buffalo was a common creature on the veldt. It was a powerful beast with few natural enemies, and if its census could have been taken by decades, it would have proved to be increasing steadily. Then toward the century's end it reached its climax, and was suddenly struck by a plague of rinderpest. Afterwards the buffalo was almost a curiosity, extinct in many parts of its range. In the last fifty years it has again slowly built up its numbers. As for man, there is little reason to think that he can, in the long run, escape the fate of other creatures, and if there is a biological law of flux and reflux, his situation is now a highly perilous one. During ten thousand years his numbers have been on the upgrade in spite of wars, pestilence, and famines. This increase in population has become more and more rapid. Biologically, man has for too long a time been rolling an uninterrupted run of sevens."

—George R. Stewart, *Earth Abides* (1949)

Chicago, Illinois
October, the First Year

Ken climbed down to Terry and said, "I sure hope this works."

They helped each other put on their packs, which was difficult in the cramped confines of the drain. They slung their rifles across their chests, with their muzzles down and with their buttstocks positioned unusually high.

They headed west, moving slowly, with the path ahead lit by just Terry's LED penlight.

The concrete storm drain had a circular cross section and had just a sixty-five-inch inside diameter. This was fairly comfortable for Terry, but it was soon agony for Ken, who was seventy-three inches tall. Walking hunched over, carrying a pack was very uncomfortable. He stopped twice in the first 300 yards, to adjust his pack. He found that repositioning the sleeping bag to the bottom of the pack and loosening the shoulder straps—lowering the entire pack—worked best.

There was no way to avoid walking in the rainwater that had collected in the low spots in the drain system. Their feet were soon wet and cold. The air in the storm drain network was warmer than up on the street. This was an effect of the ambient ground temperature. So they soon had to strip off their field jackets and stow them in their already crammed packs.

They continued westward, now with Ken leading the way, and holding the penlight. The sound of sirens and gunfire could be heard, via the storm drains, as they went. Most of it sounded fairly distant, but at one point, after walking for an hour, they heard shouting and shooting directly above them. The reverberations of the gunfire sounded very strange and muffled in the confines of the drains.

Beneath one gutter drain, they could hear a man moaning and sobbing. He was lying prone in a gutter, right next to a grille. Ken pointed his light upward briefly and could see that there was a substantial trickle of blood pouring down from the grille.

After proceeding a few blocks, Ken stopped and pulled out his Nalgene water bottle and they passed it back and forth, taking deep swallows. He asked, "Did you see all that blood?"

"Yeah. That was the most brutal thing I've ever seen or heard my whole life."

"Well, please say a prayer for that guy. I think he was dying."

Terry said in a clipped voice, "I already have."

They trudged on and on, rarely speaking. Ken counted the storm drains so that they could estimate how many blocks they had traversed. There were numbers and letters painted on the ladder shafts, but other than one number group that continually incremented downward, they were indiscernible to the Laytons.

At just after 2 a.m., they heard a deep, loud explosion. They assumed that it was a piped natural gas or propane tank explosion a few blocks away. They stopped to ponder it.

Terry asked, "How many fires are burning out of control, right now, do you think?"

"Lots. Hundreds of fires, maybe. It's a world of hurt up there, Terry. There are a lot of unpredictable explosions when there are so many fires burning. There aren't any firemen responding to half of them." They pressed on.

They reached a large four-way storm drain intersection, where they could hear the water in the pipe trickling to an area below. It was 4:12 a.m. and both Ken and Terry were exhausted. This was by far the largest junction they had yet reached. There was a catwalk decked with expanded steel mesh running across two levels above, and a staircase with metal steps leading up to a steel door. They climbed up on the first catwalk, unshouldered their packs, and sat down to rest. They shared the rest of Ken's water bottle. Next, they refilled their empty rifle magazines from the extra ammunition that they carried in bandoleers in their packs.

Terry said, just above a whisper, "I don't think I can go on much longer without some rest."

"Me neither. Let me go up and check that door, and then maybe we can get some sleep."

Carrying just his rifle, Ken walked quietly up the stairs. The door was rusty and was locked with a dead bolt on his side. It looked like it was used only rarely.

He padded back down to Terry and said, "I don't think anybody is going to come through that. We should be safe here."

"Good," Terry said gratefully.

There was sufficient room for them both to rest on the catwalk. They hung their rifles and backpacks on the looped tops of the steel ladders at both ends of the catwalk structure. Then they removed their sodden boots and socks. After wringing out the socks and hanging them on rungs of the ladders to dry, they positioned their boots on the other catwalk to dry. Lying lengthwise on the narrow catwalk, their feet nearly touched. They retrieved their rifles and kept them close at hand. At first they used their coats for padding, but feeling chilled, they then rolled out their sleeping bags. Shortly after crawling into their bags they both fell asleep. They were so exhausted that they didn't even make an attempt to have one stay up to maintain a watch.

As they rested, the situation deteriorated in the neighborhood above them. They were frequently awoken by the sounds of shots—rifles, shotguns, pistols. There were also sirens, but those became less frequent as the day wore on. By 4 p.m., the shooting became almost continuous. They could smell smoke infiltrating the storm drain system.

Ken and Terry both felt oddly isolated and immune from the chaos above. Despite the sounds of gunfire, they slept well. Terry had awoken and broken out her water bottle around noon. As they shared sips, Ken commented, "This is just surreal. Total chaos up there. We can hear it, we can smell it, but we can't see it."

Terry said forcefully, "I don't *want* to see it. Any of it. It's a two-way shooting range up there."

After a pause, she added, "I vote we keep heading west through the drain tunnels as far as we can go."

"I agree."

Shortly after, they both fell back asleep. They slept off and on—still disturbed by bursts of gunfire until just before 5 p.m.

They rolled up their sleeping bags and stowed them. After some more water with an Emergen-C packet mixed in, they put on their still damp socks and boots. Ken took a Tylenol and a magnesium tablet to help with his back spasms.

Back in the drain, they continued westward. There was gradually less gunfire, but the smell of smoke became more distinct.

They continued on, walking all through the night, stopping only briefly for water. At another pipe junction, the drain transitioned to an eight-foot-diameter pipe. Ken let out a moan of relief, and whispered, "Thank you Lord!"

They stopped and adjusted their backpack straps. As they moved on, no longer walking hunched over, they were able to pick up the pace.

Ken's back was still painful, so he took another dose of Tylenol two hours before dawn. They marched on. After what seemed an eternity, and again at the edge of exhaustion, they saw dim light ahead.

The storm drain emptied onto a jumble of riprap rocks on the banks of the Des Plaines River. There was a four-foot drop from the mouth of the pipe to the rocks below, so exiting was slow and cumbersome. With daylight rapidly increasing, they felt uncomfortably exposed. They immediately set a twenty- to twenty-five-foot interval as they walked. They walked with their rifle butts tucked into their shoulders and their muzzles down. They moved slowly and cautiously, scanning in all directions and stopping frequently to listen. Ken, in the lead, gave hand signals to Terry. This was a method that Jeff Trasel had called "TABbing"—referring to what the British army termed "tactical advance to battle" (TAB).

They walked along the river for twelve minutes until they came to a large patch of willow trees behind a jumble of fist-sized rocks. The willows were densely spaced, so Ken suggested that the center of the thicket would provide enough concealment for them to set up a cold camp. For the final fifty yards they walked carefully, stepping from rock to rock so that they wouldn't leave a visible trail.

Before heading into the willows, they refilled their water bottles from the river, dosing them with water purification tablets.

They picked their way into the thicket, trying to minimize any noise.

After clearing some downed tree branches and large rocks, they rolled out their sleeping bags. By the time they had them positioned, it was full daylight.

Ken whispered, "I'll take the first watch. You try to get some sleep."

Terry replied, "Try? No problem, trust me."

Terry awoke at midday. They divided an MRE. They hadn't eaten in more than a day, so they wolfed it down eagerly.

They then took turns cleaning their rifles and pistols. They were thorough, even unloading each magazine to dry the cartridges. Next, they removed their boots and again wrung out their socks.

Terry did a detailed inventory of the contents of their web gear and packs. Terry carried a standard LC2 ALICE pack. Ken's was a large "Arctic" variant. Both of them had Wiggy's brand Ultima Thule sleeping bags strapped on the bottoms of their packs, stowed along with their bivouac ("bivy") bags, in compression stuff sacks.

In her MOLLE pouches, Terry confirmed that she had six spare black Teflon-coated M16 30 magazines for her CAR-15. Ken carried just four spare 20-rounders for his HK clone.

She whispered each item to Ken, who was guarding their camp as she worked. She took her time carefully writing out a combined list of the contents of their packs in her notebook:

Leatherman Wave tool

2 water bottles

2 first-aid kits (one with Celox coagulant packs)

2 CAT tourniquets

.223 cleaning kit with sight tool, carbon scraper, & CAR-15 stock/1911
    bushing wrench. Spare firing pin w/retainer pin and extractor w/pin.

.308 cleaning kit with HK sight tool

.45 cleaning kit with spare firing pin, sear, finger spring, and extractor

6 sets of socks and underwear for K

8 sets of socks and underwear for T

One extra set of DPMs, for each

7 complete MREs

15 main course entrées

Magnesium pills (29 left)

Multivitamins (98 left)

17 Emergen-C packets

100 feet of olive drab parachute cord

AAA Maps: Illinois, Midwest States, Western States, Idaho/Montana

Metal Match magnesium fire starter

Gill net

Hardware wire

Hacksaw blade

Olive drab duct tape

Green bandana

2 bivy bags

Compass

Soap (1 Ivory, 1 Lava)

24 tampons (can be used as bandages)

3 camo face paint sticks

2 toothbrushes
Triple-thickness Ziploc bag of salt
Sewing kit
10 feet aluminum foil
4 black trash bags
Sierra Club cup (Ken's left in Bronco)
$23.10 face value in pre-1965 silver dimes and quarters
3 bandoleers of 7.62 Ball (one is short 20 rounds)
40 rounds of .308 150 Gr. Spire Point soft nose
1 spare HK 20-round magazine, alloy (loaded with soft nose)
4 bandoleers of 5.56 Ball (one is short 60 rounds)
1 spare 30-round AR magazine, steel (loaded with tracers)
2 match safes with strike anywhere matches
2 spare 9-volt DC batteries
T's Bible

Being thorough, she added another list below:

In pockets or carried:
LED minilight
1 tin of foot powder (half full?)
Headset radios
Gloves with liners
Tylenol (27 left)
Two bottles purification tablets (about 190 left)
DPM boonie hats
DPM jackets and raincoats
K's wallet (mine left in car)
T's sunglasses (Ken's left in Bronco)
K's key ring with Proto screwdriver & P-38 can opener (mine left in car)
Bench-made tanto pocketknife (K's Cold Steel Voyager XL pocketknife
    left in Bronco)

Wish we had:

K's study Bible (left in Bronco)

GPS (left in car)

Gerber Omnivore LED flashlights (both left in car and Bronco)

Fishing kit

Full-size tent

Fry pan

Tweezers

Hard candies

Granola bars

More food!

More ammo!

Sunscreen

Mosquito repellent

Gaiters

Better variety of plastic bags

Katadyn water filter (one left in Bronco, one left at Todd's in Idaho)

Each time that Terry mentioned something that had been left behind in the Mustang and the Bronco, Ken groaned. But then, when she'd finished the list, Ken said resignedly, "We can't worry about what we lost. We're never getting any of that back. That's just water under the bridge. I know it's hard, but we even have to forgive the people that robbed us."

Terry snorted. "I'll let you know when I feel ready to do that. Don't hold your breath."

Ken gave Terry a hug and said, "I know it's really hard, but we've got to let it go. It's the Christian thing to do."

"And shooting those guys?"

Ken answered, "That's different. They were still *in the act*. That's not revenge. And for those that lived, now it's time for us to forgive."

Terry gave Ken a kiss and said, "Okay. I'll try. I'll pray about it.

Your turn to sleep, until it gets dark. I'll wake you then—I figure that'll be about four hours."

Early in the afternoon, Terry first heard and then saw a group of people walking alongside the river, on the same bank that they were hidden. She woke Ken, pressing her index finger over his lips, to warn him to be quiet.

They lay still, watching the group as it passed by. They counted twenty-two people—fifteen adults and seven children. All of them were African American, carrying their belongings in backpacks. They moved downstream, oblivious to the Laytons' presence. The adults were carrying guns, but only the man in the lead carried his gun at the ready. He was armed with a Saiga 12 shotgun. All the rest had their rifles slung on their shoulders. Some also had holstered pistols. They had an odd assortment that included two AKs, several scoped deer rifles, an AR-180, a SIG-556, and a couple of .22 rimfire rifles. As they passed, several of the people in the group were talking loudly, debating whether the water in the river was safe to drink. Several children were complaining about the weight of their loads.

Two minutes after the group was out of sight around a bend in the river, Terry whispered, "A-mazing. Talk about an invitation to get ambushed."

Ken nodded. "Yeah, notice how they were mostly clumped up? And the guy out front wasn't acting like a real point man, either. Their spacing—er 'intervals'—sucked."

"Noise discipline was sucky, too."

Ken sighed. "I hope they don't have to learn those lessons the hard way. At least they had the sense to get out of Chicago."

Terry gave a thumbs-up and said, "Yep, bonus points for that."

"That's the way I want to see everyone from here on," Ken said. "From concealment, and preferably from a distance. Okay, it's your turn to get some sleep."

At 5 p.m. another group of refugees passed through, this time on the opposite bank of the river. Ken watched quietly, not bothering Terry, who was sound asleep.

This group was nine people, all white—four adults and five children. Like the last group, they were walking clustered together and the adults were carrying backpacks and slung long guns. One of the women was wearing a white ski jacket that, compared to most of their other clothing, stood out like a beacon.

When Terry awoke an hour later, Ken told her about the group that had passed by. He concluded with the words "Low life expectancy, no doubt."

Terry replied, "Ours isn't much better."

"Well, at least we're in all earth tone and camo clothes, and we'll be traveling at night."

"But there's just two of us. That makes us vulnerable."

Ken countered, "Yeah, but we're also not in a big, noisy *gaggle*."

Terry grinned.

Darkness was falling. They relieved themselves and buried their waste and the empty wrappers from their MRE. They applied foot powder and put on dry socks. As they were rolling up their sleeping bags, Terry whispered, "I'm starved."

"Me, too, but we've got only what's in our packs. It might be *days* before we can find a safe place to barter silver for food. So let's stick to one MRE per day."

Terry nodded and put on a glum face. She finished stowing the gear in her pack. They applied green and loam camouflage from a stick onto each other's faces and the backs of their hands. Standing in the cleared spot where their sleeping bags had been, they took turns jumping up and down to check for noise. Other than a slight slosh from Terry's canteen, their gear was quiet. Terry made a mental note to refill her canteen as soon as possible.

Weaving their way out of the willow thicket, they resumed their walk alongside the river. They began passing small refugee camps. These numbered from five to forty people. Most of the camps were lit by large campfires. There was a fistfight in progress in one of the camps. It ended with a pistol shot. Ken and Terry kept moving, leaving them wondering what had happened. The camps were easy to skirt around unobserved. At one of them, Ken recognized the woman wearing the white ski jacket. "She won't blend in until there's snow on the ground. That is, *if* she lives that long," he commented.

6

Walking by Faith

"Disaster is rarely as pervasive as it seems from recorded accounts. The fact of being on the record makes it appear continuous and ubiquitous whereas it is more likely to have been sporadic both in time and place. Besides, persistence of the normal is usually greater than the effect of the disturbance, as we know from our own times. After absorbing the news of today, one expects to face a world consisting entirely of strikes, crimes, power failures, broken water mains, stalled trains, school shutdowns, muggers, drug addicts, neo-Nazis, and rapists. The fact is that one can come home in the evening, on a lucky day, without having encountered more than one or two of these phenomena."

—Barbara Tuchman, *A Distant Mirror: The Calamitous 14th Century*

(1987)

Near Joliet, Illinois
October, the First Year

Ken and Terry continued to follow the river for two more days, moving slowly and with extreme caution. They rested during daylight in clumps of brush or far out in fields of harvested corn that had been left with their stalks still standing. Even this far out of Chicago they could still hear gunfire in the distance around the clock.

They communicated mostly via hand and arm signals. They

were often spaced as much as fifty feet apart, so they would occasionally use their pair of 500-milliwatt RadioShack TRC headset walkie-talkies in push-to-talk mode. Even though these radios
were twenty years old, they were very handy, particularly if whoever was trailing needed to contact whoever was in the lead to
alert them when they weren't looking behind.

The course of the river was mostly southwest, but it eventually turned southward—not in their intended direction, which was
west or northwest. But it offered the best opportunity to travel un-
detected and provided numerous wooded and brushy areas where
they could rest. They decided to follow the river until they got
away from the Chicago metropolitan region.

A large railroad bridge crossed over the river, just north of Joliet. "Okay, now we've finally got tracks that are heading east–
west. According to the map, if we stay on the river, it joins with
the Kankakee River southwest of Joliet and that creates the Illinois
River," Ken said.

Terry added glumly, "And that would take us down toward
Peoria and Springfield."

"Right," he agreed.

Terry gave Ken a hug and said, "Following those tracks sounds
good to me."

The tracks, they later found, belonged to the Elgin, Joliet &
Eastern Railway, a regional line. The tracks began westward, but
then curved northward. They soon intersected a set of Burlington
Northern tracks oriented east–west. They followed the Burlington Northern tracks west for several nights without incident. They
were amazed to see that even though the line they were walking
along was heretofore high volume, all train traffic had stopped.

As they got out onto the plains, the Laytons had less frequent
opportunities to find secluded places to camp. They continued to
split just one MRE per day. This required great discipline, as their
growling stomachs were a regular reminder that they were oper-

ating on a caloric deficit. They scavenged a few ears of corn at the edges of fields that had been missed during harvest, and they gnawed them clean, being careful to thoroughly chew the half-dried corn kernels so that they would be digestible.

They also occasionally found a sugar beet that had fallen from an open car hopper to the railroad ballast below. These they peeled, sliced, and ate raw. Ken called them "Manna from Heaven." Each time Ken said this, Terry would counter, "Naw, they're Manna from the Oracle of Omaha." By this, she was referring to billionaire investor Warren Buffett's ownership of the Burlington Northern & Santa Fe (BNSF) railroad.

Even with the corn and sugar beets to supplement their MREs, they were losing weight quickly. Terry had an extra ten pounds of fat on her hips but Ken was wiry, so he had little to spare. Realizing the disparity, Terry "accidentally" made sure that Ken got a larger portion of each MRE entrée and the supplemental food that they found.

The weather was growing colder. There was frost on top of their sleeping bags each morning. They bundled up, wearing nearly all of their clothes. Now out on the open prairie, they dispensed with using face camouflage paint, as they had done when "sneaking and creeping" along the river near Chicago.

Their progress was still slow and stealthy. Wanting to avoid an ambush, they stopped following the railroad tracks whenever they went though large towns. Instead, they bypassed the towns, skirting mostly through farm fields.

Near midnight, just east of Mendota, Illinois, the Laytons inadvertently stumbled into an encampment that straddled the BNSF tracks. The camp was quiet and there were no campfires burning. Terry was in the lead, twenty feet ahead. When she realized that they were passing through the encampment, she pressed the PTT button on her radio five times in rapid succession to alert Ken. By the dim moonlight, they could see at least twenty tents.

Ken quickly concluded that since they were already in the midst of the camp, it would have exposed them even more to reverse their direction. So he whispered into his radio's boom mike, "Just act brave, and keep walking. Need be, we can bluff our way through. Safeties off."

They both thumbed their rifles' safeties. A man staggered toward the tracks, obviously drunk. He unzipped his fly and looked up to see Ken and Terry walking by on the raised railroad above him. Their boots were at his face level. In the dim light, Ken could see that the stranger was carrying a holstered handgun. Ken shouldered his rifle, and centered the HK's ringed front sight on the man's chest.

Startled, the man asked, "Who the hell are you?"

Ken replied in the most macho voice he could muster, "You don't want to know, mister. Just leave us alone, and we won't waste you."

The man stood petrified, wondering how many people were traveling with Ken. Little did he know that there were just two of them.

As they passed the man, Ken and Terry turned and walked backward, keeping their rifles trained on him. The man stood still, apparently afraid to move or raise an alarm. Once they had walked this way for another forty yards, they turned and ran for about 150 yards, and then left the raised railroad ballast and cut across a field. At the far side of the field, they helped each other over a three-strand barbed wire fence and then sprinted again to take cover behind a cattle loafing shed.

Terry gave Ken a hug: "That was close!"

Ken asked, "Do you think they were looters?"

"Might've been. Maybe just refugees. Whoever it was, that sure scared me."

"Ditto," Ken added.

They waited a few minutes. There was no sound of alarm in

the camp. When they resumed their march, they paralleled the railroad for nearly a mile.

This necessitated crossing several barbed wire fences. After a while, they got good at it—not snagging their pants, and not leaving a trace. Ken always made a point of wiping off any mud clinging to the wire from their boots.

Despite their stealthy movement, they had a few unexpected scares. Twice, stray dogs darted across their path. They were gone even before they had the chance to react. Another time, Ken almost tripped over the feet of a man who was lying in a sleeping bag. The man had positioned himself with the foot end of his sleeping bag protruding into the trail. Either he was sound asleep, or dead. The Laytons didn't linger to find out which.

They reached the banks of the Mississippi during a heavy rain—the first significant rain since they had left Chicago. There was virtually no ambient light. The railroad bridge was several miles north of East Moline. It connected East Clinton, Illinois, with Clinton, Iowa. Crossing the bridge was frightening. It was dark, the bridge was wet, and it hadn't been designed for foot traffic. They knew that the chance of a train crossing the bridge was slim, since there hadn't been any trains running in days. Nevertheless, the prospect of being caught in the middle of the long bridge had both Ken and Terry very anxious.

7

Wheat Berries

"The technologies which have had the most profound effects on human life are usually simple. A good example of a simple technology with profound historical consequences is hay. Nobody knows who invented hay, the idea of cutting grass in the autumn and storing it in large enough quantities to keep horses and cows alive through the winter. All we know is that the technology of hay was unknown to the Roman Empire but was known to every village of medieval Europe. Like many other crucially important technologies, hay emerged anonymously during the so-called Dark Ages. According to the Hay Theory of History, the invention of hay was the decisive event which moved the center of gravity of urban civilization from the Mediterranean basin to Northern and Western Europe. The Roman Empire did not need hay because in a Mediterranean climate the grass grows well enough in winter for animals to graze. North of the Alps, great cities dependent on horses and oxen for motive power could not exist without hay. So it was hay that allowed populations to grow and civilizations to flourish among the forests of Northern Europe. Hay moved the greatness of Rome to Paris and London, and later to Berlin and Moscow and New York."

—**Freeman Dyson,** *Infinite in All Directions,* **1988**

Durant, Illinois
Late October, the First Year

The rain continued and it was getting colder. The Laytons were cold, wet, and miserable. They realized that they were at risk of hypothermia. Three miles southeast of Durant, Illinois, they came upon a large silo complex that belonged to Cargill Corporation. It looked as if it was designed to hold millions of pounds of grain. It was one of the largest silo operations they had seen since leaving Chicago. Oddly, there was no one there.

They walked into an open-sided terminal building that was designed to accommodate eighteen-wheel grain-hauling trucks. They were just happy to be out of the rain. The building was dark and deserted. Most of the terminal building was set up with a complex arrangement of vertical silo chutes for filling rail cars and trucks. But one quadrant of the building was a pallet and front-end loader operation. Here, there were two large forklifts and a front-end loader parked, and enormous piles of bagged and loose corn ringed on three sides by six-foot-tall concrete retaining walls. They climbed over one of these and unshouldered their ALICE packs behind a tall loose pile of corn. Next to the back wall, the corn was just a few inches deep. There, they rolled out their sleeping bags and got out of their wet clothes. Terry was shivering, on the edge of hypothermia. They laid their clothes out flat to dry. Terry estimated that dawn would come in less than an hour.

At just after 8 a.m. they were awakened by the sound of a vehicle driving into the south end of the building. Peeking over the top of the containment wall, Ken saw that it was a Sheriff's Department patrol car. But no sooner did the car arrive than they heard it leave. Ken and Terry gave each other shrugs, and then crawled back into their sleeping bags. Outside, the pouring rain continued.

They slept for most of the day. After they stopped shivering, they were comfortable. The building was quiet, except for the frequent sound of the flapping wings of pigeons. In the afternoon, they awoke and shared a meal. Ken began to methodically clean and dry their guns and magazines.

The sign hanging above the corn pile where they were camped was marked "Yellow Dent—Untreated—Super Tested." Ken knew that dent corn was used for livestock feed and that hunters used it to attract deer. Since it was untreated, he also knew that it would be safe to eat. He added heaping handfuls of the corn to two of their water bottles and left it to soak for their next meal.

At just before 8 p.m., another patrol car arrived. This time, since it was dark, a sheriff's deputy scanned the building with the car's searchlight. The car was there less than a minute and then it left.

Terry was becoming feverish and the weather was horrible, so they decided to stay. It rained steadily. The pattern of 8 a.m. and 8 p.m. vehicular patrols continued for the next three days. After that, the silo complex was completely deserted, save for the Laytons. They surmised that a shortage of fuel had curtailed patrols. Their only companions were a few pigeons, which Terry referred to as "our fellow freeloaders."

Soon, the rain transitioned to sleet. That was followed by snow. There were snow showers for two weeks. Very gradually, Terry recovered from her illness. They assumed that it had been a flu. They spent many hours in their sleeping bags talking with their faces just a few inches apart. These conversations left them feeling more connected than ever before in their marriage. The precariousness and immediacy of the situation were enormous, but they felt calm and reassured to be together. As Ken put it, he felt "ready to take on the world, just as soon as the snow stops blowing sideways."

Ken's and Terry's diet consisted almost entirely of corn soaked in water. They didn't leave the grain pile except to gather water from a downspout and to relieve themselves in a "cat hole" that Ken dug with his entrenching tool, thirty yards out in an adjoining field.

While they were there, Terry discovered that she had lost her headset walkie-talkie, most likely the day before they arrived in Durant.

Three weeks after they arrived, the sun finally peeked through the clouds one afternoon. It was still cold but Terry was again feeling healthy. They decided to press on. There were six inches of snow on the ground, and it was deeper where the snow had drifted. They filled their packs with as much dent corn as they could hold. Ken also filled the cargo pockets of their pants with corn. They planned to eat that first.

Ken left $305 in cash on top of the front of the pile of grain. He composed a thank-you note to the owner of the elevator. Realizing that it made no sense for him to continue to carry his walkie-talkie since Terry's had gone missing, he also left it as a barter payment for the owners of the grain elevator. But he first salvaged the ni-cad battery.

The temperature was 25 degrees lower than when they had left Chicago. They pressed on. It was almost unbearably cold. They took turns sleeping that night in a large open-sided hay barn located 200 yards from the nearest house. The barn was half full of hay and straw bales. It offered little protection from the wind, but they were thankful that they weren't sleeping in the snow. They weren't disturbed.

Just west of Lime City, Iowa, they decided to cross over Interstate 80. The freeway was deserted. To Ken, this seemed unbelievably strange, since up until a few weeks before, I-80 had been a major car and truck route.

Fife, Montana
Late October, the First Year

When the Crunch hit, Joshua Watanabe was woefully underprepared. His only stored fuel was three gallons of gasoline for his weed eater. His house was heated by propane, and the heater's fan was useless without grid power.

He owned only one gun, a Browning A-Bolt .30-06 that he used for hunting deer and elk. The rifle was stainless steel, and it had a matching finish Nikon Monarch 4-12 adjustable magnification scope. He hadn't bothered to buy any spare magazines for the rifle.

He had always been a "one box a year" type shooter, so as the Crunch set in, Joshua had only thirty-four rounds of .30-06 ammunition on hand. When the full implications of the Crunch became obvious, he made frantic trips to seven sporting goods stores. But he found that their inventories had already been devastated. He was able to find only three additional boxes of .30-06, and those had three different bullet weights, so he had doubts about the point of impact when using them. He bought a set of RCBS .30-06 reloading dies for $250. He was able to find 500 reloading primers (for $100), but no powder, brass, or projectiles. He also found a spare telescopic sight. It was an inexpensive 3-to-9 power scope made in China, but it was better than nothing in the event that his Nikon scope ever got broken or fogged up. Because the rifle had no iron sights, Joshua knew that if the original scope ever failed the rifle would become useless without a backup.

The sporting goods stores had hardly any guns or ammunition, but they still had a fair quantity of hunting clothes. So Joshua bought a heavy Realtree camouflage coat with a detachable hood, a set of camouflage overalls, a camouflage balaclava, and a camouflage microfleece sweater. Scouring the shelves, he also bought five rolls of rifle and bow camouflaging tape. This removable adhesive tape was intended to break up the outlines of guns or archery equipment. Since his rifle was stainless steel—with all of the metal parts looking very silvery—he felt that it was important to tone down its appearance.

Later that month, after his marriage to Kelly, Joshua's new father-in-law gave him a pistol—a Kel-Tec PMR-30 .22 Magnum. Just a .22 rimfire, it was a pitiful stopper for men, but fine for shooting squirrels and rabbits. It also had an unusually bright muzzle flash. But at least the pistol used thirty-round magazines. The Kel-Tec came with only one spare magazine. This left Joshua wishing for half a dozen more. He decided that if he ever needed to use it for self-defense he would restrict himself to taking head shots. He practiced with it, keeping such shots in mind, aiming at just the eye area of the head on a human silhouette target. Short on ammunition, he mainly did "dry practice." Because the firing pins of rimfire guns tend to gouge their chambers if they are dry-fired, Joshua made a habit of always inserting a piece of fired brass in the chamber before doing dry practice.

Not only was the pistol woefully underpowered, but he had only 340 rounds of .22 Magnum ammunition. Searching for more ammo for both the pistol and his rifle was his highest priority. The holster that came with the pistol was marginal. It was a generic nylon holster with a cumbersome thumbstrap. It took lots of extra practice to get used to quickly un-holstering the pistol with one hand.

Joshua's father-in-law's rifle was a .270 Winchester, and both Joshua's mother-in-law and his new bride owned .243 Winchesters. The family had fewer than 200 rounds between the three rifles. Jim owned the only other handgun in the family—a Ruger Redhawk .44 Magnum with a ponderously long eight-inch barrel. It was fairly well supplied with more than 600 rounds of ammunition—a mixture of .44 Magnum and .44 Special, both of which could be fired through the gun. Joshua considered it substandard as a self-defense gun—he preferred automatics—but he was hardly in a position to criticize, since he had owned *no* handgun.

Joshua's food situation was pitiful. As a bachelor, he had kept only about a twelve-day supply of food on hand, plus a couple of cases of MREs that he'd bought the year before through the base commissary with hunting trips in mind.

Joshua hadn't filled a deer or antelope tag the year before. Without any meat in his freezer, other than two pounds of hamburger and four lamb chops, he was "behind the power curve." He thawed and grilled that meat on his propane barbeque, fearing that there would soon be power failures. He was hoping to bag an elk or a couple of antelope before winter set in. This, he realized, would *not* be sport hunting. It was meat gathering, and vitally important.

The Monroes' ranch was only two miles from the A-01 MAF. Only two weeks after the Crunch, Joshua was assigned caretaker of the facility, including its outlying silos. This assignment gave him "as needed" access to JP-4 fuel from Malmstrom, to do his sporadic roving patrols of the MAF and silos. He was encouraged to do patrols roughly four times a week, but not in any set pattern. The only vehicle at the ranch that could burn JP-4 was Jim's Unimog. This at first seemed like a poor choice for patrolling the silos but it later proved ideal. The terrain around A-01 was mostly rolling hills. Because it had been set up for camping, the Unimog could be parked below the crest of hills so that it would be out of sight. Joshua could then stake out any of the silos. He could do so for days or even weeks at a time if need be.

There were no weapons or vehicles at Malmstrom that hadn't already been issued. But because of his assigned security duties, Joshua was able to obtain an AN/PVS-14 night vision monocular, issued on a semipermanent hand receipt. The monocular was a third-generation ("Gen 3") design with amazing clarity and sensitivity.

Chicago, Illinois
Two Years Before the Crunch

Just after he was promoted to assistant manager, Ken had an after-hours conversation with his boss, during which he mentioned that he objected to the foul language that had become frequent in the shop. Chet Hailey agreed, and gave Ken the authority to crack down on it. They agreed that Ken would have the say-so about behavior on the shop floor, and spent some time discussing a strategy and some new policies.

Ken waited a few days until he heard a particularly foul word that was shouted loud enough for everyone to hear. Ken shouted more loudly, "Drop your wrenches! Stand Down meeting in Chet's office, ASAP!" This was a seldom-called meeting of everyone in the shop. Heretofore, they had been called only over safety issues.

Once everyone was in Chet's office, Ken declared, "There is a problem in this shop with foul and profane language, and it has to stop. We are professionals here, and we need to treat each other with courtesy and respect. We also have to keep our customers, their kids, and the front office staff in mind. In the past few months the language here has gotten worse, *noticeably* worse. Nobody should be expected to work with that sort of language. You all know what I'm talking about, so there isn't any need to spell it out."

Tina, the shop's diminutive payroll and accounting clerk, who was listening from the office doorway, gave a thumbs-up in agreement.

The junior-most mechanic—who was also the shop's washer/detailer—voiced his objection. "You called a Stand Down over *that*?"

"Yes I did. I expect everyone to grow up, and cut out the gutter talk. There will be no more foul words used in this shop. Period. You will each be given just one warning."

Another mechanic interjected, "But—"

Ken cut him off. "This is not a subject that is open to debate or discussion. No ifs, ands, or buts. I'm laying down the law. If you don't like it, then see Tina to arrange your final pay. I've got a whole stack of applications from experienced guys who are looking for work."

At that, everyone's eyes turned to Chet, who put on a thin smile, and gave an exaggerated nod.

Ken declared, "Meeting adjourned."

8

Monroe Doctrine

"At any rate, cost what it may, to separate ourselves from those who separate themselves from the truth of God is not alone our liberty, but our duty."

—Charles H. Spurgeon

Malmstrom Air Force Base, Montana
Late October, the First Year

Joshua was a lapsed Baptist. Since joining the Air Force, he had only rarely attended church, mainly when he was at home with his parents on leave. He felt guilty about his backsliding. He often made excuses to himself and others, citing his duty schedule and the long driving distance from his rental house to the Baptist church near Great Falls that he liked best. But the truth was that he missed the interaction with his family and his old friends in eastern Washington. He simply hadn't made the effort to find the right church home near Malmstrom.

The same day that Joshua moved in, Jim took him aside and declared, "Let me lay down some Monroe Doctrine for you. I know you're a Christian. I wouldn't have blessed your marrying my daughter if you weren't. But if you are going to live in my house, then I expect you to attend home church meetings with us. We take turns meeting at different houses with the Webber and Boskill families. The circumstances these days necessitate that one of us will have to be here to guard the house at all times. So on the Sundays when the home church meeting is over at the Webbers' or at the Boskills', then either you or I will take turns staying home. Otherwise, I consider attendance mandatory. Do I make myself clear?"

Kelly had warned Joshua that whenever her father used the "Monroe Doctrine" phrase he should take him very seriously. So Joshua replied, gravely, "I wouldn't have it any other way, sir. You have my word that I will cease any backsliding."

Malmstrom Air Force Base, Montana
Late October, the First Year

Malmstrom was better prepared for economic collapse than most other Air Force facilities. It was located in a lightly populated region, so it was well removed from the urban chaos that engulfed many of the bases in the eastern U.S. and on the west coast. The base also had deep logistics stockpiles. The logistical redundancy was due to the climate, and partly because the base was spread out over such a large area of Montana.

The runway at Malmstrom had been deactivated from regular fixed-wing use many years before the Crunch, and repainted with herringboned rings of helicopter landing donut markings. The massive hangars that once handled maintenance and repair of KC-135 tankers mostly stood empty. But one hangar had been re-purposed to hold a squadron of six-seat UH-1N helicopters. These twin-engine variants of the venerable Bell Huey were reliable, but in the years following the collapse parts shortages forced them to cannibalize two of the helicopters to keep the others flying.

Three weeks into the Crunch, all of the squadrons at Malm-strom were taken off alert status, primarily due to personnel shortages. In all, nearly 40 percent of the base personnel went AWOL, because their pay was essentially worthless, because they couldn't obtain gasoline to commute, or because of worry for the safety of their family members. Of those who remained, most were soon put on "Special Reserve status," which was a polite way of saying, "We can't pay you, feed you, or house you, but we still need your help." Watanabe was in this category.

Joshua was tasked with maintaining security of the A-01 MAF and its ten surrounding silos. To accomplish this, he drove the Monroes' diesel Unimog to patrol the more distant silos, and rode his horse to the MAF and the closer silos except in the worst weather.

While many other Air Force bases were abandoned in the wholesale societal chaos of the Crunch, all of the bases that controlled nuclear weapons maintained some integrity. Brigadier General Anthony Woolson, the base commander, still showed up at his office every day to check the status of his dwindling organizations. The entire base command took on the name "Malmstrom Operations Group," and the command structure was radically streamlined. There were no longer separate wings or squadrons, there was just "The Operations Group," often simply called "The Wing."

The 341st's slab-fronted headquarters building had stylized 1960s architecture. The center section of the building had all glass walls. Because the power was frequently off, the remaining staff moved their offices to the center section so there would be enough light available to work. But after they spent the first few months bundled up in pile caps and parkas, General Woolson moved his entire staff to the 40th Helicopter Squadron's hangar. The building had originally been designed for maintenance of KC-135s, so it was built on a grand scale. Following Woolson's orders, the hangar had been retrofitted with enormous coal-fired space heaters situated in three corners of the building. The southwest corner of the hangar was dominated by a coal pile. This coal was shuttled to the heaters in wheelbarrows.

Locals had started mining a surface coal seam just west of Lehigh, a few miles southwest of Windham, and the coal was delivered in a five-yard-capacity dump truck that simply drove into the hangar when the main door was opened. The new coal mining co-op was thrilled to swap coal for JP-4, since they needed the liquid fuel to operate their heavy equipment. For lighting and for power to run tools and communications equipment, a 20-KW diesel generator set up outside was run continuously.

Most of the 341st's offices were in trailers that had been towed into the hangar and clustered around two of the heaters. Because of the trailers and the coal pile, they never lost the feeling that they were camping out inside the hangar.

General Woolson's office was spartan. A black-and-white still photo from the 1936 British movie *Things to Come* decorated the wall behind his desk. The photo showed a post-apocalyptic warlord chief in a crudely made Angora wool jacket, wearing a steel helmet, and holding a revolver. It was meant as a joke, but Woolson sometimes felt like the man in the photo, especially when the talk in the office turned to cannibalizing aircraft.

When the western power grid collapsed, the widely separated MAFs reverted to backup power. Their generators were fueled by tanks that averaged 1,800-gallon capacity. It didn't take long for Woolson's logistics planners to do the math and conclude that an order had to be given soon to shut down the backup generators. It was better, they concluded, to keep some fuel on hand for contingent needs rather than to run the tanks completely dry.

After the backup generators had been shut down, the MAFs became essentially uninhabitable. So Woolson's command had to rely on volunteer "eyes and ears" to make sure that the unmanned MAFs and LFs remained secure from intrusion. There were surprisingly few security breaches. In the first year after the Crunch began, only two deserted but locked MAFs had their aboveground offices ransacked by looters. There were also signs of a halfhearted attempted forced entry at one of the silos at the far end of Judith Basin County, but given the design, whoever had cut through the fence soon gave up on attacking the massive door.

Farmers and ranchers on the land surrounding the silos and MAFs were deputized by the 341st. They were given written "authorized deadly force" orders for anyone making forced entry. Coordination of security for each MAF and its associated silos was made the responsibility of one senior airman, usually E-5 or higher. Joshua Watanabe was one of just two E-4s entrusted with this job. The only other E-4 who had been given the responsibility was a security forces specialist.

9

Decrees

"I, as President do declare that the national emergency still exists; that the continued private hoarding of gold and silver by subjects of the United States poses a grave threat to peace, equal justice, and well-being of the United States; and that appropriate measures must be taken immediately to protect the interest of our people. Therefore, pursuant to the above authority, I hereby proclaim that such gold and silver holdings are prohibited, and that all such coin, bullion or other possessions of gold and silver be tendered within fourteen days to agents of the Government of the United States for compensation at the official price, in the legal tender of the Government. All safe deposit boxes in banks or financial institutions have been sealed pending action in the due course of the law. All sales or purchases or movements of such gold and silver within the borders of the United States and its territories, and all foreign exchange transactions or movements of such metals across the border are hereby prohibited."

—**Proclamation by President Franklin D. Roosevelt, April 5, 1933**

Bradfordsville, Kentucky
March, the Second Year

Sheila Randall owned a tidy little general store in Bradfordsville. Nearly half of the store's display cases held gardening seeds. This was the inventory that first made Sheila well known in Marion

County. The rest of the cases held a wide variety of sewing supplies, hand tools, canned foods, batteries, flashlights, fishing tackle, knives, rucksacks, and other artifacts of the recently ended age of mass production. By current standards, Sheila Randall was a very prosperous business owner. She had patiently and shrewdly built up the store's inventory, carefully trading from her initial supply of garden seeds, which had fit in one car trunk, when she, her son, and her elderly grandmother fled Radcliff, Kentucky, during the worst of the chaos in the early days of the Crunch.

Six months into the Crunch, Sheila learned that a Provisional Government (ProvGov) had been formed at Fort Knox, Kentucky. It was the brainchild of Maynard Hutchings, a member of the Hardin County board of supervisors. Although he had originally intended it to govern only Hardin County, it quickly grew beyond county lines and state lines, because it had the cooperative muscle provided by the U.S. Army units at Fort Knox. And, with the backing of the National Gold Depository, the Hutchings government had gravitas.

In Bradfordsville, ProvGov representatives delivered posters to be placed prominently at the post office, town hall, Bradfordsville Performing Arts Center, and at the old Bradfordsville School building. The latter had in recent years been turned into a senior center and designated storm shelter. The Provisional Government's new poster read:

B-A-N-N-E-D

Effective Upon Posting in a prominent place in each County and in effect until further notice, the following items are hereby banned from private possession by the recently enacted Amplified United Nations Small Arms and Light Weapons (SALW) Normalization Accord:

1. All fully automatic or short-barreled rifles and shotguns (regardless of prior registration under the National Firearms Act of 1934).
2. Any rifle over thirty (.30) caliber, any shotgun or weapon of any description over twelve (12) gauge in diameter.
3. All semiautomatic rifles and shotguns, all rifles and shotguns capable of accepting a detachable magazine.
4. Any detachable magazines, regardless of capacity.
5. Any weapon with a fixed magazine that has a capacity of more than four (4) cartridges (or shells).
6. All grenades and grenade launchers, all explosives, detonating cord, and blasting caps (regardless of prior registration under the Gun Control Act of 1968 or state or local blasting permits).
7. All explosives precursor chemicals.
8. All firearms regardless of type that are chambered for military cartridges (including but not limited to 7.62mm NATO, 5.56mm NATO, .45 ACP, and 9mm Parabellum).
9. All silencers (regardless of prior registration under the National Firearms Act of 1934).
10. All night vision equipment, including, but not limited to, infrared, light amplification, or thermal, all telescopic sights, and all laser aiming devices.
11. **All handguns**—regardless of type or caliber.
12. Other distinctly military equipment, including, but not limited to, armored vehicles, bayonets, gas masks, helmets, and bulletproof vests.
13. Encryption software or devices.
14. **All radio transmitters** (other than baby monitors, cordless phones, short-range wireless devices, or cell phones).
15. Full metal jacket, tracer, incendiary, and armor-piercing ammunition.
16. All ammunition in military calibers.
17. Irritant or lethal (toxin) chemical agents, including, but not limited to, CS and CN tear gas, and OC pepper spray.

18. All military-type pyrotechnics and flare launchers.

> Exceptions only for properly trained and sworn po-
> lice and the military forces of the UN and the Sole
> and Legitimate Provisional Government of the United
> States of America and Possessions.

> Any firearm or other item not meeting the new criteria
> and all other contraband listed herein must be turned
> in within the ten (10) day amnesty period after the UN
> Regional Administrator or sub-administrator, or their
> delegates, arrive on site. Alternatively, if Federal or UN
> troops arrive within any state to pacify it, a thirty (30)
> day amnesty period will begin the day the first forces
> cross the state boundary. **All other post-1898 produc-
> tion firearms of any description, air rifles, archery
> equipment, and edged weapons over six inches long
> must be registered during the same period.**

> **Anyone found with an unregistered weapon, or any
> weapon, accessory, or ammunition that has been
> declared contraband after the amnesty period ends,
> will be summarily executed.**

> As ordered under my hand, Maynard Hutchings,
> President (pro tem) of the Sole and Legitimate Pro-
> visional Government of the United States of America
> and Possessions.

The reaction to the decrees was almost uniformly negative. One
of Sheila's general store customers summed it up best when he
quipped: "Well, at least we can still use our fists and harsh language to stop crime. That is, until they ban harsh language, too."

10

Courting and Quirting

"If an American is to amount to anything he must rely upon himself, and not upon the State; he must take pride in his own work, instead of sitting idle to envy the luck of others. He must face life with resolute courage, win victory if he can, and accept defeat if he must, without seeking to place on his fellow man a responsibility which is not theirs."

—**President Theodore Roosevelt**

Malmstrom Air Force Base, Montana
March, the Second Year

Since the U.S. dollar was worthless and by extension any check issued by any government entity was worthless, the cadre at Malmstrom resorted to barter. The coin of the realm was JP-4 jet fuel.

One of the tenant units at Malmstrom had been the 301st Air Refueling Wing, which was inactivated in 1992. When the 301st deactivated, it left behind a huge pair of fuel tanks—S-1 and S-2. These each held 1,050,000 gallons. The year before the Crunch, a Strategic Air Command (SAC) order designated Malmstrom as an alternate base of operations for the 305th Air Mobility Wing, which was normally based at McGuire AFB in New Jersey. SAC's contingency was for KC-10s of the 305th to be able to operate out of Malmstrom in the event of hostilities in Korea or the Taiwan Strait. (For proximity, they wanted to be able to use an Air

Force base in the northwest, but runway and fuel tank farms at McChord AFB, near Tacoma, Washington, and at Fairchild AFB, near Spokane, Washington, were already in full use.) So the formerly mothballed S-1 and S-2 fuel tanks were again both filled with JP-4.

Meanwhile, Malmstrom's H-1 and H-2 fuel tanks normally used by the 40th Helicopter Squadron (each with 210,000-gallon capacity) were kept full with JP-4 and JP-8, respectively. With more than two million gallons of fuel available for their own operations and for barter, Woolson found that his units at Malmstrom could still carry on with a reasonable level of activity.

Nearly 800,000 gallons of the fuel were held in reserve for use by the 341st Security Forces Group and the 40th Helicopter Squadron, which still had four airworthy UH1-N Huey helicopters. The rest of the JP-4 was made available for barter. This was traded to local farmers and even backyard gardeners. Depending on their rank, each airman still on active duty was given vouchers for 40 to 110 gallons of fuel per month in lieu of pay, and those on "special reserve" status were given an average of 165 gallons of fuel per year. This didn't include the fuel allocated for facilities patrolling, which was variable, depending on the distances driven.

Since JP-4 and JP-8 can be used as substitutes for both diesel fuel and home heating oil, there were plenty of locals who were eager to barter. The base also bartered from the RED HORSE Squadron's enormous piles of AM-2 airfield matting. These pierced aluminum mats were designed to link together on leveled ground to form runways and taxiways. The local ranchers soon learned how to use them for livestock corral panels. The panel fences were quicker and easier to construct than building with wood.

The RED HORSE Squadron was unusual. RED HORSE was an acronym that stood for Rapid Engineer Deployable Heavy Operational Repair Squadron Engineers. It was a composite unit that included both active Air Force and Air National Guard (ANG) units, one of the first ever created by the Air Force.

Other tenant units at Malmstrom included the Air Force Office of Special Investigations, Civil Air Patrol, and the Defense Reutilization and Marketing Office. Malmstrom also had offices for on-site contractors from Boeing, Northrop Grumman, Lockheed Martin, and ATK. A few years before, when the Guidance Replacement Program (GRP) was still in progress, there had been a lot more contractors from Northrop Grumman and subcontractors out at the launch facilities, but that number had dwindled, as they reverted to routine maintenance and minor upgrades, mainly with communications systems. When the Crunch set in, all but a handful of the contractor staff evaporated.

Some of the most demanding maintenance tasks were "down hole" at the LCCs and LFs, and involved removing floor plates. These covered both battery compartments and storage compartments for survival kits.

Battery maintenance at one LCC or LF was a chore, but driving many miles between LCCs and repeating the exact same steps five or six times over and then documenting every detail of the tasks became absolute drudgery.

Joshua often used a T handle floor plate removal tool to lift up the floor plates to access the survival kit supplies and/or maintenance teams accessing the batteries. The floor plate screws were loosened using a large screwdriver. Then the T handles were screwed into the threaded holes and used to lift up the heavy floor plates. Depending on the size of the floor plate, one person could lift it, but it was easier with two.

In the capsule, seventy-five feet underground, electronics racks lined both walls. During alerts, officers sat in red-upholstered, high-backed swivel chairs. At one end was a cot with a hospital ward–style curtain designed to block light and sound so that one man could sleep, but it wasn't very effective.

The electronic equipment was a mix of old and new. Since the system was more than four decades old, some of the older components looked very 1970s. A couple of places hidden inside the racks, he found "Dharma" and "180" graffiti—references to the communications bunker in the television series *Lost*.

Fifty missile silos in Toole and Pondera counties were deactivated between 2007 and 2011, and their facilities were stripped of all useful equipment for recycling by the Defense Reutilization and Marketing Office (DRMO). When the Crunch came, some of that gear was still heaped in the DRMO warehouses, awaiting surplus and scrap sales.

The DRMO yard became the hub for Malmstrom's barter economy. In addition to trading JP-4 fuel, some glass windowpane units salvaged from Malmstrom's many disused buildings were bartered for food. Locals from all around Great Falls wanted windows for building home greenhouses. These became the rage in the post-collapse economy throughout the northern states.

After September 11, 2001, security upgrades to the Minuteman III defense system began in earnest. Contractors poured thicker concrete around the silos, while others installed new security cameras and upgraded passive IR sensors. The rapid response team from the 341st Security Forces Squadron was expanded and issued new equipment.

Great Falls, Montana
One Year Before the Crunch

Joshua had been introduced to Kelly Monroe at a church picnic, just a year before the economic turmoil engulfed the nation. Peter Blanchard, a missileer lieutenant in the 10th Squadron, had invited Joshua to come with him to the harvest picnic. They wore casual civilian clothes, so only their severe short-cropped haircuts signaled that they were from Malmstrom.

Peter Blanchard had said that he was interested in dating a young lady named Stacia, but she wasn't there. Peter and Joshua walked over to Stacia's friend Kelly. Peter said, "Hi! This is Joshua, from the base."

Kelly said hello back with a smile.

"Where's Stacia?" Peter asked.

"Sorry, she had to work today. But she should be at church tomorrow."

"Oh. So I don't suppose she'll be at the Hawk Nelson concert tonight, either."

"Nope. She said that she has to work until nine this evening. Sorry."

Peter muttered, "I don't know how I'll ever have my schedule match up with hers so we can go to a concert or a dance."

Then he elbowed Joshua and joked, "Joshua here already has Shirley, so his dance card is full."

Joshua laughed and said cryptically, "I can get Shirley to trot, but she doesn't foxtrot."

Kelly cocked her head and asked, "Are we talking about a young lady, or a horse?"

"You nailed it. Shirley is my mare."

"What breed?

"An American Bashkir Curly."

Kelly beamed. "Those are gorgeous. How tall and how old is she?"

"She's just shy of fifteen hands, and four years old. Her ground manners are a little lacking, but I'm working diligently on training her."

"My horse is a bit of a brat, too. He's a standard-bred gelding, three years old—"

"Well, my eyes are glazing over," Peter interrupted, "so I'll leave you two avid equestrians to talk while I get myself a hamburger." He stepped away.

Kelly asked, "Is he like that at the Bachelor Officers Quarters, too?"

"I wouldn't know. I live off-base. And I don't spend that much time with the officers. I'm just here because the lieutenant knew that I'm a Christian, and he thought that I'd enjoy the company."

"You love the Lord?" Kelly asked in a more serious tone.

"Oh yes, with all my heart. I was saved when I was twelve."

Kelly blinked and said, "Coming here with Peter, I just assumed that you were an officer, too."

"No. I'm just a lowly E-4."

"Is that like a corporal in the Army?"

"Yeah. It's the same pay grade."

Kelly smiled and said, "My dad was a corporal in the Army. He was in the Field Artillery. He drove a multiple rocket transport thingy. He didn't like the Army much."

Joshua liked Kelly's smile, and her expressive blue eyes. She was above average height, slender, and had a fairly plain face. There was a two-inch-long jagged upward-curving white scar on her chin and left cheek that he later learned was from when she had been thrown from a horse onto a barbed wire fence. That had happened when she was ten years old. Her hair was dark brown, worn in a ponytail, mostly hidden by a brown suede baseball cap. The hat had a stylized horse's head and shoulders with a flowing mane embroidered on it. She was twenty years old, but looked a bit older since she had spent so much time outdoors.

Kelly wore Wrangler jeans, scuffed Durango saddle boots, and a turquoise short-sleeve plaid shirt. In keeping with her no-nonsense style, Kelly wore no jewelry other than a fairly ornate silver belt buckle.

"How long've you been a rider?" she asked.

"Since I was old enough to walk."

She grinned. "Me, too."

They stared at each other's face for a while, smiling.

Joshua was so caught up in the moment, he asked, "Would you like to go for a ride somewhere tomorrow after church?"

Kelly laughed, and said, "Whoa there, cowboy. Could we get past some preliminaries first, like your family name, and the church you attend and such?"

Over lunch, they plunged into a wide-ranging two-hour conversation. As the picnic gathering broke up, they scheduled a horseback ride at Buffalo Jump State Park, ten miles south of Great Falls.

At just before two the next afternoon, Kelly Monroe pulled her pickup and trailer into the dusty extension lot at the park, beyond the pavement. There were seven pickups with horse trailers there. She could see that Joshua already had his horse saddled and waiting.

She said simply, "Hi!" and stepped out of the cab. Joshua led his horse over to the front of Kelly's horse trailer, and fastened his mare's reins to a tie-down.

"I'd like you to meet Shirley Temple," he said.

Kelly approached the big chestnut mare and exclaimed, "Oh, she's a beauty. The waves in her coat are just amazing."

"And that's just her *summer* coat. You ought to see her in the winter. It has little ringlets."

Kelly walked around and sized up the mare. She said simply, "Wow." Then she added, "Her eyes have a strange look to them. Kinda sleepy-looking."

"Yeah, that's a trait of American Bashkirs. Slanty eyes. Just like us Nipponese."

They both laughed.

Kelly asked, "How much of the Russian blood does she have?"

Joshua shook his head and said, "Oh, now I must warn you that you're veering off into myth, legend, and Breed Association marketing hype. Truth be told, and after all the genetic tests were run, the American Bashkir Curlies were proven not related *at all* to the original Russian Bashkirs. They just both happen to have the same genetic abnormality that produces a curly coat. Near as I can figure, the real root stock of the American Bashkir is just a Morgan Horse having a bad hair day. But of course that reality doesn't stop the breeders from playing up the Russian angle." Joshua chuckled. "Ready to unload?"

After so many years of practice, it took just a minute for Kelly to unload her gelding, Fritz. Tacking him up was also remarkably quick, as she worked with practiced precision. Joshua was impressed by the way Kelly had set up the inside of the front door of her horse trailer with a peg board with hooks for hoof care tools and grooming supplies, two leads, a quirt, and two sets of hobbles. The items were all in neat rows and bundled with rubber bands. After buttoning up the back of the trailer, Kelly said, "Okay, let's roll."

They mounted their horses and started off at a loose-reined walk. Since it was a hot afternoon, they never advanced the gait beyond a trot. And, as they both desired anyway, a walking pace was more conducive to conversation. They stopped frequently to drink, to check hooves, and to let the horses rest.

Kelly's horse was a seal brown, a deep brown with lighter points—what was sometimes called a "copper-nosed" brown. Fritz was just half a hand taller than Shirley. Shirley's height was considered atypical of American Bashkirs, since the mares were rarely more than fourteen hands tall.

A couple of times the horses were startled by darting ground squirrels which were present in large numbers at the park. Kelly commented, "It's a good thing my dog isn't here. She'd be going crazy."

They rode all of the trails that were open to horses that afternoon, ranging around three sides of the dramatic jump cliff at the 1,400-acre park, staying until just before the park closed at 6 p.m.

They watered their horses before loading them back into their respective trailers.

Part of how Joshua and Kelly apprized each other was through horsemanship. Both of them were favorably impressed. Kelly took particular note of Joshua's quiet humility. He wasn't a braggart or a show-off. Kelly liked that. She also thought that he had a remarkable vocabulary for someone without a college degree. Joshua felt himself drawn to Kelly like no woman he had ever met before. He felt blessed to have found a young woman who was a fellow Christian, and with whom he had so many things in common. And seeing Kelly astride her horse, handling him so expertly, greatly impressed Joshua.

Joshua's next short duty day was the following Friday. It was Kelly who had suggested a rendezvous. As well-educated Christians, they both disliked the word "dating," since both properly saw their meetings as courting for marriage. As Kelly put it, "I never get beyond the 'howdy-dos' unless I think a man is fit for marriage."

They met for dinner at Jaker's steak house. The attire there was casual, so both Joshua and Kelly dressed up only to the extent of wearing freshly laundered jeans and nicer shirts.

Two items of clothing never seemed to change, regardless of Kelly's wardrobe: a brown and black horsehair western belt from Deer Lodge, and her embroidered brown suede horse logo baseball cap. Whenever she wasn't wearing the baseball cap, she habitually carried it clipped on a mini-carabiner on a belt loop—the same carabiner where she carried her key ring. She refused to carry a purse.

When Joshua noticed that Kelly wore no makeup, his estimation of her went up immensely. Here at last was an honest-to-goodness rancher's daughter with no pretensions, even when out on the town for a dinner and talking about marriage. There was something about Kelly that Joshua couldn't pin down. It was some-

thing beyond her smile and her figure. It was also something beyond the common ground that they found in their faith in Christ.
Joshua couldn't say just what it was, but she definitely had it. And
whatever it was, Joshua was thoroughly smitten.

They nibbled on salad while waiting for their steaks. Kelly filled
Joshua in about her family's history: Her father, Jim Monroe, had
been raised on a cattle ranch a few miles south of the whistle-stop
town of Raynesford, which was fifteen miles southeast of Great
Falls. The "town" consisted of just a post office, a church, and a
few houses. The eighty-acre ranch straddled Big Otter Creek. It
had thirty-seven acres of hayfields. It also included an adjoining
320-acre seasonal grazing permit in the Lewis and Clark National
Forest. The grazing permit land stretched up toward Peterson
Mountain. This was a ten-year renewable lease. The Monroe family fenced the leased land just like their deeded acres. From a practical standpoint, the only difference was that they couldn't stop
anyone from using the 320 acres of Forest Service land for hunting, and they couldn't build any structures on it.

As the second-born son, Jim was not in line to inherit the
ranch, so he enlisted in the Army. But while he was off on active
duty, his elder brother botched running the ranch—incurring too
many debts and mismanaging the livestock, which cost the lives
of five calves.

When Jim was released from active duty, his brother declared,
"I'm just not cut out for raising cattle. I want to go into sales.
What do you say I sign the ranch and livestock over to you, in exchange for an informal note for $100,000, with payments only in
the years that you turn a profit, plus hunting on the ranch for life,
plus all the beef I need for my family for life?"

The deal was sealed with a handshake, and no papers were
signed except for the quit claim deed on the ranch. The ranch was
paid off in 2007. Kelly's uncle, who lived in Rapid City, still came
each November for elk season and to collect an aged side of beef.

Kelly asked, "What about your family?"

Joshua began, "My great-grandfather Watanabe immigrated from eastern Japan to Hawaii in 1890. He was a farmer. In 1927 he moved to eastern Washington, in what is now called the Tri-Cities area, near Kennewick. My grandparents and great-grandparents were spared the ignominy of being placed in an internment camp during the Second World War. Only Japanese families who lived in the Coastal Exclusion Zone were required to relocate."

Kelly nodded, and Joshua went on. "There was a great irony in this, though, since the family farm was just twenty miles east of the Hanford Nuclear Reservation, where plutonium was produced as part of the Manhattan Project. But very few people knew that the plutonium used in making the bomb that was dropped on Nagasaki came from the Hanford site. Most of the locals didn't find out about that until the 1950s."

He laughed, and continued, "So now, seven decades later, I'm entrusted with the maintenance on MIRVed strategic nuclear missiles that are capable of wiping out millions of people in a matter of minutes. And for all I know, those warheads include plutonium that was originally processed just twenty miles from where I grew up."

Kelly nodded again, and said, "That's doubly ironic."

"It also shows you that we are living in the greatest nation on earth. In almost every other country, immigrants get treated like dirt. Here in America, any citizen who is willing to learn English, study, and work hard can be successful."

Kelly smiled and nodded. Then she asked, "Tell me about how you got Shirley."

Joshua leaned back in his booth seat and said, "On my first leave after getting reassigned to Malmstrom—that was right after I got promoted to E-4—I told my folks how bored I was and how I missed being in the saddle. I basically begged my dad to lend me one of his Bashkir Curlies. He breeds them, you know. He said he wouldn't *lend* me one, but he would *give* me one—his 'problem child,' Shirley. Originally, he wanted to keep her as a brood mare, but she didn't get along well with the other horses, even for that. She's a biter, at least in a pasture with other mares. So my dad gave me both Shirley and his old two-horse trailer. He helped me wire the trailer lights to my pickup, and off we went. I had to board her at a stable near Belt for the first few months. Then I found the rental house out by Fife. That, of course, required permission."

Kelly cocked her head. "Permission?"

"Let me explain a recent change of policy. Traditionally, once you became an E-3 with three years of service, you could live off-base. But last year, as a cost reduction measure, anyone who was unmarried that was E-4 or below was required to live in on-base dormitories. Under the new policy, you can't live off-base until you become a staff sergeant. That's an E-5. So I guess I'm the 'exceptional exception,' because of Shirley. But I had to get permission from my squadron commander. He was willing to approve it, after my NCOIC vouched that I had, quote, 'exceptional maturity and potential for commissioning.'"

Their steaks and baked potatoes arrived and they dug in. Kelly was pleased to see that Joshua asked only for a glass of iced tea with his dinner. Their conversation shifted to religion and they spent a half hour discussing Christian doctrine. They were in full agreement on Calvinist principles except for the issue of election. Kelly believed in election, but Joshua held to free will.

"Someday, let's do a Bible study," Kelly suggested. "We'll take a concordance and go through each instance where the words 'chosen,' 'predestined,' and 'elect' are used. There are a *lot* of them, believe me. After that, I'm confident that you'll come around to my way of thinking."

Joshua countered, "So when I was twelve years old and I recognized that Christ is the Son of God and I asked for forgiveness of my sins, that wasn't *my* choice?"

"No, I believe that what we have is the *illusion* of free will. We were chosen unto salvation by God before the foundations of the earth. How can God be truly all powerful and all knowing if he couldn't see into the future who would 'choose' to be saved, and ordain it? Yes, it is mysterious, but if God truly is Sovereign then there is only one explanation. God's predestination of the Elect is a mystery that we need to accept without fully understanding in this mortal life."

Joshua grinned. "You are a woman of powerful conviction." After a moment he added, choosing his words carefully, "We may have a minor difference on election, but when it comes to the other aspects of God's guiding hand, I believe that nothing happens by chance. I want to make it clear that I am courting you for marriage. I don't believe in flirtations or trifling relationships. I wouldn't be sitting across from you right now unless I thought that you were someone worthy of marriage. And we wouldn't be having this conversation if it wasn't God's will. *Nothing* happens by chance."

Kelly threw in, "My point, exactly."

Joshua's first visit to the Monroe ranch came a week later. The ranch house had been built in the 1970s, following a chimney fire that had destroyed the original homestead cabin. The house was utilitarian, furnished with indestructible brown Naugahyde chairs and couches. Kelly had grown up hearing a standing joke about "those poor, defenseless Naugas that gave their lives for our furniture."

The living room and family room were lightly decorated with a few Charles M. Russell western prints that seemed almost obligatory anywhere within a 100-mile radius of Great Falls. The walls of the living room and family room were lined with mounted trophies and antlers from more than a dozen mule deer, elk, and antelope. There was also a black bear skin and two bobcat hides.

Kelly was the Monroes' only child. Her mother, Rhonda, was lean and energetic, and a great cook. Her health, ranching background, and her temperament made her well prepared for hard times. Jim Monroe's only active preparation, early in the Crunch, had been acquiring a four-year-old Guernsey milk cow that had always been hand-milked. He got the cow in trade for six 1,200-pound steers that were eighteen months old. Jim had grown up hearing his father and grandfather talk about the Great Depression. So getting a reliable milk cow seemed a logical thing to do. Rhonda had stocked up on canned goods, bulk rice, and beans as best she could as the buying power of their savings evaporated.

As the Crunch set in, the Monroes had sixty-eight Charolais and Charolais-Hereford cross cattle. The ranch had at one time carried more than 100 head, but Jim had scaled back, in part to discourage the advance of noxious weeds—since more intensive grazing encouraged weeds to gain ground—and in part because Jim had a bad back and could no longer tolerate the extra hours working outdoors to manage a large herd.

They also had four saddle horses, including Kelly's gelding, Fritz. Rhonda Monroe owned a Paint mare named Beverly. The horse was named after the western artist Bev Doolittle, whose paintings often featured Paint horses. The master bedroom in the house was decorated with four serialized Bev Doolittle prints, all depicting Paint horses.

As Kelly showed Joshua around the ranch, the only thing that seemed out of the ordinary was a Unimog truck. Kelly mentioned that her father had become fascinated by Unimogs when he was stationed in Germany. In 1995, he bought one from Cold War Remarketing, a military vehicle dealer in Englewood, Colorado. This Unimog had originally been a radio vehicle for the West German Bundeswehr. Jim Monroe used the "Mog" as a snowplow in the winter (with chains on all four wheels), and as a mobile hunting cabin each fall. He had equipped it with a tiny woodstove that had originally been designed for use in hunting guide wall tents.

That day they took a long horseback ride from the ranch to the ghost town of Hughesville. The town had been abandoned in 1943, but its heyday was in the 1890s, so most of the buildings were very old. Many of them were collapsed or semi-collapsed and not safe to enter. It was the first time that Joshua had been there—and in fact the first time he had been in any ghost town— but Kelly had been there many times. She showed him some interesting buildings that most tourists overlooked. One of them was a cabin that was up in a side canyon. When they walked in the door, Joshua was surprised to see that there were still some rusty pans on the stove and chairs under the table. This cabin was the highlight of the town for Joshua, because its contents were so intact. There were even a few *McCall's, National Geographic*, and *Saturday Evening Post* magazines from the 1930s and early 1940s on a shelf. Their edges had been ravaged by packrats and mice, but the magazines were still largely intact and legible. They left the cabin just as they had found it, carefully wedging the door shut with a twig to keep the weather out.

It was while they were riding home from Hughesville that Joshua first proposed marriage. Kelly rebuffed him, but Joshua was persistent and optimistic. He was falling deeply in love with Kelly, and he hoped that she felt the same. It was the pragmatist in her that triggered her first refusal.

11

Space Rifles

*"The right of self-defense is the first law of nature; in most govern-
ments it has been the study of rulers to confine this right within the
narrowest limits possible. Wherever standing armies are kept up,
and when the right of the people to keep and bear arms is, under
any color or pretext whatsoever, prohibited, liberty, if not already
annihilated, is on the brink of destruction."*

**—Henry St. George Tucker, in Blackstone's 1768 *Commentaries on
the Laws of England***

West Branch, Iowa
November, the First Year

As they entered the outskirts of West Branch, Iowa, it was dawn.
They had walked slowly all night. Ken began to ask people they
met if they knew of anyone looking for someone to hire for security for farms or ranches. Most seemed wary.

As they walked down 280th Street and reached Downey Street,
they hailed a young man riding on a bicycle. He stopped and identified himself as a member of the Society of Friends church. In
answer to Terry's queries, he said that he indeed knew of someone
who was looking for "security" for a farm. He pulled a scrap of
paper from his wallet, and wrote on it: "D. Perkins Farm, North
Charles Avenue. 2 mi. north of Main."

The young man gave them directions to the farm. This required several hundred yards of backtracking. Before riding off, the man said, "I'll let them know that you're coming."

The farmhouse sat just twenty yards back from Charles Avenue. It was far enough out of West Branch that it definitely didn't feel "in town." The farmhouses were fairly widely distanced apart, depending on the acreage. Most the farms appeared to be 80 to 160 acres. Many of the farms used traditional windmills. As with the other windmills that the Laytons had seen traversing the plains, their tails were painted with names like Aermotor, Woodmanse, Monitor, and Challenge. Terry mentioned that seeing windmill water pumps in operation was a good sign of self-sufficiency.

Ken sized up the farm as they approached it. It was 120 acres, mostly planted in corn and soybeans, now harvested. There was a large hay barn, grain storage silos, a cattle loafing shed, an Aermotor windmill, a water tower, and a dairy parlor with a low roof. There were about twenty brown cows in the pen adjoining the shed. Ken didn't recognize the breed but he could see that there were several cow-calf pairs.

The white two-story house looked like it had been built in the 1930s or 1940s. The front porch sagged a bit, but otherwise it looked well maintained and recently painted.

There were both propane and home heating oil tanks on the south side of the house. The modern touches included a DISH TV satellite dish and a CB radio antenna.

An open-sided four-bay tractor shed sat to the east of the house. In addition to a Ford tractor and its implements, the tractor shed also housed a late-model Toyota Tacoma pickup, an older Toyota Corolla sedan, and a muddy ATV. Beyond were some assorted outbuildings, two small Butler brand galvanized steel grain silos, and one forty-foot silo that looked fairly new. They later learned that the silo was more than twenty-five years old, but it was still shiny because it was constructed mostly of stainless steel.

There was a pitifully small kitchen garden plot—now heaped

with foot-deep straw mulch for winter—with a five-foot-tall fence that looked incapable of keeping out deer.

Ken and Terry reslung their rifles muzzle down so that they would look less hostile as they approached the house. Ken rapped on the frame of the front porch's outer door.

A man armed with a scoped Remington Model 760 pump action deer rifle opened the door to the house and asked warily, "Who are you?"

Seeing the rifle pointed at his chest unnerved Ken.

"I'm Ken Layton and this is my wife, Terry."

"Durward Perkins is my name. My friends call me D. We heard you were coming. Step on in."

There was an uneasy moment as they appraised each other. Perkins lowered the rifle muzzle, but it was still uncomfortably pointed at Ken's knees. As he later mentioned to Terry, he still felt like he was being "muzzled."

Perkins was in his forties, with sandy-brown hair, slightly chubby, and starting to bald.

Ken offered, "We heard that you were looking for someone to provide security."

Perkins nodded. "That's right." He lifted his free hand to his chin and asked, "Are you Christian folk?"

"Yes, we're Catholic, and we attend Mass regularly."

Perkins nodded. "We're Quakers, but we don't get to church very often."

Ken said, "We're trustworthy and we know how to use these guns. I'm also a light truck mechanic with seven years of experience—I'm ASE-certified A5, T6, and E3."

"That's all Greek to me. You've got no car?"

"We had a car and an older Bronco that I had restored and modified, but we got ambushed on our way out of Chicago. So what you see here is all of our worldly possessions."

"Do you mean to stay around Iowa City? Long-term?"

"No sir. We plan to continue on out west, next spring. We're looking for a place to spend the winter. There's a group of our friends waiting for us in Idaho. We're what you'd call preppers or survivalists."

Perkins nodded. "Uh-huh." Then he pointed to Ken's HK clone and asked, "So those black space rifles you've got—hers looks like a short M16, and what's that one you've got there?"

"It's a Vector V91—that's a clone of the German HK91 rifle. It shoots 7.62 NATO, same as .308 Winchester. Terry's is what's called an M4gery or what I still call a CAR-15. It shoots 5.56 NATO, like an M16. They're both semiauto only." After a pause, he added, "We've both put in a lot of trigger time with our rifles. We've shot competition and qualification high-power rifle matches—both CMP and Appleseed. We were also both trained by a former Force Recon Marine in our survival group—a staff sergeant named Jeff Trasel. He taught us all the tricks: perimeter security, patrolling, and small unit tactics."

"So neither of you're military veterans? Iraq, Afghanistan?"

"No sir."

Perkins gave a slight groan and said, "Well, that's what I was hoping for. But beggars can't be choosers, I guess."

There was another long, uncomfortable pause.

Terry spoke up. "Sir, you're just going to have to trust us. Some things you just have to do on faith."

Perkins nodded deeply, and then said over his shoulder, "Karen! I think we've found our hired help!"

The door swung open to reveal a petite woman holding a 12-gauge Browning pump shotgun with a goose-length barrel. She said quietly, "Hi. I'm the backup."

Durward gestured them toward the door and said, "Come on in the front room, and we'll get you some coffee."

Ken and Terry were surprised to see the top of the living room and hallway strung with dozens of wires held up by eyebolts. Hun-

dreds of strips of brined beef were hung from the wires. Karen
Perkins explained that for the past three weeks she and Durward
had been converting all the beef from their chest freezer into jerky.
The fat trimming, slicing, and brining was a labor-intensive operation that had begun even before the utility power had gone out.
Karen Perkins described it. "After we brine the meat, the strips
get blotted dry and then hung up over the kitchen sink or the
laundry room sink for eight hours. Then, after we're sure they've
stopped dripping, we move them to the wires in the hall and the
living room. It's a big, ongoing process. It'll be another week before we're done."

After more introductions, Perkins summarized his situation.
"There's only about 2,300 people in West Branch, but there's
about 70,000 in Iowa City, and they're starting to *starve*. And
there's almost twice that much population in Cedar Rapids. And
that ain't to mention all the *millions* of hungry riffraff from around
Chicago—ah, present company excepted, that is."

Glancing again at Ken's rifle, he said, "The trouble is, we're just
too close to Interstate 80. There are just *way* too many people still
following that corridor. A lot of them are on foot or on bicycles
now. Most are legitimate refugees, but a good portion of them are
looters. I hear that the worst ones are in trucks and vans. They
take gasoline at gunpoint wherever they go. They're brutal. The
looters that have been hitting Iowa City are bound to make their
way here sooner or later."

"So what exactly do you propose, D.?" Ken asked

"I'm offering you room and board, in exchange for you two
being my security staff, twenty-four hours a day, regardless of the
weather."

"So, twelve on, twelve off?"

Perkins nodded and said, "Or six-hour, or eight-hour shifts,
however you want to cover it. But I need to have someone watching the road and all around the house and outbuildings at all times.

I can fill in if either of you catch a cold or something. Otherwise, *you're it*. No pay, but we'll feed you, and house you, and I'll replace any ammo you use defending the place. Karen can wash your laundry."

Ken turned to Terry and gave her a quizzical look. Then they both nodded.

Ken looked Durward in the eye, and said with a nod, "Okay, we'll do it."

They were provided a small bedroom in the back of the house that doubled as Karen's sewing and craft room.

After surveying the property, they determined that the tallest silo had a commanding view and was in an advantageous position for a watch tower. The silo, built by the Boythorpe Company, was an unusual design. Like most steel silos, it had a caged ladder going up the side. But instead of just a typical cone-shaped roof, it had an almost flat roof and cupola structure with a five-foot-tall "Patented, All Weather" door that had a pair of hatch levers near the top and bottom. The cupola was designed to give access to the top of the silo's unloader conveyor.

The field of view from the silo's doorway included the house, and nearly all of the barnyard. It also had a sweeping view of Charles Avenue. It took only a few hours to set up the cupola as a guard post. They first laid down a forty-inch octagon that was hand-sawn from a sheet of three-quarter-inch plywood. This covered the twenty-eight-inch-diameter loading port. Because of the confines of the caged ladder, the plywood was hoisted up with a rope. They then hoisted up an upholstered chair that fit nicely through the door of the cupola.

After the first day, they added a bronze Japanese brazier, in which they burned wood scraps and dried corn kernels. The Meiji-era brazier had been brought home at the end of World War II by Durward's grandfather, who had fought in the Pacific Theater. Just ten inches high, the tubular hibachi was a fairly plain design, with a light etching of an ancient castle on one side. For many years it had just been used by the Perkins family to hold potted plants. The brazier kept the cupola warm enough to be bearable all through the winter. A crude wire rack on top of the brazier could be topped with a teapot or a small fry pan for reheating foods.

After the chair was in place, Durward asked, "What'll we use for an alarm?"

Ken answered his question with one of his own: "Tell me, D.: Do you have any scrap steel pipe?"

"Sure do, depending on the diameter."

They soon found a thirty-inch length of four-inch-diameter steel pipe. This was hung by a wire from the top of the ladder's extended top handrail loop to serve as an alarm bell. The clapper was simply a ball-peen hammer, which was kept just inside the door of the cupola. The pipe alarm bell could be heard quite distinctly from inside the house or anywhere within 100 yards.

Ken summarized the alarm bell procedure. "If it is friendly visitors, we'll ring the bell with three sets of double-taps, spaced a few seconds apart. If it is an unidentified stranger, we'll bang on it in a continuous clamor. Beyond that, let's keep it simple and ballistic: If you hear *one shot*, that serves as a warning to whoever might be approaching, *and* as an alarm to anyone who is in the house."

The routine of manning the OP (observation post) was grueling. They soon discovered that Ken preferred nights and Terry preferred days. The couple traded off at 5 a.m. and 5 p.m. The individual coming on duty would carry up a lunch, which consisted of a Tupperware container of parched corn, a one-pint canning jar half filled with cream (to agitate into butter, which was then used to top the parched corn), and either a large carrot or a turnip. Occasionally there would be a treat, like sweetened homemade tofu, or a piece of beef jerky.

Since they had binoculars close at hand, Terry developed the hobby of bird-watching while on duty. She kept a birding notebook and the Perkins family's copy of an Audubon Society bird identification book in the cupola at all times. So that there would be no risk of any lengthy distractions, no other reading materials were allowed at the OP. There were many boring hours of duty, with nothing more to do than clean pistols and trim fingernails.

A few days of each week, Ken or Terry would also churn butter with a large hand churn while standing guard. Carefully hauling the completed churn full of butter—ready for washing—down the side of the silo with a rope required someone to be standing by below, to ensure that the ceramic churn didn't hit the ground.

A 10-liter water can as well as a teakettle that fit on the brazier's wire rack were soon provided. The store-bought tea soon ran out, so they switched to willow bark to make a weak tea. There was always plenty of cream available to sweeten the tea.

The guard shifts were monotonous. There was little to do other than churn butter, so Ken and Terry often composed love letters and poems to each other, which they would leave behind when their shifts were over.

The Perkinses had eight Brown Swiss cows that were producing. Without electricity, they reverted to hand milking their cows. This turned what had been a forty-minute job (twice a day) into a two-hour job. The raw milk and cream were bartered to families in West Branch for nearly all of the Perkins family's outside needs—everything from sugar and honey to homemade washable cotton menstrual pads.

Because the front forty acres of the property were perimeter-fenced and cross-fenced for cattle, it was easy enough to simply keep the front gate chained shut and padlocked.

A great source of fear and confusion was when strangers would approach the farm, hoping to barter. Since the Laytons were new to the farm and didn't recognize neighbors and acquaintances of the Perkinses, this caused a number of false alarms. By December, this problem was largely resolved by Durward bartering only through two trusted middlemen.

The Perkinses had two young daughters, ages three and five. Out of diapers, but not yet school age, their lives was relatively carefree, concerned only with dolls, coloring books, and "helping Mommy" in the kitchen.

The Perkinses were members of a Society of Friends church that met on North 6th Street. The local church's "Yearly Meeting" doctrine remained conservative and relatively pacifistic. But the Laytons were not surprised to see that the Perkinses and the other Quakers they met always had guns close at hand. Following the Crunch, the local church clarified that their stand on pacifism mainly involved foreign wars, rather than self-defense, which they declared "a matter of personal conscience."

Once a month, weather permitting, Durward filled in for the Laytons so that they could attend Mass at the St. Bernadette Parish in West Branch, on East Orange Street. It was a two-and-a-half-mile walk, so the "Mass trips" were a six-hour exercise. Ken and Terry treated these as very special occasions. On the preceding Saturdays, Terry would give Ken a haircut and beard trim. The long walks to and from church were the only times that they had to talk with each other at length, aside from lingering together at the change of each OP shift.

Even with the combined membership of St. Joseph church in West Liberty, only about thirty people attended on average. For most, it was simply too far to travel in a world without gasoline, or people didn't want to risk leaving their houses unguarded.

At first it seemed odd seeing nearly all of the adults armed with rifles, handguns, or shotguns. One congregant regularly carried a Saiga 12 shotgun in a Kushnapup bullpup stock with a ten-round detachable magazine. Another had a Kel-Tec RFB .308 rifle—also a bullpup. Those were considered status symbols. And some of the congregants assumed that Ken and Terry were wealthy because they carried both black rifles and Colt .45 automatics.

They soon learned the new norm of sitting widely spaced apart, to leave room for guns on the pews. Ken joked that the new order of worship was "Sit, stand, kneel, sit, stand, kneel, and *sling arms*." The church was very dimly lit—the only light came in through the stained glass windows. Without enough light to read by except on sunny days, the hymns were sung by memory, rather than from reading the *Novus Ordo* Modern Missal. They often remarked that this lighting made the services seem medieval. Ken and Terry missed the Latin Mass, but Terry quipped, "Perhaps that would make it seem *too* medieval, now that we're back in the Dark Ages."

Radcliff, Kentucky
November, the First Year

It was common knowledge that Washington, D.C., was in ruins. The ProvGov filled the power vacuum left when the East Coast had a massive die-off, in part due to an influenza pandemic that particularly struck the eastern seaboard from New York to Charleston in the first winter of the Crunch. The new government rapidly spread out, "pacifying" territory in all directions. Any towns that resisted were quickly crushed. The mere sight of dozens of tanks or APCs was enough to make most townspeople cower in fear. What it couldn't accomplish through intimidation, the ProvGov accomplished with bribes.

The ProvGov soon began issuing a new currency. Hutchings administration cronies spent the new bills lavishly. Covertly, some criminal gangs were hired as security contractors and used as enforcers of the administration's nationalization schemes. Some of these gangs were given military vehicles and weapons and promised booty derived from eliminating other gangs that were not as cooperative. Hit squads were formed to stifle any dissent. These did so through abductions, arson, and murder. Nobody was ever able to prove a link, but an inordinately large number of conservative, pro-sovereignty members of Congress from the old government disappeared or were reported killed by bandits.

Some foreign troops were clothed in U.S. ACU digital or OCP camouflage. But most foreign troops stayed in their national uniforms, and were used as shock troops to eliminate any pockets of resistance. Disaffection with the new government smoldered everywhere they went to pacify.

Within the first three months of launching the new government, Hutchings was in contact via satellite with the UN's new headquarters in Brussels to request peacekeeping assistance. (The old UN Building in New York had burned, and the entire New York metropolitan region was nine-tenths depopulated and controlled by hostile gangs.) Hutchings had at first naively assumed that the UN's assistance would be altruistic, with no strings attached. It was only after the first UN troops started to arrive in large numbers that it became clear that UN officers would control the operation. Eventually, Hutchings became little more than a figurehead. The UN administrators held the real power in the country. They had their own chain of command that bypassed the Hutchings administration, and they had direct control over the military.

One closely guarded secret was that Maynard Hutchings had signed an agreement that promised a payment of thirty metric tons of gold from the Fort Knox Depository to defray the costs of transporting and maintaining a mixed contingent of UN peacekeepers, mostly from Germany, Holland, and Belgium. The gold was shuttled out of the country in half-ton increments in flights from Fort Campbell, Kentucky. There had also been the offer of Chinese peacekeeping troops, but Hutchings insisted that no Asian or African troops be used on American soil, saying, "I want it to be all white fellas that'll blend in."

12

Terminal Ballistics

"Whoever looks upon them merely as an irregular mob will find himself much mistaken. They have men among them who know very well what they are about, having been employed as rangers against the Indians and Acadians; and this country being much covered with wood and hilly is very advantageous for their method of fighting."

—Hugh Percy, 2nd Duke of Northumberland, from a letter written from America, April 20, 1775

West Branch, Iowa
Late November, the First Year

Early one morning, shortly after sunrise, Terry idly rolled a Mason jar of cream beneath her boot, churning it. Sitting in the cupola atop the silo, she was enjoying some unusually clear weather, but it was still bitter cold. There was some snow in the shady areas on the north sides of the buildings, left over from the last cold front. She wondered if it would all melt before the next front came in. Durward said the barometer was starting to fall, and that they could expect rain rather than snow in about thirty-six hours. In the month that they had been at the farm, Terry learned that Durward had a knack for predicting the weather, which was an important skill in a world that was deprived of the Weather Channel.

Terry saw a pair of full-size vans approaching on Charles Avenue from the north. Vehicle traffic had continued to gradually decrease since their arrival, so every passing vehicle had become an object of attention. The two vans slowed and then pulled up to the front gate. The trailing van was tucked up tight, yet the rear half of it protruded into the county road. That seemed odd.

Durward Perkins was feeding grain to the cows, just twenty yards from the silo. Terry yelled down to him, "D.! Do you recognize those vans?"

Perkins answered, "Nope."

She shouted, "Get back in the house, and wake up Ken and then Karen, *right now*!" Grabbing the hammer, Terry began pounding on the pipe bell. Durward dropped his grain bucket and sprinted toward the house.

Terry edged forward off the stool and sat on the plywood, raising her M4gery, resting her forearms on her knees for a good shooting position.

A man stepped out of the passenger side of the lead van with a pair of bolt cutters. Just after he cut off the gate's padlock, Terry thumbed off the carbine's safety and fired. From the dirt that was kicked up behind him, she could see that her shot went just over the man's shoulder.

Then she remembered Tom Kennedy's advice from years before: "Whenever you are shooting uphill *or* downhill, hold *low*." The man dodged to the side just as she pulled the trigger again, so she missed for the second time.

Several doors on both vans opened, and suddenly there were several AKs and ARs pointed at the house and up at the silo. The intruders opened fire, and soon there were bullets puncturing or ricocheting off the silo. Feeling unexpected calm, Terry realigned her sights on the same man's chest—holding lower—and squeezed the trigger twice more. This time he went down, kicking and screaming.

The firefight soon escalated as Ken began returning fire with his

Vector HK91 clone, firing rapidly. Shoeless and wearing just a pair of British DPM camouflage pants and a brown T-shirt, Ken leaned his elbows across the kitchen table. He was shooting through the closed kitchen window. He and Terry soon established a rapid firing tempo at the two vans.

Ken's vantage point was slightly to the left of the vans and level, and Terry's was slightly to the right and above. The vans were in a deadly cross fire. Two of the men from the rear van hesitated and held their ground, but all of the others leapt back into the vans. Realizing that her magazine was nearly empty, Terry did a rapid magazine switch. As she did, Ken's heavy fire continued to rake the vans, shattering window after window. The two men still standing outside the vans realized that they were outgunned and jumped in to join the others.

The vans quickly backed away from the gate, just as Ken was changing magazines. Terry continued to fire. She could now see blood splatters inside the windows of both vans.

As they roared away, Ken resumed firing, but he had the chance to fire just four more rounds before he judged that the vans were out of range. The looter on the ground ceased thrashing. Ken put a fresh magazine in his HK, and shouted, "Is everybody okay?"

Durward answered, "We're okay, just shook up." His daughters were wailing back in their bedroom.

Ken's ears were ringing. He hated shooting indoors without any hearing protection, but the attack had come so suddenly that he had had no choice.

With his rifle shouldered, Ken edged out through the front door, and then through the porch door. He shouted up to Terry in the OP, "What's your status?"

She answered, "Green and green!"—indicating that she was uninjured and had plenty of ammunition. A moment later, she shouted, "They left one guy on the ground. I think he's dead."

"Any stay-behinds?"

Terry responded, "I don't think so, but things were happening pretty fast."

"You did great! Okay, let's hang tight for a while to make sure that guy is dead, and we'll wait and see whether they decide to come back."

Ken asked Karen Perkins to stand guard and watch for anyone approaching the back of the house, from the vantage point of the master bedroom window. Then he retrieved his boots and coat from his bedroom and put them on.

As they waited, and watched, Durward leaned over Ken's shoulder and alternated between looking through his rifle's scope and through a battered pair of old binoculars finished with black crinkle paint. "Crimminy sakes, that's a lot of blood. He ain't moving. You expect he's dead?" He handed the binoculars to Ken.

After spending a minute looking through the binoculars, Ken said, "Yes, I think so. But I'm no expert. We should make *sure* of it. Have you got some earplugs?"

"Yeah, I'll go get them."

He returned a minute later, offering a handful of disposable foam earplugs in clear cellophane packages.

Ken opened a package and inserted a pair. As he did, he gestured for Perkins to do likewise. Then he said, "You've got the rifle with the scope."

"To make 'absa-tively' sure he's dead?"

Ken nodded. "That's right, D. Just give me a chance to warn the ladies that you're going to shoot."

It took Perkins a full minute to get ready for the shot. He laid a throw cushion from the couch on the windowsill of the window that Ken had been using to shoot from. He pulled up a dining room chair to sit on, and rested the fore-end of the Remington pump-action .270 across the cushion. He exhaled loudly. Then he cranked up the scope to 9 power and clicked off the rifle's safety. Just when Ken thought that he was about to shoot, Durward said, "Give me a sec. I'm still kind of nervous. The crosshair is dancing."

He again loudly let out a breath. A few moments later, he squeezed off a shot. Pulling the muzzle back down from the recoil, he looked through the scope and said, "I hit him just above his ear. So if he was faking before, he ain't faking now." He calmly pumped the rifle's action, chambering a fresh cartridge, and toggled the safety button to the safe position. Then he removed the rifle's magazine and topped it off with a cartridge from his pocket.

They waited another hour to see if the looters would return, Durward concerned that they might be back with reinforcements. He paced back and forth between the kitchen and the back bedrooms, consoling his wife and daughters, and giving them updates.

As they waited, Ken said, "I'm sorry that I shot right through your kitchen window."

"Shucks, that's what they make clear sheet plastic for, right? Don't you worry. . . . I'm sure I'll be able to scrounge up some replacement windows in the next few days. But before dark tonight, we'll cover the broken windows with sheet plastic. We can hold it in place with some batten strips."

Their neighbor from down the road drove up to the gate on his ATV, with his mixed breed cattle dog on the back as usual. A sporterized Springfield rifle rested in the rubberized spring steel forks mounted on the ATV's front deck. Carrying their rifles, Ken and Durward walked out to the gate to talk to him.

As they neared the gate, the neighbor asked, "You folks okay?"

Durward answered, "Yeah, we're fine, just scared spitless."

"All that shooting, and you only got one of them?"

"I think we hit a few more of them inside their rigs," Ken answered.

Durward swung the gate open and the three men closely examined the body and the surrounding ground. The gravel and the adjoining pavement were heavily littered with chunks of broken safety glass, in at least three distinct colors. There was blood on some of it. There was even more blood around the body. They found more than seventy pieces of fired brass that obviously came from AR-15s, AK-47s, and at least one AK-74. The lacquer-coated steel-cased brass from the latter captivated Durward and his neighbor. This was the first time that either of them had even heard of the smaller-caliber AK. The neighbor's dog watched all this from the back of the ATV, with its tail wagging.

The dead looter's body was partially resting on an inexpensive pair of Chinese-made bolt cutters. The man was in his late twenties or early thirties, Hispanic, and overweight. He had lots of tattoos. He had been hit twice through the lungs by .223 bullets from Terry's M4, and once through the head by Durward's .270 Winchester.

Ken said in a droll voice, "Well, D., you can sleep peacefully tonight, knowing that you didn't kill anyone. This guy was dead long before you sent that piece of 'let's make sure' through his noggin."

As they were examining the body, the neighbor's dog jumped off the back of the ATV and started licking at the blood on the gravel driveway. "That's just *wrong*," Durward said.

Seeing this, the neighbor shouted, "Bad dog! Load up!" The dog obediently jumped back onto the rear deck of the ATV.

They rolled the body over. Searching the pockets, they found the man was carrying no identification. In his pockets, they found two small rolls of clothesline twine, and a slightly rust-pitted Kershaw pocketknife.

"With both the landline and cell phones out, do you think we should try to get over to the Sheriff's Office to report this?" Durward asked.

The neighbor shook his head, and said, "No. My son-in-law Ted is a Cedar County deputy. He said that the few deputies left at both the Cedar and Johnson County Sheriff's Departments are following up on something only if it's major."

Durward asked, "So an attempted home invasion robbery and attempted murder isn't *major*?"

The neighbor again shook his head.

Ken said in a low voice, "These days, those crimes are just piddly. And killing in self-defense is just par for the course. I say we bury him, and be done with it."

The man nodded, and then said, "Yep, that's what I hear people are doing all over. We're back to vigilante days and ways." After a pause, he added, "Well, I'll leave the cleanup chores to you gents." He stepped astride his ATV, started it, and drove off with a wave.

Durward handed Ken a padlock to replace the one that had been cut, and asked, "Do you think we should sweep up all the broken glass?"

Ken shook his head. "No, we should leave it as a warning: 'This is what happens to looters.'"

They wrapped the body in a piece of used white plastic silage tarp. Rolling the looter up in the tarp was messy and cumbersome. They also found that the shrouded body was too heavy for the two of them to carry. So Durward drove his blue Ford 8N tractor out and they unceremoniously rolled it into the front scoop.

They buried the dead looter in the garden, six feet deep. Since his tractor lacked a backhoe, most of the depth was dug by hand. The tractor was able to scrape a gouge eighteen inches deep, which took them below the frost line. Even still, digging the grave took several hours.

The four adults at the farm took turns saying prayers over the grave—both prayers for the unsaved, and prayers of thanks that they hadn't been shot. There was a brief and polite theological argument when Terry said prayers for the dead looter. Perkins said that he believed that once someone was dead, it would have no bearing on their salvation. As he put it, "Either he was saved, or he wasn't. Okay, I won't try to stop you from saying prayers for his soul, post facto. But scripturally, they're ineffectual. Oh, and scripturally, there is no Purgatory. That's an extra-biblical creation of the Catholic Church."

The Perkins daughters seemed oblivious to the solemnity of the graveside prayers. They fidgeted with their mittens, pulled off each other's caps, and kicked at dirt clods.

The next day, they counted ten bullet holes in the house and twenty-five in the silo. Ken had shot out one window, and the looters' bullets had shattered two others. Several of their bullets passed though two room partitions and assorted furniture before being stopped.

Up in the silo cupola, they found that two of the looters' bullets had pierced the back of the chair and the sheet metal wall behind it, just above where Terry's head had been when she sat down to shoot. After seeing that, Terry insisted, "We need to add some *armor* to that cupola, D."

The bullet holes in the silo and its cupola were soon patched with auto body filler or, in the places where they could reach both sides, with nuts and bolts coated with auto body filler. The holes in the house's siding were filled with dowels from D.'s wood shop. It took several weeks of inquiries, but eventually all the windows were replaced. They were paid for with bartered corn, soybeans, and beef jerky.

D. made good on his promise to replace the Laytons' expended ammunition. They had fired forty-seven rounds of 5.56, and twenty-four rounds of 7.62 NATO. This took lots of searching and dickering. It eventually cost Perkins more than 1,600 pounds of bartered corn, soybeans, and scrap steel.

Ken and Terry bartered for very little while they were in West Branch. Ken swapped a nickel-cadmium 9-volt battery and a silver dime for a bottle of Break-Free synthetic lubricant, after their original had been depleted with regular gun maintenance. They also traded a pair of socks for an assortment of Ziploc bags. In their weeks traveling overland, they discovered that plastic bags were essential for keeping the various contents of their backpacks and pockets dry.

Durward said, "Well, I got my money's worth for my security force. Those space rifles sure are something. It sounded like World War III had started."

Fearing that the looters would return, they kept on high alert at the Perkins farm for the next two weeks. Temporarily, there were two people on guard at all times. They also decided that they needed better communication between the house and the silo. So Karen Perkins tapped into the local informal barter network, putting out the word that they would trade wheat for a pair of intercoms. Within three days they completed a trade of 400 pounds of wheat for a well-used but serviceable NuTone intercom, fourteen batteries, and enough three-conductor wire to reach the top of the silo. The base station was set up on the wall behind the woodstove's brickwork. This spot was chosen by Ken because he had determined that it was the part of the house with the best ballistic protection.

Two days after the dead looter was buried, they started their ballistic protection mantlet project. The steel came from an eighteen-disc offset harrow that had sat disused behind the tractor shed. This, Durward explained, was just an old spare, with a hitch that kept breaking anyway. After soaking the disc attachment bolts with penetrating oil overnight, Ken and D. were able to dismount all eighteen of the rusty discs from the harrow's frame.

They hauled the twenty-six-inch-diameter discs up to the top of the guard tower silo two at a time, with a rope threaded through the center holes of the discs. The discs were positioned in a heavily overlapping pattern at the cupola's doorway, looking like fish scales. They were held in place by a wooden framework of 2x4s.

The front and back halves of the framework were joined by long lag screws.

Just behind the tractor discs, they laid nine horizontal layers of one-eighth-inch-thickness sheet steel from Durward's large collection of scrap metal. This was designed to protect anyone in the cupola from rifle fire that was directed at a steep angle, up through the floor. As a bonus, this steel sheeting provided protection from fire in the event that the hibachi was ever accidentally tipped over.

As an afterthought, Ken and D. covered the front of the mantlet framework with a twenty-seven-inch-tall piece of plywood. Ken noted, "If anyone attacking sees just a sheet of plywood, then they'll think that they can shoot through it. I'd rather have the mantlet draw fire than have someone decide to deliberately aim over the top of it."

That same day, they repositioned the alarm bell pipe inside the cupola so that someone could ring it from behind the cover of the mantlet.

After installing the mantlet, they discovered that it retained a lot of heat from the hibachi, making the cupola even more comfortable to sit in during guard duty in cold weather.

The Monroe Ranch, Raynesford, Montana
Late March, the Second Year

Joshua Watanabe was well settled in his routine of helping with the cattle at the ranch and patrolling his assigned silos and LCC. One morning in late March, he drove the Unimog through patchy snow to MAF A-01. As was his habit, he stopped 550 yards short, behind an intervening low hill. He parked the Unimog and ambled to the top of the hill, carrying his deer rifle cradled in his arms. Unlike past patrols, he was surprised to see three vans and a pickup in the MAF's parking lot. He dropped prone and popped open his rifle's scope covers. Looking through his scope, he could see several men in civilian clothes. They were walking in and out of the building carrying boxes. He watched for several minutes, and jotted what he saw in his notepad. The vehicles had three different colored license plates. He crawled off the top of the hill toward his truck. Once he had gotten below the military crest of the hill, he rose and ran back to the Unimog. Per the security SOP, he first tried the Malmstrom security frequency on his issued handie-talkie. Just as he expected, he heard nothing but static. From this locality, the VHF radio had line-of-sight communications only when a helicopter was airborne. Then he tried the Great Falls repeater at 155 MHz. He got a response from a police and fire dispatcher. Because they lacked communications patching capability, the dispatcher had to take down a message by hand, and relay it to the 341st Security Forces Squadron at Malmstrom. Joshua asked the dispatcher to read back the message to him, which emphasized that he was the "friendly" with the vehicle, 500 meters southeast of the MAF.

As a precaution, Joshua rolled out an optic orange marker panel on top of the Unimog's radio shelter and pinned it down with a tire iron and a tow chain to ensure that it didn't blow away.

A few minutes later, Joshua was back on the hilltop, again glassing the MAF. The looting was continuing. With his other radio, Joshua made his first direct contact with a security detachment pilot, reminding him that he was located on the hilltop to the southwest of the MAF, and advising him of the local wind and cloud cover.

Soon, he heard helicopter rotors in the distance. The looters heard this, too, and they ran for their vehicles. Joshua thumbed off the rifle's safety, and centered his crosshairs on the fogged driver's side window of a van that was parked perpendicular to him. Trying to control his breathing, he squeezed the trigger. A moment later, as the crosshairs settled back down after recoil, he could see that the window had shattered.

All four vehicles started to roll out of the MAF parking lot. Joshua fired again, not expecting a hit. A UH-1N helicopter came into view to the north, flying low, following the undulations of the terrain—what the pilots call nap-of-the-earth flying.

Joshua was alarmed to see that the vehicles turned left after exiting the MAF gate. They drove south down the road toward him and the Unimog. Although he was twenty yards from his truck parked on the shoulder of the road, he felt very exposed.

He had time to fire only one more hasty shot before he heard on the radio, "We're coming in hot."

Joshua snatched his radio and shouted, "Danger close! I'm the guy twenty meters east of the vehicle with the marker panel."

He heard in response, "Roger that."

The three vans and the pickup were gathering speed. Joshua was able to line up a shot and squeeze the trigger when the lead van was only seventy yards away. They were approaching him nearly head-on. His shot was lucky, punching through the windshield and hitting the driver in the neck.

The van swerved to the left and then sharply to the right. Only sixty yards after passing the parked Unimog, the van went into the snow-filled barrow pit ditch and began to porpoise. It glanced into a three-strand barbed wire fence, and then rolled, throwing huge clods of earth into the air, tearing out T-posts, and spraying up a rooster tail of snow. The van came to a stop with its wheels tangled in the fence wire, resting on its left side.

The other vehicles continued on, still accelerating. The helicopter's 7.62mm NATO Minigun began to fire in short bursts when the pickup and the two other vans were 250 yards south of Joshua and when the helicopter was almost directly overhead. The results were horrendous. The cyclic rate of the electric Gatling gun was so high that individual shots could not be heard. It sounded like a deep, throaty animal growl.

Fired brass and links showered down on the road near Joshua

like a hailstorm. In just four bursts of about two seconds each, the three vehicles were absolutely shredded. They all coasted to a stop, flopping on punctured tires and spewing smoke and steam from their engine compartments. Surprisingly, none of the three vehicles rolled over or left the roadway. Nor did they catch fire. They simply were riddled with holes and they came to a stop at skewed angles.

As Joshua watched the strafing in fascination and horror, the rear door popped open on the van that he had stopped. A man and a woman spattered with blood crawled out. They were both carrying SKS rifles. Joshua shot them deliberately, once each through the chest, and they fell to the ground. The woman lay still immediately, but the man thrashed violently and screamed as he hemorrhaged. After twenty-five seconds, he lay still.

Joshua's attention was diverted to the helicopter, which had orbited to the east and slowed to nearly a stationary hover. The door gunner gave each of the three smoking vehicles another two-second burst from the M134 Minigun. Its 4,000-round-per-minute cyclic rate was astonishing.

"Overkill," Joshua said to himself.

As Joshua watched for any further movement from the closest van, the helicopter orbited slowly. Joshua and the pilot radioed back and forth. The pilot said that "giving it another squirt" would be a waste of ammo, so he held his fire.

They waited twenty-five minutes until the Backup Force arrived. They came in a pair of up-armored M1116 Humvees mounted with .30 caliber M240 machineguns. The vehicles stopped alongside the Unimog. The ground team, armed with M4s, dismounted and in bounds advanced to the overturned van. They approached cautiously, but found only the dead driver inside and the dead man and woman behind it. The team leader shouted, "Three looter KIAs!"

They left one man at the van and one of the gunners in the turret of the forward-most Humvee, while all the others advanced, again in bounding overwatch formation, to the remains of the other three vehicles.

The airman standing next to the van looked toward Joshua and asked, "Are you Watanabe?"

Joshua answered, "That's right."

He rose to his feet. His hands were still trembling. He refilled his rifle's magazine from a box of cartridges in his coat pocket, doing his best to look nonchalant. He closed the rifle's bolt and thumbed back its safety. He walked toward the airman, carrying the rifle muzzle down.

The airman, whom Joshua had never met, was wearing interceptor body armor (IBA) and Oakley sunglasses. He said, "Looks like they broke into the 'wrong dang rec room.'"

Joshua chuckled, recognizing the reference to the movie *Tremors*.

The helicopter departed, leaving the scene strangely quiet. Joshua's ears were ringing.

For the next two hours, Joshua and the airmen assessed the damage and searched the vehicles. Most of this could best be described as simply gawking. The destroyed vehicles looked like colanders. Two of the looters' vehicles had Wisconsin plates, one had South Dakota plates, and the other had North Dakota plates. There was little that could be salvaged from the three that had been savaged by the Minigun, but the one that Joshua had stopped yielded five serviceable guns, more than 400 rounds of ammunition (much of it in odd calibers for other guns), and a road map with markings that gave some clues about the looters' history. Two driver's licenses indicated that the gang had originated in Madison, Wisconsin. They had apparently spent the last nineteen months hopscotching through Minnesota, the Dakotas, and Montana.

They used the winch on the Unimog to pull the three shot-up vehicles off the road. Joshua filed a succinct after-action report that downplayed his own actions. A week later, he was summoned to General Woolson's office, where he was awarded a Combat Action Medal and a field commission to the rank of second lieutenant.

13

Under Escort

"Since it's not considered polite, and surely not politically correct to come out and actually say that greed gets wonderful things done, let me go through a few of the millions of examples of the benefits of people trying to get more for themselves. There's probably widespread agreement that it's a wonderful thing that most of us own cars. Is there anyone who believes that the reason we have cars is because Detroit assembly line workers care about us? It's also wonderful that Texas cattle ranchers make the sacrifices of time and effort caring for steer so that New Yorkers can have beef on their supermarket shelves. It is also wonderful that Idaho potato growers arise early to do back-breaking work in the hot sun to ensure that New Yorkers also have potatoes on their supermarket shelves. Again, is there anyone who believes that ranchers and potato growers, who make these sacrifices, do so because they care about New Yorkers? They might hate New Yorkers. New Yorkers have beef and potatoes because Texas cattle ranchers and Idaho potato growers care about themselves and they want more for themselves. How much steak and potatoes would New Yorkers have if it all depended on human love and kindness? I would feel sorry for New Yorkers. Thinking this way bothers some people because they are more concerned with the motives behind a set of actions rather than the results. This is what Adam Smith, the father of economics, meant in The Wealth of Nations *when he said, 'It is not from the benevolence of the butcher, the brewer, or the baker, that we expect our dinner, but from their regard to their own interests.'"*

—Economist and radio talk show host Dr. Walter E. Williams, from his essay "Markets, Governments, and the Common Good"

Bradfordsville, Kentucky
April, the Second Year

As the war of resistance grew, Sheila Randall took some calculated risks. She allowed her store to be used as a transit point for couriers. She also continued to trade in ammunition, donating considerable quantities to the Resistance, including any that was in prohibited categories (military calibers, full metal jacket, tracer, incendiary, or armor piercing). On three occasions, she sheltered wounded resistance fighters in the store's upstairs apartment, once for more than a week. She also passed along tidbits of information that she picked up in talking with customers.

Sheila's main contact with the Resistance was through Hollan Combs. A retired soil scientist and a widower, he said that he was the perfect resistance fighter. He reasoned, "I've got no kin, and I'm too old and crippled up to run. That leaves me just the option of standing to fight, since I'm too ornery to do anything else. This is a war that's best fought by young men who haven't yet married, and old farts like me, with nothing left to lose."

Deputy Dustin Hodges of the Marion County Sheriff's Department was Sheila's other key resistance contact. Although most of the other deputies and the sheriff himself sympathized with the Resistance, the department put on an outward show of supporting the ProvGov. Hodges regularly fed Sheila information that she summarized in handwritten spot reports. These were passed along to the couriers. It was through Dustin that Sheila got advance warning of many planned government policies. She returned these favors by letting Dustin buy certain items at cost.

West Branch, Iowa
April, the Second Year

The next few months were quiet at the Perkins farm. They had to warn off more than a dozen groups of refugees who had displayed uncertain motives. Two warning shots were fired. Most of these groups were traveling on foot. With a hand-painted sign that he posted on the gatepost, Durward directed refugees to their Society of Friends (Quaker) church house on North 6th Street. Since just after the Crunch, the Perkinses had secretly supplied the church with more than 3,000 pounds of corn and soybeans to distribute to refugees and to needy people in the community.

In most instances, refugees would stop, read the sign, and move on. But often they would try to send a "representative" to the house, hoping for a direct handout. A warning shot would usually suffice to send that individual scurrying back over the gate and the whole group packing. A few times there were hostile shouts, but inevitably the refugees would leave. Durward was mistrustful, so he kept the cows locked up in the barn every night.

In late April, as the spring rains became less frequent and the weather warmed, Ken and Terry prepared to move on. The Perkinses supplied them with as much beef jerky and pemmican as they could carry, supplemented by a few raisins and canned fruits. Durward also wrote a letter of introduction, describing their work for him. They were also given road maps for seven western states that would cover potential routes to the Idaho retreat.

At dusk on the evening of April 7, by the light of a quarter waxing moon, Ken and Terry headed west. They again traveled at night, mainly along railroad tracks and, as needed, cross-country. They skirted wide around Iowa City, via the north shore of Lake MacBride. They then walked north and followed the Canadian Pacific Railroad line westward. These were tracks formerly owned by the Iowa, Chicago, & Eastern Railroad. They followed the tracks west through a succession of small towns: Fairfax, Norway, Luzerne, Belle Plain, Chelsea, Tama, Montour, and Marshalltown.

As they approached Marshalltown, Ken pointed out a large water tower in the distance and said, "I feel sorry for towns like this, with the power grid down. Almost everywhere that you see a water tower, that means that they relied on electric pumps—to pump it up there, to create a 'head.' When the grid went down, most towns only had a four- or five-day supply of water. So except for towns that are near hydroelectric dams and that were able to reestablish power quickly, the residents were out of water. With toilets not flushing, that must be a sanitation nightmare in any town of appreciable size."

Terry asked, "So what percentage of the population of the United States is on municipal water systems that are gravity-fed, from end to end?"

"Probably less than 2 percent. The EPA raised their standards to require filtration for most water—because of turbidity testing—so they added pumps to a lot of municipal water systems that *had been* gravity-fed. Maybe they were able to take those pumps and filters out of the system and revert to all gravity flow in some places. But nearly everybody else is collecting water from rain barrels from their roofs, or gathering it out of streams and ponds. Even people with well water are going to be out of luck after they run out of fuel for their generators. People like Todd and Kevin in Idaho—with either gravity-fed spring water or a photovoltaic well pump—have got to be a tiny minority. So close to 95 percent of the population is toting water by hand every time they want to do laundry, wash dishes, or flush a toilet. Think of the collective drudgery that represents."

As they walked through the outskirts of Marshalltown, Ken and Terry were halted by two police officers who stepped out of a police cruiser with riot guns. One of them aimed a spotlight from their cruiser at Ken and Terry. The Laytons stopped and raised their hands.

"Hold it there," one of the officers warned. "Open carry of firearms is banned inside city limits."

Terry answered, "We didn't realize that we'd entered city limits."

"You haven't yet, but you will be if you cross this street."

Terry countered, "Well, can't we just unload our guns and just pass through?"

"No, then you'd be in violation of the City Council's emergency order on vagrancy. Mayor Nordyke said there are no exceptions. He laid down a zero tolerance policy for any outsiders unless they're invited here by relatives."

Ken shook his head in disgust, and said, "We're not vagrants. We're just travelers exercising our right of way. Can I show you a letter of introduction?"

The officers took a few minutes to read the letter. It seemed to soften their attitude considerably.

Handing the letter back to Terry, the older cop eyed his partner and said, "Okay, we'll just escort you out of town, and you can be on your way."

Terry asked, "In your car?"

"No, afoot. Can't spare the gas."

Ken replied, "Okay, whatever you say. Your town, your rules."

They turned off the spotlight and locked their cruiser.

The officers fell in behind Ken and Terry and they resumed walking. Ken noticed that the officers still carried their shotguns, albeit casually. They chatted somewhat nervously as they walked. The officers talked about the many close calls they'd had since October, and the many crime scenes that they had cleaned up. Just forty officers, bolstered by a new "posse" of mostly military veterans and a few retired lawmen that numbered more than 100, they said, policed the town of 26,000. The older officer mentioned that there had been more than 800 burglaries and 70 violent home invasions. He hinted that there had been some summary executions of the perpetrators. They warned the Laytons to avoid Des Moines and Omaha—describing them as scenes of chaos and starvation. The younger officer mentioned that with the currency now worthless, they had been paid wages in corn, adding, "We're all pretty sick of corn."

They reached the far side of the Marshalltown limits in just seven blocks. The older officer said, "This is where we part company. We wish you the best of luck. But if we see you back in town, you *will* be arrested. Is that clear?"

"Yes, officer, abundantly clear."

Once they were back in farmland, Ken commented, "They looked pretty lean, for cops."

"Well. You make a cop walk most places instead of drive, and take away his supply of donuts . . ." Terry joked.

Ken finished her sentence, ". . . and he just might start looking athletic."

They pressed on in the direction of Ames, Iowa. After their experience in Marshalltown, they avoided towns altogether. This often required lengthy circumnavigations. As the spring turned to summer, Ken and Terry saw fewer and fewer motor vehicles in operation. The little gasoline left was obviously being preciously guarded.

Following the advice of the Marshalltown police, they swung far around Des Moines and Omaha. From the vicinity of Ames, they walked another 650 miles west and slightly north, skirting far around Sioux City and Sioux Falls. Because of their stealthy "TABbing," they averaged only four or five miles a night.

They would occasionally find places to barter some of their handful of silver coins for food. But often, they would eat gleanings. Sometimes they would have the chance to shoot a rabbit or a pheasant on the ground with Terry's CAR-15 or with their .45 pistols. Twice, they were lucky enough to find deer to shoot. On each occasion, they spent three days camping in one place, gorging on venison and making jerky. They even cooked and ate the marrow from the large bones. And in both instances they were careful to bury the bones and gut piles so that their camp would not attract the attention of scavengers. In all, their hunting consumed only thirty-one cartridges that spring and summer. They didn't pull the trigger unless a single shot was absolutely sure to "bag a critter."

In late July and early August, they found three weeks of work harvesting pears, strawberries, and raspberries in Mission Hill, just east of Yankton, South Dakota. They were paid 25 cents in pre-1965 silver coin per day, plus one hot meal per day, in exchange for ten-hour days of hot, sweaty harvesting work.

The farm owner offered to keep their packs and rifles safely locked in his guarded house each day. This was the first time in nearly a year that they didn't have their rifles in their hands when they were outdoors. Ken and Terry felt practically naked, carrying just their .45 automatic pistols.

It was in Mission Hill that they also first started trading with Yankton Sioux. They traded two deer hides, seven rabbit pelts, and three pheasant pelts for some antelope jerky, bar soap, and salt. The natives proved hospitable, easygoing, and fair traders. But it was obvious that they were desperately poor. Ken's comment to Terry was "They were poor before the Crunch, but now all they have left is their pride."

14

In the Footsteps of Josephus

"There are certain principles that are inherent in man, that belong to man, and that were enunciated in an early day, before the United States government was formed, and they are principles that rightfully belong to all men everywhere. They are described in the Declaration of Independence as inalienable rights, one of which is that men have a right to live; another is that they have a right to pursue happiness; and another is that they have a right to be free and no man has authority to deprive them of those God-given rights, and none but tyrants would do it. These principles, I say, are inalienable in man; they belong to him; they existed before any constitutions were framed or any laws made. Men have in various ages striven to strip their fellow-men of these rights, and dispossess them of them. And hence the wars, the bloodshed and carnage that have spread over the earth. We, therefore, are not indebted to the United States for these rights; we were free as men born into the world, having the right to do as we please, to act as we please, as long as we do not transgress constitutional law nor violate the rights of others. . . . Another thing God expects us to do, and that is to maintain the principle of human rights. . . . We owe it to all liberty-loving men, to stand up for human rights and to protect human freedom, and in the name of God we will do it, and let the congregation say Amen."
—John Taylor, 1882, *Journal of Discourses*, Volume 23, p. 263

Muddy Pond, Tennessee
July, the Second Year

Life in Overton County was just starting to get back to normal when the first Provisional Government units passed through. Since the town was within the four-hour-drive-time local security radius of Fort Knox, Muddy Pond was in one of the first areas to be pacified by the ProvGov. The new administration at first seemed well intentioned and benevolent, but people soon saw its sinister side.

The nationalization programs and the controls began gradually. At first, the ProvGov seized only key industries and utilities. But later, smaller companies were taken over, some seemingly on a whim. People wondered why a padlock manufacturing company would be nationalized. And why would a silver refinery have to be nationalized?

Likewise, the wage, price, currency, and credit controls started small, but gradually grew to gargantuan proportions. Just a month after the ProvGov troops arrived, there was a dusk-to-dawn curfew, with shoot-on-sight orders for violators. But even daylight hours weren't safe, as Ben Fielding discovered.

Early one afternoon, all of Ben's family except Joseph was at home listening to some Messianic music on Rebecca's iPod dock. They often gathered in the living room to do so, on the days that the power was on. The children liked to hear the music played loudly, and they sang along and danced. Their fun was interrupted when they heard some long bursts of automatic weapons fire close by their house. They looked out their living room window and saw a convoy of UNPROFOR coalition vehicles strung out for a quarter mile on the county road. The trucks and APCs had stopped and turned out onto either side of the road in a herringbone pattern. The wild firing continued for thirty seconds. They heard a few shots hit the roof of their house. The firing finally stopped when the convoy commander in the lead Marder APC repeatedly honked his horn.

Ben and his family fearfully watched as men ran back and forth between the vehicles. They expected more trouble, so Ben took the precaution of running all the pages of his address book through his cross-cut paper shredder.

Five minutes later, a UNPROFOR patrol approached the front door. A German soldier shouted with a heavy accent, "Man of the house, come out!"

Ben walked out with his hands on top of his head, and said, "The only others here are my wife and children. Please leave them alone."

The patrol leader unslung a rifle from his shoulder and held it out. Ben recognized it as his son's .22, now missing its bolt. The *soldat* asked, "Your gun, is this?"

"Yes, I believe that is my rifle, but I'm not certain. If that is mine, then it is registered in my name, in full accordance with the law. Where did you find it?"

"It was being carried by a young, er, man, now dead."

Rebecca began wailing.

"Have you any other guns in the house?"

"No."

The soldiers spent an hour noisily ransacking the house, while others held Ben and his terrified family at gunpoint outside. Their youngest daughter, just recently out of diapers, wet herself as they waited. One team searched the house, while another searched the barn and outbuildings. Ben alternated between intense feelings of fear and anger at the situation. They watched helplessly as the soldiers carried off Rebecca's jewelry box, her iPod and dock, and many other small possessions. This included nearly 200 rounds of .22 hollow points that were taken as "evidence."

Finding nothing actionable, the soldiers left without explanation or apology.

Ben and Rebecca went inside to find the house a shambles. Several stretches of Sheetrock in the hall and master bedroom had been kicked in and the upholstery on their couches and two of the mattresses had been slashed open. Two cabinets had been pried completely off the walls, and were left dumped on the floor, coated in Sheetrock dust. There were shattered dishes and plates littering the kitchen and dining room floors. A broken pipe was spraying the front bathroom cabinet with water. Ben soon turned off the well pump and shut the valve for the service line to the house. That stopped the water from further flooding the bathroom and hall.

After a pair of honks, the UNPROFOR convoy left in a cloud of dust and diesel smoke.

Ben and Rebecca walked out to the north end of their property to look for Joseph. After ten minutes of searching, they found his body eighty yards from the county road, and about 300 yards from the house. He had been shot six times in the back and buttocks. Two gutted quail were still in his game bag. His white T-shirt was red with blood, and his blue jeans were stained red to the knees.

For a half hour, Ben sat cradling the lifeless form of his eldest son, crying and rocking. Tears ran down his face. Nearby, Rebecca and their three surviving children sat hugging each other in a huddle, crying, moaning, and praying aloud. Finally Ben stood up. He looked down at his son's corpse and said, "You wait here. I'm going to get a shovel, a sheet, some water, towels, and olive oil."

He was back a few minutes later and almost immediately began to dig. As Ben dug just a few feet from his son's body, he said forthrightly, "We'll find no remedy or recourse in the courts, Rebecca. These are tyrants, tyrants. I need to fight them."

He then continued working quietly, digging into the soil and small rocks with fervor. He didn't stop until the grave was head-height deep. Blisters were forming on his palms, but he hardly noticed. As Ben dug the grave, Rebecca washed her son's body, and rubbed olive oil onto his skin.

They gently lowered Joseph's body into the grave and Ben folded the boy's arms across his chest. They shrouded the body with a sheet. Rebecca helped Ben back up out of the grave. After saying prayers, each member of the family poured in a shovelful of earth. Rebecca then did most of the shoveling as they refilled the grave, weeping yet again.

After the grave was refilled and mounded, each family member selected a stone to mark the site. Ben found one beside Joseph's favorite fishing hole.

They recited the Kaddish, a sanctification ritual in Judaism, found in the Siddur, the Jewish liturgy book read in Jewish temples on the Sabbath and High Holy Days.

Yitgaddal veyitqaddash shmeh rabba. Be'alma di vra khir'uteh veyamlikh malkhuteh veyatzmaḥ purqaneh viqarev qetz meshiḥeh beḥayekhon uvyomekhon uvḥaye dekhol bet yisrael be'agala uvizman qariv ve'imru amen. Yehe shmeh rabba mevarakh le'alam ul'alme 'almaya Yitbarakh veyishtabbaḥ veyitpaar veyitromam veyitnasse veyithaddar veyit'alleh veyithallal shmeh dequdsha, brikh hu. Le'ella lella mikkol min kol birkhata veshirata tushbeḥata veneḥemata daamiran be'alma ve'imru amen.

(May His great name be exalted and sanctified is God's great name in the world, which He created according to His will! May He establish His kingdom and may His salvation blossom and His anointed be near. During your lifetime and during your days and during the lifetimes of all the House of Israel, speedily and very soon! And say, Amen. May His great name be blessed forever, and to all eternity! Blessed and praised, glorified and exalted, extolled and honored, adored and lauded be the name of the Holy One, blessed be He, above and beyond all the blessings, hymns, praises, and consolations that are uttered in the world! And say, Amen.)

As they walked away from the grave and back toward the

house, Rebecca carried the shovel. With both sadness and anger, she spat, "Yes, go. Fight them! You have my blessing. Don't worry about us. We will be safe and waiting here. The Lord will protect all of us, and provide for all of us."

That evening, with aching hands, Ben dug up the length of eight-inch-diameter PVC pipe buried beneath their pair of grated trash-burning barrels. The PVC cache tube contained Ben's heavily greased guns: a Galil .308 rifle, a Browning A-5 semiauto 12-gauge shotgun, and an HK USP .45 Compact pistol. All three guns were considered contraband, so they hadn't been registered under the recent edicts. Packed along with the guns there were seven Galil magazines, three 200-round battle packs of Portuguese 7.62mm ball ammunition, and seven boxes of shotgun shells, each wrapped in separate Ziploc bags. After he had cleaned and loaded the guns, Ben organized his backpacking gear. He put the Galil and magazines in a guitar case, padded by extra clothes.

As Ben organized and packed his gear, Rebecca served the children some leftovers. They had to eat sitting on the couch, because the kitchen was still littered with broken glass. After they had eaten, Ben gave each of his children lengthy hugs. He told them to be brave and reverent, and to obey their mother. He tucked them into bed and said prayers with each of them.

Back in the living room, Ben spoke with Rebecca, who was busy sweeping up glass. "The chances that they'll return our .22 rifle are about .001 percent, so I'll leave you silver that you can use to buy another .22 rifle for small game. And I'll be leaving you the 12-gauge for anything bigger, man or beast. I think under the old chest freezer would be a good hiding place for it. Did you notice that the soldiers didn't touch that? You can ask some of the neighbor men to help you patch up the house."

She set down the dustpan and came into the living room with Ben. As he continued packing, he said, "I need to be on my way, *tonight*. It is easier to fight from *outside* barbed wire than from inside it. We're lucky that I didn't get arrested today. I don't want to give them another chance. Now listen carefully: I want you to tell people that I *was* arrested and taken away tonight. Otherwise, they'll ask questions when they see that I've gone. In addition to the Army, there are at least three agencies of the ProvGov and four security contracting companies that are independently arresting people and hauling them off to camps, or I suppose for immediate liquidation. The right hand doesn't know what the left hand is doing. So by blaming them for my disappearance, you'll put yourself in the clear."

"And also make the Hutchings government look even worse," Rebecca added.

Ben nodded and said, "That's right. It's a win-win. They use psychological warfare on us, so it's only fair that we return the favor."

He let out a breath and went on. "Now I'll be going to Nashville to see some old friends. It's safer for both of us if I don't tell you exactly who."

"Okay."

Ben finished strapping his sleeping bag onto his pack. "I'm leaving you most of our silver. I can't be sure, but I'll do my best to send you money from time to time. Whenever I enclose a letter, you have to promise me that you'll burn it, right after you read it."

"I promise."

Then he shouldered his pack and gave his wife a two-minute hug and a kiss. Ben touched the mezuzah on his way out the door. On the porch he snapped closed his backpack's bellyband clasp, and picked up his guitar case. He turned to face his wife again in the doorway. "Trust in Adonai and May His *Ruach HaKodesh* (Holy Spirit) comfort you during the days you sit Shivah for Joseph. I will remember Joseph with you and will pray the Kaddish for him every day. I will pray every day for peace, safety, and that you would be comforted by the Lord, despite my absence from your side. Remember that Joseph is 'asleep.' He loved the Lord Yeshua and is with Him, at this very moment. *Ani meohev otach yoter Midai!*"

"I love you without measure as well," she said as he turned and walked out into the darkness.

15

Vigilantes

"Every man who goes into the Indian country should be armed with a rifle and revolver, and he should never, either in camp or out of it, lose sight of them. When not on the march, they should be placed in such a position that they can be seized at an instant's warning; and when moving about outside the camp, the revolver should invariably be worn in the belt, as the person does not know at what moment he may have use for it."
—Randolph B. Marcy, Captain, U.S. Army, *The Prairie Traveler,* 1859

Muddy Pond, Tennessee
August, the Second Year

After his son Joseph was killed, Ben immediately traveled to Nashville. There, he arrived on the doorstep of Adrian Evans. Adrian had been a junior partner at his old law firm. He was the firm's gun nut and had been the one who first taught Ben to shoot. He also brought Ben to his first gun show, where he bought his HK USP .45 pistol. Adrian had always struck Ben as an odd duck who was "always thinking outside the box." It was Adrian who had advised Ben to buy all his guns secondhand from private party sellers, rather than from licensed dealers. "When it comes to guns and ammunition, never leave a paper trail," he had always insisted.

Adrian, now working as a handyman and housepainter, offered to have Ben stay at his house. He promised to link Ben up with a friend who was in the nascent resistance movement.

Neither Ben nor Rebecca had any military or law enforcement experience. Ben had attended just a few Krav Maga martial arts classes, and he was only an occasional recreational shooter with no formal training. He regretted not taking more classes before the Crunch. He realized that he needed to get some training in a hurry, or he'd have a short life expectancy as a resistance fighter. So, at Adrian's suggestion, Ben sought the help of Peter Moeller, a retired neighbor who was a Vietnam veteran and longtime competitive shooter. With mostly dry practice and some .22 rimfire training in his basement, Ben became a much more competent shooter. Under Moeller's tutelage, Ben also learned the basics of combat fieldcraft, first-aid for gunshot wounds, and land navigation. Ben began running, stretching, and calisthenics every morning. He also read and reread every book that he could find on guerrilla warfare.

Diving into Adrian's book collection, as well as Moeller's, Ben read a variety of books that ranged from texts like *Guerrilla* by Charles W. Thayer, *Guerrilla Strategies* by Gérard Chaliand, and *Total Resistance* by H. Von Dach. Adrian also insisted that Ben read the lengthy novel *Unintended Consequences* by fellow attorney John Ross. As Adrian said, "This ain't your everyday novel. You'll end up taking notes. Trust me."

Through Adrian, Ben was put in touch with a resistance group that was being formed locally to conduct arson and sabotage. They called themselves the Matchmakers.

By prearrangement, Ben first met the sabotage group's recruiter at a local bar. Initially, Ben was enthusiastic about the Matchmakers' plans, but this turned to disappointment as the group endlessly built incendiaries, trained, and practiced. But their few operations were against relatively soft targets of no significance.

The Matchmakers met sporadically after-hours at a Nashville

dye plant. From the outset, Ben was not impressed with their organizational structure or their operational security (OPSEC). He thought they talked too openly of their plans and that the group was too large. With eighteen members, the resistance group's size would have been more appropriate for more overt guerrilla warfare, rather than just the sabotage that they planned. In Ben's estimation, sabotage teams should have no more than five members, and just a three-member team was ideal. He eventually convinced the unit to break into three smaller cells. Eventually, Ben left the Matchmakers after concluding that they were long on talk, and short on action.

Now physically fit and better trained, Ben moved out of Adrian's house and joined a seven-man raiding team, with members mainly from Crossville. They called themselves the Cantrell Company, in honor of Charles Cantrell, a Tennessee-born Medal of Honor recipient in the Spanish-American War. Here, Ben got his first taste of combat, in a series of raids and ambushes, most within thirty miles of Crossville. Ben developed a reputation as a daring fighter willing to take risks. Eventually, he became the team's most frequent point man. He developed a specialty in sentry removal. Eventually Ben was recruited out of the Cantrell Company to join the Old Man's reconnaissance team.

While he was first with the Matchmakers, Ben learned how to make thermite, which later proved to be a valuable skill. In addition to using some of it himself to weld shut artillery breech blocks, Ben passed along his thermite mixing knowledge to four other independent resistance groups.

The Resistance was impossible for the ProvGov to isolate and defeat because it was essentially leaderless. Anyone who tried to establish himself as a "spokesman" or "commander" was quickly and quietly told to shut up or shut down. Instead of a formal hierarchy, decentralized cells, led by subject matter experts, characterized the Resistance. This gave each resistance group a distinct personality and modus operandi. They numbered anywhere from lone wolves to teams of about thirty. Typically, however, most teams or cells were made up of three to ten people. Each team had a specialty, such as demolition, arson, vehicular sabotage, thermiting, reconnaissance, logistics, couriering, sniping, or assassination.

The beauty of leaderless resistance was that the small cells were difficult to identify, locate, or penetrate. This frustrated the Hutchings government, which had hoped for a quick solution to the guerrilla war. The lack of a hierarchical structure made it impossible to neutralize the groups. For years, the U.S. Army had emphasized social network analysis and organizational-level analysis, as taught in the joint Army/Marine Corps Counterinsurgency Field Manual. The FM 3-24 doctrine and elaborate matrixes and time-event charts were of no value when resistance was leaderless and fought primarily by small cells that intentionally set no patterns.

As part of their subterfuge, many of the resistance groups had fictitious leaders. Often they had elaborate mythologies that were sometimes so believable that they had ProvGov agents busy for weeks, chasing ghosts. For example, in Arizona, the myth of "Conrad Peters" was developed, based on the name of a real-life individual from Scottsdale who had actually left the country to do missionary work in Mexico just before the Crunch. But according to the mythology, "Peters" led a group that hid out in the Superstition Mountains east of Phoenix. In New Mexico, "The Paulson Project" supposedly had a secret arms factory in Albuquerque. There was none. In Texas, to supplement three genuine companies there were nine ghost companies of Republic of Texas militia that spread tales of fictitious troop movements throughout the state and even across the Mexican border. In Wyoming, "Colonel Reed" reputedly led the Free State Irregulars. In Utah, there were regular sightings of the enigmatic "Roger Williams," who supposedly led four sabotage teams. None of these individuals ever existed. Closer to the seat of the ProvGov, the Alvin York "Brigade" was in actuality just sixteen men and women.

Actions by other groups operating from a distance were often attributed to the fictitious groups, to sidetrack pursuing ProvGov agents and maneuver units. GPS coordinates of disused camps deep inside BLM and National Forest lands were often leaked, just to get the ProvGov to go investigate. Sometimes, these ruses would include raids on lightly manned garrisons, after their units were confirmed to have departed in search of the phantoms.

Waterville, Vermont
August, the Second Year

A tip from a confidential informant had pinpointed the house as the hideout of a resistance cell. Arriving before dawn, a French forward observer team in civilian clothes carried a tripod-mounted AN/PED-1 lightweight laser designator rangefinder (LLDR) to a hilltop. They had it set up just as the daylight was broadening and they could make out the house below. Looking through the LLDR, the team leader thumbed the designator's laser beam on and walked the pip on top of the house that matched the GPS coordinates, distance from the hilltop, and the description from his briefing the previous evening. He locked down the LLDR's manual adjustments and gave the tripod a couple of slight test bumps, and was satisfied that the pip hadn't moved. "*Bon, assuré*," he mumbled to himself.

The French *caporal-chef* radioed in, "This is FIST Three. Lima-designated fire mission, vicinity Waterville, per OPORD Sierra. I now have steady lase. Confirm target designation number Bravo-one-four-niner-eight-niner-two, at 1302, Zulu. One round, H-E Quick. Fire at will."

Less than a minute later, he heard the reply, "Shot, over."

Then, far in the distance, he heard a single bark of an artillery piece. He carefully kept the laser pip centered on top of the center of the house. Without glancing away from the LLDR's eyepiece, he pressed his handset and said, "Shot, out."

Out of habit, he started counting the time of flight in seconds in French. He saw a bright flash, as a 155millimeter artillery shell detonated in the house. Then, after a brief lag—caused by the difference between the speed of light and the speed of sound—he heard the distinctive roar of the artillery shell detonating, and the sound echoed up and down the valley.

Releasing the trigger on the designator and again keying his radio handset, he said, "Splash, over."

Dogs at a dozen nearby homes began a cacophony of howling and barking. A car alarm near the target house began warbling, no doubt set off by the shell's concussion.

The fire control center replied, "Splash, out."

The Frenchman took one last look through the scope and saw that what was left of the house was now engulfed in flames. He gave a thin smile and reported, "Target destroyed. End of mission. Packing up here. Will RTB in approximately thirty-five mikes. Out."

His two security men were French privates. They wore blue jeans, Land's End jackets, baseball caps, and sunglasses. They were both armed with *Clairons*—their nickname for FAMAS bullpup carbines. The *caporal-chef* carried only a holstered HK USP 9mm pistol. The security men helped him carry the folded tripod and the case for the LLDR down to their black 2014 Range Rover. Another successful mission, with no muss or fuss. They hadn't even gotten their hands dirty.

Brent Danley learned of the death of his parents later the same day. He was first told that the house had been destroyed by a bomb, but that was later corrected. It had been an artillery round. His parents, in their seventies, had no connection with the Resistance. His father had died in his bed, but his mother had apparently survived the initial blast and had managed to crawl out of the burning house. Her charred body was found seventy feet away, curled up in a fetal position.

It was later discovered that the confidential informant had his street addresses mixed up. There were no apologies from the ProvGov.

Brent soon decided to join the Resistance. He left his wife and six children to reside with his in-laws, who lived on a farm in Vermont's Northeast Kingdom region. They ran a dairy goat farm, near Stevens Mills, just a few miles from the Canadian border. He took his wife and kids, their clothes, and a few family mementos to Stevens Mills in his aging Ford van, towing a camping trailer that was crammed full. He left behind many of his household goods. His neighbors promised to keep an eye on the house, but that was the least of his concerns. He wanted to get to the fighting as soon as possible.

Brent traveled to Kentucky on a reliable 600cc Honda Hornet motorcycle that had been built at the turn of the century. The motorcycle was his cousin Craig's contribution to the Cause. All of Brent's motorcycle ride was through "pacified" states. He left most of his guns at his brother-in-law's home with his family. The exception was a Ruger LCP .380 pistol that he hid between two layers of one of his pannier bags.

Rather than join the Resistance in Vermont, Brent decided that the most important place for him to apply his skills was with the Resistance close to the seat of the Provisional Government. As he put it, "The quicker that we can arrest Maynard Hutchings, the better."

Volunteering for a militia in Bullitt County, Kentucky, Brent was soon dubbed their Token Yankee. While at first teased about his origin and viewed with suspicion, his tireless and skillful efforts as a medic earned him the praise of nearly everyone he met.

Brent didn't see his wife and children again until the war was over.

West of Yankton, South Dakota
August, the Second Year

Ken and Terry wanted to avoid the I-90 corridor as well as Rapid City and Sturgis, so they skirted to the north and came in on State Highway 34. They zigzagged their way through a heavily agricultural area in a checkerboard of roads to the town of Vale, where they planned to cut north on State Route 79.

At Vale, they began asking if there were any ranchers who might be looking for hired security. As they were talking to an elderly woman, they noticed two armed men approaching them from behind. As Ken turned to greet them, two more men walked around the corner from the other direction, also armed. Before they could react, one of the men shouldered a Benelli shotgun and shouted, "Put your rifles on the ground!"

With four armed men confronting them, the Laytons didn't think twice about doing as they were told. Another man shouted, "Hands on top of your heads!" Again they complied.

The four men closed in on them and pulled off Ken's and Terry's backpacks and disconnected their web gear, pulling it off and laying it on the sidewalk.

From behind one of the men asked, "What are you doing here?"

"We're just looking for work," Ken answered. "We've done ranch and farm security before, and I've got a letter of introduction in my pack that I can show you."

Two more men approached, armed only with handguns. One

of the newcomers asked, "Do you think these could be more scouts?"

Another one agreed, "Yeah, they could be spies."

Ken asked incredulously, half shouting, "Scouts? Spies? You're making a mistake."

They had Ken remove his DPM shirt so that they could check him for tattoos.

Finally, they let Ken tell them where they could find the letter of introduction from Durward Perkins.

One of them read the letter aloud. That seemed to satisfy most of them.

Terry was perplexed. She asked, "What's all this talk about spies?"

The man with the Benelli riot gun explained, "The biker gang that hit Belle Fourche last week sent some spies in first to scout it out. They weren't dressed like bikers. They were posing as a husband and wife—refugees. Now can you see why we're being cautious?"

Ken was surprised to hear the man pronounce the name of the town Belle Fourche "Bell Foo-Shay." Up until then, Ken and Terry had seen the town's name only on his road map and they had not realized how it was properly spoken. Ken nodded. "Yes, indeed I can see why you are taking precautions."

Ken then spent fifteen minutes describing where they were from, where they had been, and where they were headed. The men seemed satisfied. The leader of the Vigilance Committee apologized for detaining them, returned their guns and gear, and wished them well.

Ken and Terry continued on, still traveling in daylight. Whenever they met anyone, they asked about employment. The region was dominated by sheep ranches and sugar beet farms. At the junction of Highways 79 and 212, a sign read "Welcome to Newell, South

Dakota." Another, below it, advertised the Lions International club. Within 100 yards of passing the signs, they were again intercepted, this time by three men on horseback, who shouted, "Put your hands on your head! Vigilance Committee!"

As the men wheeled their horses around them, Ken muttered, "So *this* is how it feels to be 'Welcome' in Newell, South Dakota." They both laid their rifles on the ground.

A man with a flamboyant mustache wearing a gray cowboy hat with a high Montana peak halted his horse five yards in front of the Laytons. "Keep your hands up, and no sudden moves."

They again went through being searched and questioned. And again, it was the letter of introduction from West Branch that established their bona fides.

After the townsmen seemed satisfied, Ken asked, "We'd like to find security work around here, like we had last winter in Iowa. Do you know of anyone who might be hiring?"

The eldest man with a gray beard answered, "Yeah, you could talk to the Norwoods. I heard that they've been real worried since the big shootout in Belle Fourche. That was two weeks ago. Carl Norwood and his son have been watching their place 24/7 ever since. They're about a mile beyond the area that our committee keeps patrolled. I think he's looking for just one man, but I don't know, he might consider hiring a couple. They're cattlemen. They live out on Parilla Road, north of town."

Ken was given directions to the Norwood ranch and was told that the committee would contact Carl Norwood via CB radio to let him know to expect the Laytons. Just before the members of the Vigilance Committee left, the leader reached into his saddlebag and pulled out two lime green bandanas. He instructed Ken and Terry to tie them around their boonie hats. These, he explained, would ensure their safe passage through town. He noted, "You're expected to turn these in when you get to the committee's guard post on 9th Street, up at the north end of town. You can pick up your rifles and packs now."

As they walked the ten blocks through Newell, Terry commented, "They have a pretty clever and low-key security arrangement. It seems to work well for anyone coming in on foot, or I suppose on horseback or bicycles. But I wonder how they'd stop vehicles without a roadblock."

Ken countered, "Maybe they have some security measures we haven't seen yet."

"Yeah, given that reception, it wouldn't surprise me."

As they continued their walk through town on Dartmouth Avenue there were no motor vehicles moving, but they saw several people on bicycles, and one on horseback. The town of Newell evidenced a mix of 1950s culture and early-twenty-first-century trash culture. There was a bakery, a used bookstore, and a hardware store that all could have been from the set of *The Andy Griffith Show*. But alongside them there was a payday loans and check cashing storefront and a tattoo and piercing shop. Terry mentioned that she was happy to see the latter were both boarded up.

Most of the businesses that were open in town were repair and secondhand stores. The local abundance of wool had inspired a group of local women to open a store called the Fiber Farm. As Ken and Terry walked by, there were four women in the store's front room operating spinning wheels, chatting and treadling their way to prosperity. Signs in the window advertised "Hand-Knitted Wool Socks," "Sweaters Made to Order," and "We Trade."

Just beyond 9th Street, a young man armed with an M1A rifle and carrying a handie-talkie on his hip stepped out of a small building that looked like it had formerly been a drive-through espresso shop. The shop's windows had been painted over and prominently marked "CLOSED."

Before the young man shut the door, Ken caught a glimpse of

someone else inside, with just his head exposed over the top of a low cinder block wall. This wall was set back three feet from the building's lightly constructed outer wall.

Ken whispered, "Clever."

The young man walked up to them and asked for the bandanas.

Terry handed them over, saying, "Have a nice day."

16

Good Fences

I do not believe there ever was any life more attractive to a vigorous young fellow than life on a cattle ranch in those days. It was a fine, healthy life, too; it taught a man self-reliance, hardihood, and the value of instant decision. . . . I enjoyed the life to the full.

—Theodore Roosevelt

North of Newell, South Dakota
October, the Second Year

Four miles north of town, Ken and Terry Layton turned east on Parilla Road. The day was warming up, but the earlier chill in the air made it clear that winter was coming.

Two miles down Parilla, they came to a house on the south side with a mailbox marked in faded paint, "NORWOOD." Even before they arrived, a pair of mixed breed cattle dogs began barking at them. A large ranch house that looked like it dated from the 1960s or 1970s was located twenty yards from the road. Behind it there was a hay barn and a combination shop/tractor shed. There were various other outbuildings and corrals on either side. They could hear cattle mooing in the distance.

As they approached the gate, they heard a shout coming from inside the closest outbuilding, a woodshed: "Identify yourselves!"

Ken answered, "Kenneth and Terry Layton."

A teenager carrying an M1 Garand rifle and a large revolver in a cross-draw hip holster stepped out of the building, and declared, "Hello! I'm Graham. My dad is expecting you. Come with me, please."

Graham was lanky and had oily brown hair. He was wearing a heavy brown Carhartt stockman's jacket, black jeans, and hiking boots.

As they walked, Graham asked, "So, you're from Chicago, and you're a car mechanic, and you worked doing security for a farm last winter in Iowa?"

Ken laughed. "You seem to know all about us."

"We were briefed," Graham replied matter-of-factly.

As they walked up to the porch, he shouted, "They're here!" Then, in a quieter voice he said, "If you folks will excuse me, I got to get back to my guard post."

The front door swung open to reveal a tall man in his late forties, wearing a large-frame Glock pistol in a Kydex hip holster. He was wearing denim pants and a plaid flannel shirt. The man said, "I'm Carl. Please come in."

He motioned them in the door. "You can put your rifles and packs under the coatrack." Before leaving his pack, Ken pulled out the letter of introduction, which was protected in a Ziploc bag.

A tall, big-boned woman stepped out of the kitchen. She was also carrying a holstered Glock, but it had an unusual green polymer frame. "Hi, I'm Cordelia," she said with a friendly wave of her arm. She motioned the Laytons to sit on a couch.

Ken reached across to Carl Norwood's armchair and handed him the letter.

Carl flipped his eyeglasses up onto his forehead with practiced ease, and took a few minutes to read the letter from Durward Perkins. He held the letter just six inches from his nose, explaining, "I can never find my reading glasses, and I never got bifocals, since I can't use those shooting with a scope."

The Laytons sat quietly while Carl Norwood read the letter.

At a couple of points while reading, Carl chuckled. Finally, he flipped his glasses back down and handed the letter to Cordelia. He seemed impressed, commenting, "It sounds like you handled yourselves very well when those looters came at you."

Ken replied, "Well, *that* was mostly Terry's work. When it happened, I was late to the party, rolling out of bed. I just added a bit of accompaniment."

Terry giggled. "Yeah, accompaniment in *Bass Staccato*, as our friend T.K. would call it."

Carl grinned broadly. Then he put on a serious face. "Let me give you the layout: It's just the three of us here—my wife, my son, and I. All our relatives are in Texas and Oklahoma, and we haven't had word from them since the Crunch. We've got 320 acres, mostly paid for—although I've *no idea* what the situation is with mortgages these days." After a pause to reflect, he went on. "We're running 120 head of Angus, Herefords, and Bald-Faced Blacks."

Terry cocked her head, and asked, "We've only been around Brown Swiss, and some neighbors had Jerseys. What's a Bald-Faced—?"

Carl jumped in. "If you cross a Black Angus with a Hereford, they throw a cross called a Black Baldy or what we call a Bald-Faced Black—a black cow with a white face. They're known for their hybrid vigor. They do really well in this climate, and the cows make really good moms."

Terry nodded.

Carl Norwood continued, "We have a creek running through the property that by God's grace runs year-round. We cut hay on about thirty-five acres, and the rest is grazing ground. It's mostly good ground, and we've reseeded a lot of it in a pasture blend. The hay ground is mostly seeded in LG-31 Orchard Grass. A lot of our neighbors have had problems with Knapweed and Leafy Spurge, but we've managed to keep those sprayed out."

Ken and Terry both nodded, as Carl was now speaking in terms that were familiar to them.

"We've got three good saddle horses, two geldings and a mare. We also have a semiretired twenty-five-year-old mare, Molly. Her back isn't up to any heavy loads these days. The other three saddle horses are all less than ten years old, so they have a lot of good years ahead of them. Two of those three are bombproof. We also have Andre—'Andre the Giant.' He's half Fjord, one quarter Percheron, and one quarter Heinz. We use him for all the pulling around here. He's saddle-broke, but he's so tall that he's not comfortable to ride."

Ken asked, "Okay, I'm stumped. I know what Percheron draft horses and what Norwegian Fjords look like, but did you say 'Heinz'? What's a Heinz?"

Carl answered with a laugh, "That's like a mutt dog—Heinz 57 Varieties."

"Tell them about our firewood and fuel," Cordelia urged.

"Oh, yeah. We heat and cook mostly with wood. We have enough wood laid in for this coming winter. I'm out of gas for the chain saw, but we have friends that swap firewood for beef. We have a pickup, an SUV, and two quads, but again, no gas left to run them. We only have about 480 gallons of diesel left on hand and we're keeping that in reserve for cutting, baling, and hauling hay. I'd like to switch to haying with our horses, but I haven't found a hay mower yet. I also need more horse collars, hames, and other harness bits. A lot of the horse-drawn mowers either got melted down for scrap iron during World War II, or turned into yard ornaments. Most of those are rusted junk. So I'm still searching. You know, I had the chance to buy any one of *several* restored horse-drawn mowers that a guy from Wyoming brought to the Antique Tractor Pull that they held every September in Newell. But the Crunch of course brought an end to all those events. It's now just strictly local commerce. Our world got a *lot* smaller."

After a pause Norwood continued, "At least I had the common sense to switch our propane delivery contract to 'keep filled,' back when there was the big fight in Congress over raising the federal debt ceiling. So when the Crunch came, our propane tank was almost full. For the last year, we've been closely shepherding that supply. Right now, we're at about 70 percent. We've mainly been using that while we've been learning to cook on the woodstove. Believe me, that was quite a steep learning curve. Anyway, we won't starve, and we won't freeze. Hauling water is a pain, especially when there's snow on the ground, but we'll *live*. We've been able to trade butchered beef or cattle on the hoof for just about everything we've needed. The big surpluses around here are wool, mutton, lambs, and sugar beets. Since this is mainly sheep country and we're one of the few cattle outfits, we're in a fairly strong position for bartering. Eating mutton gets boring in a hurry."

After another pause he added, "With the power out, we get our water from the creek, and parts of each year from runoff from the roofs on the house and barn. The cattle now get their water straight from the creek. I fenced off the part of the creek that's upstream of the footbridge out back to prevent any contamination of the water. We run everything we use for drinking through a copy of a Big Berkey filter. It uses ceramic filter elements."

"Down in Newell, and out on a lot of farms and ranches, people are using water from the Irrigation District ditches," Cordelia said. "That water comes from the Belle Fourche Dam. Luckily, there's a manual emergency gate up there. Without that, the people in Newell would have been without water. The ditch doesn't go through our property, but we've got our creek."

"So, what about your security situation?" Ken asked.

Carl sighed and said, "In a word, our security situation *stinks*. I'm afraid we'll get targeted by looters. We're far enough out of town that we can't depend on the Vigilance Committee. We also don't have any neighbors that are within line of sight. So we can't depend on their help, either. The big problem here is that there's two main ways into the ranch—from both Highway 79 to the west and from Highway 212 to the east. And of course our house is so close to the county road that it hardly gives us any warning time."

Terry asked, "So what are you doing for security?"

"We have a big padded swivel chair set up in the corner of the woodshed for whoever's on guard duty. It's chilly in the winter, but we've got several washed wool fleeces—one to sit on and two others tied together like a serape to drape over you. That corner of the shed has a pretty good view up and down the road and, if you swivel around and look out the other way, you can see two sides of the house and most of the barnyard. We've got four walkie-talkies. They're just the cheap kind—FRS band, from Walmart. I got a 12-volt charging tray that can charge two radios at a time. That is connected to a pair of 6-volt tractor batteries that are wired in series. Those batteries are trickle-charged off a 20-watt photovoltaic panel that I bought a couple of years ago from Harbor Freight company. That's our only electricity here at the house. I really wish I had a few more panels. With more charging capacity, we could do a lot more than just run the CB and recharge the radios and a few flashlight batteries.

"Recently, Graham and I have been trading off with twelve-hour guard duty shifts, but we're starting to burn out. At the rate we're going, we're just getting exhausted. We don't have enough time to properly take care of the stock, and there's no way that next year we'd have the time to cut hay or put in a garden. The past two weeks, we've been concentrating on security, and that has forced us to let other things slide. The good news is that we're pretty well armed, and all three of us are good, safe shooters."

"That's right," Cordelia interjected. "We're all experienced hunters, but none of us have any military or police SWAT-type experience. We've got two .30-06 rifles with scopes, and Graham has a Garand, which is also a .30-06. Plus a Kel-Tec .223, a half a dozen bird guns—12- and 16-gauge—several .22s, and a .17 HMR, which is our ground squirrel gun."

Ken asked, "What's the depth of your ammo supply?"

Carl answered, "We've got more than 500 rounds of 06, and that includes eighty rounds of the black-tipped armor-piercing. That's all loaded in eight-round Garand clips. We've got just over nine boxes of .45 ACP, and five boxes of 9 millimeter for Cordy's Glock. We've got only about 200 rounds of .223 for the Kel-Tec, but I consider that gun kind of secondary. In open country like this, .30-06 *rules*. For the shotguns, we've got just over twenty-six boxes of shells, mostly 12-gauge. But those are all pheasant and quail loads—we don't have any buckshot or slugs, so that makes our shotguns useless for self-defense—"

Ken interrupted, "I can teach you how to cut shotgun shells. I saw a YouTube video on how to make cut shells, back before the Crunch, and my buddy Dan Fong and I did some experimenting. When you cut a shell—it's a scoring cut that doesn't quite go all the way around—it makes the whole front half of a shotgun shell go down the bore, so that it hits someone like a slug, and then it fragments. It's a very neat trick, but it's strictly for single shots and double-barrel guns. You don't want to have a shell come apart inside a pump or a semiauto. That could cause a jam at the worst possible time."

Carl looked surprised and said, "Thanks, I'd appreciate seeing how to do that! I've got a short-barreled side-by-side 12-gauge we could try that with."

Ken said, "Sorry, I jumped in there. To get back on track, how's your supply of ammo in other calibers?"

Carl answered, "We're in the worst shape on rimfire ammo—less than 300 rounds, including just two boxes for my .17 HMR. My only excuse is that it's such a long drive from here to any of the big sporting goods stores down in Rapid City that I didn't have the chance to stock up. That's a major regret, a *huge* regret. When the Crunch hit, I got fixated on finding grain and salt for our stock, and propane cylinders for our lanterns. Instead, I should've bought ammo first, before it all disappeared off the shelves. I never thought that I'd see the day when el-cheapo .22 rimfire ammo was like gold.

"Oh, I've also got several boxes of .30-30 ammo that's left over from a Marlin lever-action that I traded for a saddle a few years back. I figure that ammo will always be good to trade."

"Well, with cold weather coming and people wanting to get deer, maybe you can trade that .30-30 ammo for some more .22 Long Rifle ammo," Terry offered.

Cordelia said cheerfully, "That's a great idea."

Ken raised a finger and asked, "How old is your son, and how does he fit into the security arrangements?"

Cordelia answered, "Graham is sixteen going on twenty-six. He's been homeschooled and he's really sharp and very level-headed. He's shot two deer in the past two hunting seasons: one in the neck and one in the head. Just one shot each. I expect that he'd be up to it, if it ever comes to a real us-or-them kind of shooting situation. His one drawback is that he only weighs 140 pounds. He just needs to fill in so that he can help with the heavy chores."

Ken asked, "How are you set for handguns?"

"We've got only three: my Glock 21, Cordy's Glock 19, and Graham's .45 revolver," Carl answered. "His is an old Smith Model 1917 that belonged to my dad. It shoots .45 ACP just like my Glock."

Terry interjected again, "So two of your guns also have commonality with our Colt 1911s."

Norwood nodded.

Terry turned to Carl and asked, "So what's your worst-case scenario?

He answered with a sigh, "That would be if the bikers that

hit Belle Fourche decide to pick on us." After a pause, he added, "I don't expect you to stop an army, but I do want to be able to maintain round-the-clock security."

Ken said quietly, "Understood."

"We don't heat any of the outbuildings," Cordelia told them, "but we have a spare bed that we use out in the barn during calving season we'll bring in and put in Carl's office. The computer and phone and fax machine can't be used these days, anyway."

Carl added with a grin, "No more tax paperwork to do, either."

They all shared a laugh.

Only a few days after they had arrived at the Norwoods' ranch, Ken and Terry were like part of the family. The guard schedule was broken into three eight-hour shifts. Ken, Terry, and Graham took most of the shifts, with Carl helping as needed.

Their main security upgrade was to reorganize the woodshed, stacking the split wood for better ballistic protection. They also cut more advantageous gun ports. The firewood itself provided most of the ballistic protection, but they supplemented it with scrap steel and five 30-gallon drums that were filled with fist-sized rocks and gravel. There was no shortage of rocks on the property.

There was already a bridge across the creek that was intended for the cattle. It had been in place for decades but it sat 100 yards south of the house, which was too far for their current purposes. To provide a safe and convenient way to draw water in buckets from the creek, Carl had constructed a new bridge shortly after the Crunch set in. It was a footbridge thirty yards from the house, and was constructed mainly with 4x4s and 2x6 planks. At the center of the span, Carl had built an extended platform with a notched railing so that whoever went to the bridge to draw water would have a safe place to stand.

Typically, they put the water in four 5-gallon plastic water cans and wheeled them back and forth to the house in a twelve-cubic-foot EZ-Haul garden cart.

The next day, Graham showed them the cattle facilities. There were two large connected corrals, each sixty yards square. There was a pair of small bullpens, also adjoining. There was also a tall connecting alley built of planks, with a veterinary squeeze chute and cattle truck-loading ramp at one end. It had a swinging Y gate panel that could shunt cattle to either a high ramp or a low ramp, depending on the deck height of the arriving vehicle or trailer. The ramps themselves were inexpensively built with earth and used railroad ties. Graham mentioned that the entire property was cross-fenced, allowing for efficient grazing. This also kept the cattle out of the hay fields until after the last cutting.

"We got two hay cuttings last summer, which is unusual for here without irrigation, so we have more than enough hay for this winter," Carl told them.

"How do you deal with all the manure?" Terry asked.

Pointing his thumb at the barn, Graham answered, "We rig Andre up with a horse collar and an old road scraper. Anything in the corners of the corrals, and in the bullpens, we get by hand with a shovel and a wheelbarrow. Before the Crunch, we used the tractor for most of it, and it was a breeze. But nowadays we can't spare the fuel."

Terry sighed. "Sounds like countless hours of fun."

"Yeah, the manure scraping and hauling takes up a lot of our time. Especially now that we're penning all the stock up every night, year-round, to prevent rustling, there's a lot more manure to deal with. Between that and hauling water to the house and doing laundry by hand, the manual labor takes up several hours of our time every day. When the grid went down, it put us back in the nineteenth century."

As they walked toward the pair of bullpens, Graham asked, "You folks been around bulls before?"

Ken answered, "Yeah. We know to never turn our backs on a bull. Like they say, a bull is a bull."

"Yes, please do be careful, sir. You pour just a smidgen of grain in either feed trough, and you can get Earl to move where you want him, without any prodding. Just make sure that the connecting gate is latched before you start to shovel manure."

"Understood."

Pointing to a large manure pile just south of the larger corrals, Graham said, "There's no market for our manure these days. Even though we offer it cheap, nobody wants to burn the fuel to come this far out of town to haul it."

Terry nodded, agreeing. "Fuel is precious, and that's changed the way people do business. It has changed a lot of things."

Looking at the enormous black bull in the pen, Ken asked, "What can you tell me about your bull?"

"He's registered Angus. His name is Earl, which is short for Earl of Aberdeen. He cost Dad $24,000, and that was two years *before* the inflation kicked in."

Ken let out a whistle. "Wow."

Terry chimed in, quoting something that Durward Perkins had told her. "Well, they say that genetically your bull is half of your herd."

Graham said, "That's right, ma'am. But pretty soon we'll be line breeding, using Earl to cover, at least with our next batch of heifers that are coming up. He sired them. So Dad has made arrangements to swap Earl for a dis-related bull that belongs to a man over near St. Ogne. His bull's genetics aren't quite as good as Earl's, but at least his bull has a ring in his nose, and he's broken to lead. They say he'll follow you around like a pup. That's quite an improvement over Earl, who is the classic range bull."

Terry nodded. "Enough said. We'll be careful."

Graham continued, "The only problem is finding a way to transport the bulls, to do the swap. We're out of gas, and so is the man with the other bull. Oh well, we still have about six months to figure that out."

Terry asked, "So how are you going to get the cattle to come into the pens when the grass is up, after you've run out of grain?"

"Well, we don't need to use much grain. They come into the corral each night, pretty much like clockwork. It was Mom's idea to remove the salt blocks from all the pastures, and only give them salt in the corrals. So they have an inducement to come in every night. The cattle have gotten into a habit. Also, our dogs know the routine. They help herd any stragglers in each night. After we run out of grain, we can always use sugar beets. Those work just as well as grain does."

With the relative luxury of just eight-hour guard shifts, Ken and Terry had more time available than they had the winter before when they were working for the Perkinses.

With several common interests, Terry and Cordelia became fast friends. Terry demonstrated to the Norwoods the method that she'd seen the Perkinses use for mass production of beef jerky. Because the Norwoods had nearly run out of granulated salt, they simply placed a new fifty-pound white livestock salt block in a six-gallon food-grade plastic bucket and added water to form a salt brine. To support the drying rack suspension wires, Ken and Graham used drywall power screws, driven by hand with a Phillips screwdriver.

The Laytons were taught how to tack up and ride horses. They became good riders, but both had trouble learning how to throw a lariat. They also learned how to trim and rasp hooves, and the basics of horseshoeing.

Ken and Terry also spent many hours with the Norwoods, passing along some of the training that they had received from Todd Gray's retreat group. This included a lot of gun handling, small unit tactics, range and wind estimation for long-range shooting, and immediate action drills. Ken particularly enjoyed mentoring Graham in handgun shooting. Because ammunition was in short supply, most of their training was dry practice. For safety, this instruction was done beside the woodshed with the woodpile providing a backstop.

Graham's revolver, a Smith & Wesson Model 1917, was a veritable antique but still serviceable. Graham carried the gun in an old cavalry holster that had long before had its original full flap narrowed to just a retention strap. The holster's butt-forward configuration—originally designed to accommodate cavalrymen carrying both a saber and a revolver—was awkward, but Graham made up for this with plenty of practice. He became lightning fast at reloading the revolver, using spring steel full-moon clips that each held six cartridges. Ken observed that these were faster than any mechanical speed loader that he had ever seen used.

In his years of high-power rifle competition, Ken had considerable exposure to M1 Garand and M1A rifles. So in addition to long-range marksmanship with iron sights, Ken was able to teach Graham some of the intricacies of M1 Garand bore cleaning, gas system maintenance, and greasing of the rifle's bolt camming surfaces and the hammer.

Ken particularly stressed the importance of repeated cleanings when using U.S. military surplus .30-06 full metal jacket ball and AP ammunition from the 1940s and early 1950s. Much of this ammunition, he warned Graham, was corrosively primed. Ken also took the opportunity to cross-train the Norwoods on handling and fieldstripping their HK, CAR-15, and Colt Model 1911 pistols. The Norwoods reciprocated, teaching the Laytons how to fieldstrip all the guns in their collection.

As winter set in, they got into a regular routine for manning the OP at the woodshed. Remembering the brazier that they had used at the farm in Iowa, Ken, with Carl's help, constructed a comparable one. The base was a six-foot length of scrap six-inch-diameter well casing pipe. Rather than laboriously cutting off the pipe with a hacksaw, they simply dug a hole with a posthole digger and buried fifty inches of the pipe. This also had the advantage of creating a brazier that they knew would never accidentally tip over. The brazier itself was a mini grill that had been designed for backyard barbeques. It was brazed onto the top of the well casing pipe using a torch from the workshop of a friend who lived nearby, on KLT Road.

Several times that winter they had encounters with refugees. Thankfully, Parilla Road was a side road that received little traffic. The refugees were often seen pushing or pulling a variety of hand-carts. These included garden carts, wheelbarrows, perambulators, deer hauling carts, toy wagons, and even a wheeled golf bag. Some of the refugees were persistent beggars, and a few were even stridently antagonistic.

After the first such encounter, Ken mentioned the "safety through anonymous giving" technique that Durward Perkins had used in Iowa. The Norwoods weren't Christians, but they were moral, and they could see the need for charitable giving. In December, Ken contacted the bishop at St. Mary's Church in Newell. Two days later, with the help of three men from the church who came in a pickup, they butchered an older cow, a steer, and a steer calf. The latter had been born partially lame the previous spring.

The three men from the Catholic church arrived in a ubiquitous "mobile butcher" pickup with a small boom hoist arm mounted on the back. This arm had a hand-cranked cable hoist. Not wanting to waste any ammunition, they stunned the cattle with a pneumatic captive bolt pistol that was administered to the cows' skulls, just as they passed through a mechanical squeeze chute. They were then dumped from the chute and quickly "stuck" to bleed out. The oldest man in the group was an experienced butcher, so they made quick work of gutting the cattle and using a meat saw to remove their heads. The hearts and livers went into an ice chest. The guts, lungs, forelegs, and heads went into the manure scraper, to be hauled to the garbage pit for burial. The carcasses were hoisted onto the truck and hauled into Newell with their hides still on.

That afternoon, the meat was butchered into small cuts and hauled to the church and stored outdoors in several old chest freezers that would soon be buried in a snowbank that was formed each year by snow sliding off the church roof. Carl also donated 300 pounds of corn-oat-barley blend cattle feed to the church. When soaked in water and cooked, it made palatable breakfast mush.

Carl painted a sign for his gatepost that directed refugees to the Catholic church, which was located on 6th Street in Newell.

For handling bands of refugees, the Norwoods developed an SOP: Using the Motorola FRS walkie-talkies, whoever was on OP duty at the woodshed would alert those in the house that strangers were approaching. They would then be greeted at shouting distance from behind the small firewood pile on the ranch house's front porch. Meanwhile, the OP sentry would remain hidden and quiet. In case there was any trouble, the OP sentry would then be the ace in the hole—standing ready to engage anyone at the gate in a close ambush.

After they put up the sign directing refugees to St. Mary's Church, their interaction with them became more brief and blunt. Usually, Ken or Carl would simply shout, "Read the sign. . . . May God bless you. Now move on!"

On December 22, Graham rode his horse into town to attend a Christmas party hosted by some of his homeschooling friends. When he returned the next day, Graham gave an update on the security situation in Newell. "There's a concrete company at the south end of town that used to make pre-cast septic tanks and outhouses for the State Park Department and the Forest Service. Nobody's heard anything from the owners of the company. I heard that they went to go double up with some relatives in Montana. Anyway, there's all these vault toilet buildings sitting around, unused. So an ex–telephone lineman with the Vigilance Committee figured out a way to turn them into pillboxes. They set up a generator and used a wet diamond saw to cut gun ports. They hauled two of the vault toilets on trucks to each of the three roadblocks, and set them up on either side of the road. I saw the setup on Highway 212. They have it just east of the KLT Road junction. It is *so* sweet. They used a bunch of those modular highway concrete center divider things, and laid them out to constrict the road into three S-curves. Cars have to take the new S-turns really slowly. And all the time, they're in the line of fire of the pillboxes. It's devastating."

17

From the Oil Patch

"Never, under any circumstances, ever become a refugee. . . . Die if you must, but die on your home turf with your face to the wind, not in some stinking hellhole 2,000 kilometers away, among people you neither know nor care about."

—Ragnar Benson, *Ragnar's Urban Survival* (2000)

Waterville, Vermont
December, the First Year

Brent Danley had known the Crunch was going to be bad. He had been following the posts on a variety of survivalist blogs and forums for several years. He would have liked to be better prepared, but his tight budget kept him from working up his pantry to more than a three-month supply. Brent also saw the need to be better armed, but again cash was the constraint. He owned an older bolt-action Winchester .30-06 that had belonged to his father-in-law, a Remington 870 shotgun with a thirty-inch barrel, and two .22 rifles.

Brent worked as an emergency room trauma nurse at Copley Hospital in Morrisville, Vermont. But he lived fifteen miles away in his hometown of Waterville. He and his wife, Jennifer, owned a modest three-bedroom house on Lapland Road that was built in the 1970s. With six kids ranging from four to thirteen years old, the house was a tight squeeze. They were on well water and a creek ran through the property year-round.

Before the Crunch began, Brent made some extra money each year "sugaring"—making maple syrup, which was a family tradition. He sold most of his syrup wholesale. But he saved the best to sell retail, marketed under the trade name Northern Comfort. He was once threatened with a trademark infringement lawsuit by a company using the same name, until he mailed a photocopy of a newspaper clipping from 1946 showing that his grandfather had used the trade name Northern Comfort at least that far back. His short note hinted at a countersuit. That was the last that he heard about lawsuits.

After times got hard, Brent reanimated another one of his grandfather's ventures: an alcohol still that was built in 1931. At the same time that Brent's grandfather first operated the still, his great-uncle ran a small pharmacy in Johnson, Vermont. He sold both moonshine from his brother's still and whiskey smuggled in from Canada. Both products were sold surreptitiously to trusted customers out the back door. The extra income from the booze helped the pharmacy survive the Great Depression. It also allowed grandfather Danley to extend credit to many of his customers for many years. Later, during the Second World War, these customers gradually paid off their bills, and they expressed their gratitude.

The Norwood Ranch, Newell, South Dakota
January, the Third Year

In January, Ken caught up with some maintenance on their guns. Terry's CAR-15 had a metal rail fore-end with an Israeli folding foregrip and rubber rail covers. These covers had gradually gotten lost in their travels, with constant handling. By the time they reached the Norwoods' ranch, there were six of the gun's twelve short rubber rail covers missing. With some inquiries via the CB network, they found a man on the south side of Newell who had some spares. In exchange for two silver dimes, they got eight UTG rail covers in a mix of green, tan, and flat dark earth colors. Terry actually grew to like the odd assortment when she realized that it made her carbine blend in more than it had when the rail covers were all black. At the same time, Ken did some touch-up painting on both rifles. After more than a year of daily use, they had both lost some of their finish, mainly on their sights, muzzles, and charging handles. To remedy this, Ken was given a small bottle of flat black lacquer and a tiny brush from Durward's collection of model-making supplies that had languished since his teenage years.

They were shoveling manure out of the trodden snow in the south corral. Ken asked Carl, "What can you tell me about Belle Fourche?"

Carl chuckled. "Well, Belle Fourche is just a cow town that had a good Ford dealership, a western clothing store called Pete's, and not much else worth mentioning. It's the town where John Wayne and his crew of kids drove their cattle to, in that old movie *The Cowboys*. And did you ever see that series on cable called *Deadwood*? The Seth Bullock character in that show was the founder of Belle Fourche. Not much else to tell you. Oh, maybe I should say that the soil there is slowly moving downhill. It's what they call a 'soil creek,' which is what eventually makes all the fence posts point downhill. It is like a landslide, but in extreme slow motion. I sure wouldn't build a house there."

After another pause, he carried on, sounding more serious. "The population was about 5,000 before everything went nuts. Based on what I saw happen in Newell, I suppose the population of Belle Fourche must have increased by a few hundred last year, with people taking in their kids and grandkids and cousins, mainly from Rapid City and back east.

"And of course just two weeks before you got here, the population of Belle Fourche dropped by about 200, due to an outbreak of instantaneous lead poisoning. If you think the security is tight in Newell, then you ought to visit Belle Fourche. I've heard they've got that town locked up tighter than a drum. Any adult they don't recognize by sight gets stopped and asked for ID. If they don't have a local address then they've got a lot of explaining to do. Same thing for anyone driving a rig who doesn't have license plates with a '15' prefix—showing that a vehicle is registered in Butte County."

"How are people getting by?"

"I have no idea about the economy there now. I suppose that the town is squeaking by on barter, just like in Newell. There was a good grain mill at Belle Fourche, which is where I went to get my last bags of cracked corn before the dollar hit the fan. I don't know if it's still operating, or even if it could, without power."

Carl sparingly used his CB radio at night and at noon each day, listening to a local news relay network. One morning at breakfast he summarized what he had been hearing. "Things have changed a lot since the Crunch. There's been a big die-off. And there are actually *fewer* problems on the highway than there were six months ago. Up until recently, there was a big problem with people setting up roadblocks and pillaging people that were passing through. But after a while the only people available to be robbed were a bunch of ragtag refugees with nothing left worth stealing. Also, word got out as to where the fixed-location bandit roadblocks were located, so people just started bypassing them."

After a moment of reflection, he continued, "These days, the big problem is with large mobile looter gangs, since all the small gangs have been wiped out. But now we're hearing about big, *big* gangs with 100-plus people and 25-plus vehicles and a real bad attitude. They're like modern-day Vikings or the Mongol Horde. No town with a population of less than 10,000 is safe from them."

The Norwood Ranch, Newell, South Dakota
March, the Third Year

In March, after the snow had receded and while the Laytons were making preparations to depart, a stranger came down Parilla Road from the east. Traveling alone, the man carried a large Lowe backpack and an AK-74. He was dressed in OCP camouflage pants with a brown Army button-top sweater, and an OCP boonie hat. As he approached the gate, Terry, who was on guard in the woodshed OP, could see that the stranger was a young man with a dark complexion. She had already radioed Cordelia in the house, alerting her of the man's approach. Seeing the stranger linger after reading the sign, Ken stepped out the front door, holding his HK at the ready.

Pointing to the sign, the stranger shouted, "Can you give me directions to this church?"

Ken answered, "Sure, but first who are you, and where are you from?"

"My name's Curt Mehgai. I was working in the oil patch up in Parshall, North Dakota, when everything fell apart. I was doing pipeline and pump maintenance. But I spent the past year with a team guarding a big feed lot and elevator operation."

Overhearing Ken's questions and recognizing that this was an unusual solo refugee, Carl stepped out onto the porch to listen better to their conversation.

"Are you prior service?" Ken asked.

"Yeah, I was an 11B. That's infantry. I got out as a corporal. I was an M240-Bravo machinegunner with Alpha Company of the 2nd Battalion, 48th Infantry BCT—that's a Brigade Combat Team—from Fort Stewart."

"Any combat experience?"

"Yeah, two deployments. I've seen plenty of lead flying around, and I sent my share of lead downrange."

"Where are you headed?"

"Anywhere I can find work."

Ken looked over his shoulder to Carl, who nodded deeply in assent.

Still shouting, Ken asked, "Okay, here is what I want you to do: I want you to clear your weapon, and I'll come out to the gate and escort you to the house. There might be work for you here."

Mehgai removed the magazine from his AK, and stuffed it into his trouser's right cargo pocket. Then, holding the rifle with its muzzle upward, he flipped down its safety lever, and ejected the live round from the chamber into his free hand. He held the cartridge up over his head for Ken to see, and then stuffed it into a pants pocket. Finally, he cycled the rifle's action twice with large air guitar flourishes, demonstrating that the gun's chamber was empty.

Ken walked to the gate with his HK clone muzzle down, but with his thumb on the selector switch. As he unlocked the gate and opened it, Curt looked down at Ken's rifle and said appreciatively, "Oooh, HK-G3!"

They spent the next half hour on the front porch, quizzing Curt.

"I went home to visit my family on Guam, but I couldn't find any decent kind of job there. I knew I didn't want to go back on active duty because I'd no doubt get deployed back to A-stan, and I didn't want to go in the Army Reserve, because I'd no doubt get deployed back to A-stan. . . ." He paused to laugh, then said: "So I was doing some job hunting on the Internet and I read about the oil boom in North Dakota, so I thought, 'Why not?' It turned out they were hiring almost anyone with a strong back and who was willing to put up with winters in the Dakotas. And it didn't hurt that I was a veteran. When the economy went kerflooey, I asked around and found a job at the other end of the county, at a big grain elevator. The place is run by a family that's been there since the 1890s. They own both the elevator and a feed lot. Again, being prior service helped me get the job."

"So why'd you leave?"

"The man who owned the company kept having more and more of his relatives arrive after the Crunch. Some of them trickled in pretty late, even as recent as last November—and they told some amazing stories about how they managed to get out of the big cities. Anyways, blood is thicker than water, so I got asked to leave—politely, you know, and with plenty of notice. At least they gave me until the snow was off the roads. Nobody else in town needed a security guy, so off I went."

The questioning shifted to Carl, who asked, "Do you have any military paperwork?"

"Yeah, I've got my DD-214—that's a discharge document and service record."

Being cautious, Carl first matched Mehgai's face to his driver's license, and then the name on the license to the DD-214. The discharge document told Carl nearly everything he needed to know. Curt Mehgai had been awarded two Army Commendation medals, a Bronze Star, and a Purple Heart.

Malmstrom Air Force Base, Montana
March, the Third Year

The UNPROFOR contact team arrived at Malmstrom very quietly. General Woolson had expected that they would immediately attempt to relieve him of command, and he had a contingency plan in place to counter that. But surprisingly, Woolson was told that he would continue to command the base.

The UNPROFOR team soon took over the old headquarters building. But it took three months for several large generators to be hauled in from Wright-Patterson Air Force Base in Ohio and to get power to the building reliably.

The interactions between General Woolson's staff and the contact team became a strange ballet of probes, feints, obfuscation, and denial. Woolson was repeatedly threatened with being relieved of command for "studious lack of cooperation." He countered that he was a team player and complained that he lacked resources to provide the data and facilities access that the ProvGov demanded. Both sides in the struggle did their best to hide key facts and intentions. Their meetings went on for months. Woolson and his staff finally moved out of their trailers in the hangar and back into the headquarters building in November.

Inevitably, both Woolson and the UNPROFOR liaison team commander got what they wanted: Woolson didn't have to give up the keys to the kingdom, and the UNPROFOR team denied Malmstrom the resources required to resume operational capability (OC).

Though they were never spoken per se, it eventually became apparent that the UNPROFOR contact team had only a few key goals:

1. To maintain security of all fissile material and cryptographic systems.
2. To keep all of Malmstrom's MAFs de-alerted indefinitely.
3. To assess capabilities and to deny resources needed to improve any existing capabilities.
4. To assess how many silos had been flooded by groundwater intrusion, and how many were still dry (and hence conceivably capable of being realerted).

Rather than simply relieving Woolson of command, he was nominally put under the operational control of UNPROFOR. His "commander" was a UN major general from England. However, Woolson carefully did some picking and choosing in deciding which of his orders he would carry out, and which he would not via delays, excuses, and obfuscation. Many orders, he said, had been "put at a lower priority, or placed 'under study, due to lack of requisite resources.'"

Woolson discovered that the two highest-ranking officers on the UNPROFOR contact team had drinking problems. So he kept them well supplied with liquor. This tactic further slowed the pace of the meetings.

In a secret meeting with no UN officers present, Woolson told his staff, "We continue the tap dance and treat them like mushrooms—we keep them in the dark and spread the steer manure around liberally. We stall them, and pencil whip them, and play charades as long as possible. Most importantly, we *do not* let them have the codes so that none of the LCCs can be accessed. To make it look like we are being compliant, we will let them 'inspect' as many LFs as they'd like—very slowly and laboriously, mind you—but we make excuses so that we never, *ever*, give a UN officer access to an LCC capsule. We can walk them around *upstairs* at the MAFs and give them nice dog-and-pony shows and pretty little PowerPoint presentations until they are blue in the face. But the bottom line is that they never get the crypto keys. The LCCs stay *locked down*, gentlemen. We will deny them any launch capability."

As a contingency, Woolson ordered that thermite devices be built and secretly distributed. These were a last-ditch measure, designed to destroy both the encrypted blast door locks at the LCCs and the jackscrew mechanisms for the seven-ton "B Plugs" at the LFs. This contingency plan was given the code name "Uniform Delta," which stood for "ultimate denial."

Secretly, the UN staff had decided that there wasn't enough manpower that could be spared to secure and reactivate Malmstrom's vast missile fields. And, after all, the missiles weren't needed anyway. They had plenty of operational missiles in France, Russia, and China—at least as long as Russia and China contin-

ued to toe the line. The stated goal of "reactivation" of Malmstrom was in fact a "capability denial operation."

The key to the UN's denial strategy was the decision to delay
restoration of grid power to western Montana. The UN's general
staff had concluded that if they wanted to keep the American missiles neutered, all they needed to do was delay having the power
grid in that region reenergized.

18

Millennium Falcon

"Every body continues in its state of rest, or of uniform motion in a right line, unless it is compelled to change that state by forces impressed upon it."

**—Sir Isaac Newton's first law of motion,
from his first book of *Principia***

**Bradfordsville, Kentucky
April, the Third Year**

There was someone banging on the door downstairs. The bedside windup clock showed that it was 5:15 a.m. General store owner Sheila Randall quickly dressed and walked downstairs from the apartment to her store. A man from the Resistance whom she recognized was outside. He was shivering, standing in a heavy downpour with a dribble coming off the brim of his fishing hat. Sheila unlocked the door and the man stepped in. He was dressed in dark civilian clothes, with a brown North Face jacket. The rainwater dripping off of him made a spreading puddle on the floor.

"I'm sorry to arrive like this without any warning, but I need your help," he said urgently. "We've got a man in our truck who's been shot in the leg and in the shoulder. He's stable, but we can't get him to our field hospital in Russell Springs before daylight. Our intel says that there are Germans and Belgians patrolling the roads between here and there, there's a temporary checkpoint on

Highway 68, and there may be an ambush set up somewhere along Liberty Road. We've also heard that there might be a reconnaissance drone up later today, that they've been flying in daylight hours out of Fort Campbell. If we use a team on foot to carry him on a stretcher, it'll take a full day, and he's likely to go hypothermic. We'd rather wait until either tomorrow night or the night after and carry him by truck, even if we have to make a roundabout trip."

Sheila nodded and said, "Okay, but the last time you came here, it was just that gal with the shrapnel. I don't know how to take care of someone with major wounds."

"Don't fret, we're also dropping off a medic named Brent, to take care of him."

Sheila nodded again. "All right, let's bring him in the side door, and help him up the stairs."

As she swung open the side door, she saw her son, Tyree, descending the stairs behind her. He was wearing pajamas and carrying his shotgun. "What's up?" he asked.

"I'm afraid that you're going to have to give up your bed again."

Tyree grinned and said, "No prob, Mom. I'm an early riser, anyway."

The resistance fighter they carried up the stairs from the store to Sheila's apartment was named Jedediah Peoples. He was nineteen years old. He wore a wispy beginner's mustache and was from Westmoreland, Tennessee, near the Kentucky state line. He had been shot through the left buttock and thigh. These were large, ugly wounds, but not life-threatening. Sheila was impressed by Brent Danley, even though he wore a pair of eyeglasses that had comical-looking repairs to the bridge and one of the eyepieces. The repairs had been made with paper clips and surgical tape. Brent had thinning reddish brown hair. He was soft-spoken and competent.

Brent treated Jedediah's wounds carefully, and he gave him pain medicine—Tylenol with codeine—only as needed, following a series of "On a scale of one to ten, how would you describe the pain . . . ?" questions. Rather than attempting to stitch the wounds closed, Brent left them loosely covered with gauze to allow drainage. He explained that this was actually the safest way to treat them. "It'll leave bigger scars, but this way there's less chance of infection."

As Brent was rebandaging one of the wounds, Jedediah winced with pain and said, "I always figured we'd get raptured before we'd ever go through anything like this."

Brent shook his head slowly and replied, "You mean the collapse and the invasion? I believe that's the same thing that some people were saying in Stalingrad during World War II."

"You know," Brent went on, "in Vermont I had a neighbor who lived down the road from me. He and his family starved and froze to death the first winter after the Crunch. He and his wife were totally convinced that they'd be raptured before any disaster would threaten them. He told me that he thought that storing food in anticipation of hard times was a display of a lack of faith in God's providence. He used to give me a hard time for being a prepper."

The young man nodded, and Brent continued, "A lot of well-meaning believers have the same sort of complacency. That dispensational pre-tribulation rapture nonsense was often combined with their bogus 'Health, Wealth, and Prosperity' preaching. They have a similar eschatological basis. It is the whole 'Beam Me Up' mind-set. It goes along with the 'Feel Good, Jesus Is Your Buddy' mentality. But if the history of the church has taught us anything, it is that the life of a Christian is fraught with peril. The world hates us, and everything that we stand for. They pound on us as often as they can. Being a Christian doesn't exempt us from that. If anything, it actually means that we'll get more pain and suffering inflicted on us than non-Christians. Just look at *Foxe's Book of Martyrs*. Have you read that?"

"No."

"Well you should, if you can ever find a copy. All that bad doctrine from the new Emergent Church movement led a lot of deceived Christians to be complacent toward being prepared for themselves and their loved ones. Everyone got a rude awakening when the dollar crashed and the power grids went down. The *proper* Christian way to live is to stock up for your family, and that also gives you extra to dispense as charity."

Sheila's elderly grandmother Lily relayed messages about the care of Jedediah downstairs to Sheila, who was working at her store's front counter most of the day. Sheila asked Lily to carry up extra food and some fresh cream that she took in trade on a barter transaction.

The Norwood Ranch, Newell, South Dakota
April, the Third Year

When Curt was hired, Ken and Terry decided that it was time to press on. They felt good departing, knowing that Curt would be there to fill the security role they had occupied. They were almost ready to leave at any time, except that Ken's boots were worn out and starting to fall apart. With some inquiries via the local CB radio network, they found some tan suede military surplus boots that were snug, but his size. They were comfortable if he wore just one pair of socks, but not two as he had with his old boots. The boots were a gift from the Norwoods, who insisted that they buy them to compensate the Laytons for their many months of guard duty, manure hauling, and water hauling. They cost $2.25 in silver quarters.

Looking carefully at their maps, and after much consultation and debate, they decided that rather than trying to cross the Northern Rockies, it would be safer to veer south and get to north-central Idaho by way of the Great Basin. There were many rumors of banditry in eastern Montana. By taking a more southerly route, not only would they be traversing more sparsely populated country, but also the population would be predominantly Mormon. Given the Mormon proclivity for food storage preparedness, they anticipated they would probably be more hospitable to travelers. They also hoped that if they were able to get to Salt Lake City, they might find people with operating vehicles, as there was a large oil refinery just north of the city.

The Norwoods had cousins in Scottsbluff, Nebraska, the Bennet family. They were cousins on Cordelia's side of the family. It was decided that Graham and the Laytons would ride horseback to Scottsbluff. From there, Ken and Terry would continue west on foot. Meanwhile, Graham would return to Newell with the horses.

For the trip, they selected the Norwoods' three saddle horses, plus their old mare, Molly, to use as a packhorse. Molly was elderly, but their draft horse Andre was too valuable to the family to put at risk in a cross-country trip. Carrying a packsaddle holding the Laytons' two ALICE packs and Graham's bedroll, Molly's load would be only 110 pounds. The packsaddle was of the modern frameless type, and made of red Cordura nylon. The bright red color made Ken and Terry cringe. The untactical color was remedied by strapping a woodland camouflage quilted poncho liner over the load. This worked perfectly, since the poncho liner already had grommet tie straps spaced around its perimeter, and some extra length was simply tucked between the packsaddle and the saddle pad.

The ride to Scottsbluff was uneventful, and the weather was fairly good, with a few showers. The grazing was sparse for the horses, with just a few patches of new growth. When the horses did pass over any new growth, they would play naughty and put their heads down and pause to graze. Urging them on took some effort. For the sake of their horses, they picked their campsites in areas where there was grass coming up. As was their habit, they made cold camps each night, not wanting to attract attention. With some pasture available, hobbling was all that was necessary to keep their horses in camp.

They averaged forty miles a day. They did their best to avoid towns and any terrain that looked like it would be advantageous for ambushes. After so many months of traveling on foot and at night, travel by horseback in daylight required some adjustment for the Laytons. For the horses, the biggest adjustment was getting used to riding widely spaced apart—typically fifteen to twenty yards when on level, open ground. For the first two days, the horses would invariably attempt to bunch up. It was Molly who proved to be the magnet to the other horses. "I say that we make Molly the caboose of this outfit," Graham proposed. It was only with that resequencing and some consistent reining that the horses became accustomed to wider intervals.

Graham turned seventeen on the third day of the trip to Scottsbluff. That evening, as they made camp, Ken presented him a cloth sack containing twenty-five rounds of .45 automatic ammunition as a thank-you for escorting them, and in recognition of his birthday.

They avoided the city of Scottsbluff itself, angling in from the northeast, through ranching country. The Bennets lived on Henry Road, northwest of Scottsbluff, a stone's throw from the Wyoming state line. Arriving saddle sore late in the afternoon of the sixth day, they were warmly greeted. The Bennets lived in an older ranch-style house on four acres. Before the economic collapse, Dale Bennet had been a full-time grassland botanist with the state of Nebraska, and did the same part-time under contract for the state of Wyoming. His specialty was introduced grasses and weeds. He was also involved in a planned decades-long program to reintroduce native grasses. The Bennets had survived since the Crunch by breeding New Zealand and Rex rabbits. The acreage behind their house was dotted with cobbled-together sheds built out of scrap lumber, pallets, and recycled corrugated steel roofing from barns. The sheds held dozens of homemade wire rabbit cages.

They turned their horses out into a fenced field that Dale Bennet used for growing feed for his rabbits. Part of it was seeded in an early-sprouting grass variety, so the horses starting eating with gusto, even before they had been unsaddled.

The Bennets were overjoyed to see Graham, and thrilled to receive two lengthy letters from his mother. Graham's four cousins, ages six to thirteen, were whooping and hollering. The younger ones jumped onto his back for piggyback rides.

The Bennets celebrated the arrival and Graham's birthday by barbequing five rabbits. The barbeque party went on until late in the evening, as everyone traded stories about their lives since the Crunch.

In relating their tale, Terry mentioned that they planned to continue their journey to their group retreat by way of Montpelier, Idaho. Dale interjected, "Well, you need to talk with my friend Cliff. He's planning on taking a drive out to northern Utah, real soon."

Ken was speechless. He asked, incredulously, "Taking a *drive?*"

Dale nodded. "Yeah! We'll walk over to Cliff's house tomorrow morning, and I'll introduce you."

After a night of fitful sleep, they awoke to the smell of pancakes. The Bennets were using some of their precious supplies to make a large breakfast for Graham and the Laytons. After breakfast, just as promised, Dale escorted Ken and Terry on a half mile walk to the trailer home of his friend Cliff.

A 2009 crew cab Ford pickup sat in front of the trailer house. The house was a single-wide that appeared to be at least thirty years old. Old tires held down a blue tarp at one end of the roof.

A man answered the knock on his door with a .455 Webley revolver in his hand.

"Hey, Cliff, how are you doing?" Dale said warmly. "These are friends of my brother-in-law. Meet Ken and Terry."

Cliff invited Dale and the Laytons into the house, saying, "Pardon the mess—I've been packing." He laughed and kicked a cardboard box out of the way so that Dale and the Laytons could get to the couch.

Cliff immediately struck Ken and Terry as an odd but jovial character.

After just a few more minutes of introductions and assurances of their trustworthiness, Dale joined them as they folded out their maps on Cliff's kitchen table. "It's time to talk strategy," Cliff declared.

They calculated that the distance to Coalville, Utah, was 410 miles. Between his pickup's main and auxiliary tanks and the gas he had available in cans, Cliff estimated that he had enough fuel to travel 850 miles. Ever the optimist, he said, "So I can make it back here, even if I don't find a drop of gas around Coalville."

Cliff explained that he had been a heating and air-conditioning technician before the Crunch. Never married and living frugally, he had dabbled in energy stocks and silver, starting soon after the turn of the century. Cliff was in his late thirties, slightly overweight, and had thinning red hair and a wispy red beard. He lived alone in the sparsely furnished trailer. Neither Ken nor Terry could determine how he'd made a living since the Crunch.

Cliff summed up his desire to travel to Utah, saying, "I got word that they're alive, but I haven't seen my cousins or my aunt and uncle since before the stock market melted down. So I'd like to look in on them to see if they're all right. I'm taking *all* my stuff with me. Who knows? I might find work there—maybe at a mine, and maybe I'll even find a wife."

Dale reiterated that he had heard that there were limited supplies of newly refined gasoline available in northern Utah. He and Cliff agreed that the trip was worth the gamble.

Ken spent most of the day checking on the mechanical condition of Cliff's pickup. They had access to the inventory of an auto parts store, which had been moved to the owner's workshop for safekeeping just a mile away. At the shop, he checked the four mounted tires and the spare, adding air to two of them with a hand pump. He replaced the fuel filter and set aside an identical spare. Checking all the hoses, he noticed that the lower radiator hose felt soft. He was fortunate to find a new correct spare in the enormous pile of belts and hoses in the corner of the shop. He checked the belt tensioner and then all the fluids. He added some window washer fluid and coolant. He set aside one more full gallon of coolant to take along with them. Then he lubed the two points of the chassis that could take grease. The rest, he explained, were all "lubeless joints." Finally, noting the motor oil looked dark, he changed the oil and filter. He kept the old hose and fuel filters to carry as spares. After checking both of the pickup's fuse boxes, he also set aside an assortment of spare fuses with various current ratings.

Amid the many shelves of mostly disorganized parts, Ken found a spare serpentine belt for the pickup. "This belt runs all the auxiliaries. If this belt ever breaks, you're totally out of luck," he explained.

In all, the belt, fluids, fuses, filters, and motor oil cost Cliff just two ounces of silver and some gardening hand tools in barter. Clinching the deal, he promised the auto parts store owner, "If I'm not back here in a month, then you are welcome to my trailer house and everything left in it." He handed him an extra door key.

After the maintenance on the pickup truck was complete, they headed back to Cliff's trailer, where they ate a light dinner: three small cans of tuna and a loaf of homemade whole wheat bread that Cliff said he often bought from a neighbor. The paper labels had been removed from the cans and they had been painted in varnish, to protect them from rust. Cliff explained, "That's a trick that I picked up from a guy I knew that spent four months crewing a yacht in the Bahamas."

Looking closely at the cans before they were opened, Terry could see that their lids had "Tuna, 11/2012" written in Magic Marker, just visible through the varnish.

Cliff asked Ken and Terry to help him pack for the trip. He had remarkably few clothes, which all fit into just two large cardboard boxes. He also packed a large Tupperware box that he explained contained some photocopies of family history and genealogy documents that his late mother had made before the Crunch.

Then they started digging. Using a rusty shovel with a broken tip, they dug up three hidden caches in the yard. The first was very shallow. A sheet of plywood, a thin layer of soil, and a large pile of used wooden pallets covered it. This cache contained seventeen 5-gallon gas cans painted various colors, mostly red. The cans had been positioned on top of an odd assortment of scrap wood blocks to keep their bottoms from rusting. All the gas, Cliff said, had been treated with PRI-G gasoline stabilizer.

As they pulled the cans up out of the hole, Cliff said, "You know, this gas was the fruit of four months of hard dickering and bartering. I'm hoping that there'll be gasoline back in production soon. I heard there's some sort of 'Provisional' national government, headquartered at Fort Knox, Kentucky, and that they're getting things straightened out."

The second cache, deeper than the first, held more than twenty military surplus .30 caliber, .50 caliber, and 20mm ammo cans containing various ammunition and some hand tools. Atop the ammo cans, there were some canned foods, stowed in two Sterilite brand plastic tote bins. All had been varnished and hand-labeled, just like the tuna cans.

The third cache, nearly three feet down, contained three guns in a capped piece of eight-inch-diameter PVC pipe, and two more .30 caliber ammo cans. The latter, Cliff said, held what he called his "silver trove."

They spent that night in their sleeping bags on the floor of

Cliff's living room. Ken and Terry were so excited that they were scarcely able to sleep. Cliff roused them an hour before dawn. The gas cans had already been loaded in the back of the pickup the night before and covered with a tarp. They quickly loaded all the ammo cans and the rest of the gear. The heap filled up the entire bed of the pickup truck, most of the rear seat, and nearly all the passenger-side front seat and floor.

Terry opted to be tail gunner, sitting on top of the backpacks just behind the cab, but forward of the gas cans. She bundled herself up with both her unrolled sleeping bag and Ken's sleeping bag. She wore gloves, a muffler, and a pile cap to keep her head warm. She sat facing rearward, with her CAR-15 in her lap.

Ken, meanwhile, sat in the seat directly behind Cliff. Remembering how all the windows of their Mustang and Bronco had been shot out, Ken ordered, "At the first sign of trouble, you hit all four buttons to roll the windows down. We don't want them getting shot out, and besides, the way this HK ejects brass, it's a window smasher."

"You got it!" Cliff replied.

On the seat next to him, Cliff carried a folding-stock Ruger Mini-14 Ranch Rifle with a thirty-round magazine. Two spare-loaded twenty-round magazines were placed within reach in the center console, along with Cliff's ancient Webley revolver. Beside it were four full-moon clips of .45 ACP ammunition. Seeing this, Ken surmised that Cliff's revolver had been converted to .45 ACP.

Ken positioned his HK butt down on the floor between his legs, and both his pack and web gear were next to him on the seat. He debated removing his M1911 pistol from its holster, but then, remembering an account that he'd read of the FBI's 1986 Miami shootout, he decided that the pistol might get misplaced if they came to a sudden stop.

Cliff started the engine and shouted, "Y'all ready?"

Ken and Terry both shouted back, "Yes!"

Cliff turned on the headlights, and they started down Henry Road toward the freeway. Cliff popped a cassette tape into the pickup's tape and CD player. The voice of Hank Williams Jr. came from the speakers, singing "A Country Boy Can Survive." Ken laughed uproariously. The situation seemed so surreal.

After Cliff turned west on State Highway 26, the sky behind them was starting to lighten. Cliff set the pickup's cruise control to fifty miles per hour. He said forthrightly, "I'm keeping it under fifty-two, for fuel economy. I read somewhere that's the magic number." The sensation of speed was overwhelming to both Ken and Terry. They had spent so many months on foot that fifty miles per hour seemed alarmingly fast. Ken laughed and exclaimed, "Woo-hoo! I feel like we're in the *Millennium Falcon*, and you just shouted 'Punch it, Chewie!'"

Recognizing the reference to the movie *Star Wars*, Cliff retorted, "Well, we both got red hair, so doesn't that make us *both* Wookies?"

Ken laughed again and yelled, "Wookie suiters of the world, unite!"

The landscape of Wyoming raced by as the daylight grew. At Torrington, they turned south onto Highway 85. At this junction and south of it, they saw dozens of burned-out hulks of cars on the shoulder. As they approached the cars, Cliff slowed to twenty miles an hour and sounded serious for the first time. "I gotta watch for any scrap metal in the road. There was a looter roadblock here last year. It cost us five men's lives to clean those looters out."

Beyond the destroyed cars, Cliff sped up and again set the cruise control to fifty. Terry tapped on the back window and grinned at Ken. She gave an exaggerated thumbs-up.

Ken sat in silence, listening to "Tennessee Stud," "The Coalition to Ban Coalitions," and other songs that were unfamiliar to him. The tape began playing "A Country Boy Can Survive" for the second time. Looking in the center console box and in the glove box, Ken searched for other tapes or CDs, but he found none. He realized that not only was the audio system set to repeat, but also that Cliff had only one cassette tape in the vehicle. Ken shook his head and grinned. Cliff was a bona fide character.

They hadn't seen a vehicle heading in either direction all morning. The barren plains of eastern Wyoming were now in full daylight. The engine was running smoothly.

Ken said, "Say, Cliff, you never mentioned your family name."

Cliff answered ambiguously, "That's right."

"Well, I noticed the mailbox there was marked 'Larson.' So is that your name?"

Cliff answered with a laugh, "Well, it *might* be."

Ken laughed and shook his head. "Oh well . . . How about them *Cubs*?"

"I'm a Red Sox fan, personally, but I don't think there's going to be a baseball season next summer. Folks are using their baseball bats for other purposes these days."

Cliff seemed distracted, and didn't continue. He slowed and turned west onto County Road 218.

Cliff was looking anxious and he regularly scanned the sides of the road and his rearview mirrors. Finally, Cliff explained, "This route that we're taking will bypass Cheyenne." Then he gestured over his left shoulder, and said, "You do *not* want to go through Cheyenne. Last I heard, that city was in the hands of the bad guys, and they will eat you for breakfast." After loudly drawing a breath, he added, "Literally."

Cliff took several more turns on small roads, some of them gravel, for the next hour. Several times, Cliff stopped and consulted his maps to be certain of his route. They finally got back on the Interstate just east of Laramie. "From what I've heard, it should be smooth sailing from here on," he reassured Ken.

They stayed on I-80, heading west, transiting the Rockies. In places the mountains loomed above them. There were a couple of places where rocks had rolled into the road, and there was one small slide two miles west of Green River that partially blocked the right lane. Otherwise, the highway was in remarkably good condition, considering that it had gone through two winters without any maintenance.

They pulled off the road just past Green River to check on Terry. Cliff left the engine running. Ken handed everyone strips of jerky and bottles of water. Terry had rosy cheeks, but seemed exuberant. "Why did we get off the highway onto all those small roads back there?" she asked.

"Just a shortcut," Ken told her, not wanting to darken her mood. "Don't sweat it. Say, do you want to switch places?"

She shook her head and said, "Nah. I want to do the *whole* width of Wyoming out in the open, soaking it all in. I'm in a big, happy dream right now."

They continued their descent from the western slope of the Rockies. The air was now comfortably warm. Other than abandoned cars on the shoulder that had run out of fuel in the midst of the Crunch and a few tumbleweeds, the Interstate was clear of any obstructions. But they could see the recent ruins of some ranch houses near the freeway. With most of these, there was little more than a stone chimney and a blackened patch of earth left as a silent testament to the chaos that had reigned over the past year and a half.

As they crossed the Utah state line, Ken did some math in his head. In just over eight hours, they had covered more distance than they could have traveled by foot in more than two months.

Late in the day, they reached the junction of Interstate 80 and Interstate 84. In the distance, they could see the odd blue color of Echo Reservoir to the south.

"Well, here you are," Cliff announced.

He slowly brought the pickup to a stop in the right lane of the freeway, not bothering to pull onto the shoulder. They had still not seen another vehicle in motion all day long. Cliff turned off the engine.

Ken and Terry thanked Cliff repeatedly. After pulling out their packs, they helped him refill the pickup's main fuel tank, emptying six of the 5-gallon cans. Ken dug into his backpack and pulled out a brown twenty-round box of Federal 5.56mm ball ammunition and handed it to Cliff, saying, "This is just a token for all the gas that you burned today. Thanks."

Cliff nodded, accepting the gift, and said, "Don't mention it."

Ken and Terry shouldered their packs. Cliff started the pickup's engine and shouted, "Thanks for the ammunition, pardner!" He gave a wave, and drove away.

"What a lunatic," Ken said with a laugh.

"Well. Let's thank God for the kindness of the lunatics in our lives," Terry said.

19

A Bump in the Road

"He doubted whether they could survive the winter, even though they piled broken furniture into the fireplace. Some accident would quite likely overtake them, or pneumonia might strike them down. They were like the highly bred spaniels and pekinese who at the end of their leashes had once walked along the city streets. Milt and Ann, too, were city-dwellers, and when the city died, they would hardly survive without it. They would pay the penalty which in the history of the world, he knew, had always been inflicted upon organisms which specialized too highly."

George R. Stewart, *Earth Abides* (1949)

North of Coalville, Utah
April, the Third Year

Again on foot, Ken and Terry walked on the rough service road paralleling the railroad and highway. They walked two miles before making camp for the night. Nearby, the Weber River roared in a spring torrent. Ken had developed a hot spot on his left foot.

After they had set up their camp, he pulled off his boots and socks. A blister had formed on the projection at the widest part of his left foot, near the head of his right-most metatarsal bone.

As he powdered his feet, Ken told Terry, "These new boots haven't been broken in well enough. I think that we're going to have to take it easy and only do a couple of miles each day for the next couple of days."

He decided that the left boot needed stretching to improve its fit. So he spent ten minutes walking around barefoot, looking around the campsite at various small rocks. He eventually found a lozenge-shaped rock that was just slightly wider than his foot. He carefully inserted the rock into his boot, wedging it in, just where he thought the boot was too tight. As an afterthought, he wet that part of the boot leather to help it stretch.

They awoke before dawn. Ken applied moleskin to the blister on his foot. As they rolled their sleeping bags and packed their gear, he consulted their Utah road map. A tiny dot on the map ahead on their route was marked "Henefer." Just after sunrise, they skirted around the small town of Henefer, following Echo Road. The town appeared to have just a few hundred residents. Two dogs barked at the Laytons, but otherwise they attracted no interest. Their progress was slow, both because of their stealth and because of Ken's blister. They camped up a side canyon, two miles from Morgan City. The canyon was steep, so it took them an extra half hour to set up camp, arranging rocks to make level spots for their sleeping bags. A seasonal creek trickled down the draw. Ken muttered as he pulled off his left boot. The blister was larger and starting to redden.

The next day they decided to hunker down, in deference to Ken's blister. It was a pleasant spring day, and they had fresh water close at hand. There were a few spring wildflowers dotting the hillsides. They took turns napping and nibbled at dried fruit and jerky. In the afternoon, they watched Blue Bellies—western fence lizards—dart around the rocks. Terry thumbed through her well-worn Missal, saying, "Well, there are worse ways to spend a day."

Ken roused her at 4 a.m. the next morning. By the light of Terry's tiny LED light, they could see that Ken's blister hadn't improved, and that it now extended beyond the moleskin. So he applied a larger piece of the protective covering, hoping for some improvement.

They buried their trash beneath some rocks and erased the signs of their camp. They were back on the trail by 4:30 a.m. Their progress was slow and agonizing. Ken winced each time his left foot hit the ground. In six hours, they advanced only one and a half miles.

They set up camp in the afternoon in the tall grass of what had been the Round Valley Golf Course. In the distance, they could see that the west end of the golf course had been fenced, and now contained a flock of horned sheep. Terry took the first watch while Ken tried to sleep. The blister was very painful and looking even more red.

The next morning, Ken declared, "I think it is infected."

He put on a clean sock and then painfully put on his boot.

"We need to find a place to stay and let that heal," Terry suggested.

"Maybe we can do some more security work. Let's head for a farm that reeks of prosperity," he answered.

They made slow progress toward Morgan City. Ken was in agony. The verdant fields of the valley floor contrasted the brushy and sparsely wooded hillsides above them. Most of the fields appeared to be hay grass, but there were also some row crops. They were surprised to see and hear tractors operating.

Spotting a tall, gleaming grain silo north of town, they headed for it. The silo was at a tidy farm with several large fields. A sign at the county road proclaimed, "L. & L. Prine Farm, Hay Sales By Appointment Only," with an 801 phone number. The stylized outline of a beehive was painted beneath the phone number. Ken knew that this symbol indicated that the family was associated with the LDS Church.

Down the lane, on the porch of the farmhouse a dog barked, already aware of their presence. They walked slowly with their rifles slung muzzles down. Another dog joined in on the barking. A teenage girl stepped out onto the porch, armed with a lever-action carbine. Another girl, slightly younger, soon joined her armed with a Mossberg .22 rifle. The front door opened again, and a portly man stepped out, carrying both a scoped rifle and a holstered revolver. "We don't want any trouble," the man warned.

"We're not trouble," Terry said. "We're the *antidote* to trouble." She and Ken made a show of laying down their rifles, packs, and web gear.

Larry Prine interrogated the Laytons for twenty-five minutes. While they spoke, Larry's wife, Lynda, and more and more of their family emerged from the house. Soon, six children ranging from five to sixteen were lined up, listening intently. Larry was curious, and seemed to take pity on the Laytons. He read the letters of introduction from Durward Perkins and Carl Norwood.

After their interrogation, Terry asked, "How are things here in Morgan City?"

Prine leaned back against the wall casually and replied, "We've gotten by a lot better than most towns, since we have irrigation water from the river. We've prospered, but we've been shorthanded. When those derivatives imploded and the dollar collapsed, the town Elders panicked and got a little overzealous. They sent home *every* student enrolled at Weber State, and they ran all the migrant farm workers out of town. They did the same to the druggies and drunks at the halfway house. At least that move made sense. But as it turned out, we could have used the help from the college kids for the next summer's harvest, and for security, too. If they hadn't been in such a rush, they could have taken their pick of the students from the college. For instance, they could have kept all the ROTC cadets and criminal justice majors, and some of the ag students. That was very shortsighted of them. But like I say, everyone was very panicky when the hyperinflation kicked in and the riots started in the big cities."

"So how have things been recently?"

Prine scratched his chin and said, "The last few months, things have been getting dicey, with the looter gangs that have come up from Nevada and west from the Plains states. Some of 'em have armored vehicles—mostly old bank armored cars. I heard that St. George and Vernal both nearly got destroyed. More than half the houses in both those towns burned down. And in Richfield there was a gang that moved in and stayed for *months*, just brutalizing everyone in town. Then that same gang moved on to Price, and did the same thing, and they're still there. Hopefully the new government in Kentucky will send the Army to come and clean them out."

"What about here, around Morgan?" Terry asked.

"This is an agricultural community, so we apparently draw from quite a large radius. Burglaries, mostly. But once in a while there's a really wicked home invasion. Looters will sneak into farms in the middle of the night. They catch a family sleeping, and then . . ." He glanced down at his row of children and said tersely, ". . . Well, you know what happens. It ain't pretty."

After glancing at his wife, Larry said, "If you are willing to both put in eight-hour guard shifts, you're welcome to stay for at least a couple of weeks while your blister heals up."

It took a full week for Ken's foot to heal. Then he spent many hours each day in the Prines' fields, weeding with a hoe. He developed a technique that he called speed weeding. His goal was both to eliminate thistles and other weeds, and to toughen up his feet. He would sprint to each weed he spotted and then come to a sudden stop and start hoeing. Then he would sprint to the next patch. It looked comical, but it worked. Day after day of this exercise toughened up his feet.

Just when Ken felt that his feet were ready for him to resume their journey, Terry had an accident. After more than a week of doing her guard duty from ground level, she decided to try manning a shift from atop the Prines' silo, just as she had done at the Perkins ranch. Coming down the ladder at the end of her shift, she reached the bottom of the caged section, turned, and absentmindedly hopped off the ladder. But unlike the ladder at the Perkinses' silo in Iowa, the transition to the caged section of the ladder began eleven feet off the ground instead of six feet. She landed on her right knee. Recognizing the intense pain, she realized that she had broken it.

She shouted for help, and soon Ken and several of the Prine children were standing over her. "I feel like an idiot," she said, grimacing. "There's nothing stronger than habit. At the Perkins place, I got used to turning and jumping off the ladder just when my head got below the caged part."

Five weeks after Ken and Terry's arrival, Mrs. Prine's sister Kate, her husband, Roy, and their two sons arrived from Oak City, Utah. They were seeking refuge because the town had been savagely attacked by looters just a few days before, and it was feared that the looters would return and burn the rest of the town. Their arrival made the already crowded house even more crowded. Several of the children were sleeping on the carpeted living room floor in sleeping bags.

For two weeks, Ken and Terry had been trying to get a message through to Todd Gray's retreat group in Idaho, via the regional CB radio network, but they found that it didn't extend any farther than southwestern Idaho and Bozeman, Montana.

Next, Ken and Terry spent several hours composing a letter. It read:

Dear Todd, Mary, and Whoever Else Arrived:
Terry and I are writing to let you know that we are safe

and living temporarily at a farm three miles north of
Morgan City, Utah (twenty-five miles northeast of Salt
Lake City—see enclosed strip map). We walked most
of the way here from Chicago. We had planned to stay
here only a week to rest up and then press on to the
retreat, but Terry took a bad spill off a ladder, breaking
her kneecap. That was nearly two months ago. I'm afraid
that the break is not healing properly. I don't believe
that there is any way that we will be able to continue on,
at least not on foot. We hope that all is well with you.
This is the third letter that we couriered up your way. If
you got either of the previous ones, I apologize for the
redundancy. However, we figured that sending multiple
letters by different couriers would be the best bet in
getting our message through to you.

We are staying in a spare bedroom at the Prines'
farm. They are wonderful people. Like most of their
neighbors, they are Mormons, and thus were relatively
well prepared for the collapse. To earn our keep I am
being employed as a night security guard on the farm.
I also help out with the heavy work during the day
(mending fences, splitting wood, etc.). Terry is still
confined to bed most of the time.

Because of Terry's injury, the Prines have agreed to let us
stay on as long as we'd like, but we don't want to wear out our
welcome and their stock of supplies. (Mrs. Prine's sister and
brother-in-law and their two teenage boys moved in three
weeks ago, and the stored food supply will soon be critical.)
Is there any way that you could provide transportation to the
retreat? I realize that this is asking a lot, and would involve
considerable risk, so feel free to say no.

To avoid missing you, we promise that we will stay
here until we either hear from you or somebody shows

up. Please send word via courier or by radio if you get a
chance. Do you have the nighttime CB voice message relay
network set up? Well, that's all for now. Once again, we
hope that all is well with you. God bless you all.

Ken Layton and Terry Layton
D.V.—Ps. 37

Terry then wrote out five copies of the letter and map by
hand. Her hand felt cramped when she was done. She and Ken
added their signatures and Ken appended his characteristic stylized "D.V.—Ps. 37" logo, which was short for "*Deo Volente*,
Psalm 37." For many years, he had penned this logo on all his
personal letters.

They sent the letters out via couriers over the course of the next
three weeks. Two of the letters went with traveling traders, two with
refugees heading toward Idaho, and one with a circuit-riding Baptist
minister. They hoped that at least one of them would get through.

Fort Knox, Kentucky
January, the Fourth Year

Maynard Hutchings was scheduled to present his State of the Continent speech, as part of his weekly *America's New Dawn* morning show recording, for later distribution over the Red and Blue
networks. (The two networks had the same staff, but different
names were given for a feigned show of balance.) When Hutchings, his staff, and bodyguards arrived at the Fort Knox television
studio in their Boxer APCs, they found that they were locked out.
The studio staff had arrived a half hour earlier and found the
door lock jammed. So they had summoned the Fort Knox MPs
together, and they were furiously working on the building's steel
doors with a sledgehammer and crowbars.

One of the President's aides jogged over to the MPs and demanded, "What's going on here?"

"Somebody used Krazy Glue on the door locks!" the ranking MP answered.

With special funding directed by the President, the station staff had recently upgraded the physical security at the broadcast studio building. They had two teams of contractors install heavy vault-like steel doors, and anti-vehicular barricades designed to stop suicide drivers or remotely controlled vehicle-borne IEDs (VBIEDs). But imprudently, there had not been a corresponding increase in manpower, to provide someone to guard the building 24/7. The building was left unoccupied and unguarded between 1 and 5:30 a.m., five nights a week.

An empty tube of cyanoacrylate epoxy was found near one of the doors and bagged as evidence. The lock cylinders of every door were frozen in place. After resorting to using a cutting torch, they finally got into the building just twenty minutes before Hutchings was scheduled to go on the air.

Once inside, the studio staff found some of the inner door locks similarly jammed, but they were less of an obstacle. A couple of quick blows from a sledgehammer opened each door. The staff fumbled with flashlights, trying to determine why the lights weren't working. They soon found that the saboteur or saboteurs had removed all the circuit breakers from the main breaker box. The floor cameras had their lenses smashed, but a spare handheld camera from the mobile van was brought in and set up on a tripod. Maynard Hutchings finally went on the air twenty-five minutes late, "due to technical difficulties," and without his usual makeup.

Wearing a tailored suit that couldn't conceal his ample girth, Hutchings began his speech:

> My fellow Americans: The United States is slowly recovering from the greatest tragedy in its history. I

have recently been provided a detailed report on the extent of the catastrophe from the administration's chief scientists. Some of the report's findings are as follows: In the past three years, an estimated 160 million of our citizens have died. Most died from starvation, exposure, and disease. Of the deaths by disease, more than 65 million were caused by the influenza pandemic that swept the eastern seaboard. Without antibiotics available, the disease ran rampant until there were no more hosts left to attack in the heavily populated regions.

At least 28 million are estimated to have been killed in lawless violence. In addition, more than five million have died of complications of preexisting medical problems such as diabetes, heart disease, hemophilia, AIDS, and kidney disease. Hundreds of thousands more have died of complications of tonsilitis, appendicitis, and other ailments that were heretofore not life-threatening. The distribution of population losses ranged from in excess of 96 percent in some northeastern metropolitan areas to less than 5 percent in a few areas in the High Plains, Rocky Mountains, the intermountain areas of the West, and the inland Northwest. Order has been restored in only a few states, but we are making rapid progress.

As you are no doubt aware, the economy is still in complete disarray. The formerly existing transportation and communications systems have been completely disrupted. In the coming months, our biggest priority will be on revitalizing the petroleum and refining industries of Oklahoma, Texas, and Louisiana. Next, we will strive to get electric power back online in as many areas as possible. With bulk fuel, natural gas, and electrical power available, it is hoped that agriculture and the many industries critical to our nation's economic health will be re-established.

Here at Fort Knox, we have taken the lead in rebuilding a new United States. Already, with the help of security forces from other United Nations countries, we have pacified the states of Kentucky, Tennessee, Mississippi, and Alabama. But there is much more to be done. America must be put back on its feet again economically. Never again can we allow the economy to get so out of control. Strict economic policies will ensure that there will never be a repeat of the Crash. Wages and prices will, by necessity, be controlled by the central government. Many industries will have to be government-owned or government-controlled, at least in the foreseeable future. Reasonable limits on the press will stop the spread of unfounded rumors. Until order is completely restored, the federal and state constitutions have been temporarily suspended, and nationwide martial law is in effect. The single legitimate seat of power is here at Fort Knox. It is only with central planning that things can be put back in order rapidly and efficiently.

Kentucky, Tennessee, Mississippi, and Alabama are already under the control of nine United Nations subregional administrators. I will soon be dispatching UN regional and subregional administrators to the other areas that have independently reestablished order. These include Maine, New Hampshire, and Vermont, the southern portion of Georgia, most of Texas, part of Louisiana, most of Colorado, southwestern Oregon, all of Idaho, all of Utah, eastern Washington, all of Wyoming, and most of North and South Dakota.

The UN regional administrators will oversee the many tasks required to accomplish a complete national recovery. For example, they will be setting up regional police forces, which will be under their direct control. They will oversee the issuance of the National ID Card. They will appoint judges that they deem properly qualified. Each regional administrator will bring with him on his staff a regional tax collector and a regional treasurer who will handle issuance of the new national currency. Rest assured that the new currency is fully backed by the gold reserves of the national depository. I hope that you, my fellow citizens, will do everything in your ability to assist your new regional administrators, the subregional administrators, their staffs, and those that they appoint under them. Only with your cooperation will America be able to quickly restore itself to its former greatness.

The applause from the small audience was digitally augmented to make it sound like a huge crowd.

There was then a staged question-and-answer session, with low-level ProvGov cabinet staffers posing as journalists.

The first stood and asked, "Mr. President, how would you summarize our government's relations with UNPROFOR, and how would you characterize the current security situation in the country?"

Hutchings cleared his throat and responded, again looking at his notes. "I have been gratified to see the outstanding cooperation shown by the UN Partners for Peace. Our recent victories over the bandits in Michigan and Colorado and the rapidly decreasing rates of terrorist acts and banditry indicate that we are winning and the terrorists are losing ground. Things are getting better."

Another pseudo-reporter took to his feet and asked, "Mr. President, when will elections be scheduled?"

Hutchings beamed. "There will be regional elections real soon. But the security situation in certain parts of the country, particularly west of the Missouri River, might preclude other elections for a while."

After the live airing, they decided to have him repeat the speech the next day and do another digital camera recording, with makeup and better preparation.

Five days after Hutchings's speech, a firing squad from the Fort Knox Provost Marshal's Office executed the television studio saboteur. He was the thirteen-year-old son of an Ordnance Corps major who was stationed at the fort and lived off-post in Radcliff.

The boy's mother worked as a secretary at the television station. With access to his mother's purse, the boy stole her keys and her address book that had the building's alarm system passcode. Unbeknownst to his parents, he bundled up in warm clothes and slipped out of the house at midnight. He rode his bicycle to a gap in the Fort Knox perimeter fence—known to all the teenagers in their subdivision—and then rode to the station. He then spent two hours smashing equipment, stealing circuit breakers, and gluing door locks. His mother found the backpack full of circuit breakers, and he soon confessed what he'd done, explaining that he'd been inspired by seeing the movie *Max Manus*, about the Norwegian resistance during World War II. "I'm like Max," he told his father. "Sometimes you have to be daring and do what you think is right, regardless of any risk of getting caught. So I decided I'd just go for it."

Two days after the boy's execution, the major and his wife were also executed by a firing squad. They were shot at the remote and rarely used Yano Tank Range. There were no digital photos taken to document the executions. Their bodies went into unmarked graves. President Hutchings later explained: "Parents should be held accountable for their children's actions."

windowless back room. She, her son, Tyree, and her grandmother Lily lived in the apartment upstairs.

Sheila was quick to react to changes like the ProvGov's new currency and gun laws. One of the new gun laws was a restriction on arsenals that put a limit of 500 rounds of ammunition per home. This absurdly included .22 rimfire ammunition that had long been sold in retail boxes of 500 or 550. Sheila benefited from an exemption in the ammunition law for stocking stores. This allowed her to have up to 40,000 rounds on hand at any given time. Sheila seized this as an opportunity, offering to trade ammunition for any of her inventory. Within a week, the value of her inventory jumped, as people rapidly made trades to react to the changing legal landscape. When townsmen dumped their excess ammo in trade at Sheila's store, it added tremendously to the volume of her business.

Recognizing the significance of the exemption for pre-1899 guns from the new registration requirements for rifles and shotguns, Sheila bought every antique gun that she could find. Her landlord, Hollan Combs, loaned her a printout of a Pre-1899 Firearms FAQ from the Internet that he had put in his file cabinet before the Crunch. It listed the serial number thresholds for guns that would allow her to determine which ones had receivers that were made in or before 1898, and those that were 1899 or later. Any modern guns required registration under the ProvGov's new law. Sheila photocopied the FAQ on a day that the utility power was on so that she could return the original to Hollan. She posted the FAQ in document protectors, tacked up immediately below her store's rack of antique rifles and shotguns.

As resistance to the new government grew and the Gun Amnesty deadline loomed, her customers soon migrated into two distinct camps. The first camp were those who scrambled to get rid of any guns that were banned or any supplies of ammunition that exceeded the 500-round arsenal threshold or that was of a restricted

20

Fire Mission

"Money is a mirror of civilization. Throughout history, whenever we find good, reliable noninflated money, we almost always find a strong, healthy civilization. Whenever we find unreliable, inflated money, we almost always find a civilization in decay."
— Richard J. Maybury, *Whatever Happened to Penny Candy?* (2010)

Bradfordsville, Kentucky
December, the Second Year

Sheila Randall's general store had prospered since the Crunch. As the proprietor of the only store in town that showed the flexibility to barter and with the courage to stay open amid the chaos, she had attracted customers from a wide radius. She had opened the store shortly after the Crunch began, soon after her husband had been murdered. A savvy barterer, Sheila had parlayed a small pre-Crunch investment in gardening seeds into a burgeoning inventory of everything from locally produced honey and sorghum to tools, ammunition, kitchen utensils, canning jars and lids, bolts of cloth, gloves, cans of kerosene, home-canned vegetables, rat traps, garden and mechanic tools, and dozens of other items. Starting with an empty storefront and with just the help of her ten-year-old son and her spry eighty-five-year-old grandmother, Lily Voison, her inventory soon grew to fill the store's display room. Sheila then built up a substantial overstock that eventually filled the store's

type. The other camp consisted of those who were trying to rapidly build up batteries of guns for resistance to the government.
To them, the arbitrary ammo quantity limit and the distinction of
the pre-1899 exemption meant very little, so they willingly traded
their antique guns to Sheila for full-capacity magazines and large
quantities of military-caliber ammunition. They sought calibers
such as 9mm Parabellum, .45 ACP, 5.56 NATO, 7.62 NATO, and
.30-06. The 5.45x39 and 7.62x39 ammunition for Kalashnikovs
was also highly sought after. This put Sheila in a key position as a
middleman and launched her into a blur of activity that caused her
store's inventory to rapidly shift and grow.

Since they were sympathetic to the Resistance, the local sheriff's deputies turned a blind eye to the gun and ammunition trading that took place at the store. Many of these trades were made
after-hours, in the store's back room. As guerrilla activity grew, a
huge array of guns that had been hidden—some since as far back
as 1934—began to be pulled out of basements and de-greased and
oiled. The citizens of Kentucky and Tennessee had long been no-
torious for owning unregistered machineguns. Sheila was amazed
when she was asked to find magazines for BARs, Thompson sub-
machineguns, M3 Greaseguns, M2 Carbines, MP40 Schmeissers,
a Swedish K, and even a French MAT-49. Here again, Sheila acted
as the middleman and prospered. She realized that she was taking
some risks, but she wanted to take full advantage of the amnesty
time frame. Thankfully, the amnesty in Kentucky, as the seat of
the new national government, was extended to sixty days. Those
sixty days were some of the most hectic days of her life.

Before the window of opportunity for the amnesty closed,
Sheila had accumulated more than 6,000 rounds of assorted ammunition and sixteen antique guns. These included three early-
production Winchester Model 1897 shotguns, five double-barreled
shotguns from various makers, a Burgess pump shotgun, a Colt
Lightning pump rifle in .38-40, nine lever-action Winchesters in

various calibers, a Winchester Model 1890 pump-action .22, two Marlin lever-actions, and a Model 1894 Swedish Mauser carbine that had been rechambered to .257 Roberts. Most of these guns soon filled the rack on the back wall of the store, to the amazement of her customers. For each, she could document their "exempt" status, so she displayed them with impunity. A prominent sign above the gun rack read: "Pre-1899 Antique Guns. Trade for Ammo or Silver Coins Only!" Realizing that their exemption from the new gun law made them a rarity, Sheila put very high prices on the guns.

She set aside three of the antique guns for her own use: A Model 1892 .44-40 carbine that she kept loaded behind the front counter, a Winchester Model 1897 12-gauge takedown shotgun with a nineteen-inch barrel (for Tyree to use while standing guard in the back room), and the Swedish Mauser (dated 1895 on the receiver ring) that she kept upstairs. Since .257 Roberts was an odd caliber, she set aside all of it that she had acquired for the store inventory—just sixty rounds.

There were just two guns that she had to make disappear before the registration amnesty ended. These were her Remington 20 Gauge Model 870 "Youth" gun, and her .41 Colt revolver. She hid the revolver in a seed broadcaster among the clutter of merchandise that hung from nails on the walls of the back room. She had Tyree coat the shotgun inside and out with automotive grease and bury it in a fifty-two-inch length of six-inch-diameter PVC pipe in the hills just outside town. Also greased and packed away in the same tube was an assortment of twenty-three rifle and pistol magazines that she hadn't sold or traded away quickly enough. Most of the excess space in the tube was taken up by boxes and socks filled with 20-gauge shotgun shells. She also included $40 face value in silver dimes, quarters, and half dollars for a cash reserve. Her wise grandmother Lily had urged including the silver coins, reasoning that they shouldn't keep all their eggs in one basket.

The caching tube was glued shut with standard end caps, using clear PVC cement. Sheila would have preferred to use a threaded end cap at one end, but those were almost impossible to find after the Crunch. To eventually open the tube she would have to use a hacksaw. Before the tube was glued shut, Sheila inserted six large silica gel desiccant packets to absorb any moisture inside the container.

The length of PVC pipe was buried next to a large, distinctive boulder at the edge of an abandoned dump. Tyree reasoned that the boulder was unlikely ever to be moved, and that the clutter of rusty cans in the dump would make it impossible for anyone to ever find the cache with a metal detector.

The Prine Farm, Morgan City, Utah
June, the Third Year

Just seventeen days after they had sent out the last of the letters to Idaho, Ken was helping Larry Prine clean his chimney. As Larry was threading on another rod section, he heard a vehicle approaching. Glancing up to size up the situation, Larry shouted down from the roof, "There's a vehicle coming in!"

Ken grabbed his rifle and stepped to the front door to investigate. An older Ford Bronco pulled into the Prines' lane and approached the house. The Bronco's roof had been removed, and its windshield was flipped down and covered with burlap. Two men in camouflage uniforms and wearing Kevlar helmets were in the front seats. As the vehicle got closer to the farmhouse, Ken recognized his friend Tom Kennedy's vehicle—despite the fact that it was being driven with its windshield flipped down and it had a new cable cutter attached to its front bumper. Then he recognized the faces of Dan Fong and Kevin Lendel. Without hesitation, he ran out to greet them.

Ken was wearing a huge grin as Dan Fong braked the Bronco to a halt and shut down the engine. "What, only two of you came?" Ken joked. "I figured you'd have at least three or four guys."

Kevin looked down, fighting back tears. Then he replied, "We *were* three, but we're just two now."

He motioned with his thumb at the pair of jungle boots protruding from the end of the rolled-up ponchos.

After a few moments, Kevin blinked his eyes heavily and said in a broken voice, "It's T.K."

The expression on Layton's face melted.

Ken walked back to the tailgate and stared down at Tom Kennedy's shrouded body. With his voice wavering, Layton said, "If I'd known something like this was going to happen, I'd have never sent word to the retreat. This . . . this is all my fault."

Dan shook his head and said, "It wasn't your fault, dude. It's rough wherever you go out there. We all knew the risks. But we're your friends. Some things are a lot more important than your personal safety. It was a matter of honor."

Ken took some time to stand over Tom Kennedy's body and pray. Kevin and Dan stood a polite distance away. As Ken turned back toward them, they could see tears running down his cheeks. They shared a three-way hug.

Terry hobbled out the front door of the farmhouse on a pair of homemade crutches. Ken went to her and explained what had happened. "I've never been so happy and so sad at the same time before in my life," he said.

While refueling and packing up the Bronco early the next morning, Kevin Lendel gave the Prine family the sealed plastic buckets of food that they had brought along, as well as four gasoline jerry cans, one of which was still partly full. This provided enough room for the Laytons and their gear. Dan liked the idea of getting rid of the empty gas cans, explaining that emptied gas cans containing vapors were more explosive than full ones.

After making their goodbyes, packing Ken and Terry's gear

was quick and easy. All that they had were their rifles, web gear, ALICE packs, and Terry's new crutches. Ken and Terry gave the Prines hugs, and they were off. None of them could avoid occasionally looking at T.K.'s shrouded body. It served to subdue what otherwise would have been an animated conversation.

As they began their drive, Dan Fong explained what had happened. "We ran into two looter roadblocks on the way down here. T.K. got shot when we got stopped at the second one. Not much more to say, except that we snuck back there that same night, and made those SOBs pay for it."

The trip to Todd Gray's ranch near Bovill, Idaho, was uneventful. From the experience of their trip down, Dan and Kevin knew how to pick their return route to avoid trouble. More than halfway home, they made a cold camp about ten miles from where they had camped two nights before. They consciously avoided using the same spot twice.

Todd's ranch was just as the Laytons had remembered it. The undulating hills of the eastern Palouse region were here mostly covered by timber. Everyone at the retreat house ran outdoors for what turned out to be a bittersweet reunion.

They buried T.K. the next day.

Bloomfield, New Mexico
June, the Third Year

L. Roy Martin, who owned the Bloomfield Refinery, formed a resistance cell. Martin had been disgusted to see the Provisional Government act like errand boys for the United Nations, bowing to their every demand. It sickened him to see the nation's sovereignty discarded for the sake of convenience and exigency. With service experience as an Army Strategic Communications (STRATCOM) officer, L. Roy thought that his skills could best be used to help develop signals intelligence for the Resistance. As a man of action, it was just a short step for him to transition from his hobby of monitoring the radio spectrum haphazardly for his own interest to monitoring it actively and systematically to gather intelligence for the Resistance.

As the UNPROFOR army approached New Mexico, L. Roy moved his amateur radio equipment to a thirty-foot-long CONEX overseas shipping container near the back of the refinery complex. This became a Communications Intelligence (COMINT) intercept and analysis facility. Martin and his men bolted equipment racks to the walls in case the CONEX ever had to be moved in a hurry.

Martin led a team of five ham radio operators, a traffic analyst, and three courier runners who manned the CONEX container mini–field station twenty-four hours a day, gathering and summarizing signals intelligence. Their summaries were then relayed to other resistance organizations via the couriers, mainly using USB thumb drives. On rare occasions, they also sent some urgent messages via encrypted packet radio from vehicle-mounted ham rigs. When they did so, they were always careful to be in motion and at least fifteen miles away from the intercept site whenever they transmitted. They didn't want to become the victims of their counterparts within the UNPROFOR.

The gear inside the field station CONEX included a pair of R-390A HF receivers, two Sherwood SE-3 synchronous detectors, four hardwired demodulators, a half dozen multiband scanners, several digital audio recorders, two spectrum analyzers, and seven laptop computers that were loaded with demodulators, digital recorders, and decryption/encryption software.

In the back of the CONEX was a large map board with United States and Four Corners region maps and a large whiteboard. The whiteboard was used by the traffic analyst (or "TA"). His job was to analyze the "externals" of the message traffic, to try to determine the relationships between the units and their missions—namely, who was subordinate to whom, and hopefully from this more about their locales, intentions, and order of battle. His references were the U.S. Army's TA-103 Traffic Analyst course book, and the Air Force Security Command (AFSC) Radio Traffic Analysis (RTA) manual, which had both been declassified just a few years before the Crunch.

The AC power for the field station—to run the radios, lights, and heater/air conditioner—came from the refinery's co-generated power, but it could just as well have used grid power, or power from mobile generators. It was also possible to use less stable power from generators because everything in the CONEX except the air conditioner and heater used "cleaned up" power. This was accomplished by passing the current through an uninterruptable power supply (UPS).

Martin had his dipole and sloper antennas rigged so that they could rapidly be disassembled and hidden. He had "MTBE," "MSDS #3557," and "Toxic—Keep Out" spray-stenciled on the CONEX's doors in large letters. Below, a sign in smaller print read:

> **Warning: Methyl tert-butyl Ether (MTBE). EXTREMELY FLAMMABLE—EYE AND MUCOUS MEMBRANE IRRITANT—AFFECTS CENTRAL NERVOUS SYSTEM—HARMFUL OR FATAL IF SWALLOWED—ASPIRATION HAZARD. Do not open this container unless wearing respirator and protective suit! Per MSDS 3557: High fire hazard. Keep away from heat, spark, open flame, and other ignition sources.**
>
> **Contact may cause eye, skin, and mucous membrane irritation. Avoid prolonged breathing of vapors or mists. Inhalation may cause irritation, anesthetic effects (dizziness, nausea, headache, intoxication), and**

respiratory system effects. If ingested, do NOT in-
duce vomiting, as this may cause chemical pneumonia (fluid in the lungs).

The team left a dozen empty 55-gallon drums sitting just outside the CONEX doors. These drums also had convincing-looking
MTBE markings stenciled on them and they all had their bungs
sealed shut. In the event that the team had to camouflage their operation from officials, they could pile up the barrels just inside the
door, blocking the view of the electronic racks and chairs, which
sat farther back, behind a blackout curtain. A pint can of paint
thinner was kept handy, so that the floor inside the doors could be
doused to give the CONEX a convincing aroma.

Several times, Martin's team practiced disconnecting the antennas and "shore power" to the CONEX and securing the rolling
chairs. They then loaded it onto an eighteen-wheel truck that had
a self-loader. Their goal was to be able to displace tactically with
just fifteen minutes notice. They eventually got their time down
to sixteen minutes. In the event that it ever became necessary to
relocate where there wasn't grid power, they also had two pickup
trucks towing generator trailers that would go with them.

Once the UNPROFOR troops had entered the Four Corners region, L. Roy opted to leave the CONEX on the truck at all times,
giving them the ability to displace even more quickly. They soon
became accustomed to climbing the ladder to access the CONEX,
regardless of the weather.

After word came that the Federals were on their way to Farmington, they relocated the CONEX to a large gas drilling equipment yard halfway between Bloomfield and Farmington. There, the
CONEX was lost in the clutter of rusting compressors, drip tanks,
boom trucks, stacks of pipe, and other shipping containers.

A 250-vehicle UNPROFOR convoy rolled into Farmington.
They soon established smaller garrisons in Bloomfield and Aztec.

A "protection team" was dispatched to L. Roy Martin's refinery, escorting Chambers Clarke, a former fertilizer salesman who was the deputy minister of information for the Hutchings administration. Clarke had been specially tasked with securing key strategic assets, such as refineries and large power plants, as the UNPRO-FOR's pacification campaign continued.

In a private conversation with his plant manager, Phil McReady, three days before the UN forces arrived, Martin had said, "The guys from the pacification contact team from the Fort Knox government will be here tomorrow. What I want you to do is quietly tell everyone to just play along, and carry on operations as usual. We want to lull the ProvGov to sleep, thinking that our refinery is safely *their* refinery and that the Navajo coal mine and the power plants are *theirs*, too. We need to make them assume that there won't be much resistance in the Four Corners region. That way, they'll leave just a small garrison and move on. But right under their noses, we'll be diverting fuel and lubricants to resistance groups all over the Southwest. I've already discussed this with the tribal elders."

McReady nodded, and Martin continued, "So tell everyone: *Do not* sabotage any equipment or interrupt any processes. We're the only ones who know how to operate this plant, so it will continue to be ours. It's a lot like things were in Italy under the fascists."

Phil grinned hugely and said, "So the trains still run on time, even though we're plotting against *Il Duce*, and providing logistics for *la resitenza*."

L. Roy shouted, *"Minuziosamente!"* They shook hands.

The next day, L. Roy's conversation with Chambers Clarke lasted less than an hour. Clarke came across as a saccharine-sweet character, full of promises about ProvGov protection and sumptuous benefits in exchange for nationalization of the refinery and its associated pipeline infrastructure.

Recognizing the UNPROFOR's disproportionate firepower, L. Roy feigned a cooperative, pro-Hutchings attitude. But he bargained hard for salaries for all his employees, even carving out a concession that part of their pay would still be in the form of bartered fuel. Only two days after the Federals arrived, L. Roy turned day-to-day operations of the refinery over to Phil McReady.

Martin publicly announced that he planned to take "a well-deserved and much delayed fishing vacation." But after just two days at his ranch, he started working two twelve-hour shifts each week at the CONEX. Later, once it was clear that his actions weren't attracting suspicion, he increased his workload to four twelve-hour shifts per week.

Just as he had been doing before the UN forces arrived, Martin kept his SIGINT team small, realizing that one any larger was sure to be detected or infiltrated. The core of Martin's team was Pat Wicher, a retired Air Force senior master sergeant (SMSgt) who had for many years been on the cadre of joint service field stations for the Air Force Security Command (AFSC). Wicher had worked all over the world at both tactical and strategic levels, communications intelligence (COMINT), and electronic intelligence (ELINT) intercept and analysis. A good portion of the gear at the refinery's intercept site came out of the collection in Wicher's garage and attic. Wicher had squirreled away an impressive array of electronics. Most importantly, he owned two spectrum analyzers—a continuous swept-tuned analyzer and a wideband snapshot analyzer. These were crucial for the mini–field station's mission. With them, rather than simply scanning through the spectrum, they could see signal spikes where they could then quickly tune. Wicher even knew how to use an oscilloscope to realign receivers. L. Roy was constantly amazed at the breadth and depth of Pat's knowledge.

Partly because the ProvGov could no longer rely on an intact technological infrastructure to keep encrypted and frequency-hopping radios working, and in part because of their arrogant condescension, they made many transmissions "in the clear" and they used obsolete encryption methods such as Four-square and Playfair substitution ciphers, which were easily broken. Because they assumed that the Resistance was not listening in some bands or that their ciphers could not be broken, the ProvGov and its army often had its communications compromised. This yielded a wealth of practical intelligence to the Resistance.

L. Roy Martin's team very rarely transmitted, and only then in the HF band via skywave, because it was very difficult to locate via direction finding other than via groundwave in the immediate vicinity of the transmitter.

Bloomfield, New Mexico
August, the Third Year

At their ranch near Bloomfield, New Mexico, Lars Laine and his brother Andrew launched into another one of their conversations about resistance to the Provisional Government. The brothers were both Army veterans. The elder brother, Lars, had been given a disability discharge in the aftermath of a roadside bomb explosion. That incident cost him a hand, an eye, and the hearing in one ear. The younger brother, Andy, had been released from active duty as a captain at the end of his six-year contractual obligation, just as the Crunch was unfolding. He was stranded in Germany, with all military and commercial airline flights grounded. He resorted to buying a bicycle and trailer, and pedaling across Germany and France. On the coast of France, he used part of his dwindling supply of small gold and silver coins to pay for passage to England on a French fishing boat. From there, he pedaled up the east coast, finally finding work as a hired security man on a yacht that would soon sail for Belize. In Belize, following an ambush by bandits that left him with a broken leg, Andy bought a horse and made his way by horseback up through

Mexico, crossed into Texas, and finally made his way back to the family's ranch in New Mexico.

Lars and Andy had spent the evening in the "radio shack" corner of the master bedroom, listening to the massive Scott SLRM multiband radio that had belonged to their late father. The old vacuum tube radio was originally designed for use on U.S. Navy ships, just before World War II. It was a very robust boat anchor design that weighed eighty-five pounds. The radio's most distinguishing feature was that it had a green cathode ray tuning eye. The front of the cabinet was stained yellow-brown with tobacco smoke from its original Navy service. The radio was powered by an isolation transformer, which was considered a must for safety with these radios, because of the shock hazard of running one without isolation.

Lars and Andy had spent the evening tuning through the 40-meter and 80-meter amateur bands on the Scott radio, listening to ham conversations about the Provisional Government. The consensus seemed to be that the new government was illegitimate and had a penchant for larceny. Although both Lars and Andy had ham radio licenses, they rarely keyed up, preferring to gather intelligence without raising their profiles.

Lars turned off the big radio and they launched into a fairly loud conversation about the ProvGov. When Lars's wife, Lisbeth, and Andy's wife, Kaylee, overheard this talk they sat down on the edge of the bed and listened intently.

Bloomfield, New Mexico, is just east of Farmington, in the Four Corners region, where the boundaries of Colorado, Utah, New Mexico, and Arizona meet. The region was rich in natural gas and coal. The only child at the farm was Lars and Beth's daughter, Grace, who was six years old when the Crunch began. They also had three young hired men who worked as their in-house security and ranch hands.

Lars and Andy debated how to best resist the Provisional Government and their "guest" UN peacekeepers. They discussed some options, including sabotage, establishing a clandestine newspaper or radio station, computer viruses, and even raids or ambushes. They briefly discussed assassination. Lars compared the looting of the country with armed robbery, saying, "The only thing that can stop a bad man with a gun is a good man with a gun."

"That's true," Andy countered, "but there are a couple of problems. How would someone get close enough? And more importantly, from what I've heard, Hutchings is a figurehead. The real seat of power is at the new UN headquarters."

Eventually, the conversation turned to reconnaissance of Fort Knox itself. Lars mentioned that Fort Knox had traditionally been the home of the U.S. Army's Armor Corps, but that role had shifted to Fort Benning, Georgia, in 2007. Then, just before the Crunch, the tanker school had been moved back to Fort Knox for political reasons. Lars said, "Things have been so fluid, it is difficult to get a grasp on their order of battle. We need to know where the units are, and any planned troop movements, adjustments to TO&Es, and specific task organization changes or operational control arrangements."

"Well, somebody's got to go there to scope things out," Andy insisted.

"I could go," Lars offered.

"No, after your trip to Arizona to whomp on the looters, it's my turn for some travel. Besides, I'm the one with the pink Army Reserve ID card. You've got a retiree's card. You'd have to argue your way past your injuries. It's more logical for me to go."

Lars cocked his head and asked: "What are you talking about?"

"I'm talking about going back on active duty."

"What? Are you serious, actually *join* the ProvGov army?"

"That's right," Andy answered. "There's no better place to gather intelligence than right in the belly of the beast. Anything less would just be some halfhearted poking around at the periphery—you know, sort of like the old fable about the blind men feeling different parts of the elephant. If we really want to get a clear picture of what's going on and send back some meaningful intel, then it's the most logical thing to do."

His wife, Kaylee, chimed in: "You can go, but only if I'm going with you."

Before they departed, Andy and Kaylee made contact with her family, the Schmidts, in New Braunfels, Texas. Being sympathetic with the Resistance, they agreed to help courier messages. They already had contacts in Kentucky, and they were confident that they could help set up a courier network.

Andy soon put out the call locally for purchase or donations of USB flash memory thumb drives or pen drive sticks. Within a few days, they had accumulated almost 200 of them. More than half of these were 2-GB sticks that were silkscreened with a Nacel Energy logo. These were leftovers from a trade show giveaway, donated to the Resistance by a former Nacel marketing department employee.

Packing up took only a day and a half. They were satisfied the ranch would be safe in their absence. The Laines' three teenage hired hands—the Phelps brothers—were gaining confidence, competence, and strength as time went on. But more than anything else, Andy was concerned with the well-being of his sturdy gelding horse, Prieto. He had ridden the horse all the way from Belize to New Mexico, so he was particularly fond of him. Lars promised to groom and exercise Prieto regularly.

The box trailer behind Andy Laine's pickup was completely full of gas cans. In all, they carried twenty-three cans. Theoretically, between the gas in the cans and what was in the pickup's tank, they could drive 1,914 miles.

They brought only three guns with them: Andy's SIG P228 pistol, his Mosin-Nagant bolt-action, and Kaylee's Browning

Hi-Power. The latter, along with 100 rounds of ammunition, two spare magazines, and a holster, was hidden wedged inside a mounted spare tire. It would take a bead-breaking tool (which they also carried) to access the gun, but they felt confident that it would not be found even in a rigorous search. To conceal it, they chose their one tire rim that was painted differently from the others to avoid any confusion.

For emergency communication with the Resistance, Andy also brought his Elecraft KX1 QRP shortwave transceiver. This low-power transceiver could be used to transmit Morse code in the 20-, 30-, 40-, and 80-meter ham radio bands. Powered by six AA batteries, the ten-ounce radio was capable of transmitting around the world when ionospheric conditions were right. It put out just 1 to 2 watts of power on the internal batteries, or up to 4 watts if using an external 12-volt battery or AC power adapter. Using his 200-watt Kenwood HF transceiver in Texas, Lars had had several successful two-way contacts with Andy when he was in Afghanistan, even though his younger brother's transmitter put out only "flea power."

Andy knew that the transmitter would be vulnerable to radio direction finding if he used it within forty miles of Fort Knox or any other HF intercept site. So he decided that he would use the transmitter only briefly, and then only in the event of an emergency.

21

TDY—Temporary Duty, Yonder

"You must never confuse faith that you will prevail in the end—which you can never afford to lose—with the discipline to confront the most brutal facts of your current reality, whatever they might be."
—Vice Admiral James B. Stockdale, a former prisoner of war in North Vietnam, as quoted by James C. Collins in his book *Good to Great* (2001)

Amarillo, Texas
August, the Third Year

They knew that they had crossed over into UNPROFOR-controlled territory when they crossed the Texas state line. But they didn't see any signs of the UNPROFOR occupation until they reached the outskirts of Amarillo. Someone had spray-painted a concrete highway overpass with the words "U.N. Out!!!" A half mile beyond that they began to see powder-blue billboards that read, "U.N. Partners for Peace. Building a Better Tomorrow." On one of them, someone had expertly vandalized the sign with spray paint to instead read, "U.N. Partners for Piss. Building Maynard's Tomorrow."

At the Georgia Street exit, there was a sign added that read: "UN-MNF HQ." Andy took the off-ramp and said with a gulp, "Well, this is it."

The UNPROFOR outpost was in a large parking lot beside an abandoned Walmart Supercenter with a collapsed roof, at the corner of Georgia Street and Canyon Drive.

The fence around the outpost was seven strands of concertina wire piled three courses deep, erected in a defensive donut. A light blue UN flag hung limply on a pole near the front gate. Most of the vehicles inside the wire were HMMWVs, but there were also a few Caiman and MaxxPro mine-resistant ambush-protected (MRAP) vehicles.

A sign proclaimed:

322nd M.P. Bde.
Force Prot./Civil Affairs
"Bad to the Bone"
UN-MNF Command
UNPROFOR Region 6
No Civilians Beyond This Point

Andy Laine parked the pickup and trailer 100 yards away from the concertina wire. It was a hot, still day. They cracked open the windows for ventilation. Andy said resignedly, "Okay. Wish me luck."

Kaylee kissed his cheek and said, "Not luck. I'll be praying for you."

Andy was wearing a set of ACUs—faded from many washings—and an ACU boonie hat. He had black "railroad track" captain's bars pinned on his hat and Velcroed in the center of his chest on his ACUs. He wore a "Laine" nametape above his right breast pocket, but just a blank Velcro patch above the left pocket, since he had heard that wearing a "U.S. Army" tape was considered an offense. Empty-handed, Andy carried only his holstered pistol.

He approached the gate guards and pulled his Army Reserve ID card from his pocket. He handed it to a pimply-faced PFC who was wearing an MP shoulder brassard and carrying a well-worn M16A2 with a badly scratched polymer P-MAG. The soldier was well enough trained to know how to salute with his rifle, bringing it smartly parallel with the centerline of his body. Andy returned the salute and said, "I need to talk with your S1."

The young MP answered, "Yes, sir. You need to go to the longest trailer, there on the left. I'll get you an escort."

The brigade headquarters consisted of four single-width trailers of the type that Andy had formerly seen used at construction sites. A generator set whined in the distance. HESCO bastions filled with sand ringed the perimeter. The scene reminded Andy too much of what he had seen in the Middle East. But now *he* was an insurgent.

Laine was ushered into a spartan trailer office with steel furniture. Two box fans roared in open windowsills. A first lieutenant wearing OCP camouflage utilities, with a "UNPROFOR" nametape, sat behind the desk. A hand-inked sign taped on the front of his desk read: "1LT Taylor—S1." He rose to his feet when he saw the captain's bars on Laine's chest.

The lieutenant offered Laine a seat, and then gave him an expectant look. Laine handed the lieutenant his pink Army Reserve ID card, saying, "I'm here to volunteer to go back on active duty."

Across the room, the MP brigade commander—a full colonel—listened in on their conversation as he worked sorting a stack of papers.

Lieutenant Taylor asked, "Where did you go to school?"

"Texas A&M."

"Were you 'Band' or 'Corps'?" Taylor retorted.

Andy flashed a grin of recognition at a fellow Aggie. "Corps of Cadets. I was on a four-year ROTC scholarship. I got branched Ordnance, but after OBC, I was mainly given branch immaterial slots. You know, to fill 'the needs of the Army.' I did a tour in Afghanistan with Task Force Duke, as the S4 for a Stryker battalion. The Crunch came down just when my active duty obligation ended."

Lieutenant Taylor nodded, and said, "I see."

"So, are you looking for Reserve officers for active slots?" Andy asked.

"Absolutely. We have far more active duty positions than we have qualified officers. There are detached companies out on the frontier that are bringing back every former commissioned officer who is willing—even some retirees in their late fifties. I even met a former Coast Guard officer who's now a commissioned Army officer, leading troops."

"So how do I come on board?"

"That's at the CO's discretion—any commanding officer of a brigade or higher can make the call. There are no review boards or any of that bureaucratic bravo sierra."

Glancing down, Taylor continued, "Sir, before we proceed, I have to ask you to surrender that pistol. Civilian pistols are contraband."

Andy raised his index finger and said, "Wait just a minute, I've got a hand receipt for it."

Andy opened his wallet and pulled out a soiled and deeply creased document. The lieutenant examined it and looked up at Laine. "Sir, this hand receipt is on the Old Army form and it's dated *three years* ago."

"I can explain. Before I left active duty in Germany, I had T.I.'ed my M4 Carbine and TA-50 gear. But since things were so chaotic, I kept the SIG out on hand receipt for my personal protection while I was in transit. You have no idea how FUBAR things were at the time in Germany."

Lieutenant Taylor nodded, and Laine continued. "At that point all commercial flights were grounded and there were no MAC flights. So I literally got on a bicycle and pedaled across Germany, across France, took a fishing boat to England, got back on my bicycle, and rode up the English coast until I found a sailboat that was heading for Central America. Then, from

Belize I rode horseback all the way up through Mexico and back to my home in New Mexico. I haven't been to a U.S. military installation in three years. So, you can see, I had no opportunity to T.I. this pistol."

"Well, you can turn it in now, under the general amnesty, since you've been living outside pacified territory."

"I'm willing to do so, but I'd like you to immediately reissue it to me. Again, for my personal protection."

"That's the commander's call."

Andy said, "Fair enough." He unholstered the pistol, ejected its magazine, and cleared its chamber, locking the slide to the rear. He handed the well-worn SIG P228 to the lieutenant, butt first.

Taylor examined the pistol's serial number and compared it with the serial number on the hand receipt. He looked down at the hand receipt's signature block and gave a blink. "*Olds*? Colonel *Edward* Olds? There's a brigadier general named Edward Olds at Fort Knox. He commands a mech infantry brigade."

"If that general is the same Ed Olds," Andy said with a smile, "then he can vouch for my bona fides."

Taylor nodded.

"So, is there some sort of procedure or reg that I need to follow?" Andy asked.

Taylor gave a dismissive wave, saying, "No, sir. Regs and paperwork have gotten a lot simpler in the New Army. There is no more FORSCOM, no PERSCOM, no more echelons above Corps, and no more Officer Efficiency Reports. All the 201 files are now kept at the brigade level, and most promotions are handled internally. There are basically just *six blank forms* for everything we do, and beyond that just a few types of cards and passes."

He passed Laine a blank sheet of typewriter paper. "Take a close look."

Andy held the paper up to the light. There was a small holographic square embedded in the upper-right corner of the page. Holding the sheet up to the light, he could see that it was also watermarked "UN-MNF" at the top and it had an enormous numeric "1" watermark that covered most of the page.

Taylor explained, "The One watermark is for all personnel paperwork, Two is for intelligence reports, Three is for operations, and so on. The numbering follows all the traditional S-shop numbering."

Andy nodded.

The lieutenant opened his wallet and pulled out his ID card, a weapons card to show Laine, and continued, "The days of separate cards for TRICARE, for dining facilities, military driver's license, and all the others are *over*. Now it all comes down to just an ID card and a weapons card."

Across the room, the commander looked up from his laptop screen and said, "Go ahead and issue this gentleman both an ID card and a weapons card for his sidearm."

Taylor answered, "Will do, sir."

"That's it—that simple?" Andy asked incredulously.

"Yep, welcome to the New Army. You'll take an oath of office and have to do some bravo sierra paperwork further up the chain, but as you can see, 'Commander's Discretion' carries a lot of weight these days."

Later that week, wearing a fresh OCP uniform and a new pair of tan boots, Andy walked into the dayroom of the 1st Composite Mechanized Infantry Brigade headquarters. "Captain Laine to see General Olds, if he is available," he announced.

A gruff voice from behind him shouted, "*You bet* I'm available. Good to see you, Andrew!"

Ed Olds, wearing starched MultiCams, took two steps forward and clasped Andy around the shoulder. "I always knew that we'd cross paths again. So you're back on active duty?"

"That's right, sir."

Olds looked much the same as Laine remembered him in Germany, except that he had gone completely gray and now had a livid scar running up half the length of his left jaw, starting from just behind his chin. The single star of a brigadier general punctuated the front of his uniform. Olds motioned Andy into his office and he shut the door behind them. He pointed to the chair in front of his desk, and took his own—a massive leather swivel chair that looked antique. He glanced at Andy's upper arm, and noticed the lack of a unit patch.

Olds asked, "Do you have a duty assignment?"

"Not yet, sir."

"Well, I already have a good Loggy, but I could use someone in Plans and Operations, since my S3 is about to go out on maternity leave. Are you interested?"

"It would be an honor to work for you again, sir."

Olds reached across his desk and unplugged the cord from his telephone and the ethernet cable from his closed Dell laptop. Then, in a quieter voice, he said, "I have to ask you this BLUF—bottom line, up front: What are your feelings about the ProvGov?"

"Frankly, sir, my feelings are mixed. I want to see law and order restored, but I don't like seeing people's rights get trampled. Maybe I'm too much of a freedom lover to fit in, in the New Army."

Olds gave an almost imperceptible nod. "I'm glad to hear you say that. If you hadn't, I would've had doubts about you. You'll find that there are a lot of ruthless bastards in the New Army and in the coalition forces. We are going to face some tough issues in the months to come. And just between you and me, I want to let you know that my first and highest loyalty is to the Constitution, not to some buffoon from Mayberry named Maynard."

Laine whispered, "Likewise, sir."

Olds opened his desk drawer. After rifling through it, he pulled

22

Belly of the Beast

"The government consists of a gang of men exactly like you and me. They have, taking one with another, no special talent for the business of government; they have only a talent for getting and holding office. Their principal device to that end is to search out groups who pant and pine for something they can't get and to promise to give it to them. Nine times out of ten that promise is worth nothing. The tenth time is made good by looting A to satisfy B. In other words, government is a broker in pillage, and every election is sort of an advance auction sale of stolen goods."

—H. L. Mencken, *On Politics,* a posthumous collection of essays published in 1956

Fort Knox, Kentucky
August, the Third Year

The brigade had just one company of Stryker IFVs. All the rest of the vehicles were German Boxer wheeled APCs. Outwardly, they looked similar to the Stryker, but they differed substantially, mechanically. Built by Krauss-Maffei Wegmann & Rheinmetall, the thirty-three-ton eight-wheeled German APCs had a mix of 40mm grenade launchers and .50 caliber machineguns for their primary armament.

The Boxers dwarfed the eighteen-ton Strykers. But since the brigade's Strykers all had slat armor appliqués, they looked nearly as big as the Boxers.

out a handful of Velcro-backed divisional patches and then a bundle of small gold Oak Leaf patches—insignia for the rank of major. He slid them all across the desk toward Andy and said in a louder voice, "The job comes with a bump to O-4." After a pause, he added with a nod and his characteristic squint, "'Commander's Discretion.'"

The brigade had a "fluid" Table of Organization and Equipment (TO&E) and a polyglot of troops: roughly one third American, one third German, and an odd mix of Dutch, Belgians, Lithuanians, Estonians, Bulgarians, and Britons. A few of them wore beards. Most carried either M4s or AK-74s, although a few had FN P90 bullpup carbines. There was an assortment of handguns carried in hip or shoulder holsters, mostly Beretta M9s, Glocks, HKs, and SIGs. But there were also a few ostensibly "civilian" pistols like FN FiveSevens, FN FNPs, Springfield Armory XDs, HK USP Compacts, and a Taurus 24/7. Andy was dismayed to see that there was no standardization of uniforms or web gear, either. The net effect was that they looked like a band of mercenaries rather than a professional army. And, as Andy later described the scene to Kaylee, that is exactly what they were: mercenaries.

Andy's first walk-around in the motor pool meeting the troops and seeing the mix of vehicles and equipment was enlightening. Andy was led by the brigade's Belgian *Adjudant*—the equivalent of a U.S. Army first sergeant (E-8). The *Adjudant* was also called a *Stabsfeldwebel* by the brigade's German troops, since that was the equivalent rank in the Bundeswehr.

The vehicles were in a mix of paint schemes: Woodland CARC, desert tan, flat olive drab, and the Bundeswehr's desert camouflage. Andy was surprised to see the interiors of the IFVs were crowded by a large number of locking Hardigg boxes. They looked similar to the cases used for storing M4 carbines that Andy had seen at remote outposts in Afghanistan. But each of these was stenciled with the name and service number of an NCO or officer. And each of these cases was chained to the floor down the center aisle of each Boxer and Stryker vehicle, and secured with an assortment of padlocks. These boxes were each slightly larger than a standard footlocker. When he asked the *Adjudant* about the Hardigg boxes, Andy was told, "The ProvGov got those when they first went in to try to pacify Massachusetts. That's in the depopulated region on the East Coast—where they got hit worst with the flu and the arson riots. They cleaned out the abandoned Hardigg factory in Deerfield, Massachusetts, and came back with *truckloads* of those cases. The Hardigg box is one of the perks for everyone that's pay grade E-6 and higher, for personal property." He added with a wink, "We are promised that they are never subject to inspection." Laine concluded that seventeenth-century-style piracy had been revived in the New Army.

Seeing the AK-74s as well as a few Russian GAZ-3308 trucks in the motor pool, Andy asked if there were any Russian troops in the North American UN peacekeeping force. He was told that there were only a handful of Russian technical advisors. These were mainly "he comes with the equipment" types that accompanied specialized vehicles and electronics. Later, in reading some strategy papers, Andy learned that there were no Russian troop units because their army was badly bogged down in fighting rebels in Ukraine and the Stans. But there was a substantial quantity of Russian and former Soviet Bloc equipment brought in from Europe via Roll-on, Roll-off (RORO) ships. Most of these were older-generation second-line vehicles, including a large number of Russian and Ukrainian BTR-70 APCs, as well as the German equivalent—the SPW 70 (*Schützenpanzerwagen*).

Andy was caught up in a blur of activity as he settled into his new job. The major whom he was relieving was anxious to start her maternity leave, so she was briefing Andy nearly nonstop. He furiously took notes on a yellow legal pad. Late in the afternoon of the first day, Ed Olds rapped his West Point ring on Andy's open office door and said, "For most of my PT sessions, I run out to Heard Park and back, four days a week. Meet me in your sweats in front of my quarters tomorrow morning at 0600."

"Will do, sir," Andy answered.

The next morning, Andy walked up General Olds's driveway just as Olds was coming down the steps. Both men were dressed in well-worn Army PT sweats, with black bottoms and gray tops.

"Good to see you, Andrew. You're prompt, as always."

After wordlessly doing some stretching exercises, Andy and the general started out at a lope, running side by side. They soon settled into a steady, familiar "Jody" running pace. There was no vehicle traffic.

Ahead of them, a platoon of soldiers ran in formation singing a familiar "Jody" tune—but with some lyrics in German and Dutch. The platoon crossed the intersection in front of them, heading toward Agony Hill. Seeing them reminded Andy of when he was posted at Fort Hood five years before. The only difference was that they had dispensed with the road guards in optic orange vests, and instead they now had four soldiers with loaded M4s—two ahead and two behind the formation—as ATEs—Anti-Terrorist Escorts.

After the sound of the platoon had faded into the distance, Olds said in a casual voice, "It's good to be able to talk freely without a lot of European backstabbers listening."

Laine nodded, and Olds continued, "Let me fill you in. The New Army is essentially a sham. It is a cover for a foreign occupation force. Don't have any illusions: The UN is calling the shots. Anyone that steps out of line gets shown the door—that is, if they're lucky—or they conveniently disappear—with that blamed on resistance kidnappers—or they have a sudden 'heart attack,' or they 'commit suicide.'"

Andy groaned and said, "That's not too surprising."

"You've probably heard that the ProvGov is expanding in all directions, and now controls about half of the land area in CONUS, and 70 percent of the population. The motivation is loot. Everyone right down to the infantry privates gets some loot. The Tooth-to-Tail Ratio has been stretching more and more toward bureaucracy and do-nothing general staffs, as everyone and his uncle want to share a piece of the action."

Olds shook his head from side to side, saying, "Someday this institutional sickness has to end."

They continued on, at a comfortable and familiar pace. Andy was glad that they were running early in the morning, before the temperature rose. Fort Knox was famous for its hot, humid summer weather. General Olds seemed deep in thought. They jogged on in silence for several minutes.

Finally, Olds commented, "All this looting . . . They don't need any encouragement from the higher echelons. You see, once they occupy a region, they start to strip it of any valuables that are compact and portable, mostly gold and gemstones and guns—especially handguns. But they're even after jewelry, elephant ivory, high-end electronics and e-book readers, things of that nature. Silver is just too heavy to carry, so if they get any, they very quickly try to swap it twenty for one or even thirty for one for gold or platinum. They want *compact* but valuable loot that they can take with them when they go back home, O-CONUS."

"I see."

"In the Plains states, it was essentially a race between the unit commanders to see who got to loot each city first."

"In-credible."

"The modus operandi is hideously simple," Olds continued. "They roll into a town and declare it 'pacified.' Then they start interrogating and find out where all the jewelers, coin dealers, and gun dealers live. Those that don't agree to be 'taxed' to the tune of 40 percent of their inventory get either shot or arrested for being 'terrorist sympathizers.' "

Olds snorted to himself. "At first, I was hoping that all this would soon stop, but it hasn't. It's actually become institutionalized. We have independent infantry brigades out there that have practically gone rogue, that have been out of contact with us for months at a time, hopping from town to town. When they do cycle back to Knox, they come home packing heavy."

"That's unconscionable."

"But that's not all, Andy. There are also the rapes and the child molestations. There are some very sick puppies in the UN forces, and within the civilian rank and file of the ProvGov. It seems to attract the sickos. Some of the worst of them gravitate to the frontier, where they can get away with more. We call it the 'leading edge' or the 'bleeding edge.'"

By the tone of the general's voice, it was apparent to Andy that he was fully sympathetic to the Resistance. Olds seemed to have drawn the same conclusion about Andy Laine. They ran on for several more minutes, in silence. Then Olds asked, "What's your view of the strategic situation?"

"The Army seems to be getting stretched thin," Andy answered. "There's almost 3.8 million square miles in the United States. As the Army spreads out, it has to leave garrisons in each region. The troops are getting spread thinner and thinner. It's like the board game Risk, but for real."

Olds nodded in agreement. "Speaking of risks, just before I rotated in from Germany, an infantry colonel and two MI majors here at Knox tried to plan a coup, but they were detected and shot, very early on. I don't know whether it was bad OPSEC, or bad COMSEC, or just a talkative wife, but the whole operation got blown. They drove those three officers out to the North Range maneuver area, and shot them in the back of the head. They tucked them into a ditch with a backhoe. The ProvGov didn't even try to make a secret of it. I think they wanted it to be known: 'This is what happens to any *Valkyrie* wannabes.' Things have been very quiet since then."

"So now?"

"Now we watch, wait, and coordinate some plans, *very* quietly," Olds replied.

23

Up Close and Personal

"Courage is not the absence of fear, but rather the judgment that something else is more important than fear."
—James Neil Hollingworth (aka Ambrose Redmoon), manager of the band Quicksilver Messenger Service

Five Miles West of Leitchfield, Kentucky
December, the Second Year

Ben Fielding had no previous military experience and just a bit of field experience with the Matchmakers. And of course there was the incident behind the Full Moon Saloon, long before the Crunch. But that occasion he considered just instinctive self-defense and God's protection. Despite his lack of formal training, Ben soon excelled at patrolling. He had keen senses and better-than-average night vision. He learned how to move almost silently. He originally carried his big Galil .308 rifle, but he later began carrying a suppressed MP5-SD slung with a single-point sling instead. He sent the Galil home for the safekeeping of his family in Muddy Pond, via a courier. He enclosed a note that read simply: "All is well. Keep the faith. B."

Ben habitually wore a sniper's camouflage face veil/scarf that had been "liberated" from a dead Austrian sentry. He liked the versatility of the scarf. In cold weather it could be worn as a muffler. And he found that he could quickly don it as a face veil when he was approaching UNPROFOR positions. This obviated the need to put on face paint.

While most of the members of the reconnaissance team wore Woodland or MultiCam pattern BDUs or OCPs, Ben wore all civilian clothes. His clothes were typically green denim jeans and a brown shirt. In cold weather he added a brown Australian's oilskin drover's jacket with a corduroy collar that had been given to him by Adrian. Because he didn't like the way they blocked his peripheral vision, Ben never wore hats with brims. Sometimes, when the weather got unusually cold, he would wear a green knit cap, but never over his ears. To Ben, all his senses were crucial. For wet work, situational awareness often could make a split-second difference between life and death.

By wearing civilian clothes, Ben hoped he could ditch his MP5 and web gear and then quickly blend in with the general population when necessary. But he also realized that by not wearing a uniform he could be shot on sight as a spy or terrorist. On the other hand, given the UNPROFOR's tendency to ignore the Geneva Convention and other laws of land warfare, wearing a uniform wouldn't provide any guarantees of good treatment if he were taken prisoner. He often said resignedly, "They'd just shoot us, anyway."

Even Ben's boots were civilian—a pair of W. C. Russell hiking boots that had been a college graduation present from his father. In his nearly three years with the Resistance, he had the boots resoled twice.

Ben's favorite close quarters weapons were the short-handled light blacksmithing hammer that Adrian had given him years before the Crunch, and a large Cold Steel Magnum Tanto XII fighting knife that some would call a short sword. The knife was taken from the web gear of an UNPROFOR Armored Cavalry scout who hadn't been as quick or alert as Ben. Since he was more focused on function over form, Ben kept the knife very sharp, but spray-painted its blade and sheath green after each sharpening. His backup knife was a big CRKT Hissatsu folder. That had come from the pocket of a German officer who, as Ben explained, had no further use for it.

The hammer turned out to be very effective for eliminating ProvGov soldiers who were manning LP/OPs. Ben always aimed his swings at the neck and head. The sentries rarely made any noise before they went down, usually after just the first blow.

Although he owned the HK pistol, he didn't carry it after his first week of patrolling and probing lines. For stealth and speed, he found that he liked to carry only minimal gear. All that he carried was a CamelBak hydration pack, a MOLLE vest (without hard ballistic plates), three spare MP5 magazines, a night vision monocular pouch, an oversize belt pouch for his hammer, and his sheathed Cold Steel knife.

In two years with the Recon Team, Ben fired fewer than 100 rounds through his Galil and his MP5. In all, he had killed thirty-two UNPROFOR soldiers, but twenty-six of those were dispatched with either his hammer or his big tanto knife. He often said that killing was the surest "at bad breath distance." Ben killed so many sentries in messy hand-to-hand work that he got into the habit of carrying a spare clean shirt in a plastic bag, stowed inside his CamelBak bag. Some of the resistance fighters gave him the nickname "Bloody Ben," out of respect for his accomplishments. But he disliked this sobriquet, so it wasn't used in his presence.

Near Leitchfield, Kentucky
September, the Third Year

The newest recruit in the Mulholland Company was young, scared, and uncertain of himself. He clutched an old H&R 12-gauge single-shot shotgun and eyed everything going on around him in the camp warily. Ben had taken him under his wing at the small camp where they were temporarily co-located with the Mulholland Company. They bivouacked there just one night as they prepared to raid a small UNPROFOR garrison in Leitchfield, Kentucky.

As they often did, some of the other men at the resistance camp were reminiscing about the things they missed—like coffee, tropical fruit, and iPod downloads. Ben had told the recruit to hang tight while he got him a more capable weapon.

He came back three hours later with an M4 carbine and a MOLLE body armor vest with a ceramic armor plate that was "shingled" with a half dozen magazine pouches. As he handed the vest to the recruit, he said, "Sorry about the blood. It'll wash out."

The next morning, the recipient of the carbine and field gear came to Ben's tent to again thank him. "It's an honor to have this rifle," he said. "I promise you that I'll use it fighting the good fight. And I'd appreciate your prayers. I just wish I could be as fearless as you."

Ben shook his head. "I'm not fearless. I'm just *determined*. There's a difference between the two. I'm nothing special."

After motioning for the young man to sit down next to the tent, Ben continued, "You know, I read a lot of books about the Holocaust and the people who survived the death camps to go on and fight for the independence of Israel. They had to fight the British first, and then the Arabs. Those men and women could be very fierce and determined, because most of them had nothing left to lose."

The recruit nodded, and Ben went on. "When I heard that the ProvGov was setting up concentration camps, just like the Nazis, I very quickly decided that I'd never get dragged into one of them. I'd rather die on my feet with a rifle in my hands—"

The recruit interrupted, "—than on your knees."

"Yes, precisely. My attitude, as a Christian, is that I know that this mortal life is short, and that I already have life eternal in heaven. So it is all a matter of keeping perspective. I have confidence that you'll fight the good fight. Never forget this conversation."

Depending on the tactical situation, the five-man Recon Team was often loaned out to work with Hammond's Hellhounds, the Mulholland Company, the Fawcett Company, Gunners Against Illegal Mayors (GAIM), the Gillian Group, the Morris Maquis, the Lexington-Versailles Company, or the Alvin York Brigade. All these were independent militias that operated in western Tennessee and western Kentucky. They numbered between nine and twenty-eight members, mostly men.

The Recon Team's specialty was locating enemy positions and lines—and crossing them, if need be. They would then guide militia companies to vulnerable points to attack. The Old Man handpicked all of his fighters from other units. He recruited Ben Fielding shortly after his team's point man had been killed by an exploding land mine. The Old Man selected men who were exceptionally well tempered, physically fit, experienced in the field, and who had perfect uncorrected vision. Ben and Brent were the only members of the reconnaissance team that didn't have prior military service. Most of the others had been Army Rangers or Army Cavalry scouts, one had been a Force Recon Marine, and another was a former Navy SEAL.

When Ben asked the Old Man his name, he answered dryly, "You don't have a need to know, son. Besides, it's safer for *both of us* if you don't know it."

The Recon Team was famous for never taking more than a one-week break from operations in two years of the resistance war, and most of those were after actions when several team members were wounded. The Old Man was the only member who made it all the way through the war. All of the others were replacements for those who had been killed or wounded. Like Ben, all of them were sworn to secrecy. Further, all were under orders to never mention their surnames to each other. At one point, there were two members on the team named Jim. They were called "Old Jim" and "Young Jim" to avoid confusion.

Brent joined the Recon Team much later in the war than Ben, just nine months before the UNPROFOR collapsed. He replaced a medic who had been killed in an ATACMS missile strike.

From the vantage point of his leaky pup tent, Brent sized up the Mulholland Company. They were a ragtag bunch, with few recognizable leaders. With twenty-nine members, it was one of the larger resistance militias. Recent experience had shown that larger units were easier for the UNPROFOR to detect and engage. In fact, the trend was to split resistance units into groups no larger than fifteen. The Mulholland Company had not yet done so, but a split was already under discussion. The members of the company had a wide assortment of weapons, uniforms, and equipment. A good portion of their gear was captured.

Like many other resistance units, there was a preponderance of young men—many still in their teens and as young as sixteen— and men in their late fifties and early sixties. Most of the married men in the ages in between had feared for their families' safety and therefore didn't feel free to join the fight. Both in their forties, Ben Fielding and Brent Danley were in the minority. Like many men their age in the Resistance, Brent and Ben had both lost family to the ProvGov's actions, so their motivation could be attributed partly to revenge.

And, like many others their age, Brent and Ben had a deep-seated hatred of the ProvGov, and this made them some of the most motivated and tireless fighters. One of Brent's most common sayings was "I'll only relax when Hutchings is six feet under, and we have a Constitutional government again."

The militias that tried using armored vehicles found it made them targets for airstrikes or laser-guided artillery rounds. So after taking heavy casualties in the first few months of the resistance war the goal became to destroy UNPROFOR vehicles, rather than capture and use them.

The most effective use of vehicles by the Resistance was to drive abandoned or stolen civilian cars and SUVs for high-speed covert movement of troops, to mass for short-duration raids. Often their weapons would be hidden in the vehicles in case they had to pass checkpoints.

Most resistance units preferred 7.62mm NATO battle rifles, such as M1As, AR-10s, FN/FALs, and HK91 clones. These gave them better range than the M4s, M16s, and AK-74s used by the UNPROFOR army, yet they were still light enough to carry on long patrols. Light belt-fed weapons such as the M249, MG4 (the German equivalent of an M249), and the M240B were also highly prized. The other weapons that they did their best to procure were Claymore mines, LAW rockets, AT-4s, and the various generations of Russian RPGs. These were used to great effect in anti-vehicular ambushes.

A few resistance units in urban areas found that they could carry M4 carbines broken down into two halves concealed beneath heavy coats and jackets. Assembling the guns took just a few moments. This modus operandi often resulted in gaining the element of surprise when ambushing UNPROFOR troops who were off duty or otherwise in a low state of readiness.

24

Mole Tunnels

"The qualities of a good intelligence officer:
- *Be perceptive about people*
- *Be able to work well with others under difficult conditions*
- *Be able to distinguish between fact and fiction*
- *Be able to distinguish between essentials and non-essentials*
- *Possess inquisitiveness*
- *Have a large amount of ingenuity*
- *Pay appropriate attention to detail*
- *Be able to express ideas clearly, briefly and very important, interestingly*
- *Learn when to keep your mouth shut*
- *Understanding for other points of view, other ways of thinking and behaving, even if they are quite foreign to his own*
- *Rigidity and close-mindedness are qualities that do not spell a good future in Intelligence*
- *Must not be over ambitious or anxious for personal reward, and the most important quality: What motivates a man to devote himself to the craft of intelligence?"*

—**Allen Dulles,** *The Craft of Intelligence,* **1963**

Fort Knox, Kentucky
December, the Second Year

With a quiet word from the Resistance, Kaylee soon got a job working the front counter and cash register at a bagel and pastry bakery on Knox Avenue in Radcliff. The owner was sympathetic to the Cause. His bakery was in the building that had been occupied by the Better on a Bagel bakery before the Crunch. It was located near the junction of Knox Avenue and North Wilson Road. When it reopened, the bakery was called Bullion Bakery, and had a metallic gold painted sign in the shape of a gold ingot.

Because Kaylee would be in contact with so many people each day, it was the perfect place for her to be able to surreptitiously pass notes, memory sticks, or even small parcels to couriers. In the event that she had to deliver a note or memory stick to a courier after-hours, she had two dead drop locations: one inside a carved-out copy of the book *Soil Survey of Hamblen County, Tennessee* in the dusty stacks at the Radcliff Public Library, and one in a Ziploc bag beneath the cigarette butts in the top of a steel fence post in the parking lot of Cho's Snack Corner on North Wilson Road.

Andy was often up late in the night, preparing intelligence reports on Kaylee's aging Pentium laptop. His greatest fear was that someday he'd be identified by a ProvGov mole within the Resistance. He spent many hours reading books on espionage tradecraft, and implementing the concepts he had learned. As a mole himself, he went with the assumption that there would be one or more ProvGov moles in the Resistance who would see his reports. For this reason, he was careful to just *summarize* the contents of ProvGov and UNPROFOR documents, rather than duplicate them.

"One of the oldest counterintelligence tricks is to create multiple versions of a document," he explained to Kaylee, "with a pattern of very subtle differences—even just a comma that is changed to a semicolon or an extra space, for example. They carefully keep track of which suspected agent is provided a particular version of the document. Then, when a mole at the far end gets a copy of the document he forwards it back to the government, and they can then analyze it and deduce who leaked it. Back during the

Obama administration, that technique was even used within the White House to identify members of the staff who were whistle-blowers."

Andy's reports covered a wide range of topics—everything from the latest troop movements and flight schedules to power politics within the ProvGov. The more technical reports detailed things like radio protocols, the range and effectiveness of various UNPROFOR weapons, vehicle vulnerabilities, radio direction finding, and the ProvGov's diminished access to spy satellites.

The Resistance was particularly interested in the specifications of radio-controlled IED (RCIED) countermeasures systems. They were already fairly familiar with American-made jammers. These included the Duke cell phone jammers mounted on Humvees, and the Guardian man-portable counter-RCIED system. But they knew much less about the Rhino II and Rhino III passive counter-passive infrared systems. These systems used a glow plug mounted on a boom that caused passive IR-initiated IEDs to pre-detonate before a vehicle passed over them. And, until they later captured some for analysis, they also knew hardly anything about the German-, Dutch-, and French-built IED jammers.

Many of Andy's reports were instrumental to resistance planners, both tactically and strategically. To the geographically scattered group leaders of the Resistance, he was known only as "Confidential Source #6."

At the other end of the chain was the intelligence network of officers and ProvGov civilians, coordinated by General Olds. He used Andy Laine as the coordinator and compiler for this information. Most of the reports were in text files that were copied onto older 1- or 2-GB memory sticks for a courier to pick up from Kaylee the following day. His supply of empty memory sticks was kept inside the pedestal of a round oak table. He made a habit of leaving out no more than ten empty sticks at any time, in case his apartment was searched.

After each night's work, Andy copied the "Games Backup" folder from Kaylee's laptop onto a pair of Ironkey 8-GB thumb drives, and hid these in a secret compartment in the bottom of one of his SIG pistol magazines. The Ironkey drives were uniquely designed so that if anyone without the correct password made multiple attempts to open the files, the files would be automatically erased. After he had written new files to the Ironkey drives, he erased the requisite sectors of the laptop's hard drive clean, with special "Wiper for Windows" software.

Whenever Andy needed to copy a file from his laptop at the brigade headquarters, he would use a third Ironkey drive that he kept in a hidden compartment beneath a drawer in his office desk, or he would remove one of the other Ironkey drives from the SIG magazine while in a restroom stall. The same compartment in his desk held a Panasonic Lumix ultracompact digital camera that he used on the rare occasions when he needed to photograph a map or a piece of equipment. He kept a cable at home that allowed him to transfer the images to Kaylee's laptop and then in turn to a thumb drive.

Andy would have preferred to have used all Ironkey drives, but because the courier runs were so frequent and one-way, he had to rely on less-secure standard thumb drives. Andy always kept a can of WD-40 lubricant on his desk. After writing files to thumb drives for Kaylee to deliver to the couriers, he would give each of them a squirt of WD-40. He had read that this coating made it almost impossible for them to retain fingerprints that could be lifted.

As Andy became accustomed to his brigade staff job, he consciously reminded himself to avoid making friends with other officers on the brigade staff. As General Olds put it, "Friends mean confidences and confidences are always risks." Because he spoke some German, he was popular with the German officers. But Andy consistently turned down offers to attend social functions with them. He said, accurately, that he liked spending all his free time with his wife. The other officers seemed to take this at face value, and didn't take offense.

Deep down, Andy was glad that he didn't get to know any of the German or Dutch officers well. He reasoned that if all went well, he'd be part of deporting them in less than a year. And for all he knew, he might even be gunning for them.

Andy and Kaylee Laine's espionage activities were very stressful, particularly to Andy. He constantly felt like he was playing a role in a stage play. He had to control his facial expressions when attending briefings or when reading dispatches. For him to even display the slightest pleasure at the news of an UNPROFOR setback might unmask him. He had nagging fears of being detected. His dreams were a tangle of what he called "bad scenes": getting caught with classified documents, being arrested and beaten, being tortured. He often resorted to taking a couple of valerian root capsules at bedtime to help him sleep.

It was Kaylee who helped him keep his balance. They had long, cathartic talks about the happenings in the brigade and even global politics. Andy was certain that if Kaylee weren't with him at Fort Knox, he wouldn't be able to handle the stress that he was under.

Ed Olds was cautious about security for his intelligence team. They never met in groups of more than three, and in fact none of them except Olds himself knew the names of all of the members. Whenever he had to mention another team member, he would use euphemistic names like "Mister Black," "Mister Green," "Our man in the administration," "Our man in the Signal Corps," or "Our man in the G2 Shop." He was so consistent about using the "Mister" and "Our man" monikers that Andy did not learn until years later that there were two women in his intelligence-gathering cell.

Many of Andy's surreptitious meetings with Olds were during morning PT sessions, or after-hours at Olds's home, while his DVD player played a science fiction movie with the volume turned up loud. Ed Olds was a serious sci-fi fan, with more than seventy movies and television series in his collection. Andy feigned being a science fiction devotee to explain his frequent visits to the general's quarters.

One of their key conversations came when they discussed endgame strategies for the war of resistance. General Olds stated forthrightly, "I've concluded that the ProvGov and the UN peacekeepers are doomed, for four reasons. First, as we've discussed before, they've overextended their reach and have thereby spread their forces too thin. Second, they are being confronted by a guerrilla army of resistance that is leaderless, so it cannot be isolated and eliminated. Third, like the Nazis in World War II, they've embarked on a campaign of mass arrests and reprisal killings, which is alienating any support that they might have once enjoyed. And lastly, they've attempted to disarm the populace. That is an idiotic and futile endeavor."

"I agree that their goal is futile," Andy said. "Before the Crunch, we were a nation of, as I recall, around 328 million people, with around 250 million guns. There were 4.5 million guns manufactured each year, but meanwhile fewer than one million guns were worn out, exported, or melted down in those stupid 'turn in your gun for concert tickets' programs. Who would be so moronic as to trade their birthright for a gift certificate from Toys-R-Us? But now, after the big die-off, we are a nation of perhaps 100 million people, still with around 250 million guns. There is absolutely *no way* that we'll ever be disarmed. From a demographic standpoint, the ProvGov is so outnumbered and so outgunned that it's almost comical. The handwriting is on the wall."

25

El Tesoro

"Three-fifths to two-thirds of the federal budget consists of taking property from one American and giving it to another. Were a private person to do the same thing, we'd call it theft. When government does it, we euphemistically call it income redistribution, but that's exactly what thieves do—redistribute income. Income redistribution not only betrays the founders' vision, it's a sin in the eyes of God."

—Dr. Walter E. Williams, in his essay "Bogus Rights," from *Townhall*,

February 8, 2006

Near Sedona, Arizona
May, the Fourth Year

Ignacio García's looter gang, La Fuerza, had gone mobile just as the Crunch began, cutting a swath from near Houston, west across Texas, through southern New Mexico and Arizona. García's gang had specialized in invading small towns and stripping them clean. One of their trademarks was using armored cars, both former bank transport armored cars, and wheeled military surplus armored personnel carriers (APCs). At its peak, García's looter gang was a small army, numbering 212 with fifty-three vehicles.

La Fuerza was quite successful until they reached the vicinity of Prescott, Arizona. There, a group of local citizens bolstered by a small contingent from New Mexico carried out a daring nighttime raid on Humboldt and Dewey, Arizona, with Molotov cocktail firebombs, destroying all of their armored vehicles and half of their unarmored ones. In the raid forty-four of the gang members were killed or wounded.

A retaliatory raid on Prescott—in which nearly every building in the city was burned—cost the lives of another forty-seven gang members. Soon after that, seven members left the gang. They stole away in the night, in two groups.

North of Williams, Arizona
June, the Fourth Year

Three weeks after burning Prescott, Ignacio decided to cache all his precious metals and gemstones. With just his wife and his trusted lieutenant, Tony, he drove four miles off Highway 64 into federally owned rangeland that his maps showed was administered by the Bureau of Land Management (BLM).

They found a rusted abandoned tractor frame that looked like it had been there for more than fifty years to use as a landmark. He wrote down the GPS coordinates. Then he stretched a piece of twine from the tractor's steering column to a large, distinctive boulder 100 feet away. With a tape measure he measured exactly forty feet down the string from the tractor and scratched a large X on the ground with the tip of a digging bar. They brought a pick and two shovels from the pickup and started to dig.

The dry, rocky soil made digging difficult. Ignacio's original plan had been to dig a hole five feet deep. But as the day warmed up and blisters began to form, he revised his plan to dig a trench just two feet deep. The gold and platinum coins as well as a large assortment of jewelry and gemstones had already been packed in eighteen U.S. military surplus .50 caliber ammo cans. The greatest value was in loose diamonds and diamond wedding rings. García's wife had lost count at just over 300 stones, so she estimated that there were at least 350 diamonds. The cans were so heavy that they were difficult for a man to lift and carry.

Before placing the cans in the hole, Ignacio opened them and applied a coating of Vaseline to the rubber gaskets on their lids. After taking a few minutes to admire his treasure (*tesoro*), he resealed the cans. They laid the cans in the bottom of the trench, covered them with two thicknesses of trash bags, and then refilled the trench. They spent thirty minutes scattering the excess dirt and smoothing over the site to make it look undisturbed. Then they dragged some scrap metal they found near the tractor and placed it on top of the cache to serve both as a reminder of where the cache was located and to foil anyone who might someday use a metal detector.

He wrote down the precise GPS coordinates for both the tractor and the cache on two pieces of paper. He then trimmed them to the size of business cards and laminated them on both sides with clear packing tape. He had his wife sew one of these into the lining of her fur coat, and one into his leather belt.

In June, García's gang drove into Colorado, following their time-proven hit-and-run tactics. They gathered trucks and vans to replace some of the vehicles lost in the Humboldt and Dewey, Arizona, fiasco.

In each town they hit, they began to hear more and more about the ProvGov. Generally called the Federals—or as García's men termed them, *los federales*—they were a great concern to García and his lieutenants. They were told that Fort Carson was the headquarters for the UNPROFOR in Colorado.

One of García's men approached him and said, "These *federales*, they're going to squash us like a bug."

García shook his head. "Not if we become security contractors. As contractors, we'll just have to give up a little piece of what we take, but we'll have *legitimacy*. Under the martial law, it will all be official. We'll be employees of the ProvGov."

So they dubbed themselves Force Two Associates, or simply F2. Carlos, who had been a graffiti tagger before he'd joined La Fuerza, cut a handsome sixteen-inch-tall "F2" stencil for painting the doors, hoods, and tailgates of their trucks. They used glossy black spray paint. Some of the camp followers carefully embroidered the F2 logo on some stolen tan baseball caps to match.

Negotiating with the regional administrator at Fort Carson went rapidly. García quickly hammered out a mutually acceptable charter. The UNPROFOR's cut was 20 percent of all loot. The regional administrator took a further personal commission of 2 percent, although that was not mentioned in the charter contract. But he made it clear that if he didn't get his cut, in gold, he would leave García twisting in the wind.

Fort Knox, Kentucky
September, the Third Year

To Andy, joining the New Army seemed simultaneously familiar and strange. For example, when he drew his issue of field gear, it was still called "TA-50" gear, but it was an odd assortment of field gear that included a set of U.S. interceptor body armor (IBA), a German sleeping bag, a Dutch tent, Belgian waterproof over-boots and parka, a French backpack, and a battered Russian mess kit. At the same time, he was handed a chit for an "Article 4 Exemption" Hardigg locker. This, he was told, could be picked up at the Army Community Service (ACS) and Army Emergency Relief (AER) Outreach Office on Binter Street. The ACS office was not far from the Commissary and Exchange stores. It seemed strange to him that the ACS charity would issue a piece of military equipment.

Andy drove to the ACS/AER office on his lunch hour. As he entered the building, he walked by two contract civilian security guards who were armed with laser-mounted M4s. The men were lounging in overstuffed chairs in the foyer. By their clothes and mannerisms, they looked like XE Corporation toughs or at least XE wannabes.

Inside the building, Andy expected to see a utilitarian office. But he was stunned to see that the office was overfurnished with ornate antique furniture. Every bit of wall space was lined with fancy chairs, armoires, china cabinets, and marble-top tables. He handed the chit to a plump secretary who wore too much eye makeup. As she rose from her chair, Andy observed that she was armed with a *wakazashi* Japanese short sword, carried in a sash-like *obi* belt. She escorted him to a room with a pile of empty Hardigg lockers and said matter-of-factly, "Take one. You'll have to provide your own lock and chain."

Andy shouldered one of the lockers and carried it out to his pickup. When he opened the locker to examine it, he found a silk-screened sign the size of a bumper sticker lacquered inside the lid. It read:

> Inspection Exempt Items, Per Art. 4, ProvGov-UNPROFOR Agreement. Please **give generously** to A.C.S./A.E.R. When this locker is too full to hold any more, then it's time to give. Thank You.—Ft. Knox A.C.S.

When he got back to his quarters that evening, Andy discussed the locker with Kaylee. He said, "I feel like I've been transported into an alternate universe. The AER office used to be just a place for penniless wives of junior NCOs to get the bare-bones necessities of running a household, like diapers and dishes, and stew pots. But now the place looks like something out of an antique furniture auction catalogue. It's bizarre. Do you remember when we borrowed my dad's set of the old *Star Trek* television series on

DVD? There was that parallel universe episode where Spock had a beard?"

Kaylee nodded and said, "Yeah, it was called *Mirror, Mirror.*"

"Yep, that's the one. Well, I haven't met a bearded Mr. Spock yet, but today I met Uhura with a dagger. The world has been turned inside out. Since when is a charitable organization given control of excess loot?"

26

Trampling Out the Vintage

"Freedom is never more than one generation away from extinction. We didn't pass it to our children in the bloodstream. It must be fought for, protected, and handed on for them to do the same, or one day we will spend our sunset years telling our children and our children's children what it was once like in the United Stated where men were free."

—**President Ronald Wilson Reagan**

Fort Knox, Kentucky
January, the Fourth Year

As the Resistance continued to gain ground, the ProvGov tried to sound upbeat in their propaganda broadcasts. The UN's Continental Region 6, which included the territory that had been the United States, Mexico, and Canada, was in a losing war with the guerrillas. There was resistance growing throughout the region. The resistance ranged from passive protest to sabotage and overt military action. The UN was steadily losing control of Region 6.

It was becoming clear that resistance was the strongest, the best organized, and the most successful in rural areas. Unable to wipe out the elusive guerrillas, the UN administration and their quislings began to concentrate on eliminating the guerrillas' food supplies.

In areas where resistance was rampant, "temporary detainment facilities" were constructed to house anyone thought to be politically unreliable. Special emphasis was placed on rounding up suspect farmers or ranchers, or anyone remotely connected with food distribution businesses. When farmers were put into custody, their crops were confiscated, plowed under, or burned. The authorities carefully monitored bulk food stocks.

Despite the ProvGov's efforts, the guerrillas rapidly gained in numbers. As the war went on, resistance gradually increased beyond the UN's ability to match it. Every new detainment camp spawned the formation of new resistance cells. Every reprisal or atrocity by the UN or federal forces pushed more of the populace and even federal unit commanders into active support for the guerrillas. Increasing numbers of commanders decided to "do the right thing" and abide by the Constitution. The decision to support *The Document* rather than the Provisional Government's power elite at Fort Knox was becoming widespread. Units as large as brigade size were parlaying with the guerrillas and turning over their equipment. In many instances the majority of their troops joined the Resistance.

County after county, and eventually state after state, was controlled by the Resistance. The remaining loyal federal and UN units gradually retreated into Kentucky, Tennessee, and southern Illinois. Most held out there until the early summer of the war's fourth year. Militias and their allied "realigned" federal units relentlessly closed in on the remaining federal territory from all directions.

Fort Knox, Kentucky
Early July, the Fourth Year

The opportunity for the Constitutionalist underground within the UNPROFOR to round up the foreign troops at Fort Knox came on July 3, when there was a German art film scheduled to be shown at the old Waybur Theater. The movie had been produced two years before the Crunch. It was titled *Die jungen gefangenen Karrierefrauen* ("The Captive Young Career Women"). The movie could at best be called soft pornography. The film was in German, with Dutch subtitles. A large number of UN officers and NCOs were expected to be there. Since it had been a very popular film in Germany, the first showing at the post theater was restricted to officers and NCOs only.

"It should be perfect," Andy told General Olds. "It is bound to draw a full house. I heard that it shows lots of skin, so the foreign officers are already starting to talk about it, and they're giving each other the elbow nudge. They all want to be there."

"Have them bring as many riot shotguns as you can muster," Olds recommended. "Those scare the heck out of the Germans and the Dutch."

The Waybur Theater, constructed in 1936, was built of brick. It had seats for 674 people. Even after it had been restored in 2009, it still had a 1930s look and feel. Many of the building's original terrazzo floors were intact.

Two days before the roundup at Fort Knox, the planning got a lot easier. Maynard Hutchings and most of his staff—including Chambers Clarke, Major General Clayton Uhlich, and as well, the two-highest-ranking UN officers at Fort Knox—suddenly boarded night flights to Brussels on the pretense of "attending meetings." So the coup committee members who had been assigned to arresting Hutchings and his cronies were reassigned to arresting UN officers, or to the Waybur Theater raid itself.

Andy was tense the day of the theater raid. He forced himself to appear casual and nonchalant, putting in a normal day of pushing paper at his S3 desk. Only his 42 Alpha Human Resource Specialist assistant (called a "Clerk/Typist" in the Old

Army) picked up on his tension. To explain his agitation, Andy told him that he'd had a lengthy argument with his wife the night before.

That evening, Andy positioned himself just inside the right-rear fire exit door—at the end of the theater closest to the screen. He waited until twenty minutes of the film had rolled. Then he unsnapped the thumbstrap on his SIG's hip holster, said a brief silent prayer, and toggled the handset on his handie-talkie three times. Then he immediately pushed the bar on the fire door, opening it from the inside. One hundred sixty men—the equivalent of one and a half infantry companies—took over the building, rushing it from every entrance. They soon lined the walls of the theater, and shouldered their rifles and shotguns at the audience. Eighteen men covered the exits from outside while the rest rushed down both aisles—half from the front lobby, and half from the rear fire doors. Engrossed in the film, the audience was taken completely by surprise. One fire team was sent to clear each of the restrooms. The projector stopped and the house lights came up.

Andy jumped up onto the theater's restored wooden stage and pulled out a PylePro electronic bullhorn that had been hidden behind the curtains. He turned it on and flipped it to the siren setting for two seconds, getting everyone's attention with its piercing warble. Then he flipped its switch to talk and announced to the frightened audience: "Put all your weapons on the floor, now! *Alles gewher, alles pistolen, Mach Schnell!* Take off your pistol belts and drop them, right now! Drop everything on the floor, right now: guns, knives, tear gas, PDAs, cell phones, CrackBerrys, iPads, everything! After you've dropped your gear, then put your hands up. *Hande hoch!*"

While nearly all the assembled officers hesitantly dropped their pistol belts to the floor, an obese Dutch colonel in the third row named Dekker panicked. He drew his HK USP pistol and leveled it at the American soldiers nearest him. He was breathing heavily, almost gasping. Within a few moments, there were four laser dots dancing around his eyes and forehead. Then Dekker shouted *"Smeerlappen!"* just before he turned his pistol around, shoved it into his mouth, angled it upward, and pulled the trigger. His body collapsed between two rows of seats, spraying blood on those standing nearby.

"That was stupid," Andy announced on the bullhorn. "Nobody else does anything stupid, and we'll get along nicely. Now, I want everyone in the front row, and the front row *only*, to slowly exit, back through the lobby—*die Diele ausgang, bitte*. Keep your hands on top of your heads."

Andy continued ordering the moviegoers out, gradually, row by row. Outside, they walked into the blinding glare of five mobile floodlights on generator trailers, courtesy of some resistance sympathizers in the Kentucky Highway Department. Immediately outside the theater's covered wooden entryway, three strands of concertina wire had been strung out to form a rectangular corral measuring 80 by 300 feet. Armed troops and resistance fighters ringed the enclosure, and their intent was clear. There were no attempted escapes.

In all, there were 663 prisoners, mostly men, although there were twenty-six women and two infants. All the adults were put in flex cuffs. Almost immediately, there were pleas for mercy and claims of innocence. After everyone was cuffed, nine high-ranking officers were singled out and taken to the stockade cells at the 34th Military Police Detachment headquarters in Building 204, on Old Ironsides Avenue.

One German captain who had recently been disciplined for making anti-UN statements as well as nineteen Americans were immediately released, after other officers and NCOs vouched that they were anti-ProvGov. But this left a large number whose status was deemed "ambiguous." This included several women who claimed to be dates or spouses of UNPROFOR officers. But at least two of the women claiming this were recognized as foreign officers dressed in civilian clothes. There was a huge uproar, and shouted calls for various people to be released. Andy's solution was swift. He shouted, "We take them *all* to the Abrams Auditorium and sort them out later."

Through some careful coordination, at the same time as the Waybur Theater roundup, all the radio and television stations inside the collapsing area of UNPROFOR control began broadcasting resistance victory shows and playing patriotic music. Resistance forces congregated at the broadcast studios and transmitter sites to prevent UNPROFOR interference. Meanwhile, newspapers across the country were preparing Fourth of July victory editions. Announcing that all UN units had conceded defeat and were laying down their arms—although it wasn't completely true—was a strategic masterstroke of PSYOPS, since it was a self-fulfilling prophecy. This was a fait accompli on a grand scale.

As the news of the impending victory spread, more than 10,000 militia unit members from as far away as Georgia, Arkansas, Iowa, Michigan, and Pennsylvania began overnight drives to Fort Knox. They had a celebration to attend.

There was a long delay before the prisoners from the Waybur were loaded onto eighty-passenger personnel carrier vans, since each one had to be individually searched. Not counting the 416 pistols and revolvers that had been dropped to the floor of the theater, the troops found eighteen pistols in shoulder and waistband holsters, eighty-four pocketknives, fifteen boot knives, twenty-nine sheath knives, two garrotes, seven saps, three pairs of brass knuckles, four nunchakus, three hand grenades, and twenty-six containers of pepper spray or tear gas. There were also more than 100 cell phones and radios confiscated, forming a large pile on the pavement.

The personnel carrier vans, each towed by a tractor truck, were a familiar sight at Army forts where basic training and Advanced Individual Training (AIT) were conducted. These replaced the older "silver side" cattle cars, but still looked very utilitarian. The vans also worked fine for hauling prisoners when they had their doors chained shut. Escorting Humvees bristling with guns ensured that none of the prisoners tried to leap from the windows.

At the same time that the arrests were going on at the Waybur, many Hutchings cabinet staffers and UN officers were also arrested. Some who were considered high-risk were jailed in the Building 204 Stockade.

By dawn, the group at the Abrams Auditorium swelled, with an additional 416 foreign officers and NCOs arrested on- or off-post during the rest of the night. By the next evening they began shuttling the prisoners in groups of thirty to a new makeshift prison camp that was set up in the old Basic Combat Training (BCT) Disney Barracks complex—the area commonly called "Disneyland."

Creating the prison fence around the barracks complex took all three companies of the 19th Engineer Battalion two full days. Almost 200 pallets of concertina and razor wire were strung out and stacked six courses high. Some of the NCO prisoners were ignominiously detailed to help string the wire for their own prison camp. Three days later, the temporary concertina wire fence was supplemented by an array of passive IR sensors. Then a chain link fence was added, also topped with concertina wire.

Of the UNPROFOR troops who were arrested during the summer of victory, there were a few suicides by known rapists and "liquidators" who feared being brought to justice. After some debate, the Restoration of the Constitution Government (RCG) issued a general amnesty to UNPROFOR troops for embezzlement, theft, possession of stolen goods, and possession of stolen military property, but for no other crimes. The logic was that even some ostensibly good officers and NCOs had been given a share of loot. The prevailing culture in the New Army, it was argued, was to accept a share of loot, or else be suspected of disloyalty.

27

Anthem

"Statesmen, my dear Sir, may plan and speculate for Liberty, but it is Religion and Morality alone, which can establish the Principles upon which Freedom can securely stand. The only foundation of a free Constitution is pure Virtue, and if this cannot be inspired into our People in a greater Measure than they have it now, They may change their Rulers and the forms of Government, but they will not obtain a lasting Liberty. They will only exchange Tyrants and Tyrannies."
—John Adams, Letter to Zabdiel Adams, June 21, 1776, in *Letters of Delegates to Congress: Volume 4, May 16, 1776–August 15, 1776*

At just before noon on July Fourth, everyone congregated at the Brooks Field parade ground. They quietly lowered the UN flag and raised Old Glory without much fanfare. Resistance soldiers cut up the UN banner into small swatches for souvenirs.

A mobile PA system was set up, with a pair of speakers and a microphone stand. There was no time to arrange for a band to play or for an artillery salute, but a bespectacled former Marine with a double chin and an amazing singing voice gave an a cappella rendition of all four verses of "The Star-Spangled Banner":

Oh, say can you see by the dawn's early light
What so proudly we hailed at the twilight's last gleaming?
Whose broad stripes and bright stars thru the perilous fight,

O'er the ramparts we watched were so gallantly streaming?
And the rocket's red glare, the bombs bursting in air,
Gave proof through the night that our flag was still there.
Oh, say does that star-spangled banner yet wave
O'er the land of the free and the home of the brave?

On the shore, dimly seen through the mists of the deep,
Where the foe's haughty host in dread silence reposes,
What is that which the breeze, o'er the towering steep,
As it fitfully blows, half conceals, half discloses?
Now it catches the gleam of the morning's first beam,
In full glory reflected now shines in the stream:
'Tis the star-spangled banner! Oh long may it wave
O'er the land of the free and the home of the brave!

And where is that band who so vauntingly swore
That the havoc of war and the battle's confusion,
A home and a country should leave us no more!
Their blood has washed out their foul footsteps' pollution.
No refuge could save the hireling and slave
From the terror of flight, or the gloom of the grave:
And the star-spangled banner in triumph doth wave
O'er the land of the free and the home of the brave!

Oh! thus be it ever, when freemen shall stand
Between their loved home and the war's desolation!
Blest with victory and peace, may the heav'n rescued land
Praise the Power that hath made and preserved us a nation.
Then conquer we must, when our cause it is just,
And this be our motto, "In God is our trust."
And the star-spangled banner in triumph shall wave
O'er the land of the free and the home of the brave!

This was the first time the Ben had ever heard the usually omitted later verses. Like many others who were gathered, the lyrics moved him to tears.

Then Andy Laine stepped up to the microphone and pulled a sheet of handwritten notes from his ACU shirt pocket. "My only regret," he began, "is that I didn't join the Resistance sooner. I'm from New Mexico, and it took a long time for the ProvGov to become a threat to our liberty there. If I had only known the full depth of the ProvGov's crimes, I would have joined the fight sooner."

Andy cleared his throat, and went on:

> I'm not an eloquent speaker, so I don't have the proper words for this sort of momentous occasion. I will just let the words of our Founding Fathers express my sentiments. First, I'd like to quote from George Washington, the man who could have been appointed our nation's king, but who humbly demurred. In his farewell address to his cabinet, Washington said:
>
> "Of all the dispositions and habits which lead to political prosperity, religion and morality are indispensable supports. In vain would that man claim the tribute of patriotism who should labor to subvert these great pillars of human happiness, these firmest props of the duties of men and citizens. The mere politician, equally with the pious man, ought to respect and to cherish them. A volume could not trace all their connections with private and public felicity. Let it simply be asked: Where is the security for property, for reputation, for life, if the sense of religious obligation desert the oaths which are the instruments of investigation in courts of justice? And let us with caution indulge in the supposition that morality can be maintained without

religion. Whatever may be conceded to the influence of refined education on minds of peculiar structure, reason and experience both forbid us to expect that national morality can prevail in exclusion of religious principle. . . . Observe good faith and justice toward all nations. Cultivate peace and harmony with all. Religion and morality enjoin this conduct; and can it be that good policy does not equally enjoin it?"

Next, a brief quote from Alexander Hamilton, from one of his many writings in *The Federalist Papers*:

"The fabric of American empire ought to rest on the solid basis of the consent of the people. The streams of national power ought to flow from that pure, original fountain of all legitimate authority."

And finally, a quote from Thomas Jefferson:

"The people of every country are the only guardians of their own rights and are the only instruments which can be used for their destruction. It is an axiom in my mind that our liberty can never be safe but in the hands of people themselves, that, too, of the people with a certain degree of instruction."

Andy bowed his head and prayed aloud solemnly, "Almighty God, we beseech thee, oh Lord, to again extend thy covenantal blessings on America. We realize that we deserve only your righteous wrath. But we have repented and we beg ye, oh Lord, for thy mercies upon us. We pray for thy providence and protection, as well as that by thy Holy Spirit that thou would grant wisdom and restraint for the new Congress that we elect. We pray this in the name of Christ Jesus, Amen."

Then Ed Olds stepped up onto the base of the flagpole. With

many people recognizing him, the crowd began cheering. Like Andy, Ed's MultiCam uniform now had a full-color American flag patch on the right shoulder, and a "U.S. ARMY" tape where the "UNPROFOR" tape had been a day earlier. He raised his hand in a slow wave, and waited for the crowd to quiet down.

With the mobile PA system, Olds announced: "Ladies and gentlemen, here we stand, on Independence Day, once again independent."

This inspired a huge wave of applause and cheering that went on for nearly two minutes. Finally, Olds continued. "The war of resistance was leaderless, so this puts us in an interesting position. Rather than have some individual declare, 'I'm in charge,' we are recognizing that *we*, the People, are in charge. As an active duty soldier, I recognize that you are our employers. *I'm* certainly not in charge, and I'm the officer who relieved the post commander. He was a quisling and a crony of Maynard Hutchings. The officer corps certainly isn't calling the shots. That's *your* job, ladies and gentlemen. I urge you to re-form a limited, and in fact *minimalist* Constitutional government, from the grass roots up. The county governments are key to this."

A woman in the crowd shouted loudly, "That's right!"

Olds continued, "We don't need a *new* Constitution. The existing one—the one that was briefly discarded—can still work fine, if the separate powers can be kept in check, and the original intent of the Framers is heeded. So once again, as Ben Franklin said more than two centuries ago, I'm here to announce: 'It's a Republic, if you can keep it.'"

There was a huge round of applause.

The applause finally died down and Olds added, "And *beware*. I'm glad Andy Laine quoted George Washington—because he was very prescient. Washington wisely advised us to beware. He once wrote: 'Government is not reason; it is not eloquence; it is force. Like fire, it is a dangerous servant and a fearful master.'"

There was a cascade of applause, and a man in the crowd shouted, *"Veritas!"*

Immediately after the anthem and speeches, Ed Olds and Andy Laine were introduced to some of the militia members, including Ben Fielding, Brent Danley, and the Old Man. It was not until they discussed where they had been operating that Andy recognized the men from the intelligence dispatches. He had an "aha" moment when he realized that Ben was the resistance fighter known variously as "Mister Green Jeans" and "Bloody Ben," in reports.

Ben, Brent, and the Old Man had infiltrated into Fort Knox five days before on foot. But they departed in a liberated Ceradyne Bull mine protected vehicle, with Brent behind the wheel. There was heavy traffic in both directions on Bullion Boulevard—traffic like none of them had seen since before the Crunch. The traffic was slow, as revelers honked their horns and slowed to watch spontaneous celebrations and fireworks.

As they passed the Chaffee Gate, Ben leaned forward from the rear seat and asked the Old Man, "So now that we've won, how about you finally let us know your family name? I'd like to keep in touch."

The Old Man made no reply. He dipped his head and looked deep in thought.

Brent turned the vehicle south onto the Dixie Highway, and glanced over at him. He continued to look contemplative. Finally, the Old Man shook his head and said with a laugh, "I've told you before, Ben, you don't have a *need* to know. I think it's best that now we all just humbly fade back into the woodwork. *Especially* our recon team. After what we've done—I don't know about you—but I've got some mixed feelings. We killed almost as many men from Shreveport and San Antonio as we did from Stuttgart. So I'd rather just put it all behind me and make a fresh start."

They drove on in silence for another minute, and then the Old Man asked, "Say, can you drop me off down at the Cav Store?"

Brent answered, "Sure, my pleasure."

A few minutes later, they pulled into the U.S. Cavalry Store parking lot. A group of teenage boys and girls were there, setting off smoke grenades and launching military pop flares, with many hoots and hollers. The group was boisterous, with one of the boys shouting, "A Fourth of July to remember!" In the distance, they could hear the sporadic detonations of artillery simulators and what they presumed were grenade simulators.

The three men stepped out of the vehicle and reached into the rear cargo compartment to pull out the Old Man's MOLLE vest, rucksack, and well-worn suppressed MP5-SD submachinegun. To do so, they had to move a couple of cases of hand grenades and un-tangle the slings of eight captured guns, including a German MG4 light machinegun. Without any flourishes, the Old Man shoul-dered his gear. They shook hands and he said quietly, "See you on the other side, gents. God bless you." He turned and strode away.

Brent and Ben sat lost in their thoughts for a while before Brent restarted the engine. They were both blinking, fighting back tears. Then Ben asked, "Can you give me a ride home?"

"You betcha. Where would that be?"

"Muddy Pond, Tennessee. It's about a four-hour drive from here. I'd love to make it back there this evening."

"My pleasure."

Ben grinned and said, "I'll introduce you to my wife and kids. I got word that they're doing just fine."

As Brent pulled out of the lot and back onto the Dixie High-way, again heading south, he said, "Okay, but I can't stay long at your place. I've got a long drive home to Vermont."

They pressed on through Radcliff amid the revelry, including several UN flags being burned. Boom boxes and car stereos were playing mostly patriotic music. Appropriately, on one street corner a boom box was playing the old Roger McGuinn song "Dixie Highway." At various places they drove through clouds of smoke in white, red, yellow, and violet. "How'd they get hold of so many smoke grenades so quickly?" Ben asked.

"Oh, I suppose the same way that you accumulated your little gun collection back there." Ben thrust his thumb over his shoulder toward the vehicle's cargo compartment for emphasis, and said laconically, "They weren't nailed down, so they just mysteriously ended up in private hands."

"I noticed that you snagged a couple of extra M4s complete with PVS-14s, that TAM-14 thermal sight, and a few Claymore satchels, too," Brent countered.

Ben nodded. "As they say, 'To the victor go the spoils.' They're just a few war trophies that double as insurance."

"Insurance?"

"Yeah, an insurance policy for my family to keep at home. Just in case another joker like Maynard Hutchings ever pops up."

Brent let out a breath. "God forbid that should happen in our lifetimes, or in our children's."

28

New Guards for Future Security

"If the representatives of the people betray their constituents, there is then no resource left but in the exertion of that original right of self-defense which is paramount to all positive forms of government, and which against the usurpations of the national rulers may be exerted with infinitely better prospect of success, than against those of the rulers of an individual State. In a single State, if the persons intrusted with supreme power become usurpers, the different parcels, subdivisions, or districts of which it consists, having no distinct government in each, can take no regular measures for defense. The citizens must rush tumultuously to arms, without concert, without system, without resource; except in their courage and despair."

—Alexander Hamilton, writing as Publius,
The Federalist Papers, Number 28

Fort Knox, Kentucky
Mid-July, the Fourth Year

The UN's own barbed wire internment camps made a convenient place to put the UN soldiers while they were waiting to go home. It took more than a year to send the UN forces back to Europe by ship and airplane. All of their vehicles, aircraft, and weapons stayed in the United States. This caused nearly as much acrimony as the reparations and the delays in returning their troops.

The Europeans chafed at being billed for the demobilization

and troop transport. The "return bounty" reparation was fifty ounces of gold per enlisted soldier, 200 ounces per officer, and 500 ounces per civilian administrator, payable before delivery.

Recognizing that the foreign troops would soon be out of the United States, the RCG scrambled to reestablish NORAD and its nuclear deterrent. Trident missile submarines returned to port, and the nuclear missile silo LCCs at Malmstrom AFB were re-manned.

Maynard Hutchings spent seven months in hiding in Brussels. He committed suicide just before his scheduled extradition hearing. Most of his civilian staff and a few divisional and brigade commanders were eventually extradited from Europe, given trials, and shot. Hundreds of lower-ranking military officers and local quislings were arrested and similarly put on trial. Sentences included head shavings and brandings. In a few rare cases, there were death sentences.

Only a few UN troops who professed fear of retribution if they were returned to their home countries were granted asylum. Each of these individuals was given a separate hearing by the RCG. Most of them eventually bought citizenship.

The first elections since before the Crunch were held in all fifty states in the November following the federal surrender at Fort Knox. The Constitution Party and Libertarian Party candidates won in a landslide. A former Wyoming governor—a Libertarian—was elected President. Based on rough population estimates, the new House of Representatives had just ninety seats.

There was a new emphasis on personal liberty at all levels of government. Under the RCG, elected representatives trod lightly, fearing the wrath of their constituents. There was a clear demotion of the federal government and a simultaneous resurgence of State Sovereignty. It became the norm to again use capital letters for the words "State" and "Citizen." The terms "resident," "taxpayer," and "individual" were stricken from many laws and replaced by the word "Citizen," always with a capital C.

In the three years following the elections, there were nine Constitutional amendments ratified by the state legislatures in rapid succession. The document went through some major changes.

The 28th Amendment granted blanket immunity from prosecution for any crimes committed before or during the Second Civil War to anyone who actively fought for the Resistance.

The 29th Amendment repealed the 14th and 26th amendments. It also made full state Citizenship a right of birth, applicable only to native-born Citizens who were the children of Citizens. It allowed immigrants to buy state citizenship. It clarified "United States citizenship" as having effect only when state Citizens traveled outside the nation's borders, and outlawed titles of nobility such as "esquire."

The 30th Amendment banned welfare and foreign aid, removed the United States from the UN and most foreign treaties, capped federal spending at 2 percent of GDP, capped the combined number of foreign troops in the fifty states and on federal territory at 1,000 men, and limited the active duty federal military to 100,000 men, except in time of declared war.

The 31st Amendment amplified the 2nd Amendment, confirming it as both an unalienable individual right and as a state right, repealed the existing federal gun control laws, preempted any present or future state gun control laws, and reinstituted a decentralized militia system.

The 32nd Amendment repealed the 16th Amendment, and severely limited the ability of the federal government to collect any taxes within the fifty states. Henceforth, only tariffs, import duties, and bonds could fund the federal government's budget.

The 33rd Amendment outlawed deficit spending, put the new United States currency back on a bimetallic gold and silver standard, and made all currency "redeemable on demand."

The 34th Amendment froze salaries at $6,000 a year for House members and $10,000 for senators, limited campaign spending for any federal office to $5,000 per term, and repealed the 17th Amendment, returning senators to election by their state legislatures.

The 35th Amendment restored Common Law and invalidated most federal court decisions since 1932, and clarified the inapplicability of most federal statutes on state Citizens in several states.

The 36th Amendment reinstated the allodial land title system. Under a renewed federal land patent system the amendment mandated the return of 92 percent of the federal lands to private ownership through public sales at one dollar in silver coin per acre.

The nation's economy was slowly restored. But with the nine new amendments, the scope of government—both state and federal—was greatly reduced from its pre-Crunch proportions. Small government was almost universally seen as good government. For the first time since before the First Civil War, it became the norm to again refer to the nation plurally as "these United States," rather than singularly as the United States. The change was subtle, but profound.

29

To Dust

"The moment the idea is admitted into society that property is not as sacred as the law of God, and that there is not a force of law and public justice to protect it, anarchy and tyranny commence. If 'Thou shalt not covet' and 'Thou shalt not steal' were not commandments from Heaven, they must be made inviolable precepts in every society before it can be civilized or made free."

—John Adams, *A Defence of the Constitutions of the United States Against the Attack of M. Turgot,* 1787

Fife, Montana
August, the Fourth Year

As the ProvGov capitulated, there were a few UN army units and "contractors" who went renegade and refused to lay down their arms. Without support from the crumbling Fort Knox government, the holdout units were increasingly demoralized, depleted logistically, and hemmed in by steadily growing resistance forces.

The remnants of García's Force Two Associates gang was by then down to just twenty-three men and fourteen camp followers. The Resistance killed his friend Tony, who had been with him since the beginning. This was when they were looting the town of Lame Deer, Montana. The F2 gang had moved into Montana two weeks earlier, hoping that the lower population density would mean they'd meet less organized opposition. But instead the Resistance seemed only stronger and better organized. The F2 gang was reduced to making a few nighttime raids for food and fuel, and laying up each day in parklands or at abandoned ranches. No longer able to bluff their way into towns under color of law, they avoided being seen in all but the smallest towns.

An abandoned ranch on Enger Cutoff Road, a few miles east of Great Falls, seemed like a good place for F2 to spend a day. They pulled in an hour before dawn. A windmill kept a stock tank full so they'd have drinking water. And they were able to conceal their vehicles in a large hay barn—now empty except for a few bales that had turned black with mold. But what they didn't realize was that a neighbor a half mile away who owned a small dairy farm had seen their headlights. The dairyman was up early for his morning milking. He knew that the adjoining ranch had been abandoned for more than two years. Curious, the dairyman stealthily approached the house and ascertained that the vehicles belonged to F2. He got back to his own farmhouse just as dawn was breaking, and immediately reported seeing the looters by telephone.

As the security coordinator for that end of the county, Joshua got the word just a few minutes later. He hung up the phone and began jotting down notes.

Kelly, who had overheard his end of the conversation, asked, "What's your plan?"

"Just MSU."

Kelly laughed. The standing joke answer to all difficult questions in Kelly's business classes at Montana State University had been "MSU," which referred to an alternate use of the acronym for the school's name: "Make Stuff Up."

"Really?" she asked.

"I won't be able to say what the plan is until I see the lay of the land," Joshua said. "I'll make up a plan on the fly. We'll just gather at the Fife junction, and then we'll probably cram ourselves into a smaller number of vehicles. We'll stop about a half mile short of the farm, and walk in from there. Sometimes MSU beats elaborate planning and multilevel interagency coordination. And it certainly does when time is of the essence."

"Air support?"

"None available. The Hueys and most of the 341st Security Forces Squadron are way back beyond the east end of the missile fields. They got called in to support the handover of command of an artillery unit that capitulated a few days ago. Then they got tasked with mopping up a bunch of looters even farther east. With refueling and all, it would take them a minimum of fifteen hours to get here, and by then the bad guys will probably be gone."

Joshua got to Fife twenty minutes later driving the Rust Bucket. The Fife junction was close to his old rental house, which now sat empty.

The ranchers soon began to arrive. They were armed mostly with scoped deer rifles. One of them had a scoped M1A semiauto, which Joshua thought was perfect for what he had planned. The majority of them wore jeans and camouflage hunting jackets. A few of them wore complete camouflage ensembles. Three airmen from the 341st—two E-3s and one E-4—arrived, all armed with M4 carbines. Joshua considered their carbines inadequate "pop guns" for what he had envisioned. He recognized two of the airmen from his security forces cross training, where in the past year he had learned the rudiments of small unit tactics.

Joshua began his briefing. "Gentlemen, I'm Lieutenant Watanabe. What we have planned today is to reconnoiter and possibly engage a group of looters that just rolled into an unoccupied farm over on Enger Cutoff Road. I'm in command, and I'll lead the main group. You three from the 341st will cover the rear of the farm from the south, act as our backup, and likely provide a diversion. I haven't yet scoped it out, but I anticipate that the rest of us will set up an ambush position on the north side of the road. We'll coordinate on the Guard frequency."

One of the ranchers raised his hand and asked, "So are we going to assault the farmhouse?"

"No. That would put us at risk of taking too many casualties. Frontal assaults are the ProvGov's style, not mine. My plan is different: We make them come to us, and we just shoot them."

Noticing smoke grenade canister pouches strapped on the MOLLE vests worn by the three airmen, Joshua said, "I see you guys have some pyro with you. Those will probably come in handy. More on that later."

Approaching stealthily, Joshua reconnoitered the farmhouse and barn. He set up his spotting scope just over 300 yards away. Seeing the F2 logo on the tailgates of two of the pickups confirmed his suspicions. He radioed his instructions to the team from the 341st. It was now just after 11 a.m. and the day was warming up.

Joshua gave his men a briefing on the situation and he sent a runner back to their parked vehicles, to get a pickup equipped with a winch. Using the winch, they pulled out the cattle guard at the entrance road to the farm. With the help of five men, Joshua flipped the heavy steel cattle guard over and back into the ditch at an odd angle, facing inward. They left the pickup parked at a sharp angle, and its winch cable stretched parallel across the top of the cattle guard to form an additional barrier.

Seeing the upended cattle guard and the cable, Joshua declared, "Nobody is getting through here in a hurry. Okay, let's get into position."

They crossed the road and began to climb the low hills on the opposite side. As they walked, Francisco Ortega, a young ranch hand that Joshua had met only once before, asked, "Lieutenant, can't they just go around the cattle guard and crash through the barbed wire fence?"

Joshua shook his head and said, "That's a Hollywood myth.

I saw a looter van going fifty miles an hour glance into a barbed wire fence a couple of years ago. The fence *stopped* that van. And my father-in-law was in the Army. He told me that even tracked vehicles like tanks and APCs have trouble going through a three-strand barbed wire fence. Most cars might get fifty feet, pulling up a few T-posts, but then they almost always end up in a big wad of wire around the wheels. And usually the wire doesn't break, either. So a barbed wire fence is the perfect stopper for a car or a pickup."

Francisco nodded, and Joshua went on. "If anybody steps out of those rigs to cut the fence wires, we shoot them. Or if they try to crash though and get tangled up, we shoot them. And if they try to back up, we shoot them."

Francisco chuckled. "I noticed that all three of those ended with: ' . . . we shoot them.' "

Watanabe chuckled as well. "I can see that you were paying attention. You may have a future in the militia."

They picked out prone shooting positions on the two small hillocks that were respectively 200 and 250 yards from the cattle guard, on either side of the creek that flowed south and through a culvert into the dairy farm. Their "far ambush" positions provided a decent cross fire to engage anyone at the cattle guard, and a good distance in either direction on Enger Cutoff Road. Francisco, armed with a scoped .300 Weatherby Magnum that had belonged to his grandfather, was lying five yards to Joshua's left. Joshua again glassed the farmhouse and barns with his spotting scope. Their activity at the cattle guard had not been noticed, since it was 600 yards north of the house, and some intervening terrain blocked the line of sight.

Joshua pressed the PTT bar on his handie-talkie and said, "Okay, pop smoke and light 'em up."

Moments later, two red smoke grenades were set off by the backup team. A light breeze from the west pushed the red smoke eastward.

Soon, there was a flurry of activity as the Force Two men sprinted to their trucks in the barn.

Bursts of automatic fire came from the trio of airmen, and a hail of 5.56mm bullets pierced the walls and roof of the barn and farmhouse.

Not wanting to stay for a fight, the F2-marked vehicles soon pulled out of the barn in an impromptu convoy, and they quickly drove north to the gate. They stopped five yards short of the over-turned cattle guard.

Joshua thumbed his rifle's safety forward. Absently, he remembered that he had shot only ten rounds of .30-06 since the Crunch began. Together, those ten shots accounted for stopping one looter van and dropping five mule deer.

The Mad Minute began. By prearrangement, Watanabe's team first shot up the engine compartments and tires on the rearmost pickup. Then they shifted their fire and systematically shot out the tires on all the other vehicles. Joshua fired sixteen rounds, paus-ing once every four rounds to flip open the rifle's bottom-hinged magazine and refill it. When they switched to shooting out the vehicle windows, the occupants panicked and ran. Caught out in open ground in a cross fire, most of them were shot within twenty seconds. A few of the looters tried running east on the road. They, too, were cut down.

Joshua toggled his handheld, ordering the three-man backup from the 341st team to sweep northward.

Confused and not realizing that the shots were coming from two different hills, García and three other men ran northeast, di-rectly toward Joshua and half his team. The last of them dropped before they were within 100 yards of where Joshua and the ranch-ers lay prone. The firing died down to just a few sporadic shots from Joshua's men.

Joshua shouted, "Okay, everyone top off your guns! Show me a fist when you're done."

He heard the sound of guns being reloaded. He stood and scanned his men. They soon all raised a fist. Joshua then swept his arm forward and shouted, "Shoot anything that moves. Follow me!"

They advanced at a slow walk. As they descended the two hills, there were only two coup de grâce shots fired. Joshua and Francisco then came upon Ignacio García, who was bleeding badly. As García lay bleeding heavily, he began to babble in Spanish. His last words, ending in a shout, were *"Dónde? Dónde está mi tesoro? Mi tesoro!"* Then his chest stopped heaving.

"What's that he said?" Joshua asked.

Francisco translated. "He was asking: 'Where is my treasure?'"

"Well, his worldly treasures won't help him where *he's* gone."

They continued down to the road and crossed it, checking the bodies of the Force Two gang members for signs of life. Some of the men began to search the shot-up vehicles, which sat in green puddles of radiator water. They shut down the engine of one vehicle that was still sputtering.

The three enlisted men from the 341st trotted up to see what had happened. Joshua said simply, "We covered the rest of it from our positions. Good work on providing the cattle prod, guys. That was a job well done."

As they passed by the body of García's wife, who had been shot through the neck, Joshua instructed, "Save anything that looks useful for turn-in. Burn the rest."

Still standing beside the body of García's wife, Francisco picked up the collar of a full-length mink coat with the tip of his rifle barrel, and asked, "What about this fur coat, sir?"

"No. It has blood all over it. Burn it."

30

The Second Age of Steam

"In the face of the basic fact that fossil fuel reserves are finite, the exact length of time these reserves will last is important in only one respect: the longer they last, the more time do we have, to invent ways of living off renewable or substitute energy sources and to adjust our economy to the vast changes which we can expect from such a shift.

"Fossil fuels resemble capital in the bank. A prudent and responsible parent will use his capital sparingly in order to pass on to his children as much as possible of his inheritance. A selfish and irresponsible parent will squander it in riotous living and care not one whit how his offspring will fare."

—**Rear Admiral Hyman Rickover, 1957**

North of Williams, Arizona
178 Years After the Crunch

Pastor James Alstoba set the parking brake on his Alliance Motors Elec-Truck. He stepped out and flipped down the side-mounted PV panels on both the truck and the trailer, giving the panels full exposure to the south, and he tilted up the rack on the truck's roof to a 40-degree angle, giving that set of panels the best possible solar exposure as well. Unless the sky clouded up, the vehicle would be fully recharged by 3 p.m.

He paused to pray as he did before each day of detectoring,

asking for God's providence. James depended on the detector work for his support. He spent five days a week with his church responsibilities at Grace Baptist—which included Sunday services, several Bible studies, outreach, and sermon writing—but just two days on detectoring. That was usually Mondays and Tuesdays, but that could be shifted if there was bad weather. Early on in his ministry, he had decided to work two days a week in detectoring, rather than begging for support. To his mind, begging was bad Christian witness. He'd rather sweat a bit.

His helper that day was twenty-two-year-old Mickey Johnson. Mickey was likable, but his broad facial features, vapid expression, and nasal voice immediately marked him as someone with Down syndrome. He would never surpass the mentality of an eight-year-old. But he was an amiable, cheerful worker. Some of Mickey's sayings made James laugh. James also appreciated Mickey's childlike wonder when examining a rock or an insect. And a couple of his observations on human nature were so unknowingly accurate that James had later mentioned them in his sermons.

James had to constantly remind Mickey to drink water and to wear his big sun hat. Mickey helped haul some of the detectoring finds to the trailer—mostly scrap aluminum and steel. But most importantly, Mickey went with him to be ready to radio for help in case of an accident. That was the first thing that Pastor Alstoba had taught him to do when Mickey replaced Alstoba's son as his helper.

The front of the Elec-Truck was decorated with a painted cross and the words *"In Omnia Paratus."* To James, that phrase had a double meaning: both physical preparedness, and spiritual preparedness. The trailer had been hand-built by a member of his congregation. The vehicle itself was ten years old and nearing the end of life for its second set of 6-volt batteries.

James had been in prayer that he'd soon make a big detectoring find and hence have the funds to buy the new set of batteries without having to ask anyone for donations. With new batteries, the old truck would be back to its full potential range, and hence it would open up a wider area available for his detectoring.

James checked his holstered 5-7 and spare magazine. The pistol had been passed down to him from his grandfather. It was a relic from back in the lead bullet days. By the late 2100s, most projectiles were either copper-jacketed steel or all copper. Lead was too valuable for use in batteries to waste it in making bullets. It would be a shame if the projos weren't recovered for re-cy.

James strapped on the battery pack and then the Steady Harness for his detector. The detector was an expensive new model from Minelab. He had upgraded to the new detector with the proceeds from a providential streak of one-eighth-ounce to one-quarter-ounce gold nuggets that he had found the previous year. The Australians still made the best detectors. This one had a nice backlit display and had great sensitivity and selectivity. The detector's display could distinguish between various coins, pieces of fired brass, aluminum soda cans, spent bullets, or gold nuggets. Finally, he put on his Clarke headphones. They, too, were state-of-the-art, and even had automatic noise canceling if he ever took a shot at a rabbit or a deer.

James ran the detector's Built In Test and Calibration "bitsy" sequence. The display indicated green in all segments. He was good to go. Then he consulted his tablet-comp, and used a stylus to mark the next area of the map grid that he planned to search. It zoomed in to display a composite satellite image overlayed with old map data. The tablet comp's GPS subsystem then kept track of what ground he had covered, and beeped a reminder if he missed a spot.

As Pastor James swept the detector's trapezoidal head slowly left and right, his mind soon began to wander, as it often did when detectoring. He thought about his son, Matthew, who was off training with the 3rd Liberator Brigade. The brigade was famous for freeing slaves and fighting Islamists all over the world.

James was very proud of his twenty-year-old son. Matthew had already mastered several languages, including English, Navajo, and Spanish. Now he was also learning Arabic, to ready himself for crusading. James was hoping that Matthew would return to Arizona after his militia service, but Matthew was already talking about settling in Wyoming. The lure to go there was strong. But, inevitably, like everything else, where he settled would be up to God's plans.

James's father, Alan Alstoba—the great-great-grandson of General Alstoba of World War III fame—was a prospector and celebrated *detectorista*. He had become wealthy by finding and patenting a uranium mine. But most of the old man's cattle and fields had been passed down to his firstborn son, Jonathan. As the second-born son, James inherited only a one-tenth share of the cattle, and a few guns from the household armory. But James had become a successful detectorist in his own right, despite the fact that he devoted only two days a week to the art.

Most of the younger Alstoba's finds on public lands over the years had been modest. But he had often found gold nuggets, iron meteorites, vehicle body panels and engine blocks, and long discarded car and truck batteries. Those had each been days to celebrate.

As always, he worked under a broad-brimmed canvas hat that had been made back east at one of the Amish communities. The hat had originally been white, but it was now badly stained by sweat and accumulated grime. As James's wife put it, the hat had "character." Living in Arizona, the sunshine was both a blessing and a curse. Economically, the strongest regions were the Pacific Northwest, the northern Rockies, and the Midwest. The Northwest was envied for its vast forest lands (a fantastic source of constantly renewing fuel for steam power), its wind farms, its hydroelectric dams, and its farmlands—most of which didn't require pumped irrigation water.

The Midwest was nearly as prosperous because of its rich farmlands and its growing network of canals. But people in the arid Southwest were doomed to a lower standard of living. The Southwest's greatest sources of wealth came from its coal mines, natural gas wells, and a few uranium mines. But without regular rains, living in the Southwest was always a struggle. At least the Mexican Border Wars were a thing of the past.

Alstoba had read that the planet was coming out of the Second Little Ice Age. For a century and a half, there had been unusually cold weather. But now some climate scientists were warning that there might finally be the long predicted global warming, as the glaciers again began to retreat. This was a great source of debate, both in scientific and political circles.

By James's generation, there were still fifty states, but no more "capital" cities. The early twenty-first century, in addition to the First Great Die-off, was also remembered as the beginning of a monumental decentralization trend. Americans learned the hard way that large cities—especially capital cities—were targets for nukes and dirty bombs by Islamic terrorists. So the population spread out. All elections were held via the Net, and legislatures met only virtually.

Because of transportation costs, most goods were transported by ship, barge, and steam train. Steam, sail, and nuke-powered ships dominated the high seas. These days, more than half the dwindling oil production was dedicated to making lubricants rather than fuel.

By the late twenty-second century, the silver-to-gold price ratio had dropped to 5 to 1. This shift took place because silver was being used up in various industrial processes like building PV panels, and the re-cy processes couldn't recover much of this silver. Inexorably, the price of silver rose in relation to gold.

The Islamists had made territorial gains throughout the twenty-first century, but in the twenty-second, when *their* oil ran out, they were forced to retreat on all fronts.

By the late 2100s there were just 50 million people living in the United States, which was deemed to be just about its long-term sustainable carrying capacity. Excess population was being shunted into the African colonies. These colonies had been developed in an attempt to repopulate the African continent, and to push out the Islamists. The Islamists had been stopped, and then pushed back, starting in Rhodbabwe, early in the twenty-second century. The rallying cry in World War IV had been "Push them back across the Zambezi." But by Alstoba's generation, five decades later, it was hoped that the Islamists could soon be pushed entirely off the African continent.

James heard a "whirrr!" in his headphones. Digging with his weeding probe, the target turned out to be a four-inch-long steel bolt. He put the rusty bolt in his collection bag, and resumed scanning. Two paces forward, a large hit showed up on his detector's screen. This one turned out to be a four-foot length of rusted one-inch steel pipe. This piece alone would have made his day worthwhile. Then he found an old steel T-post, also just below the surface. This got him excited, because three years earlier he had followed one hit after another on an old fence line and had recovered seventeen T-posts in just one day. That was considered a pay dirt day.

Next, James got into an odd patch of soil, roughly rectangular, where the detector indicated a high level of diffuse iron oxide. From his past experience, he knew that this meant that a vehicle had sat there rusting for many decades before it had been hauled away for re-cy, long before James was born.

He kept searching, still finding useful nuts and bolts and other bits of rusted steel. There was enough scrap here to warrant him stopping and moving his vehicle and trailer closer, to obviate making tiring trips back and forth.

He knew he'd come upon a productive patch for finding steel. He could probably dig up valuable base metals here for several days. He pulled out his tablet and triple-tapped the stylus on his currently indicated position and said, "Good patch for scrap steel." The icon of a human ear appeared on the screen, indicating that a new voice annotation had been made to the map.

He moved his truck and trailer in close, to an adjoining patch that he had already scanned as clear. He again flipped the PV panels down. The charge controller showed the batteries were already back up to 47 percent. The skies were still sunny, so he would have enough juice to drive home within a couple of hours. This was shaping up to be a good day.

He eyed his lunch bucket on the seat but decided to go back to scanning. He didn't want to leave a productive patch so soon. Out of habit, he reran the detector's bitsy sequence and put his headphones back on. After finding a couple of steel shards, some nails, and a few aluminum cans, the detector went quiet. Apparently, he was leaving the scrap field. He plodded on, and his mind began to wander again. His tablet beeped and said, "200, reminder." That was a preprogrammed reminder that he had traveled 200 meters past the last registered hit. So he stepped two paces to his right, made a 180-degree turn, and walked back toward the productive scrap patch. After walking 150 meters, he was back in the thick of it. He dug up so many nails and cans that he had to have Mickey help him shuttle the load back to the trailer. He took a long pull from his canteen, and thought again about taking a lunch break. But he decided to press on.

When he was just fifteen meters from the rectangular patch of iron oxide, his detector started to howl. The only other times it had done this was when he found something big, like an engine block. The Minelab's display showed a strange blinking "Fe-Pt-Au-Ag???" indication. Walking over the spot from three directions showed him that the indicated spot was about a half meter wide, and one and a half meters long. James was excited, but he didn't lose his cool. He pulled out his tablet, triple-tapped the stylus, and said, "Large, metallic target, near surface. Could be good."

Knowing that the target was large, James set down his detector and headphones. He pulled his entrenching tool out of its belt pouch and flipped it open. He had dug down only ten centimeters when he uncovered a rusty steel plate. Then, widening the hole, he recognized the familiar outline of the folding handle of an ammunition can. He tried pulling the handle up with his fingers, but it was rusted in place. So he pried the handle up with the tip of the e-tool.

He tried pulling the can up out of the ground, but it wouldn't budge. When he used the tip of his e-tool on three sides to wedge it free, he could then see that it was just one of several ammo cans that had been buried together in a phalanx. After prying the can free from the surrounding caliche soil, he was finally able to lift it. He was surprised at its great weight.

He set the rusty can down beside the hole, and, using the tip of the e-tool for leverage, he flipped its latch open. And then, with considerable force to overcome the rust on the hinge, he swung open the lid. He was stunned to see that the can was filled with gold coins, ten-ounce silver ingots, and diamond rings. James looked skyward, and said, "Thank you, thank you, Lord, *Jehovah Jireh.*"

Twenty minutes later, he had excitedly dug up eighteen cans and lined them up in a row, at close intervals, and had pried them all open. James was dumbfounded. With this much gold, he'd be able to support dozens or even hundreds of missionaries for decades.

Mickey walked back from the truck where he had been napping to look at what James had found. Gazing at all of the glittering gold in the ammo cans, Mickey clapped his hands, and declared, "Yeah, yeah! Do you know what this means, Pastor?"

"No, what?"

"We can buy ice cream!"

Acknowledgments

As a novelist, I've been influenced by Pat Frank (the author of *Alas, Babylon*), George Stewart (the author of *Earth Abides*), and Larry Niven and Jerry Pournelle (the coauthors of *Lucifer's Hammer*). When I was a young man, those four novelists provided me some important formative "what if?" images of possible futures for America. I am in their debt.

Above all else, it takes faith and friends to survive. I've been blessed with a lot of friends, and they have helped strengthen my faith in Almighty God.

This novel is dedicated to my new wife, "Avalanche Lily," for her inspiration, encouragement, and diligent editing. She has filled a huge gap in my life after Linda ("The Memsahib") passed away.

My sincere thanks to my editor, Emily Bestler. This novel wouldn't exist without you.

My thanks to the other folks who encouraged me, who contributed technical details, who were used for character sketches, and who helped me substantively in the editing process: Aviad, Azreel, Ben, Brent F., Chris F., Cope, Daniel C., "The Other Mr. Delta," Grizzly Guy, Reggie K., Ignacio L., Jerry J., J.I.R., Johannes K., Keith K., Dr. Mark L., CW3 J.S., Dave M., Michael H., Dean R., Jim S., D.S., "SNO," and Terrie.

James Wesley, Rawles
The Rawles Ranch
July 2012

"Because I have called, and ye refused; I have stretched out my hand, and no man regarded; But ye have set at nought all my counsel, and would none of my reproof: I also will laugh at your calamity; I will mock when your fear cometh; When your fear cometh as desolation, and your destruction cometh as a whirlwind; when distress and anguish cometh upon you. Then shall they call upon me, but I will not answer; they shall seek me early, but they shall not find me: For that they hated knowledge, and did not choose the fear of the LORD: They would none of my counsel: they despised all my reproof. Therefore shall they eat of the fruit of their own way, and be filled with their own devices. For the turning away of the simple shall slay them, and the prosperity of fools shall destroy them. But whoso hearkeneth unto me shall dwell safely, and shall be quiet from fear of evil."

—Proverbs 1:24–33 (KJV)

Glossary

10/22: A semiautomatic .22 rimfire rifle made by Ruger.

1911: See **M1911**.

9/11: The terrorist attacks of September 11, 2001, which took 3,000 American lives.

AAA: American Automobile Association.

ACP: Automatic Colt Pistol.

ACS: Army Community Service.

ACU: Army combat uniform. The U.S. Army's "digital" pattern camouflage uniform that replaced the BDU.

AER: Army Emergency Relief.

AFB: Air Force Base.

AFSC: Air Force Security Command.

AK: Avtomat Kalashnikova. The gas-operated weapons family invented by Mikhail Timofeyevitch Kalashnikov, a Red Army sergeant. AKs are known for their robustness and were made in huge numbers, so they are ubiquitous in much of Asia and the Third World. The best of the Kalashnikov variants are the Valmets, which were made in Finland, the Galils, which were made in Israel, and the R4s, which are made in South Africa.

AK-47: The early generation AK carbine with a milled receiver that shoots the intermediate 7.62 x 39mm cartridge. See also: **AKM**.

AK-74: The later generation AK carbine that shoots the 5.45 x 39mm cartridge.

AKM: "Avtomat Kalashnikova Modernizirovanniy," the later generation 7.62 x 39 AK with a stamped receiver.

AM: Amplitude modulation.

AO: Area of operations.

AP: Armor-piercing.

APC: Armored personnel carrier.

AR: Automatic Rifle. This is the generic term for semiauto variants of the Armalite family of rifles designed by Eugene Stoner (AR-10, AR-15, AR-180, etc.).

AR-7: The .22 LR semiautomatic survival rifle designed by Eugene Stoner. It weighs just two pounds.

AR-10: The 7.62mm NATO predecessor of the M16 rifle, designed by Eugene Stoner. Early AR-10s (mainly Portuguese-, Sudanese-, and Cuban-contract, from the late 1950s and early 1960s) are not to be confused with the present-day semiauto-only AR-10 rifles that are more closely interchangeable with parts from the smaller caliber AR-15.

AR-15: The semiauto civilian variants of the U.S. Army M16 rifle.

ASAP: As soon as possible.

ATF: See **BATFE**.

AUG: See **Steyr AUG**.

AWOL: Absent without official leave.

B&E: Breaking and entering.

Ballistic wampum: Ammunition stored for barter purposes. (Term coined by Colonel Jeff Cooper.)

BATFE: Bureau of Alcohol, Tobacco, Firearms, and Explosives, a U.S. federal government taxing agency.

BBC: British Broadcasting Corporation.

BDU: Battle dress uniform. Also called "camouflage utilities" by the USMC. Most BDUs were made in the Woodland camouflage pattern.

Black rifle/black gun: Generic terms for a modern battle rifle—typically equipped with a black plastic stock and fore-end, giving these guns an "all black" appearance. Functionally, however, they are little different from earlier semiauto designs.

BLM: Bureau of Land Management, a U.S. federal government agency that administers public lands.

BLUF: Bottom line, up front.

BMG: Browning machinegun. Usually refers to .50 BMG, the U.S. military's standard heavy machinegun cartridge since the early twentieth century. This cartridge is now often used for long-range precision countersniper rifles.

BNSF: Burlington Northern & Santa Fe Railroad.

BOQ: Bachelor officers quarters.

BP: Blood pressure.

BTR-70: A Russian eight-wheeled armored personnel carrier, designed in the 1960s.

BX: Base exchange.

C-4: Composition 4, a plastic explosive.

CAR-15: See **M4**.

CARC: Chemical agent resistant coating. The paint used on most U.S. military vehicles.

CAS: Close air support.

CAT: Combat application tourniquet.

CB: Citizens band radio. A VHF broadcasting band. There is no license required for operation in the United States. Some desirable CB transceivers are capable of SSB operation. Originally twenty-three channels, the citizens band was later expanded to forty channels during the golden age of CB in the 1970s.

CLP: Cleaner, lubricant, protectant. A mil-spec lubricant, sold under the trade name Break Free CLP.

CO: Commanding officer.

CO$_2$: Carbon dioxide.

COD: Collect on delivery.

COMINT: Communications intelligence.

CONEX: Continental Express. The ubiquitous twenty-, thirty-, and forty-foot-long steel cargo containers used in multiple transportation modes.

CONUS: Continental United States.

COPS: Committee of Public Safety.

CP: Command post.

CPY: Ham radio shorthand for "Copy."

CRKT: Columbia River Knife & Tool.

CU: Ham radio shorthand for "See you (later)."

CUCV: Commercial utility cargo vehicle. The 1980s-vintage U.S. Army versions of diesel Chevy Blazers and pickups, sold off as surplus in the early 2000s.

DE: Ham radio shorthand for "From." This is used between call signs.

DF: Direction finding.

DMV: Department of Motor Vehicles.

DPM: Disruptive pattern material. A British military camouflage pattern, with colors similar to the U.S. Army's defunct Woodland BDU pattern.

Drip or drip oil: The light oil or hydrocarbon liquids condensed in a natural gas piping system when the gas is cooled. Sometimes also called natural gasoline, condensation gasoline, or simply "drip." A mixture of gasoline and drip oil can be burned in most gasoline engines without modification. Pure drip oil can be burned in some gasoline engines if the timing is retarded.

DRMO: Defense Reutilization and Marketing Office.

E&E: Escape and evasion.

ELINT: Electronic intelligence.

E-tool: Entrenching tool (a small military folding shovel).

F2: Force Two Associates.

FAA: Federal Aviation Administration.

FAL: See **FN/FAL.**

FAMAS: *Fusil d'Assaut de la Manufacture d'Armes de Saint-Étienne.* The French army's standard-issue bullpup carbine, chambered in 5.56mm NATO.

FBO: Fixed base operator. Typically, a small private airport's refueling facility.

FEMA: Federal Emergency Management Agency, a U.S. federal government agency. The acronym is also jokingly defined as: "Foolishly Expecting Meaningful Aid."

FFL: Federal firearms license.

FIST: Fire support team.

FLOPS: Flight operations.

FN/FAL: A 7.62mm NATO battle rifle originally made by the Belgian company Fabrique Nationale (FN), issued to more than fifty countries in the 1960s and 1970s. Now made as semiauto-only "clones" by a variety of makers. See also: **L1A1.**

FOB: Forward operating base.

FORSCOM: U.S. Army Forces Command.

FRS: Family Radio Service.

FUBAR: Fouled up beyond all recognition.

Galil: The Israeli battle rifle, based on Kalashnikov action. Most were made in 5.56mm NATO, but a variant was also made in 7.62mm NATO in smaller numbers.

GAZ: Gorkovsky Avtomobilny Zavod. A Russian car and truck maker.

GB: Gigabyte.

GCA: The Gun Control Act of 1968. The law that first created FFLs and banned interstate transfers of post-1898 firearms, except "to or through" FFL holders.

GDP: Gross domestic product.

Glock: The popular polymer-framed pistol design by Gaston Glock of Austria. Glocks are a favorite of gun writer Boston T. Party.

GMRS: General Mobile Radio Service, a licensed UHF-FM two-way radio service. See also: **FRS** and **MURS**.

GMT: Greenwich Mean Time.

Gold Cup: The target version of Colt's M1911 pistol; has fully adjustable target sights, a tapered barrel, and a tighter barrel bushing than a standard M1911.

GOOD: Get out of Dodge.

GPS: Global positioning system.

Ham: Slang for amateur radio operator.

H-E or HE: High explosive.

HF: High frequency. A radio band used by amateur radio operators.

HIMARS: High mobility artillery rocket system. The wheeled variant of the MLRS rocket launcher, which is normally mounted on tracked carriers.

HK or H&K: Heckler und Koch, the German gun maker.

HK91: Heckler und Koch Model 91. The civilian (semiautomatic-only) variant of the 7.62mm NATO G3 rifle.

HQ: Headquarters.

HR: Ham radio shorthand for "Here."

Humvee: High-mobility multipurpose wheeled vehicle, spoken "Humvee."

IBA: Interceptor body armor.

ID: Identification.

IED: Improvised explosive device.

IFV: Infantry fighting vehicle.

IV: Intravenous.

K: Ham radio shorthand for "Go ahead."

Kevlar: The material used in most body army and ballistic helmets. "Kevlar" is also the nickname for the standard U.S. Army helmet.

KJV: King James Version of the Bible.

KL: Ham radio nickname of Kaylee Schmidt.

KN: Ham radio shorthand for "Go ahead." (But *only* the station that a ham is already conversing with.)

L1A1: The British army version of the FN/FAL, made to inch measurements.

LAW: Light Antitank Weapon.

LC-1: Load Carrying, Type 1. (U.S. Army load-bearing equipment, circa 1970s to 1990s.)

LDS: Latter Day Saints, commonly called the Mormons. (Flawed doctrine, great preparedness.)

LF: Launch facility.

LLDR: Lightweight laser designator rangefinder.

LP: Liquid propane.

LP/OP: Listening post/observation post.

LRRP: Long-range reconnaissance patrol.

M1A: The civilian (semiauto-only) equivalent of the M14 rifle.

M1 Abrams: The United States' current main battle tank, with a 120mm cannon ("main gun").

M1 Carbine: The U.S. Army semiauto carbine issued during World War II. Mainly issued to officers and second-echelon troops such as artillerymen for self-defense. Uses ".30 U.S Carbine," an intermediate (pistol-class) .30 caliber cartridge. More than six million were manufactured. See also: **M2 Carbine.**

M1 Garand: The U.S. Army's primary battle rifle of World War II and the Korean conflict. It is semiautomatic, chambered in .30-06, and uses a top-loading, eight-round en bloc clip that ejects after the last round is fired. This rifle is commonly called the Garand (after the surname of its inventor). Not to be confused with the U.S. M1 Carbine, another semiauto of the same era, which shoots a far less powerful pistol-class cartridge.

M1911: The Model 1911 Colt semiauto pistol (and clones thereof), usually chambered in .45 ACP.

M2 Carbine: The selective-fire (fully automatic) version of the U.S. Army semiauto carbine issued during World War II and the Korean conflict.

M4: The U.S. Army–issue 5.56mm NATO selective-fire carbine (a shorter version of the M16, with a 14.5-inch barrel and collapsing stock). Earlier-issue M16 carbine variants had designations such as XM177E2 and CAR-15. Civilian semiauto-only variants often have these same designations, or are called "M4geries."

M4gery: A civilian semiauto-only version of an M4 carbine, with a 16-inch barrel instead of a 14.5-inch barrel.

M9: The U.S. Army–issue version of the Beretta M92 semiauto 9mm pistol.

M14: The U.S. Army–issue 7.62mm NATO selective-fire battle rifle. These rifles are still issued in small numbers, primarily to designated marksmen. The civilian semiauto-only equivalent of the M14 is called the M1A.

M16: The U.S. Army–issue 5.56mm NATO selective-fire battle rifle. The current standard variant is the M16A2, which has improved sight and three-shot burst control. See also: **M4.**

M60: The semi-obsolete U.S. Army–issue 7.62mm NATO belt-fed light machinegun that utilized some design elements of the German MG-42.

MAC: Depending on context, Military Airlift Command or Military Armament Corporation.

MAF: Missile alert facility.

Maglite: A popular American brand of sturdy flashlights with an aluminum casing.

MG3: A German belt-fed light machinegun, chambered in 7.62mm NATO.

MG4: A German belt-fed light machinegun, chambered in 5.56mm NATO.

Mini-14: A 5.56mm NATO semiauto carbine made by Ruger.

MIRV: Multiple Independently targetable Re-entry Vehicle.

MLRS: Multiple-launch rocket system.

Molotov cocktail: A hand-thrown firebomb made from a glass container filled with gasoline or thickened gasoline (napalm).

MOLLE: Modular lightweight load-carrying equipment.

MP: Military Police.

MRAP: Mine-resistant ambush protected (military vehicles).

MRE: Meal, ready to eat.

MSDS: Material safety data sheet.

MSS: Modular sleep system.

MTBE: Methyl tert-butyl ether. An oxygenating additive for gasoline.

MultiCam: See **OCP.**

MURS: Multi-Use Radio Service. A VHF two-way radio service that does not require a license. See also: **FRS** and **GMRS.**

MVPA: Military Vehicle Preservation Association.

MXG: Maintenance group (USAF).

Napalm: Thickened gasoline, used in some flame weapons.

NATO: North Atlantic Treaty Organization.

NBC: Nuclear, biological, and chemical.

NCO: Noncommissioned officer.

NFA: The National Firearms Act of 1934. The law that first imposed a transfer tax on machineguns, suppressors (commonly called "silencers"), and short-barreled rifles and shotguns.

NiCad: Nickel cadmium (ni-cad) (rechargeable battery).

NiMH: Nickel metal hydride (rechargeable battery) improvement of NiCad.

NWO: New World Order.

O-CONUS: Outside the Continental United States.

OCP: Operation Enduring Freedom Camouflage Pattern, commonly called by its civilian trade name, MultiCam.

OP: Observation post. See also: **LP/OP.**

OPORD: Operations order.

OPSEC: Operational security.

PCS: Permanent change of station.

PERSCOM: U.S. Army Personnel Command.

PFC: Private, first class.

Pre-1899: Guns made before 1899—not classified as "firearms" under federal law.

Pre-1965: U.S. silver coins with 1964 or earlier mint dates, usually with little or no numismatic value. They are sold for the bullion content. These coins have 90 percent silver content. Well-worn pre-1965 coins are sometimes derisively called "junk" silver by rare coin dealers.

ProvGov: Provisional Government.

PSYOPS: Psychological operations.

PT: Physical training.

PTT: Push to talk.

PV: Photovoltaic (solar power conversion array). Used to convert solar power to DC electricity, typically for battery charging.

PVC: Polyvinyl Chloride (white plastic water pipe).

QRF: Quick-reaction force.

QRP: Ham radio shorthand for "low-power" (less than 5-watt) transmitters.

RCD: Race car dynamics.

RCG: Restoration of the Constitution Government.

RCIED: Radio-controlled improvised explosive device.

Reg: Slang for "regulation."

RORO: Roll-on, Roll-off—a type of ship designed for transporting vehicles.

ROTC: Reserve Officers' Training Corps.

RPG: Rocket-propelled grenade.

RTA: Radio traffic analyst. See also: **TA.**

RTB: Return to base.

SBI: Special background investigation.

SCI: Sensitive compartmented information.

SIG: Schweizer Industrie Gesellschaft. The Swiss gun maker.

SIGINT: Signals intelligence.

SOCOM: Special Operations Command.

SOP: Standard operating procedure(s).

SRT: Security response team. Spoken "Sir-Tee."

SSB: Single sideband (an operating mode for CB and amateur radio gear).

Steyr AUG: The Austrian army's 5.56mm bullpup infantry carbine. Also issued by the Australian army as its replacement for the L1A1.

S&W: Smith and Wesson.

SWAT: Special Weapons and Tactics. (SWAT originally stood for Special Weapons Assault Team until that was deemed politically incorrect.)

TA: Traffic analyst. See also: **RTA.**

TA-50: Table of Allowances 50. The listing of the U.S. Army's field gear authorized for issue to individual soldiers. TA-50 typically includes a rucksack, sleeping bag, helmet, magazine pouches, MOLLE vest, canteen, etc.

TAB: Tactical advance to battle.

TAD: Temporary assigned duty.

TARPS: Tactical aerial reconnaissance pod system.

TDY: Temporary duty.

Thermite: A mixture of aluminum powder and iron rust powder that when ignited causes a vigorous exothermic reaction. Used primarily for welding. Also used by military units as an incendiary for destroying equipment.

TI: Turn in (of issued equipment).

T.K.: Tom Kennedy.

TO&E: Table of organization and equipment.

UAV: Unmanned aerial vehicle.

UN-MNF: United Nations Multinational Force.

UNPROFOR: United Nations Protection Force.

UPS: Uninterruptible power source.

VAC: Volts, alternating current.

Valmet: The Finnish conglomerate that formerly made several types of firearms.

VDC: Volts, direct current.

VW: Volkswagen.

WD-1: U.S. military–issue two-conductor insulated field telephone wire.